WHERE FLOWERS GROW

A Novel

BARBARA ANNE KING

Where Flowers Grow
A Novel
Barbara Anne King

Copyright 2021
First Edition
Cypress Point Press
Print ISBN: 978-1-7335369-7-4

Book Cover Design by Jenny Q, Historical Fiction Book Covers

CONTENTS

The last thing Richard Bankston was looking for was a wife. Later, he would regard the marriage as the biggest mistake of his life. But once their eyes met and sparks flew, he was powerless to resist.

Richard had been in Boston taking a special engineering course at MIT (Massachusetts Institute of Technology). When he learned about the crew race, he headed for the Charles River to watch Stanford face off against the top Ivy League rowers. As he maneuvered through the crowd, he grazed a young woman who turned her head, fixing her big brown eyes on him. All he remembered from that encounter was the fireworks that passed between them. Then a whirlwind courtship ensued, resulting in a wedding a few months later. After a honeymoon in Maine, Richard returned to California to await his wife, who had been left behind to pack up her belongings and bid her old life goodbye.

CHAPTER ONE

Richard was lost in thought when Jack Overton stepped into the office and tossed a report on his desk. "The boss requested I deliver this to you pronto."

"Huh," Richard said, giving his head a shake.

"Don't tell me you were daydreaming about your new bride. Is it this weekend that the Mrs. arrives?"

"I pick her up at the airport first thing tomorrow morning."

"She'll be somewhat shocked when she first sees our little town."

"I plan to ease her in. We'll be spending the weekend in San Francisco. I want her to know she'll not be that far from civilization."

"That's smart. But it could set up false expectations. Anyway, I've got to get going. Can't wait to hear about your weekend on Monday."

Richard mulled over Jack's words as he packed his briefcase, glancing at the report marked state college project. I hope Jeremy doesn't want my analysis by Monday. That would put a crimp in my weekend.

Richard stood up and turned toward the window to watch the sunset over the land, sensing his connection. He spotted brown bodies still squatting in the soil—most were Mexican farmworkers, others Japanese sharecroppers. This place is so different from the East Coast. He wondered how his bride would take to Watsonville, coming from Boston—a city of sophistication, intellectual curiosity, and style. He shuddered to think what her reaction might be. But Gina was the woman he had chosen, the one who never failed to turn him on, the one he needed to achieve his dreams. In his experience, a man without a good woman behind him didn't amount to much. And on that same note, a good woman could help a man reach heights never thought possible.

On the way to his car, Richard glanced up at the sky, a habit he had developed as a navy pilot. He noted it was clear, winds gentle—the gods were smiling on his weekend. He drove toward the highway, passing miles and miles of apple orchards, fruit that had turned Watsonville into the Apple Capital of the World. The trees' branches were straining under their burden, begging for relief as workers picked the fruit by hand—the only means to ensure the apples would not get bruised and rot. Richard wondered how much labor was required to bring these crops to market, knowing apples from one tree could fill twenty crates. He heard the population in town doubled at harvest time—men eager for work and wages.

Richard's thoughts drifted off to Gina and their wedding day. She had taken his breath away when she walked down the aisle dressed in a vintage gown fashioned out of French Chantilly lace. And the Ryans had spared no expense for the reception that followed at their summer home on Martha's Vineyard. Dom Perignon champagne flowed while appetizers of Beluga caviar and fresh seafood were offered in abundance. Joe Ryan had made his fortune in the stock market. And Theresa spent it in style.

The extravagance of it all had sent Richard the clear message that the bar was set high.

Richard made it to the arrival area just as Gina was making her way down the corridor. As soon as she passed through the gate, Richard wrapped his arms around her and pulled her close while his lips met hers in a deep, heartfelt kiss. "Welcome home," and he continued to kiss her. "I missed you. It's too bad check-in time is still hours away."

"Don't worry, darling, we'll make up for lost time," Gina said, pressing herself against him.

Richard loved the feel of Gina's body against his. She had womanly curves that appealed to both his sense of sight and touch. Gina also had a pretty face, her eyes the focal point—set wide apart and fringed with thick, dark lashes. The golden hair that framed her face made a striking contrast to her big, brown eyes. Then there were the high cheekbones, turned-up nose, and full bow lips that came to life when she smiled, displaying her only flaw, front teeth that crossed ever so slightly. But the flaw only made her more human, more real. He always was a sucker for a pretty face.

After claiming the luggage, Richard and Gina walked back to the parking garage, hand in hand with a porter in tow. After tipping the porter, they settled into their seats.

"Do you mind if I have a cigarette?" Gina said, not waiting for Richard to respond as she pulled one out and lit up. She took a long drag, letting the smoke out slowly. "That's better. Now, I can finally relax."

Richard let out a cough to clear his throat. "So, how's your family?"

"Mom and Dad are fine. They send their love and look forward to visiting soon. Annemarie is dating a new guy, and we think it's serious."

"Another Harvey?"

"No, this one's a Yale grad. She's tired of Harvard men. She finds them all about ego and ambition. And I agree."

"Is that so? What's a Yalie like then? They do all right for themselves—they must have some ambition."

There was silence while Gina considered her answer. "They have more creative minds and a better sense of humor. They're just as ambitious, but they don't wear a sign saying so."

"And what is the stereotype of Stanford men?"

Gina took another puff before answering. "It's too early to tell. But I'll come up with one."

Richard gave her a wry smile. "That brings me to a choice you have between touring Stanford University to take a sampling or heading to the world-famous Fisherman's Wharf for lunch and people watching, a favorite pastime there."

"I know you're proud of your alma mater, Richard, and I'd like to see it, but not today. I'm starved, and besides, we might get into our room early to make the most of our day."

Richard checked the rear-view mirror as he began backing up. "All right then, next stop Fisherman's Wharf. But you're not off the hook. This fall, we'll go to a football game, and I'll give you the grand campus tour."

"And in the meantime, you'll be my only sample of Stanford men. And so far, so good."

Richard found his way back to the freeway and into downtown San Francisco. "Let's park the car and take a cable car down to the wharf." After they mounted the cable car, he said, "Hold on tight. This could be a wild ride."

Once the cable car stopped, Richard stepped out, offering his hand to Gina to help her down. "This is the world-famous Fishermen's Wharf—home of the sidewalk Dungeness crab cocktail. Let's grab one and keep on walking." Richard held onto Gina's elbow, guiding her to Alioto's seafood bar, and ordered two crab cocktails. "These crabs differ from the ones you get on the East Coast—the meat is sweeter, more tender." The vendor handed a cocktail to Gina, then to Richard.

Gina dipped her fork in to taste the fresh crab. "This is delicious. I could get addicted."

It was summer, and the wharf was packed with tourists and street artists—musicians, painters, and mimes dressed up like the tinman, a cowboy, even an Egyptian Pharaoh, standing still as a statue.

Gina could not take in enough of the sights, turning her head from right to left as she clung to Richard's arm. "It's like a freak show down here, isn't it?" Richard said.

"I love it. It's something I've never experienced."

"Get your fill now because home is nothing like this."

Gina didn't understand what he meant by that comment. She loved all the variety of sights and sounds in San Francisco. She hoped home would not be boring.

"Are you still hungry?" asked Richard.

"A little."

"Let's get some chowder—that'll hold us until dinner."

Richard led Gina to a harbor view restaurant with outdoor seating. A table had just freed up, and he hustled to claim it. Gina followed. They sat down while the server signaled a bus boy to clear the table.

When the waiter stepped up to hand them menus, Richard waved them off. "We'd like two bowls of cioppino, a basket of sourdough bread, and a couple of beers." He nodded, leaving to fill the order.

"What's cioppino?" Gina asked.

"It's a seafood stew made with a red sauce. I didn't dare order New England style clam chowder—there's no competing with the best."

The waiter returned with the order and placed the steaming bowls of chowder in front of them while setting the bread basket in the center. "I'll be back with the beers. We have Miller on tap. Will that suit you?"

"That'll be fine. Now, let's dig in."

Gina spooned up some chowder, careful not to spill a drop on her new white blouse. "This reminds me of bouill-abaisse."

"It's similar. The Italian version. Didn't your mother ever make it?"

"I have no memory of it. But she made bouillabaisse. Sometimes she preferred the French version of things." Gina grabbed a piece of bread, taking a bite. "Now, I know why this is considered sour—it makes my mouth pucker. I think I'll stick with Italian bread or, better yet, a French baguette."

"Not once you realize how much healthier it is for you. It has many benefits including improved digestion, and the bread doesn't have all the additives the other breads do."

"People out here sure like to be healthy."

"That's right. We're at the cutting edge of things. We like to look good and feel good. By the way, you should lose that smoking habit of yours."

Gina gave Richard a frown. "Please, don't start in on my smoking. I've done it since I was a teenager, and it may be too late to stop." She took another bite of bread. "Maybe I'll try to cut back and munch on sourdough bread instead," she said as she took another bite while grimacing.

Richard let the moment pass. "Let's eat up and head back, so we don't have to cut our evening short."

Gina caught the desire in his steely blue eyes, set in a face of chiseled features that made him appear so vitally masculine, so sexy. But it was the blond forelock that fell across his brow, giving him a playful look, that made her fall in love with him.

They took another cable car, and once they arrived at their destination, they disembarked and walked toward the car. "Before we go to the hotel, I want to show you something." They entered the City Club, taking the stairs that led to a large mural that took up a wall and part of the ceiling. "This is known as *The Riches of California*, painted by the famous Mexican muralist Diego Rivera."

"It's amazing," Gina said as she stepped back to get a better view. "I feel like it has gathered me up into the scene."

"Let me explain the images in it and teach you something

about California history. The large woman is the Goddess Calafia, who legend tells us ruled the mythical island of California. Notice she is digging into the rich earth with one hand and holding up a variety of fruit in the other."

"It reminds me of the biblical phrase 'fruit of the vine, work of human hands.'"

"Possibly." And Richard continued. "It also depicts the economy of California, including engineers who helped build the state and miners who dug for gold."

"And don't forget the sun smiling down from the ceiling, blessing everything."

Richard nodded. "The funny thing is that no one quite knew what Rivera would paint since his art reflected his political leanings—he was a communist. He even hosted Trotsky when he was exiled. He sympathized with the struggles of the working class, which are themes in his paintings."

"They're in this one. The hands tell the story—they're the focus. But beyond that, the colors he used are mesmerizing."

"He learned the art of frescos in Italy, and that's the method he used. If you've seen enough, we better be on our way. We're going to be staying on Nob Hill tonight."

Gina turned toward Richard. "Nob Hill—that's a funny name. How did it come to be called that?"

"Nob is short for the Hindu word Nabob, which means conspicuously wealthy. This was where the four railroad barons, including Leland Stanford, built their mansions, and other rich folks followed."

"Will we have time to see them, the mansions, I mean?"

"They burned down during the 1906 earthquake. The only things left were the fire-resistant granite walls. The mansions were made of wood. That's why you take a materials course in engineering. If those mansions had been made of stone, they would have survived. The Flood mansion did—but the fire gutted the insides."

"Earthquakes," Gina said as she gave a little shiver, "what a terrible natural disaster they are."

"Yes, but they don't happen very often, and we've developed better construction methods for handling them. Engineers are great problem solvers."

"If you do say so yourself."

"We're coming up on the Mark Hopkins, named after one of the railroad barons."

Gina had been in many fine hotels in Boston, but this one was especially elegant. The lobby, painted in peach and cream tones, showcased Oriental rugs covering the parquet hardwood floor and had large crystal chandeliers hanging from the ceiling. Several artfully arranged groupings of French-style furniture filled the room, beckoning guests to relax. The reception desk, a long, carved piece of mahogany, was polished to perfection. The bellman led them to room 628, holding the door to allow Gina to step in first. It was a beautifully decorated room in the same style as the lobby, a large picture window covered with sheers the focal point. Gina couldn't contain her excitement while she unmasked the window, filling it with a view of the Golden Gate Bridge surrounded by the choppy waters of San Francisco Bay. "Oh, Richard," she said, "this is breathtaking."

The bellman quickly took his leave as Richard bent down to kiss Gina, building their passion until they moved to the bed, still wrapped in each other's arms. They couldn't undress fast enough, wanting to feel the heat of skin on skin. It didn't take long before they were both in ecstasy yet yearning for more. After they had satisfied themselves, Richard left the bed to check out the mini bar. He opened the small refrigerator and began pulling out some miniature liquors. "What's your pleasure, ma'am?"

Gina perused the bottles. "Gin and tonic's my pleasure, sir."

"Then gin and tonic it will be." Richard found two glasses and poured the drinks. "Cheers."

Gina took a sip and smiled, showing her satisfaction. "Mind if I smoke?"

"No, go ahead. I know you need a cigarette by now."

Gina got out her pack, slid out a cigarette, and lit up. She put it to her mouth, taking a deep inhale. Then she looked around for an ashtray and seated herself in the chair next to it. "What do you have planned for tonight?"

"Some dinner and dancing. We can do all that right here in the hotel. After the hectic day we've had, I thought it would be better to have a relaxed evening. And I know you're tired from the long flight. We could turn in early if you can't hold up."

"Don't worry about me. I'll get a second wind—I always do."

They finished their drinks as Richard looked at his watch. "We better get dressed for dinner. Why don't you take a shower first since you need more time?"

After showering, Gina stood in front of the mirror to touch up her makeup and restyle her hair. She brushed her teeth, sprayed on Chanel No. 5, her favorite scent designed for femininity, and searched in her makeup case for her lipstick—Rouge Jolie—red lips are always so alluring. She pulled out matching red nail polish to coat her nails as well. The black lace dress she planned to wear would be more dramatic with red lips and nails. Then, she stepped out of the bathroom. "All yours." Richard gathered his necessities and headed for the shower.

When Gina heard him step in, she opened the mini bar and grabbed a vial of vodka she had spied earlier. She liked vodka because it left no telltale sign, being both colorless and odorless. That was a lesson she learned as a teenager and had never forgotten. She poured the vodka into her used glass, lit another cigarette, and sat in a chair to savor the moment. She liked to down a couple before going out—then she was ready for anything. When she heard Richard turn off the water, she tidied up and took out the dress she had bought for the occasion. Gina put on her garter belt and carefully slipped on her stockings to ensure the seams were straight and then connected them to the fasteners. She hated garter belts. The fasteners often poked her legs when she sat. And if she had terrible luck, one would pop, and her stocking would droop. She preferred to go bare-legged whenever she could. Next, Gina slipped on the sheath-style lace dress that clung to her body, emphasizing her womanly curves. With the low back, she couldn't wear a bra, so she'd have to go braless—her breasts were small and firm and, as the French like to say, just the right size to fit into a champagne glass—she could get away with it. She pulled out her black pumps and clutch purse. Now for the jewelry. She always liked pearls with lace and chose a single white pearl strand. She put a trio of gold bangles on one wrist and a gold watch on the other. Then she chose gold and pearl dangling earrings to complete the look. She was ready but would wait to put the pumps on until the last minute. She crossed her fingers, hoping her feet would not already be too swollen from all the walking...and drinking. When she heard Richard turn off the sink faucet, she finished her drink and replaced the glass in its original position. Then she eased into her shoes, relieved they were not tight. She stood up to the mirror for a full-length view and liked what she saw—sexy and sophisticated. She had no doubt Richard would be captivated.

The bathroom door opened, revealing Richard in his tighty-whities, hair still wet, face shaved. He took one look at Gina and let out a wolf whistle. "I can't believe I have the honor of escorting you tonight," he said.

Gina just smiled, a hint of mystery behind it.

They took the elevator to the 19th floor, known as Top of the Mark. As soon as Gina glimpsed the scene, she let out a gasp. Windows surrounded the famous lounge, offering spectacular views of the Golden Gate Bridge and the hills of Sausalito beyond. Richard gave the maître d' his name, and they were shown to a prime table. "I don't think I've ever laid eyes on a more glamorous sight," said Gina.

"It certainly is something. I never get over the thrill of being up here. During the war, servicemen came here before shipping out to the Pacific Theater for their last look at San Francisco. If they were lucky enough to return, they would have a drink from their squadron's bottle, which would be awaiting them behind the bar. Now, this is where the celebrities come—you might even see one tonight."

The waiter stepped up to their table. Richard said, "Martinis are the signature drinks—they have about a hundred different kinds." Then he ordered two Golden Gates.

While the waiter was getting their drink order, Gina asked Richard, "Why were there so many servicemen in San Francisco?"

"Both the Presidio and Navy Shipyard on Mare Island are here. In fact, this is where I usually do my training weekends. But sometimes I go to the Naval Postgraduate School in Monterey instead."

The waiter appeared with their martinis and set one in front of each of them. Then he disappeared again. Gina lifted the glass to her lips and took a sip. "I taste chocolate," she said.

"That's right. There's crème de cacao in here along with Jack Daniels and a squeeze of lemon."

Gina took another sip, then pulled out a cigarette. Richard struck a match and lit it for her. Gina took a long inhale, leaned her head back, and let out a stream of smoke. She could not resist a cigarette with her drink.

The band had set up. Their first number had the rhythm of a tango. Gina couldn't wait to be taken into Richard's arms as they headed to the dance floor. He knew how to take control of his partner and move her through the prescribed steps of a number of dances. Richard had been on a ballroom dance team in college, where he had developed his talent. He made a good spare at gatherings during his navy years—officers' wives appreciated his skill. And now, as Richard dipped and twirled Gina around the room, she experienced his mastery. By the time the music ended, she was breathless. The next song the band struck up was "As Time Goes By"—their wedding song. Richard pulled her in close as he sang along. Gina was more in love than ever.

They headed back to their table, and Richard looked at his watch. "Almost time for our dinner reservation. Would you like another quick cocktail before we go downstairs?"

"After that tango, I'm famished. Let's eat."

The French Chateau-style dining room featured Louis XVI chairs, crystal chandeliers, gilt-framed mirrors, and paintings of Paris. The maître d' showed them to a corner table while the server brought them menus and a wine list. "May I recommend one of our California vintages? They rival anything else on the menu, including French wines."

"Please," Richard said. And the waiter pointed out some selections and left for the wine cellar.

When he returned with a bottle of chardonnay, they put in their orders. It was a magnificent four-course dinner–scallops St. Jacques to start, followed by a green salad with avocado and hearts of palm and rack of lamb with bordelaise sauce. A Grand Marnier souffle, sweet and airy, provided the perfect finish to the feast. Gina batted her long lashes and looked Richard in the eyes. "Is this the lifestyle I can expect from you?"

He held the eye contact. "It will take several years, but this is what I aspire to."

"Do you have a plan to achieve all this?"

"Yes, of course. And you are part of it. We'll build an empire together."

Gina gave Richard a speculative look. She did not know what to make of this. She knew Richard was always planning ahead—always striving for something more. But she didn't understand what part he wanted her to play. She had a feeling she was about to find out.

They were both weary when they entered their room. Richard took off his jacket and hung it in the closet. Next, he loosened his tie and removed it. Gina kicked her heels off, feeling relief at last—they had started a stranglehold on her feet that she was glad to escape. "Richard, could you unzip me, please?"

He moved behind her, then slowly unzipped her dress and pushed it past her shoulders, allowing it to slip into a puddle at her feet. Gina turned to face him. She had nothing on except her garter belt and stockings. Her breasts were bare, nipples standing erect. Richard's eyes slowly swept every inch of her body. Overcome with passion, he scooped Gina off her feet and carried her to bed. The night was still young, and he was going to make the most of it.

CHAPTER TWO

Richard took the scenic route home along the coast, but the fog was still eclipsing the ocean view. Gina laid her head back on the seat and closed her eyes to rest. "Wake me when the Pacific becomes visible." It wasn't until they reached Santa Cruz that the fog let up to reveal the glorious ocean, a sapphire blue, white caps sparkling like diamonds.

Richard let out a yell, startling Gina. "See how the coast bends around—that's Monterey and Carmel over there. Night becomes magical with a myriad of twinkling lights."

"How much longer?"

"Not long. Maybe half an hour. I don't know whether I told you, but our neighbors, Tom and Margery, plan to drop by to meet you when they spot us driving in."

"It's nice to know our neighbors are friendly."

"I think you'll find a lot of friendly people in town. I hope you're not worried about being alone."

"My family and everyone else I know will be far away. But I'm looking forward to meeting your friends and making my own as well."

"This is a small town. You'll have no problem doing that. And you're outgoing, which will help."

Gina was glad to know she might have one friend immediately who lived right next door.

The road sign announced Watsonville. It got Gina's attention, and she sat up straight in her seat. She didn't want to miss any part of their arrival. As Richard exited onto the town road, a large patch of dark earth filled with lettuce appeared. "Look at that field. That's some of the richest farmland in the world, known as the Salad Bowl of the Country because of all the vegetables and fruits grown here."

"Who are the people in the fields?"

"They're migrant workers up from Mexico for the season. They're part of the Bracero program."

"Bracero. That must be a Spanish word. What does it mean in English?"

"Arm. They're lending us their arms in return for money that they'll take back to their families in Mexico after the harvest."

"Oh, Richard, there's a farm stand ahead. Can we stop and buy some fresh produce?"

Richard hesitated while he checked his watch. "I'd like to get home so you can settle in. Besides, the neighbors are waiting for us. Don't worry. This won't be the last farm stand—they're all over."

They crossed the bridge over the Pajaro River and headed toward Main Street. In the center of town stood a plaza with a bandstand surrounded by benches. "That looks just like pictures I've seen of Mexico."

"There's a lot of Spanish influence in California. A Spanish Jesuit priest, Junipero Serra, founded missions up and down the state, creating the first settlements. The Mexicans come to the plaza on Sunday afternoons to dance and socialize. During the week, old men come here to play cards or read the newspaper while they bask in the sun."

Gina became quiet. She was thinking about how different California was from the East Coast and wondered if she would enjoy living here. She loved San Francisco, but Watsonville was a far cry from the City on the Bay. As they moved down the street, she spotted a movie theater, department store, and even a hotel. Who would spend a night there? When they came to the end of Main Street, where it intersected Route One, the Catholic church came into view. "Oh, Richard, it's named St. Patrick's. I'm starting to feel like I'm home."

Richard turned the corner and drove past the town rec center with tennis courts and a pool, past a shopping center, and through one of the best residential sections—tree-lined streets with a mix of colonials, Tudors, and Spanish revivals, until they reached Buena Vista Drive. He turned onto it, stopping at number 717, a white California bungalow with blue shutters framing a bay window. "We're here," he said as he pulled the key from the ignition.

Richard made his way to the other side of the car and held the door open for Gina. She got out with a bounce in her step. They walked hand in hand up the curved brick pathway that bordered the sprawling front yard, entering through the patio gate. The patio was all brick as well, with bougainvillea climbing up the wall that separated the area from the street. In fact, it was more of a courtyard since it was enclosed on the other three sides as well—two by the house that formed a right angle and the other by a high hedge providing privacy between neighbors. The sun was still shining down on the courtyard, radiating heat from the brick.

"This is where I'll put my lounge for sun bathing," Gina said. "And we need a patio set for alfresco dining. There's nothing like having a wonderful meal in the fresh air."

Richard smiled as they climbed up the front steps. He slid the key in the lock and pushed the door ajar. "We need to do this right," he said as he wrapped Gina in his arms and carried her over the threshold. "Welcome home." He set her down, and they fell into a loving embrace until Gina stepped back, signaling it was time to take inventory of the rooms.

The entrance hall connected the dining room and living

room into an airy L-shaped space filled with windows. "We're going to have wonderful dinner parties here. The space naturally lends itself to that."

Next, she headed toward the kitchen. It was white, with good, clean lines. "I can do a lot with this plain canvas to evoke an Italian theme. The windows just need patterned swags and, with some artfully placed Italian pottery, the look will be complete."

"I'm glad you like the house, and your design ideas will turn it into a showplace."

"Getting the house decorated will be my first priority. I want this to be a home you can be proud of."

Before Gina could check out the master suite, the doorbell rang. "I bet it's Tom and Margery. They said they would watch for our arrival. I'll get the door."

Margery was tall with shoulder-length chestnut hair, hazel eyes, and straight, white teeth that sparkled when she smiled. Tom was tall but not much taller than Margery and appeared older. He had dark wavy hair with a few streaks of gray at the temples and green eyes—almost the color of jade. Dimples appeared when he smiled, giving him boyish appeal. Richard made the introductions. Afterward, Margery handed a freshly baked apple pie to Gina. "I thought we'd enjoy dessert and coffee while we get acquainted. This pie was made with apples from our own tree. Although, any apples you get around here will be delicious. In case you haven't heard, Watsonville supplies most of the apples to the world."

Gina bent over the pie and took a whiff. "Yum. I'll go make the coffee."

Gina headed into the kitchen, where they could hear the cupboards opening and closing. That was Richard's cue to speak up. "The pot is on the counter, and the coffee is in the cupboard to the left of the sink." Lowering his voice, he said, "Why don't we go into the kitchen and sit down while we wait."

Once they had their pie and coffee in front of them, Richard spoke first as he held up his coffee cup. "Here's to friendship. Good neighbors are worth their weight in gold."

"Mm, mm," said Gina. "The pie is as delicious as it looks. I'd like your recipe."

"It's a pretty basic apple pie, but it's the fruit fresh from our tree that makes the difference. In fact, cooking is a pleasure here because there's so much fresh produce available it's hard to go wrong. Do you like to cook, Gina?"

"Yes, and I learned all the trade secrets from my Italian mother, who can turn a few boring ingredients into a masterful dish."

"I can probably learn something from you. My mother is German. I'm a great baker, but my cooking is much more basic —lots of roasts and potatoes."

Richard chimed in. "I'm getting an urge for king crab legs. Let's go to the Naval Post Graduate School for dinner and a little dancing next Friday night. They fly the crab legs in fresh from Alaska every week for the buffet."

"I haven't had king crab since my army days in the Aleutians," said Tom. "I'd go over to our sergeants' quarters whenever it was on the menu. And guess who I'd see there—Dashiell Hammett— he was a sergeant, too, working on the *Stars and Stripes*."

"Dashiell Hammett," said Gina. "I've read the *Maltese Falcon*. He's quite a writer."

"That's what I hear," said Tom. "Anyway, after spending time in Alaska, I gained a lot of respect for crab fishermen. It's rough work fishing for crab, and the waters can be treacherous."

"I didn't know you served in the war," said Richard.

"Got drafted at twenty-eight. Then I went to Camp Pendleton for basic training before shipping out to the Aleutians."

"The Aleutians seem like an odd destination," said Gina.

"They expected the Japanese to mount an attack, which never happened—only a few skirmishes. I was lucky."

The four chatted a while longer until Margery looked at her watch and called time. "My roast needs to be taken out of the oven. But tomorrow morning, I'll expect you for coffee, Gina— around ten a.m."

The four said their goodbyes. Gina watched the neighbors walk through the patio and out the gate. "I like them. My instincts tell me Margery and I are going to be good friends."

"I'm off to work. Enjoy your day. I'll leave the keys to your car on the kitchen table."

Gina let out a sleepy sigh. "Thanks, Richard." And she turned over and fell back asleep. When she awoke, it was only eight a.m. She padded into the kitchen and started the coffeemaker. After locating her cigarettes, she sat down and lit one, taking a slow inhale to relax. Her new life was interesting... but nothing was familiar. She poured herself a cup of coffee and felt herself coming back to life. After another drag on her cigarette, she stumped it out in the ashtray and searched through the cupboards for something to eat but came up empty-handed. *I might as well get dressed and go out to look around. I'm not due next door for an hour.*

Gina threw on a pair of capris, a plaid cotton shirt, and flip-flops. She grabbed her purse and the car key, locked the door, and headed down the path to the garage. The door was heavy and difficult to open, but when she succeeded, she stood there dumbfounded. A station wagon. *I gave up my BMW for an Oldsmobile station wagon.* She wanted to let out a primal scream but feared arousing the neighbors. Instead, she did a slow burn. *What was he thinking?* But this was the only car available, and she would have to drive it—at least for now. She opened the door, slid in, and turned on the ignition while she glanced at the dashboard. *There's a full tank—thank goodness for small favors.* Gina put the car in reverse and edged out of the garage, careful not to scrape on either side. It was a tight fit, but she made it without mishap.

Now, which way should I go? She turned the car toward the nearby corner, stopped to look both ways, then made a right onto Martinelli Street. She took it all the way until it dead-ended. Straight ahead, a large white Victorian house stood in the middle of an apple orchard. It looked very misplaced. That house must have a tale to tell. She turned left and passed mile after mile of apple orchards where workers picked fruit, packed crates, and loaded them onto trucks. Watsonville must still grow apples to supply the world. She was feeling out of place, just like that house. Boston is civilization. Watsonville is still the Wild West—it's nothing like San Francisco. Finally, Gina spotted a large farm stand called the Corn Castle and pulled in.

She grabbed a basket and began filling it with an abundance of produce—lettuce, tomatoes, asparagus, onions, garlic—the fresh vegetables had inspired her to make pasta primavera for dinner. A salesman saw her hesitating. "I haven't seen you in here before. Are you new to town?"

"Yes, I only moved here yesterday."

He gave her the once over before speaking again. "Where did you move from?"

"Boston."

"Oh, Boston…I know the Red Sox."

"Everybody does."

"May I help you find something in particular?"

"Pasta."

"It's over on the far shelf."

"That's convenient. I'm making pasta primavera tonight, and that's the only other thing I need except cheese. Do you carry parmesan?"

"With so many Italians around here, we have to stock it."

Gina put her groceries on the counter, and as the salesman rang them up, she pulled out a credit card. "I'll help you out with these bags," he said. And he stowed them in the trunk.

Gina hurried home, driving back the same way to avoid getting lost. When she pulled into her driveway, she glanced at her watch—almost ten a.m. *I'll be on time if I can make quick work of these groceries.*

On her way next door, she caught sight of Margery through the kitchen window. She looked up and waved Gina in.

"Thank you for inviting me over this morning. I needed to talk to someone."

"Would you like some coffee before we start getting more acquainted? I just made a fresh pot."

"That's exactly what I need right now, along with a cigarette. Do you mind if I smoke?"

"Not at all. I've gotten used to it. Tom is a heavy smoker—three and a half packs a day."

Gina lit her cigarette, took a puff, and blew rings into the air.

"Here's some coffee to go with your cigarette. I understand they're a natural pairing."

"That's right. They both seem to take the edge off."

Margery sat down and picked up her cup. "Tell me, how do you like our lovely town so far?" she asked as a wry smile crossed her lips.

"Boston, it's not. This morning, I drove around and saw nothing but miles and miles of apple orchards. Although, there was one curious sight."

"Oh, what's that?"

"A large Victorian home set in the middle of an orchard. It didn't fit in."

"That's the Rodgers' home. He's an apple farmer, and his wife is the eldest sister of novelist John Steinbeck. *In Dubious Battle* may have been inspired by an apple strike in an orchard near here out on San Juan Road. His brother-in-law could have provided some insider information."

Gina's eyes opened wide. "Steinbeck. A friend gave me *East of Eden* to read. She thought it would prepare me for my new life."

"Did it?"

Gina took another puff of her cigarette and brushed her hair back while she considered her response. "The only thing I remember from the book is Watsonville was where the sheriff dumped off an old prostitute."

"And don't forget he mentions that our wonderful citizens tarred and feathered a Pole during the war, mistaking him for a German. He made us out to be real bumpkins."

Gina let out a laugh. "Well, Richard holds this place in high regard, and I hope he's right."

"I came from the East Coast, too, Buffalo, so I know how you feel, even though Buffalo is not in the same league as Boston."

They shared a chuckle as they compared the differences in lifestyle until a cry interrupted them. "Is that a baby I hear?"

"Yes, she's two months old and probably wants to eat again. I'll get her and be right back."

Margery returned with the baby in her arms. She sat down, unbuttoned her blouse, and put the baby to her breast. Gina watched the maternal scene with awe. Margery seemed such a natural mother. It wasn't long before the baby was through feeding. "I have plenty of milk," Margery said. "It flows fast. Betsy hardly needs to suckle."

"I guess it's best to breastfeed if you can."

"It certainly is. Babies get better nutrition, and they bond better, too. Excuse me a moment while I put her back down, and we can talk some more."

Gina helped herself to another cup of coffee and was lighting a cigarette when Margery returned.

"Now, what questions do you have for me?"

Gina let out the smoke she had inhaled. "Tell me about the neighbors. Who's living around us?"

Margery paused before she spoke. "Across from us are the

Crawfords. Their two children are older, maybe in college. Ben is retired from the air force and manages the airport."

"Airport manager. I wonder if Richard knows he lives right across the street."

"On the corner are the Yamamotos. They have three boys who are near high school age."

Gina raised her eyebrows. "They must be Japanese."

"Yes, we have a large Japanese population. Most of them are in the flower or strawberry business. The Yamamotos grow flowers. They invite the neighbors for a Japanese New Year's celebration and put on a feast."

"That sounds interesting. I hope we get an invitation."

"If not, we'll bring you along. On the other side of you are the Cunninghams, who own a trucking business."

"What an assortment of characters," Gina said.

"That's a small town for you. A Chinese family lives across the street from the Yamamotos. But so far, we don't have any Mexicans in the neighborhood. That will be coming."

"Richard told me the Mexicans come up for the harvest and go back home afterward."

"Not anymore. The families discovered how good life is in the USA and have set up home. They want their babies to be born here, so they qualify for citizenship and all the benefits that come with it. When I worked maternity at the hospital, there were few Mexican babies. Now, they fill the ward."

"America is one big melting pot. I'm proof of that, being half Italian and half Irish."

Margery nodded in agreement. "What else can I tell you?"

Gina looked at her watch. It was almost noon, and she knew Margery was due at work in a couple of hours. "Let's save it for tomorrow. I'd like to make coffee with you a regular habit."

Gina prioritized her day as she walked home. I've got about six hours before Richard returns. I have to cook, but more importantly, I need to buy a chaise lounge. She set it up on the patio and spent the next few hours reading in the sun. This is the life. What would I be doing in Boston now? Probably packing up my summer wardrobe and getting out the boots and woolens.

Gina spent her remaining free hours in the kitchen chopping, stirring, and tasting to correct seasonings. This pasta primavera is one of my better renditions. It was now getting close to six o'clock. Time to get the pasta boiling. Next, she pulled out a couple of Italian print placemats and set the table with wine goblets along with a pair of candlesticks. As if on cue, Richard walked in the back door. "What's that delicious smell?"

"It's pasta primavera. You're going to love it."

After taking off his boots, he padded his stocking feet into the kitchen and put his arms around Gina. "Not half as much as you."

They ate their pasta by candlelight while the wine flowed. "What did you do with your day?" Richard asked while he rolled pasta onto his fork.

"I took a ride, bought some produce at the Corn Castle, and had coffee with Margery."

"Oh," Richard said, raising an eyebrow, "did she pass on any words of wisdom?"

"She told me about some of the neighbors. Did you know the airport manager lives across the street?"

"You mean Ben Crawford? No, I didn't. What a coincidence. Let's invite him and his wife for dinner sometime."

Gina swallowed her mouthful of pasta before she answered. "The two of you would have a lot in common between flying and the military."

"I'll leave it to you to arrange something. Gina, you're going to need more than Margery's company to stay busy. I'd like you to join the Women's Club. It would give both of us a chance to meet some new people."

"I'll look into it. But I'd also like to sing in a choir—maybe at the church. Music is important to me."

"You can do that, too. By the way, I noticed a new chaise lounge on the patio."

"I also went to a patio store. An outdoor dining set will be delivered later this week. Then we can have the alfresco meals I've been promising you."

"A dinner like this one at the kitchen table suits me just fine. To show my appreciation, let me help you clear the table."

"You don't have to do that. I know you've had a hard day."

But Richard had already stood up. "I've read that men who share household chores with their wives are rewarded with better sex lives."

The pair cleaned up the kitchen in no time and headed off to the bedroom while the evening was still young.

Gina showed up on Margery's doorstep around ten the next morning. "Hi. Can I borrow a cup of coffee?"

"You're in luck. There's still some in the pot."

Gina had already lit a cigarette. "I can talk better with this in my hand," she said as she gazed down at the cigarette. "Before I forget, I want to remind you about our date for king crab legs at the Naval Postgraduate School. Richard made reservations, so we should leave about six p.m. And we'll take his business sedan, not my station wagon."

Margery put her cup down and looked straight into Gina's eyes to gauge her meaning. "I take it you don't like the station wagon."

"Let's put it this way, it came as quite a surprise after driving a BMW for years."

"You're a housewife now. A station wagon is practical."

"Well, I don't plan to look like a housewife on Friday night. I'm going to wear my sexiest dress."

The baby started crying, then quieted down. "My mother's here."

"You're lucky your mother is nearby to help you. But from what I saw yesterday, you're an expert already for a first-time mom."

Margery looked down, composing herself before responding. "Of course, I've had my share of experience on the maternity ward. But Betsy is not my first child. My first child died when he was only a year old."

"I'm sorry…I…I didn't know."

"Mark will be gone a year in October. I'm not sure how I'll deal with the anniversary," Margery said while tears welled up in her eyes.

"Had he been ill?"

"He was one of the healthiest baby boys around—big, blond, almost beefy looking. On the day he died, I had to work, and Tom was watching him. He had put him in his swing in the back-yard. Unbeknownst to him, our neighbor was about to spray his roses that bordered the fence along our property lines. He always sprayed them when the wind blew our way. And just like a man, Tom put Mark in his swing and went about his yardwork. Who knows how long the baby had been inhaling that poison? Not long after I got home, he stopped breathing. I gave him CPR and worked on him until the ambulance arrived. With each compression, Tom was yelling, 'Save him. Save him.' He knew I had saved many babies in the hospital, but I couldn't save our son."

Gina put her arms around Margery and hugged her tight.

Tears were rolling down Margery's face when they separated. "I'm sorry. It's still so emotional for me. I often think about how different things would have turned out if I hadn't worked that day. My baby wouldn't have been in that swing unattended."

Gina stayed silent.

Then Margery continued. "You know, around here, they're spraying poison on the crops all the time to kill insects. But God only knows what the poison is doing to people. Sometimes the crop dusters dump part of their load on cars, spraying them with white powder. I can only imagine what would happen to someone in a convertible. Mark my words. One day, people are going to die because of it."

Gina left for home in a state of shock at Margery's revelation. It was common for people to lose infants, but not the way Margery lost hers. Gina wondered what other shocks were in store for her new life.

CHAPTER THREE

At six p.m. sharp, Margery and Tom arrived at the Bankstons' door. Richard was ready while Gina lagged. "Hurry up," Richard called to her.

"I'm coming," she shouted back and appeared dressed to the nines. She wasn't kidding when she said she was going to be her sexiest. Gina wore a red chiffon sleeveless dress that nipped at the waist and flared at the hips. She had on red pumps to match and even wore red on her lips.

"You look fabulous," Richard said. Then he grabbed her wrap off the dining room chair and pulled it around her. "Let's go."

Richard drove, and Tom rode shotgun with the girls in the back. They headed down Main Street, over the Pajaro River bridge, and onto the road that would take them to Monterey. "This is a road I know like the back of my hand," said Tom. "I used to come over here before the navy took control of the Del Monte Hotel for the war. Big bands played there, and everyone from presidents to movie stars came to hear them. Bing Crosby used to come here a lot—he has a sister in Watsonville."

The stacks of the Moss Landing power plant were now coming into view. "Believe it or not, Moss Landing has an annual shark derby. The bay is so deep they come in close to shore," Tom said.

Then it was Castroville, the Artichoke Capital of the World. The fields were filled with the plants growing on long thistle-like stems. "There's the Giant Artichoke," said Margery. "Anybody interested in fried artichoke hearts?" But there were no takers. Beyond that lay the Fort Ord Army Base on the left and large sand dunes on the right, tumbling down to the sea. Then it was on to Seaside, Marina, and finally Monterey.

"We're almost there," said Richard. He turned toward the guard's gate, showed his ID, and proceeded in. He found a parking space in the lot and turned off the engine. "All ashore who's going ashore," he said.

They put smiles on their faces as they walked toward the Spanish-style building with its red tile roof and stucco façade. "You may have known this as The Hotel Del Monte," Richard said to Tom, "but now the navy calls it Hermann Hall. Although, it still serves as a hotel of sorts for the military."

The foursome entered through the grand door. Richard led the way down the hall. "I thought we'd have a drink first at the Trident—it's known for its wide selection of beers." When they entered the bar, the girls were taken aback. It was all wood paneling and stained-glass artwork, with a bar fashioned out of a massive piece of oak. "Step up and name your poison," Richard said.

"I don't care for a beer—make mine a martini," Gina said.

"I'll have that, too," said Margery. Tom and Richard ordered drafts.

Meantime, Tom surveyed the room, trying to recall past times there. He recognized Ben and Sylvia Crawford, who waved the group over. The foursome approached the Crawfords, who asked them to stay and join them for drinks. The server spotted their new location, bringing the martinis on a tray along with two large mugs of beer capped with foam.

After they got settled, Tom said to Ben, "I believe you have met Richard at the airport, but did you know he lives across the street?"

"Is that a fact?" Ben said.

"And he's military, too," said Tom. "Navy."

"I had my career in the air force. That's the reason I took the manager's job at the airport. Richard, did you know Watsonville used to be known as a navy town?"

"Yes, that's one reason the town attracted me. I believe the old airport served as a Naval Auxiliary Airfield during the war."

"That's right. It was one of only two on the West Coast. Airships deployed on sub patrols and air and sea rescues. The bay is so deep that subs could sneak right up to the coast."

"I guess it's good the war is over. Now, the whales and sharks don't have to share the space with subs," Tom said.

They all laughed and turned to listen in on the girls' conversation. But before they could tune in, another couple approached the table. "These are our friends, the Masons." They all shook hands and exchanged greetings. Richard looked at his watch and announced it was time to move to the dining room.

Richard gave his name to the maître d' who checked the reservation book. "This way, please, Lt. Bankston." He led the group to a large table surrounded by four Spanish-style chairs. The white-clothed table was set with an ornate silver pattern and crystal-cut goblets. An arrangement of mixed flowers paired with wrought iron candlesticks added to the Spanish style elegance. The waiter came by and handed each member of the group a menu, leaving the wine list for Richard. "Since crab is the star tonight, shall we go with a white wine?"

"Let's start with white, but we might want to switch to red afterward. I noticed a leg of lamb on the buffet table. That calls for red," said Tom.

Remembering what the server at the Mark Thomas had recommended, Richard ordered a California chardonnay. The group headed to the buffet table for their salad course. They all filled their plates with a large romaine salad. They added asparagus wrapped with prosciutto, mushrooms stuffed with crab, marinated mussels, and fried artichoke hearts. "Thank goodness we didn't stop at the Giant Artichoke," Margery said. "Gina, try the sautéed abalone—it's a local specialty. After a pounding, it is tender and sweet. There's nothing like it."

Gina took some on her plate. "A million sea lions can't be wrong," Tom said. "They love the stuff." Gina smiled.

With plates piled high, the group made their way back to their table to eat their salad and appetizers. Richard filled the glasses with the chardonnay that had arrived table-side, chilling in a bucket. The waiter rushed over to pour, but Richard waved him off. Then he offered a toast, "To friendship. May we always be good neighbors."

"Hear, hear," said Tom, as they clinked glasses all around.

They headed back to the buffet for the pièce de résistance—Alaskan king crab legs, so long that they extended out over the plates. "These seem like they'll be more difficult to eat than lobster," Gina said.

"Don't worry," said Richard. "I'll demonstrate."

"We'll have to compare techniques since I learned mine closer to the source," Tom said. They chuckled and headed back to the table. Margery looked around the room. Several of the men were in military uniform, but she didn't see the Crawfords yet.

Richard started the conversation off, talking about his time in the navy and his weekends in the reserves. "I'm hoping to make commander before I retire."

That was just like Richard, Gina thought, always setting goals. It was what she both loved and loathed about him. But no doubt goal setting had helped to put him on the path to success.

The band had played some mood music for the dinner hour. Now they were starting up with dance numbers. Richard took

Gina by the hand and led her to the dance floor. Tom and Margery took the cue and followed. The dance floor was spacious, and few couples were on it, allowing them to move freely. When a tango came on, Richard held Gina tight—dipping and twirling her around the floor as her skirt whirled about her. Margery and Tom had settled back into their chairs to watch. When the couple returned, Margery said, "Richard, where did you learn to dance like that?"

"I was in a ballroom dance club in college. We competed up and down the West Coast. Gina's a good follower, so she makes us look good."

"I grew up dancing. We were always going to big weddings or some other affair. My father was the one who taught me. The Irish love their dancing."

"That's not all they love," said Richard. "But we won't talk about that."

Tom and Margery gave each other a quick glance and remained silent.

Then Margery noticed Ben and Sylvia on the dance floor. Ben, tall and broad-shouldered with gray hair, had the bearing of a military man and the face of a warrior, strong features set in a square face with a prominent jaw. When he bore down on you with his pale blue eyes, he could put fear in both man and beast. Sylvia, thin and elegant, wore her silver hair in a bob but moved with the grace of a younger woman. She pointed them out, saying, "Don't they make a nice-looking couple." Tom took that as a hint and led Margery out to the dance floor.

Now alone, Gina said, "I don't know what you meant by your comment, but I don't like you making derogatory remarks about my heritage."

"It was only a joke. Do you care to dance again? We make such a nice-looking couple."

"Oh, you," Gina said, slapping Richard playfully on the arm. "I guess your sense of humor is too subtle for me. But let's dance. Everyone's out there."

Richard took Gina's hand in his, brought it to his lips for a kiss, then led her to the dance floor.

They danced until the band shut down, switching partners occasionally. All the women in the room were secretly hoping to dance with Richard, but only Margery had the chance. And she stayed in his arms as long as she could, although she didn't have the stamina to keep up with him.

"This has been a great evening," said Tom. "I feel like I'm back at the Del Monte. Those were the good old days."

"It's hard not to be nostalgic when times have passed. But we're in the springtime of our lives," said Richard.

"When do you have to be home for the babysitter?" Gina asked.

"No particular time. My mother's watching the baby, and she's planning to spend the night. But there's church tomorrow morning, so I don't want to stay out too late. Gina, would you like to join Tom and me?"

"Yes, thanks for asking. I want to find out about the choir and meet the priest."

"Oh, you're going to love Father O'Leary."

"O'Leary. St. Patrick's. Is this little Boston?"

Both Margery and Tom laughed. "No," Margery said, "but there are a lot of Irish around here. I believe they built the church."

Richard looked at his watch. "Let's call it a night so you can get off to church in the morning." They all rose from the table, making their way out of the dining room to the coat check. Tom and Richard handed their claim checks to the attendant and helped the girls with their wraps. Fall was on its way.

Everyone was quiet on the ride back, lost in their own thoughts after the memorable evening. Richard remarked on the lights as they came into view, highlighting the northern section of the bay.

They made it home before midnight. Margery reminded

Gina about church. "Be ready by quarter to eleven. We'll pick you up."

Gina was ready on time, wearing a blue suit, hat, and heels. She liked the church ritual and had fond memories of singing in her church choir, performing in the Christmas pageant, attending too many church socials and fundraisers to count, especially bingo night. Tom parked the car in the back lot, and they entered through the side door. They found seats in the nave's mid-section. After saying their prayers, Margery whispered to Gina, "They named the church St. Patrick's because construction started on the saint's day."

The Mass was about to begin. They stood for the entrance hymn, and Gina smiled, liking what she heard from the choir. She could see herself fitting in. Father O'Leary stood on the front steps, greeting everyone as they left, giving Margery an opportunity to introduce Gina. He looked her straight in the eyes. "An Irish lass. St. Patrick is smiling today."

"I'd like to join the choir," Gina said.

"Ah...and she sings, too. Come on Thursday night at seven p.m., and we'll find a place for you."

Gina flashed her warmest smile. "I'll be there."

"Isn't Father O'Leary wonderful?" Margery asked.

"He reminds me of some of the priests from home. About half are like Father O'Leary, all mirthfulness and light. But the other half breathe fire and brimstone."

"We have the luck of the Irish in this parish," Margery said.

Richard was waiting at the door when she returned. "I take it church was successful."

"I'll start singing with the choir on Thursday."

"That's good. But don't let it consume you. You need to save room for the Women's Club."

. . .

Gina was on Margery's doorstep early Monday morning, ready for coffee and conversation. She was barely in the door when she said, "Richard wants to give a dinner party this Saturday evening. I don't know how I'll pull it off. The house isn't decorated, and I've never given a dinner party."

"Don't worry," said Margery. "First, the décor won't be a problem once the guests show up. They'll not only fill up the room but decorate it, too. I discovered that secret when I had a Christmas party in a semi-empty house. And second, I can help you plan." In no time, the pair had put together a menu worthy of a king.

"Do you have everything ready?" Richard asked. "Can I do anything to help?"

"The coq au vin is in the oven. Dessert is made. The appetizers and salad are in the refrigerator. Champagne—I bought an entire case. Can you put a couple of bottles on ice?"

Richard was listening while he perused the dining room. "The table looks great." It was covered with a white damask cloth topped with their new sterling flatware, an ornate Old-World pattern, and glimmering Waterford crystal goblets. A silver vase, filled with a mix of garden flowers, was the centerpiece, flanked by crystal candlesticks.

Richard had just gotten the champagne chilled when the doorbell rang. "I'll get it." Meantime, Gina took off her apron, reapplied her lipstick, and powdered her face to take away the shine from sweating over a hot stove.

Gina made her way to the entrance hall and turned on her charm. "Steve and Sue, I'm so glad you're here." Steve Hillman had been one of Richard's fraternity brothers in college. He grew up in Watsonville and now served as town attorney. He looked bookish with his signature wire-rim glasses, page boy haircut, and small, smooth hands that had not known a day of manual work. The other two couples arrived right behind them—Rob and Jane Thomas and Jack and Lynn Overton. Richard played tennis with Rob, who was branch manager of Wells Fargo. Rob had the portly look of a banker and was getting a receding hairline as well. But he had a kind-looking face and a ready smile that always won the day. Jack was an engineering colleague at Blackrock Construction. He wore his hair in a crewcut and always kept a slide rule handy in his pocket. Tonight was no exception. The wives were all a version of the California Girl—tan, toned, and blonde. Richard introduced Gina and said, "Let's sit down in the living room while we have appetizers."

Gina returned to the kitchen and reappeared with a tray of assorted canapés, which she placed on the cocktail table. Richard had already popped the cork on the champagne and was filling everyone's flute. Steve stood up, raising his glass. "To Gina and Richard, may your lives be as happy and fruitful here as ours have been. And may our friendship grow with time." They clinked their glasses and took a sip.

Rob looked up in surprise after his first taste. "This is the best champagne I've ever had," he said.

"Veuve Clicquot," Gina replied, looking smug. "It's my favorite."

"You are bringing real class to town," Steve said. "Lord knows we need it."

They moved to the table where the first course had already been plated. "Shrimp cocktail," said Sue. "It's my favorite starter." Richard refilled the champagne glasses, and the conversation flowed from town politics to construction issues with a dose of gossip thrown in. Gina excused herself, then reappeared with a steaming platter of coq au vin, which filled the room with its earthy aroma.

While Richard did the honors serving, Gina returned to the kitchen for the salad and bread. As they were talking, Richard brought up Gina's interest in joining the Women's Club since the three women were members.

"You'll have to come to our next meeting," Jane said. "It's

going to be at Esther Rodgers' home. She had a luncheon a while back, and it was lovely."

"She's John Steinbeck's sister, isn't she?"

"Yes, but she doesn't advertise it. Although, you'll notice him in some of the family photos displayed around the house."

"Please, give me the details and date, and I'll plan to attend. I'd love to meet more women in town."

After a dessert of chocolate mousse, the party moved into the living room. Richard approached the stereo to put on some dance music, but Rob sat down at the piano and began fingering the keys. When Richard heard him play, he put the records away. "I didn't know you played," said Steve, who tickled the ivories himself.

"Banker by day, boogie-woogie man by night," Rob said. The singing and dancing continued all night until someone mentioned they were due home for the babysitter.

Gina made her way to Margery's on Monday morning and let herself in. Her appearance was now expected, and she no longer felt the need to knock. As Gina walked into the kitchen, she noticed a fresh lemon meringue pie on the counter, then Margery appeared from the other room. "Good morning. I've been wondering how your party went over the weekend. I didn't see you in the choir on Sunday."

"I had a sore throat in the morning," Gina lied. "It had to be from all the singing I did on Saturday night. Are you aware that Rob Thomas plays the piano? He's quite a musician."

"Rob appears so stuffy in that three-piece suit he wears at the bank. I never imagined him with a musical bone in his body."

"They might all be from what I witnessed. He told me he once played at Pat O'Brien's in New Orleans when he was on a college road trip to attend Mardi Gras. Apparently, he was so good they asked him back the next night and offered him a long-time stint. Instead of a banker, he could be living the life of an artist in the French Quarter." Gina let out a snicker.

"Life has its twists and turns. But tell me, how did the dinner turn out?"

"Everyone loved the coq au vin." Then Gina gave a detailed report of the evening.

"Glad to hear the party was a success. Was Richard pleased?"

"He certainly was. He told me before the dinner party that he wanted to cultivate these people, and afterward, he said good seeds had been planted."

Furrowing her brows, Margery asked, "What type of harvest does he plan to get?"

"I'm not sure. He and Steve might go into business someday, and Rob would be able to help with the financing. And Jack is a good check on his ideas, especially when it comes to land. Richard fancies himself a land owner one day—even one of the growers in this valley."

"Growers and shippers dominate the area. They may seem like country folk, and most are not well-educated like Richard, but they wield power. And not just here. In Washington, too. I've heard they have a lot of influence with our congressman."

"Richard moved here for opportunity. He won't settle for an engineer on someone else's payroll."

Margery gave an understanding nod. "He has the market cornered on brains. Now, he needs connections, and that's where you can be helpful."

"All the women we had over are in the Women's Club. I'm not sure if it was a coincidence or if Richard planned it that way. He wants me to join to become acquainted with those women. The next meeting is going to be on Friday—a luncheon at Esther Rodgers'."

Margery peered out her kitchen window and spotted Gina in her driveway, dressed up for the Women's Club luncheon. She walked out her front door and called to Gina, "Don't you look like a bit of California sunshine." Gina was dressed in orange from head to toe—an orange sleeveless sheath dress, orange sandals, orange wide brim straw hat, and orange handbag. Even her lips wore orange.

"Everything I'm wearing is from Ford's," Gina said. "The saleswoman assured me this would be the perfect ensemble for the luncheon. Is it too much orange?"

"With your golden hair and skin tones, it really becomes you. It's always better to be bold than blend in like a wallflower."

On that parting note, Gina got in her station wagon, cursing Richard under her breath, and headed for Esther Rodgers'. She drove through the iron gate and parked in the large gravel driveway. As she made her way up the walk, she observed the house—a two-story white Victorian with black shutters and a porch. The second floor had a front balcony with a spindle railing. To the right of the house stood a water tower. And in the back, Gina glimpsed a gazebo. She loved gazebos. They reminded her of F. Scott Fitzgerald and the jazz age. She imagined Zelda there with a mint julep in her hand. Could this be a sign my time in town is about to change?

Gina waited eagerly for Richard to return home that night. As soon as he walked in, she was there to greet him. "Guess what?" Excited, she didn't wait for his reply. "Not only was I asked to join the Women's Club, but I was asked to sing the 'National Anthem.'"

Richard hugged her. "I bet you were a hit like the other night. Once the word gets around, you'll be booked for so many singing engagements that you won't have time to make me dinner."

"The women know who I am now, even Esther Rodgers. She had family photos displayed all over the house, including one of brother John carving the Thanksgiving turkey. And that reminds me, we're meeting the Crawfords for dinner tomorrow night. Now, about dinner tonight. I was out all day and singing besides. It's just going to be an omelet and salad. Is that all right with you?"

"It will have to be."

CHAPTER FOUR

Richard and Gina met the Crawfords at the Pleasant Valley Golf Clubhouse. Ben and Sylvia were avid golfers and could be found on the links most days. Richard spotted the pair at the 19th hole already having cocktails. As they walked over, Ben stood up and held a chair out for Gina. "Glad you could join us. We share a lot in common."

"Yes," Richard said. "Flying and the military, for starters."

"Starters—that's about all there is."

Ben took the California chardonnay from the wine bucket, poured it into goblets, and passed them around. After a toast, the women and men broke off into their own conversations. Sylvia asked Gina how she was getting along in Watsonville.

While the girls talked, Ben said to Richard, "I understand you're in the Naval Reserves."

"I go up to San Francisco once a month for training. My goal is to stay in long enough to make commander."

Ben took a gulp of wine. "What rank are you now?"

"Lieutenant."

Ben smiled, reflecting on his own climb up the rank ladder to colonel. "On another subject, what's your opinion of our little airport?"

"It's convenient. I fly to Sacramento every Wednesday to put in Blackrock's bids on state projects."

"I didn't realize you used it that often. You own a share in a plane, correct?"

"There are four of us in on it. But there never seems to be a conflict."

Ben paused before he spoke again, letting the silence signal the importance of his next comment. "I want to float an idea by you. What do you think about the airport hosting a fly-in? Other parts of the country put one on."

Richard took a moment to mull over Ben's idea. "That would bring visitors to the town. Have you talked with town officials or the Chamber of Commerce about it yet?"

"No. This is only in the conceptual stage."

"I'm good friends with the town attorney, Steve Hillman. He and I were fraternity brothers at Stanford."

"Stanford. You hear that, Sylvia. That's another thing we share in common. Let's go up to watch a football game some weekend. But getting back to the fly-in, I would like to speak with Steve if you could arrange a meeting. He'd know about liability."

"Tell me when you're available, and I'll set it up."

On the way home, Richard said to Gina, "You haven't been up in the plane yet. Come with me to Sacramento on Wednesday, and we'll eat in the capitol dining room after I put in the bid."

"I'd like that, Richard. Thanks for suggesting it."

Richard wanted Gina to meet some of the key people in state government with whom he was dealing. And he wanted her to appreciate what he and his company any did. He knew she was not impressed with the small town of Watsonville. But once she saw how he fit into the larger picture, she would better understand her role as his wife. They were going to go places. And he needed Gina to help him.

. . .

"Where were you hiding the past couple of days?" Margery said.

"Richard took me to Sacramento yesterday, and I had to do a million things to get ready."

"You're in luck today. I have some fresh pumpkin bread to go along with the coffee." She got out a chef's knife and sliced the loaf.

"Pumpkin...it's getting to be that time of year. I'm going to miss the holidays in New England—the leaves changing colors, the chill in the air, the snow—"

"Snow," Margery groaned. "After growing up in Buffalo, I don't miss the snow. But there is something about holidays in New England—they're right out of a storybook. But here, we don't have to worry about nasty weather spoiling plans."

"I suppose you're right."

"Don't you remember some of the power outages we had during the war? No lights on the Christmas tree, no roast cooking in the oven, and no warmth or water in the house. That's no way to spend the holidays."

"Anyway, about our trip to Sacramento." Gina pulled out a cigarette, lit it, and took a puff before she began telling Margery her story. "Lunch in the state dining room was the highlight. Lots of people stopped by our table to say hello to Richard— even the governor. I had no idea how many politicians he knows."

"He plays an important role in a company that builds big state projects."

"After lunch, we stopped by a few legislators' offices, so he could introduce me. Blackrock Construction is planning to host a holiday party up there this year, and he wants me to come along as a hostess."

"That's sounds exciting. I have to admit I'm envious."

Richard and Gina's social life continued to expand. Ever since their first dinner party, when word spread about their fun-filled gathering, they had been at the top of everyone's guest list. Now, the invitations were pouring in for the holidays—dinner parties, cocktail parties, and even cookie parties. One invitation stood out—it was from the Yamamotos. Gina opened the origami invitation designed in the shape of a flower and unfolded it to reveal the invitation inside. *A traditional Japanese New Year's feast*, the invitation read. This must be the party Margery had mentioned.

When Gina arrived at Margery's back door, she was not in the kitchen, and she let herself in as she called for her. Margery appeared, smoothing her top down. "I was breastfeeding. The baby just went down for a nap, so we won't be interrupted. Can I get you some coffee?"

"Of course. Coffee and cigarettes to start the day." Gina lit up and took a long inhale while she awaited the coffee.

"What's new?" Margery said as she set the coffee on the table. "Are you ready for that holiday party in Sacramento?"

"Oh, that. Yes. We'll be going next week. The company has hired a party consultant to handle most of the details. They're expecting a lot of legislators, but Richard says they'll probably get staffers instead."

"The legislators could be busy with competing events this time of year. But since staffers do most of the work, it'll be worthwhile meeting them."

"Speaking of parties, I received the invitation to the Yamamotos' New Year's Day party."

"We got one, too. Isn't it a beautiful invitation? Ann made it herself. The Japanese seem to be gifted with artistic talent. But I want to mention something about the Yamamotos before you meet them."

That got Gina's curiosity up as she paused smoking her cigarette. "Tell me."

Margery inhaled a deep breath before starting. "The war took a toll on everyone. The Yamamotos were sent to an internment camp for a few years. In fact, Sam and Ann met and married there. The authorities let them out for a week to take a honeymoon in Salt Lake City. Armed guards watched everyone, but they issued compassionate leave. Since their relatives were still in the camp, I suppose they had no doubt they would return. Their first son was born there."

"Oh, my," Gina said. "I never heard about that part of the war. Thank you for telling me."

"This is something no one talks about. The Japanese are very proud people and want to put everything behind them. But it was hard on them. Many lost their businesses and had to start all over again."

"That's terrible."

"The Yamamotos are good neighbors, and we are blessed with a large Japanese community in town. There's a Buddhist temple on San Juan Road."

"I assumed the building was a church. It's lovely."

"The minister, Reverend Fukuda, is rumored to have been trained as a kamikaze pilot, but his turn never came up—the war ended first, and I suspect he had some sort of conversion."

"Like St. Paul on the road to Emmaus."

Margery nodded. "Something like that, and now he lives here among us. I've only met him once, but he seems to be a wonderful man—very humble and kind."

"You've given me a lot to consider today."

Gina was stirring a pot at the stove when Richard returned. "Hi, honey. Dinner will be ready in a minute. You can take a place at the table after you wash up."

As soon as they were both seated, Gina said, "Richard, it's already December. We need to get a Christmas tree. When can we go to a tree farm and cut one down?"

"Why don't we just pick a nice one out at a lot? We could even go tonight."

On the way to find a Christmas tree, Richard brought up the holiday season. "Gina, we're going to be pretty busy this month.

Besides the company party in Sacramento, I've seen several other invitations come in. In addition, one weekend is my Navy Reserve duty."

"Somehow, we'll manage. I'd much rather be busy than not have anything to look forward to. By the way, we got an invitation to a New Year's Day party from our neighbors, the Yamamotos. Margery said they put on a real Japanese feast."

"That sounds interesting. It'll be a good way to get to know them better as well as the other neighbors."

"Margery told me that the Yamamotos spent time in an internment camp during the war."

"Were they sent to Manzanar down near Bakersfield?"

"It must have been one near Salt Lake City because they were let out for their honeymoon at the Great Salt Lake. It was terrible that they sent Japanese families, even citizens, to those places."

"That's war. It's a necessary evil. But it wasn't just Japanese who were interned. Germans were, too. In fact, some of my mother's relatives were questioned by authorities, but they didn't make them relocate. And Italians were also suspect."

Italians, she thought, remembering some of the discrimination she grew up with. "You're right. War is evil."

"But it's kept us free. Never forget that."

They both were silent for a long time until the Christmas tree lot came into view. "Let's try this place," Richard said as he turned to pull in. "I've spotted some attractive trees."

On Friday, Richard hurried in from work to change into his navy uniform. Gina had a plate waiting for him on the table, but he waved her off since he was running late. "I'll just grab a bite once I get there."

Gina saw Richard to the door and kissed him goodbye. "There'll be a surprise waiting for you when you return."

"I'll look forward to that all weekend. It's not that much fun playing weekend warrior when I'd rather be here with you."

"Me, too," Gina said while thinking she was glad to have the weekend to herself. She wanted to get the Christmas decorations up with no interruptions.

By the time Richard returned late Sunday afternoon, the halls were decked and ready to welcome him back. He spotted the tree lights twinkling in the bay window and smiled. This kept her busy and not thinking about what she was missing back home. A wreath with a big red bow hung on the front door, and jingle bells rang out when he entered. Gina ran over to kiss him. "I found these bells at a Christmas shop in Carmel—they're authentic sleigh bells. Their sound brings back memories."

Gina led Richard into the living room. His eyes went to the tree and then to the fireplace mantle in the center of the room, where the nativity was set over a blanket of assorted greens— white pine, cypress, balsam fir, and sprigs of holly and juniper.

"I love the scent of evergreens," Richard said. "They take me back, too. I spent a lot of time in the woods in Connecticut, crushing needles under foot. It's a fragrance you never forget."

"I'm sure your family always put up a tree."

"Of course, my mother is German—Christmas is in their blood. One day, we'll visit Germany during the holidays. Talk about a wonderland—there is nothing like it. And the Christmas markets are a holiday shopper's dream."

"I'd like that. Why don't you change while I finish getting dinner together?"

Richard noted the pleasing aroma coming from the kitchen. "What are we having?"

"Something special. Now, get changed."

Richard padded off to his room as told.

Gina had made veal banquette—something comforting to relax him. She opened a Chianti to go with it. While she waited for Richard, she poured herself a glass and sat down at the table to smoke a quick cigarette before he arrived.

"I smell something," he said, "and it's not something I want to eat."

"I'm sorry. Next time, I'll smoke outside. But don't let a little odor spoil things."

Richard sat down, and Gina placed a hot plate of the veal stew in front of him. "This has always been one of my favorite dishes."

"I know. Your mother told me. She filled me in on a lot of your passions."

"I'm sure she missed out on one of my big ones," Richard said with a wink.

When they were getting ready for bed, Gina opened the music box on her night table that she had purchased in Carmel, and the tune "As Times Goes By" began to play. She got the expected reaction out of Richard. "May I have this dance," he said as he pulled Gina into his arms. They danced, clung together until the song ended. Then Richard lifted Gina up, placed her on the bed, and made passionate love to her. It was one of the best nights Gina had ever had. The cost of the music box was money well spent.

Gina was still in bed when Richard nudged her to wake up. "I'm getting ready to leave for work," he said. "This is going to be a busy week for both of us. Remember, the party in Sacramento is on Thursday night. And I want you prepared to charm and disarm my boss."

"Are you talking about the president, Jeremy Edwards?"

"He's the one. I know he's going to take a liking to you, so it won't be difficult."

When she heard the jingle bells, Gina knew Richard was out the door, and she got up. *I better take an inventory of my closet. There's no doubt I will need a new dress. But first things first.* She made coffee and got out her cigarettes.

. . .

Gina and Richard's holiday season was a social whirl of sights, sounds, food, and good cheer. The Blackrock party in Sacramento was the highlight—succulent appetizers, lavish buffet, champagne, entertainment, and enough politicians to make the whole thing a success. Gina sang in the choir at Christmas Eve Midnight Mass and the eleven o'clock Mass on Christmas Day. Her rendition of Ave Maria was a thrill to hear—Margery gave her five stars. New Year's Eve was coming up next. "What are the plans?" Gina asked Richard.

"We could do something low-key like dinner with a few friends. Or, we could go to one or more of the parties that are awaiting our RSVP."

"I'm a little too young for a low-key New Year's. Let's go through the party invitations and decide which ones to choose." Gina picked up the invitations—there weren't all that many. "Let's do the rounds—let's do them all."

"Are you serious? We'll be a wreck by midnight."

"Who cares? The next day is a holiday—we can take the time to recover."

"But we don't want to go to the neighbors all hung over."

"That's what coffee's for. And beer to bring up the equilibrium. Make sure there's a six-pack on hand."

"You think of everything, don't you? Something tells me you've had experience in this area."

Gina flashed him a smug smile and thought, is it that obvious?

New Year's Day, Richard and Gina woke up late—they were both hung over. It had been quite a night, and they got home late. Besides, Gina opened the music box, which caused the night to linger into the wee hours. Richard arose first and jumped into the shower. A tepid shower always helped revive him. He dressed and headed to the kitchen, retrieved a beer from the refrigerator, and popped open the brew. The first quaff always tasted best. After a few, he could feel himself coming back to center and chugged the rest of the can while the coffee brewed. When it was ready, he entered the bedroom and tore the sheets off Gina. "Up and at 'em."

Gina groaned. She lay sprawled on the bed, naked and limp. Richard opened the curtains to let the light flood in. Then he lifted her out of bed, placed her in the shower stall, and turned on the water, which blasted out cold. "What are you trying to do? Kill me?"

"No, just getting you ready for our next event—remember the Japanese New Year's at the Yamamotos'—it starts in two hours. Here's a towel and robe. The coffee's ready."

Gina took the towel and began drying herself. Afterward, she wrapped her head in it, slipped on her robe, and padded to the kitchen. Richard had the coffee poured with her cigarettes sitting next to it. He popped open another can of beer. "Try to get all this down. It will make you feel better. I know it did me."

Gina took the can in her hands and just let the beer slide down her throat as fast as she could swallow. "Let's never repeat that New Year's Eve." She picked up her coffee, took a sip, lit a cigarette, and inhaled deeply. "I need to eat something before making an appearance at the neighbors'."

"You stay put. I'll scramble some eggs and make toast. But, save room for the Japanese feast. We don't want to offend the Yamamotos. They might not understand about New Year's Eve."

It took the entire two hours to recover, but Richard and Gina got themselves together. When they opened the door to leave, the jingle bells rang out as the sun flooded in, temperatures almost balmy. "What a different feel to the holidays," Gina said.

"Is it better or worse?"

"It is a beautiful day. But I'm a traditional girl. And now I'm about to eat Japanese food on New Year's. My mother always served sausage and lentils for good luck. I doubt that will be on the menu at the Yamamotos'."

"Let's just keep an open mind. That's what the west is all about—open-mindedness. There are so many cultures out here, and they blend almost seamlessly. Most westerners want to learn new things from others. Let's try to do that today."

After a short walk, they were at the Yamamotos', ringing the doorbell. Ann answered and invited them in. "We are honored by your company." Ann wore a traditional kimono in a pine tree motif, her hair drawn back in a chignon style with hairpins and flowers. "Please, follow me," she said as she took tiny steps in her zori sandals toward the living room. Several people were already there, including Tom and Margery. Sam stood up to shake their hands and welcome them, making introductions all around. Gina and Richard sat down and eyed the delicacies covering the table before them.

"May I get you some Japanese beer or wine?" said Sam, who was also wearing a kimono in a solid dark blue color.

Gina and Richard chimed "beer" in unison, then stole a glance at each other, hoping no one would notice.

Not missing a beat, Tom and Margery shot them understanding smiles. They knew better than to let on.

Sam delivered the beers, and then he took a seat near Richard. "I understand you are an engineer."

"Yes, a civil engineer for Blackrock Construction."

"I am impressed. So much knowledge of math and science is necessary for a degree in engineering. You must be very smart."

"I don't know how smart I am, but I've worked hard. You can often make up for lack of talent with more effort."

"That is Japanese philosophy. Work hard, and then rewards follow. We try to instill this in our children."

Richard paused a moment to take a sip of beer. "I've heard you're a flower farmer."

"Yes, my family has been growing flowers in California for almost one hundred years. My ancestors came around the Gold

Rush and settled in San Francisco. Later, they migrated down here because of good soil."

"Where is your farm located?"

"Off San Juan Road near Buddhist Temple. You should come by sometime, and I will show you my operation." Sam smiled as a burst of pride welled up, causing him to blush.

"I'll do that. But tell me, what type of flowers do you grow?"

"We grow many carnations. They are popular with florists for bouquets. But we also grow chrysanthemums, which are special in Japan. They are symbols of sun and perfection. Also, rejuvenation. Did you know that Emperor's royal house is called Chrysanthemum Kingdom?"

"No, I didn't, but I'm glad you told me. I'll remember that whenever I see chrysanthemums now."

"That will please me. Now, eat. There are many delicious foods here for you to sample. But we tried to take your pleasure into consideration." Sam pointed to the delicacies as he continued, "There's sushi which I am sure you will enjoy, grilled sea bream which symbolizes auspicious event. Then we have pickled vegetables, grilled lobster, and herring roe which you must eat—it brings blessing of many children."

Richard jerked his head back. "Perhaps, we should pass on that this year."

Sam laughed. "Ann is about to bring out more tempura. And here she comes with platter, right on time."

Richard and Gina tasted most of the offerings while Margery and Tom loaded their plates as if they were at the last buffet. Gina enjoyed the shrimp and vegetable tempura but wasn't fond of the sushi with raw fish. However, she made herself eat one and appear to be enjoying it. When Sam noticed his guests were satisfied, he brought out the Saki and little cups. He poured one for each guest and gave a toast to good luck and friendship. Likewise, the guests toasted the Yamamotos in appreciation of their hospitality. Gina thought about Sam's toast for friendship and how, not long ago, he must have felt he had no friends to prevent him from being interned. Like the song, time goes by, and things change. It appeared they had all changed for the better.

On the way home, they ran into the Crawfords. Gina said, "We just came from a wonderful New Year's feast at the Yamamotos'. Is that where you're headed?"

Sylvia appeared to go white and looked nervous, glancing at Ben as if pleading to let the moment pass. But Ben had no hesitation in answering. "I have nothing to do with Japs. I don't care that we're at peace now. During the war, they treated our prisoners of war cruelly. Some of them cannibalized our soldiers they captured on islands like Chi Chi Jima. I will never forget. And I have not received the grace to forgive."

Gina gasped in shock. She couldn't imagine people as nice and kind as the Yamamotos would be capable of such inhuman acts.

Richard intervened to break the stifling silence. "War is hell. It turns men into animals, even worse—devils. But there's always a silver lining. We made great strides in aviation. Isn't that right, Ben?" Richard tried to strike the right note to divert the conversation.

"As an air force man, I can attest to that. The war focused this country, and we produced amazing aircraft that both men and women helped produce. Without those planes, we wouldn't have won the war."

"That reminds me. I'll set up that meeting with my friend Steve Hillman, the town attorney, to discuss your plans for a fly-in. The younger generation needs to learn about the history of aviation and the ingenuity that made it possible to preserve our way of life. Maybe it will inspire more kids to go into engineering."

"I'll look forward to that meeting. Let's make it soon."

They all said their goodbyes and wished each other Happy

New Year. Sylvia had come back to life, and Gina, too, recovered.

But as they headed up their walk, Gina was lost in thought. They opened the front door, and the jingle bells gave off their cheerful sound. One minute we're talking about horrific war crimes, and then the next minute, we're stepping into Santa's fairyland. How strange life is with all its contradictions.

Gina had been silent after hearing Ben's comments. "Gina, don't pay a lot of attention to what Ben had to say. Some men can never put the war behind them. They are one of its ongoing tragedies. Some incur physical wounds, some mental wounds, and some are wounded in spirit. This is the price of war and why we should never enter one casually."

"I was a child during the war, which protected me from all the horrors. Besides, few Japanese live in Boston, so the subject never came up. At least not when I was around."

"Remember, Sam's family has been in America for more than a century. But he and his family paid an enormous price during the war. Even though they were citizens, they were sent to internment camps, and many lost whatever businesses they left behind. They thought it was their patriotic duty to leave—one way they could help the war effort. But the conditions at the camps were grim, and they had little to pass the time. We try to forget. Now the Japanese are some of our most productive citizens. They work hard and raise good children."

CHAPTER FIVE

Gina burst into Margery's house without even a warning knock. "I've got a big announcement."

Standing at the sink, Margery turned her head as Gina tumbled in and took off her rubber gloves and apron to welcome her. "Let me get the coffee first. Okay, now that I'm sitting down, tell me."

"Sam was right about the herring roe."

Margery furrowed her brow as if trying to remember what he had said about the fish eggs, but she could not recall it.

"I'm pregnant. Remember, Sam said that the herring eggs would bring many children."

"Now, I remember. Well, that makes two of us."

"What? You're pregnant, too?"

"Due in October."

"You appeared to be putting on pounds, but I chalked it up to all the baked goods you make."

Margery frowned. "Weight is necessary for a healthy baby. When is your baby expected?"

"End of February." Gina stood to show Margery the profile of her stomach. "As you can see, not much there yet."

"It's early. But you'll be showing soon. Purchase some maternity clothes and get the nursery ready while you can."

"You're right. But the timing of this baby really stinks. I'll be too big to fit into any of my holiday dresses for the Christmas season, and I won't be able to ski. I love our weekends up at Yosemite."

"That's what being a mother is all about—self-sacrifice. Is Richard excited?"

"He seems to be, but he doesn't say much. He's always too wrapped up in his job."

"You're lucky he's a good provider. That'll mean you won't be required to do double duty and work, too."

"I guess we always take what we have for granted. Richard said he wants a son."

"All men do. And some women, too."

Gina walked home, reflecting on Margery's last words. She must ache for her son. I hope this next baby is a boy. He might help mend her heart, unlike Betsy had done. Now that Gina was pregnant herself, she could more understand the loss of a child. She was already looking forward to her baby and imagining what it might look like...what it might become. An infant's death, even a miscarriage, is not only the loss of a baby but of an entire lifetime of dreams.

At last, Gina was at her door. Her thoughts had exhausted her. She walked into the kitchen and made another fresh pot of coffee. She sat down and lit a cigarette while she waited for it to brew. Once the coffee finished dripping, she poured herself a cup and planned her day. I should look for some maternity clothes while I can still get around.

Richard arrived home on time, entering through the back door. After a quick dinner, he headed off to the meeting at Ben's, crossing the street and following the paved brick walk to his front door. Sylvia answered. "Good evening, Richard," she said in the gracious hostess voice she had honed when they lived on military bases and entertained officers and their wives. "Ben and Steve are waiting for you at the kitchen table. The coffee's on, and I will bring it out when it's done percolating."

As Richard entered the room, Ben stood up. "Thanks for being here. I realize you're busy, but this fly-in is important to me. You're going to be key to getting it off the ground, so to speak."

Richard laughed, and Steve joined with a smile. "Take a seat, Richard. Steve and I were only shooting the bull, so you haven't missed anything."

Richard and Steve exchanged greetings while Richard took a seat. "Thanks for being here, Steve. Your input is going to be very helpful from the town perspective." As town attorney, Steve understood liability and what went into gaining support from the town council.

"We're ready now," Ben said. "Let's begin. But first, I want you both to know how close to my heart this fly-in is. Not only is it an opportunity to showcase airplanes to our folks in town, but it is also an opportunity to remember the role the Watsonville Airport played in the war and in preserving our way of life. Years from now, no one will remember that our airport served as an Auxiliary Air Naval Station where dive-bombing was taught, and search planes were based to protect our coast from subs. We were one of only two naval stations on the West Coast. Our role was critical to the war effort. In fact, for a time, we had two stations."

"Many people have already forgotten," Steve said. "In fact, remind me what planes flew out of here."

Ben squinted his eyes and bore down on him. "There were Corsairs, Avengers, Dauntless, and Hellcats. Our boys left from here to fly missions in the Pacific. Watsonville was known as a navy town back then. A decade later, it's back to being a snug little farming berg. Nobody thinks anything important ever goes on here or ever did. We need to remind them of our history. It could come around again."

"Ben, you expressed yourself well. Steve and I share your sense of mission. Now, let's put together a plan. We can contact the Los Angeles show at Dominguez field that has been taking place since 1910—right after the Paris Air Show began. It would give us a sense of the scope of what needs to be done to, as you stated, 'get this thing off the ground.'"

"That's right," Steve said. "And I can look into the liability for the town on holding an event like this. But it could also mean additional revenue, which council members always love. It takes a lot to run the town. Anything that can contribute to the bottom line without adding to the tax burden is viewed favorably." Steve took a sip of coffee while he waited for a response.

Richard took control. "Now, for the action steps. Ben, you need to spell out your vision. Steve, check on the liability insurance. I'll come up with some ground rules for pilots and planes we'll allow to take part. Someone needs to contact the Dominguez airshow. Ben, do you want to do that?"

"Yeah, I should do it. Whatever I learn will help me put together a plan for us."

"At some point, we'll want to expand our committee," Steve said. "We should bring on some local veterans and town leaders, as well as some folks with deep pockets. But we also need people who can fulfill certain roles, not simply act as a mouthpiece for their own agenda."

"We should play this close to the vest for now," Ben said.

"Ben's right," said Richard. "We should do our research and put a plan together before we expand our group. With a projected budget, we will be prepared to answer all questions, including the ones that could deep-six us."

"You're thinking just like a military man," Ben said.

"Or an engineer whose specialty is estimating and submitting good bids," said Steve.

"We each have our expertise," said Richard. "And it's complementary, which makes us an excellent team."

Using his fist as a gavel, Ben pounded it on the oak table. "Okay. I'm going to call an end to this meeting and order you to do your duty. Now, will you join me in a drink to the success of our mission? There's a special bottle of Scotch on the counter waiting for us."

Ben got up, grabbed the bottle, spread three shot glasses around the table, filled them with liquid gold, and raised his glass. "To success." He tipped his glass, slugging it down in one gulp.

Richard and Steve raised their glasses and followed suit. When Richard finished, he let out a satisfying sigh. "That's special. What is it?"

"Well, it ain't torpedo juice," Ben said. "Whiskey—Glenfiddich—one of the best. I was saving it for a special occasion."

Richard and Steve said their farewells, and the pair walked back toward the street where Steve parked his car. "Richard, Ben has a high regard of you, and tonight, you only added to your luster. The way you took charge and made assignments was impressive. Before you arrived, Ben was saying you'd be right for a position on the town Planning and Zoning Commission, that it would be a springboard to bigger leadership positions in the town. He feels with your background and Gina's social connections, you'd be a very electable candidate."

"That's very flattering, Steve, but other priorities take precedence. Let's first focus on the fly-in."

"You've always had big plans for yourself, so take what I said seriously."

"It's all about timing. Did I tell you that Gina's in the family way?"

"No, you didn't. Weren't you planning to hold off children until you were on firmer financial ground?"

"I was, but her diaphragm slipped. Anyway, fatherhood's

beckoning. I can't spread myself too thin, or the family will suffer."

"Well, congratulations to you and Gina. I'll tell Sue. She'll want to visit Gina and talk about babies. That's how women are. But, back to your goals, the P&Z only meets once a month. Of course, there's always some homework to do, but it doesn't need to take a lot of time. Besides, with your engineering expertise, you wouldn't be too far behind on the learning curve—and probably ahead of it. You'd establish yourself as an expert right away and leader. It could fast-track you to your dreams."

As Richard walked home, he considered Steve's comment. Steve had known him since college and understood he was ambitious. Moving to this town had been the first rung on that ladder. He could be a big fish in a small pond, yet the pond covered a valuable mine, waiting to deliver more payload. Gina had been another rung on his ladder. She balanced him out and was an asset in society. A position on a town board could lead to even more rungs on the ladder. But he didn't want to jump in too soon and be in over his head. Besides, he had his career to consider. Blackrock Construction was on the move, and he would be, too, if he played his cards right.

In October, Margery had the baby, another girl they named Angela. When Gina stopped by to visit, Margery was sitting in the kitchen breastfeeding while Betsy rolled around in her wheeled chair. Gina bent over Margery and kissed her on the cheek. "I hope you had an easy time. The baby is beautiful, darker than Betsy."

"Usually, a third is easy to deliver but sometimes not. If it's bigger than the others, it could be more difficult to push out."

"You look good. I wouldn't have known you just had a baby. I brought you a couple of presents—one for Angela and one for you. A mother needs something, too. And I almost forgot. This one is for Betsy. We don't want her to become jealous of all the attention shown the baby."

"Thank you. When I'm done here, I'll put Angela back down and open them. I can't wait to see what's in these pretty packages."

"Now, enough about me, how are you?"

"A little tired. I try to take a nap every day so I can make it through the day, but there's always so much to do."

"You should take care of yourself. I hope you're eating well."

"There are times I'm not up to cooking, and we have a quick meal, like a frozen TV dinner."

"Please, don't do that. Give me a call. I'll double our dinner and share it with you."

Margery refilled their coffee cups. She took a sip before speaking. "Gina, how far along are you now?"

"The baby is due at the end of February."

Margery held up her hand and counted on her fingers. "That means you're about five months along, but you look much bigger. Are you sure you aren't having twins?"

Gina's eyes opened wide, considering the possibility. "The doctor hasn't mentioned it, and they don't run in the family, at least not that I know of."

"Only fraternal twins are hereditary. Identical are random chance. But next time you go to your doctor, ask him to listen carefully to the heartbeat and different parts of your belly. I just have a premonition."

The holiday season passed in the usual fashion. Gina was getting bigger by the moment and wondered how she was going to make it to her due date. The maternity clothes she had were getting snug, and she still had about a month to go. She needed a couple of big house dresses—something roomy and comfortable. Gina waddled down the walk to her car and headed for Ford's on Main Street.

When she returned home, Gina left her package at the door, dropped into an easy chair, and pulled out her cigarettes and lighter. *I know I'm supposed to be cutting back, if not quitting, but I need one to relax. At least, it will keep me from having a drink.* After the first inhale, Gina felt better and sat back in the chair. She almost fell asleep with the butt still in her hand. If it hadn't been for the mantle clock sounding twelve o'clock, she might have set herself on fire. The thought put the fear of God in her and increased her belief in guardian angels. *My poor angel always has to do double duty. My antics in college alone could have done me in if not for her grace. God must have some purpose in mind for me, but I don't have a clue what it is.*

Gina's stomach growled. *I better get up and find something to eat.* She put her hands on the arms of the chair and pushed herself up to a standing position. She paused to take a breath. *That was hard work. I just don't know how I'm going to make it one more month.* Almost as soon as that thought crossed her mind, a trickle ran down her leg. She looked back at the chair cushion and noticed a wet spot. *Oh, God, my bladder's giving way.* And she lumbered as fast as she could to the bathroom. But too late—liquid came gushing out.

Even before she called the doctor or Richard, Gina called Margery, who she knew would be home and within arm's reach. "My water just broke. What should I do?"

"Stay calm and take some deep breaths. I'm coming right over but call your doctor and tell him."

When Margery arrived, she found Gina collapsed on her bed. She was sweating and anxious. "I'm afraid."

"Don't worry. You're going to be fine. The baby is going to be born soon. Once the water breaks, it has to be born one way or the other before infection sets in."

Richard entered the maternal scene undetected and surprised them. "Oh, I'm so glad you're here. The doctor said we should go to the hospital when the pains are five minutes apart."

"Put your hand here, Richard," Margery said, "and when you feel the contraction, start timing until the next one comes."

Richard did as he was told. "I got eight."

"Good. Just keep timing them every couple of minutes, and when you get to five, that's your signal to move out. Gina, do you have a bag ready?"

"It's in my closet. I packed it last week."

"I'll get it and put it by the front door." When she returned, Richard announced the pains were now seven minutes apart.

"You're progressing. I'm going home now. But Gina, you're in good hands with Richard. I'll just be next door—a shout away. Don't hesitate if you need me."

It seemed to Gina and Richard that it took forever for her to progress to pains five minutes apart. But it took less than two hours. When Richard got the number he was looking for, he let out a "bingo" and helped Gina out of the chair, guided her down the walk, and loaded her in the car but not before sliding the passenger seat all the way back to make room for her oversized belly. The hospital was only a few minutes away.

When he pulled up to the front door, there were no other cars. Richard turned off the ignition and entered the hospital to alert the staff he was bringing Gina in to give birth. An orderly came out with a wheelchair and rolled her into the maternity ward, where several other women were already in various stages of childbirth. The duty nurse told Richard to take a seat in the waiting room and that the doctor would come by when he had something to report. He walked down the hall to a room painted institutional green. It was furnished with a couple of brown Naugahyde sofas and wooden chairs. Expectant fathers populated the room—most migrant Mexican workers straight from the fields. Wearing work clothes that were shabby and dirt-stained, they held cigarette butts between their thumbs and forefingers, smoking one after the other. Richard felt out of place, although he had no choice but to find a spot to sit down. The three men stared at him, their dark eyes penetrating. Richard raised his hand in a friendly salute. They nodded. One uttered something in Spanish that Richard did not understand since it came out muffled. This was going to be a long wait...I wish I had a book.

Soon, a doctor appeared, rattling off Spanish with the proficiency of a native, although it was clear he was not. The new father got up and shook his hand, thanking him as he left the room to inspect his new baby. The doctor looked at Richard and held up his hand with five fingers spread. His fifth child, and he doesn't look older than a teenager, Richard mused. How in the world do they manage? In time, the other two men left the room one by one. Their wives were built for babies. Now, alone with his thoughts, he tried to manage them as he'd always done. It did no good to let them run wild. As he sat there, he cleared his mind while he concentrated on his breathing. At last, the doctor appeared. "Congratulations, Mr. Bankston, Gina did well. You have twin sons."

"Twins," Richard said, astonished.

"Yes, two babies. Both a good weight and healthy."

"We didn't know we were having twins."

"Sometimes, it's a surprise. One must have been overshadowed, and we just didn't pick him up. That happens from time to time. But from my point of view, you got two for the price of one—a bargain."

Somehow, Richard didn't consider it a bargain. He started doing a mental tally in his head—two times the diapers, two times the formula, two times pediatricians visits—it was more than he had bargained for.

"Richard, are you there?" asked the doctor. "I know it's a shock, especially on the first pregnancy. But once you see your beautiful sons and wife, it will all be worth it."

Richard stepped into Gina's room, where she lay resting. Her face was flushed. Her hair hung in wet clumps. The lack of makeup and standard-issue hospital gown made her appear sickly. He had not expected this, and it scared him, but he hoped this was normal. "Gina," he whispered so as not to wake the patient in the other bed.

Upon hearing his voice, she turned her head and smiled. "Hi. Did you see them yet?"

"No, not yet. I wanted to see you first."

It was then they heard the carts filled with babies rolling down the aisle, making a racket too loud to ignore, as if announcing their imminent arrival for a feeding. Three baskets came into their room—two for them and one for the mother on the other side of the curtain. Richard peered into the baskets at the tiny, pink-faced bundles. Their heads were covered with blond fuzz, and they were swaddled in blue and green blankets. One appeared to be asleep. The other was starting to fuss. The nurse, a middle-aged spinster, built like a stevedore, said, "This is how it will always be. You won't ever have them both on the same schedule. Father, would you like to hold one?"

Richard blinked. Before he could answer, she handed him a crying baby. "What am I supposed to do now?"

"Just hold the baby next to you and rock him a bit. But don't worry if it doesn't work—it is not you who has what he wants."

Holding back a wry grin, Gina watched Richard, who seemed ill at ease in this new world.

Gina and the babies spent a week in the hospital. The day they arrived home, Margery came by to offer some tips. She brought a bouquet and also what she called a "Mom's Survival Kit." It contained everything from Pedialyte to a pack of beer, which helps increase breast milk.

"Gina, how are you feeling?"

"Exhausted. I've only been home a few hours and have not rested more than a few minutes. If it's not one baby crying, it's the other. I don't think I can handle this alone."

"Few mothers can, even if it's only one baby. You need a baby nurse."

"Baby nurse? I wish you were available."

"I do, too, but my hands are full with my own babies."

"Do you know a baby nurse who would be available? But I'm not sure Richard will go for it—he's so thrifty."

"I'll check around. She doesn't need a nursing degree—just be good with babies."

Waah!

"There they go again."

"You stay put. I'll wash my hands and find out what the fuss is about."

Margery returned from the nursery with a baby in her arms. "Which one is this? He's wearing a blue tag."

"Matthew, the firstborn but smaller twin. Michael is tagged green."

"How's Richard holding up?"

"He manages to sleep and gets to work on time. I don't think he realized how much babies would change his life. But he's glad they're boys...someone to build a future with...sons to follow in his footsteps and move beyond them. He's thinking dynasty already."

"I understand. With girls, your hopes are pinned on a good marriage. With sons, you can mold them into what you want them to be—within reason, that is."

"I hope you're right, Margery. But somehow, I already feel they're marching to their own drummer."

"When do you plan to baptize them?"

"In April, right after Easter. My folks are planning to come out for it and Richard's, too."

"That will give you time to get things under control. I better go now. Do you want Matthew, or should I settle him back in his crib?"

"You better hand him over. There's a chance he'll be happy if I hold him. He seems to be a real mama's boy."

. . .

When Richard arrived home, it was clear he should not expect dinner. Dishes were piled in the sink, the counters were cluttered with empty soda cans, coffee mugs, and used tea bags, and there was no pot simmering on the stove. He opened the refrigerator to determine if there was something he could scavenge. Not much—just a couple of beers remaining from a six-pack. *What in the world is going on here?* The house was quiet for once—that was a blessing at least. He walked to the living room and found Gina lying on the sofa, half asleep. "It looks like you've had a hard day."

"Oh, you're home already. I lost track of time." Gina struggled to sit up. "The babies keep me going nonstop."

Richard eyed her skeptically. "It looks like they're asleep now."

"Maybe the beer soothed them. Margery brought a six-pack over in her Mom's Survival Kit. She said it's good for milk production."

"I'd say it's good for more than that. I better go check on the boys."

Richard marched down the hall, shaking his head. He valued order above all else. He wanted his home to be shipshape, like the naval vessels on which he had served. When he reached the nursery, he breathed a sigh of relief. The twins were still sleeping and looked more content than he had ever seen them. Thank goodness for small favors. Then, he retreated to his study across the hall.

A couple of minutes later, Gina appeared in the doorway. "I'm sorry. I know I should provide dinner for you when you come home and make the house presentable, too. After I adjust to the babies, I should be able to do a better job. Margery says I need a baby nurse to help me get through these early weeks."

"Let me think about it."

"The problem is, there's no family nearby to help. Most

people in our situation rely on someone. I never valued family more than I do now."

"You're right. I can see you need help. I'll do some asking around."

"Now, about dinner tonight, could I persuade you to order a pizza? I can make a salad to go with it."

"Don't worry about me. I can make do with whatever is in the cupboard. Peanut butter and jelly would suit me just fine."

Things kept spiraling out of control at home. Richard hadn't gotten a decent dinner all week, and next weekend would be his naval duty. Gina would have a two-week span with very few extra hands on deck. There was no choice but to find a baby nurse. One evening, after Gina and the babies were settled, he walked next door to speak with Margery. She and Tom had finished dinner, so his timing was right.

"Gina told me you mentioned she needs a baby nurse. Honestly, our house is in a state of chaos. The babies are so demanding, they're taking up all of Gina's time, and she's exhausted. We need to get some help in to get through this crisis. Do you know of anyone available?"

"Not off-hand. But I can put out the word. An LVN I know, a Mexican woman, has a wide network of women who do this type of work."

"Are they all Mexican ladies?"

"Yes. But they're very good with babies."

"Do they speak English?"

"I'm sure they speak enough. But Gina needs someone who can help with the babies. They're naturals when it comes to handling infants, and they don't need a lot of instruction. And, besides, they'll take wonderful care of Gina, too—make sure she eats and gets her rest."

"What do they charge?"

"Not too much. But whatever you have to pay, it will be worth it."

As Richard walked home, he contemplated how quickly his life had changed. Nothing was going to plan—he spent most of his time troubleshooting. He wondered if this was just the way life is, and he had been lucky up to now, or if something was terribly wrong. He'd have to have a talk with Steve after their tennis game this weekend. Steve would have insight into the situation. He'd been along this road before, and he seemed to come out of it on top.

Marta arrived on Gina's doorstep early one morning, not long after Richard's visit with Margery. She spoke English well enough to make Gina understand she was there to take care of the babies. Marta appeared to be about forty years old, with jet black hair streaked with gray and tied back in a ponytail. Her eyes were a rich, soft brown, and when she smiled, a gold tooth revealed itself, glistening in the light. She wore jeans and a peasant top with gold hoop earrings.

Gina invited her in as the babies wailed in the background. Marta found her way to the kitchen, washed her hands, pulled an apron out of her bag, tied it on, and put a clean dish towel over her shoulder. When she reappeared in the hallway, all Gina needed to do was point, and Marta followed her direction as well as the babies' cries. It wasn't long before Gina heard the babies settling down. Marta brought the green baby out first. She went back, swaddled the blue baby, and cooed to him until he relaxed. "Marta, you're a godsend. I feel so much better now that you're here. You work wonders with babies."

"I've known babies since I was young. I had my first at sixteen."

Gina's mouth opened wide in shock. "Sixteen. How many do you have?"

"I have six and four grandchildren."

Gina did some math on her fingers. "How could that be?"

"My four daughters had babies at sixteen, too. We multiply fast," Marta said with a broad, proud smile.

"I should say so. I guess that makes you a baby expert."

Marta nodded. "I have to leave at five o'clock, but I will be back tomorrow morning."

"How much do you charge?"

"Two dollars an hour, is okay?"

Gina did the math in her head. "Eighty dollars a week."

"But could you pay every day, please, in cash?"

It was then that Gina realized what living hand to mouth meant. Some people live that close to the edge. It was not a way of life she was familiar with. "Of course," she said. When it came time for Marta to leave, Gina handed her sixteen dollars. "See you tomorrow, Marta. Thanks so much for your help." Martha smiled, her gold tooth gleaming, and she turned and headed down the walk. Gina noticed she stood at the sidewalk as if waiting for a ride. Sure enough, a pickup truck pulled up, and she got in and drove off. I'm learning about a different way of life. Marta is going to teach me a lot, and not even realize it.

For the next few weeks, Marta came right on time. She bathed and dressed the babies, prepared them for their feedings, changed their diapers and bedding, and put them down for their naps. In between, she cleaned the kitchen, made breakfast and lunch for Gina, and brought her coffee in the afternoon with a few cookies to tide her over until dinner. Marta also got dinner underway before she left—arroz con pollo, pork stew, enchiladas. Gina loved the new aromas coming out of her kitchen. And Richard loved the Mexican food he became accustomed to in college. Sometimes, Marta brought leftovers from her Sunday dinner, too. Chicken mole was something that could not be made on the spot. It took hours to blend the complex ingredients of peppers and chocolate to make a mole sauce. It was a treat when chicken mole was on the dinner menu. Marta worked nonstop from the time she arrived until the time she left. Single-handedly, she righted the ship, and it was now smooth sailing. Richard was grateful that life, as he expected it to be, was back to normal.

One day, instead of Marta showing up for work, it was Rachel. She explained she was Marta's sister and that a family emergency prevented Marta from coming.

With both eyebrows raised in surprise, Gina asked, "What's wrong?"

"Oh...Marta's husband, Carlos, got a knife wound."

Gina jerked like she'd been struck by a body blow. "Knife wound? How did it happen?"

"He was at the Frontera Bar on Sunday night after the fiesta. Some chicos got drunk, and one stabbed him," she said with sad, downcast eyes.

"Is he going to be all right?"

"I don't know, but he's in the hospital right now."

This is like something out of the Wild West, Gina thought. The Frontera Bar is on the south end of Main Street—it's not hidden off somewhere. Gina wondered again about the town she now called home.

"Rachel, thank you for coming in Marta's place because the babies need the extra pair of hands."

"Let me wash up and put on an apron, and I will get started."

"The kitchen is that way," Gina said while she pointed.

Rachel appeared in the living room, ready for work. "Please, show me to the babies."

"Go down the hall. The nursery is the last room on the left." Rachel shook her head, not understanding. Then a baby cried. "Ah, now, I know how to find them." In moments, she appeared with the green baby in her arms. "He's hungry, Mama—time to feed him." She helped Gina get him settled and retrieved the blue one who was still sleeping. The day passed seamlessly. Mexican women seem to know what is needed, doing it without a fuss. Gina hoped Marta would be back soon, but if not, Rachel would get the job done.

Marta returned a few days later. She seemed unfazed by her husband's injury. But Gina noticed she did not smile as much and tried to keep to herself when she could. If she took a break, she prayed the rosary. Gina had been afraid to ask about her husband, but now that it was the end of the day, she felt she could not let her go home without expressing some concern.

"How is your husband? Rachel told me he was injured and in the hospital."

Marta bowed her head. "He dead, Miss Gina."

"What? You mean he died from the knife wound?"

"Si. We bury him a few days ago."

"I'm sorry. Is there anything I can do for you?"

"Thank you. But I will be fine. My family takes care of each other."

"What about your children?"

"They are all grown now and working. Thank goodness for that."

Marta gathered up her things and headed to the sidewalk to wait for her ride. Gina noticed it was not the pickup truck that picked her up today but a van. The pickup truck must have belonged to her husband. But life had moved on, and she found another ride.

Gina was eager to tell Richard what she had learned about Marta's husband. She thought he might have some insight into the situation since he knew more about the town's culture than she did.

He was on time as usual and came into the living room where Gina was holding Matthew. When she saw Richard, she got up, kissed him, and walked back to the nursery to put Matthew down. When she returned, Richard asked about her day.

"Marta was back, so everything is back to normal, more or less."

"That's good."

"Except her husband died."

Richard turned serious. "I didn't want to say anything to alarm you, but often these guys in knife fights get an artery cut near the heart."

"She didn't tell me what happened, but he's already buried."

"Is she going to continue to come here and help you?"

"Yes, it appears life just goes on for these people. She told me she has a big family to help her. We could learn something from them."

Richard checked his watch. "Not to change the subject, but I'm due at a meeting at Ben's about the fly-in soon. Can we eat now?"

"Marta has dinner ready. Follow me into the kitchen, and I will get it on."

Gina took a peek into the pot on the stove—it was chicken mole—probably left over from the funeral reception.

CHAPTER SIX

Ben answered the door, wearing his signature Hawaiian shirt, and welcomed Richard in. "I'm glad you arrived first because I wanted to have a word."

"What about?"

Ben lowered his voice as if he was about to reveal a secret. "Remember, I mentioned you would be a great fit for the Planning and Zoning Commission? A little birdie told me there might be an opening coming up that would require an appointment. Interested?"

"Maybe, but I would need to learn more such as the commission's duties and responsibilities as well as qualifications to serve."

"Don't worry about qualifications. You already have those covered. I will get information to you on the responsibilities. That's the doorbell. It must be Steve. Let's keep this to ourselves for now. I don't think it's widely known yet that an opening will be coming up."

After they had all settled around the kitchen table, Ben said, "Now, let's start with what I learned from talking to the LA show guys." And he filled Richard and Steve in.

Next, he asked Richard about pilot qualifications and types

of planes to allow. Richard handed Ben and Steve a report he had put together.

"I like how thorough you are," Steve said. "It'll be much easier to get liability coverage and the council's support."

They discussed all the details and considered a date in May for the debut.

"Isn't that a little too soon?" asked Steve.

"We can make it based on what I found out. The first show can be a small one—sort of a warm-up to the big one next year."

"It'll give us a chance to test everything out before the real thing," said Richard.

"That's right," said Ben. "By the way, do you know Chuck Cunningham?"

"I don't think so. Why?"

"He lives next door to you."

"Oh, that guy. I never see him. His front door and driveway are on the other street. What about him?"

"He approached me about being in the air show."

"I didn't know he could fly."

"Apparently, he has a license."

"What type of plane does he want to bring?"

"A Korean War fighter jet."

"That's a lot of airpower. Unless he has good flying credentials and has racked up hours in that aircraft, we shouldn't let him in the show."

"Exactly my thoughts," Ben said. "Do you want to tell him, or should I?"

Richard paused a minute. No use getting on Chuck's bad side. "Why don't you tell him since he asked you about it?"

"Okay. I'm used to the buck stopping with me. But the sooner we have ground rules drawn up, the easier it will be to deal with these wannabe flyboys."

"I'll get on it," said Richard.

"Now, before you head out, I've got something else for us to taste." Ben reached for a bottle on the counter. "This is a

Macallan single malt." He poured three tumblers and passed them around. "Tell me what you think."

"I'll tell you what I think," Steve said. "Let's hold more meetings at your house. You really know how to put closure on one."

Gina was set to leave when Marta arrived. She wanted to drive by the Frontera Bar on Main Street and see it for herself. She never went to that end of town, although she had passed by a couple of times on the way to Monterey but hadn't noticed the landscape as she drove by. "Marta," Gina said, "I'll be home around lunchtime. I just fed the babies, but there's pumped milk in the refrigerator if you need some."

Gina checked her watch after she got into the car. It was a little past nine a.m. She had plenty of time to do her sightseeing and get back to talk it over with Margery.

She headed to Main Street, which was lined with shops—shoe stores, jewelers, photographers, and, of course, Ford's department store—the only real game in town. Beyond that was the Fox Theater and the famous plaza laid out in a circle with a bandstand rising above it all. The western façade of the post office stood guard behind, and to the side of it was the library, a pair of sentinels presiding over the little enclave that gave the town some stature. Further on the left were a couple of Mexican restaurants—one named El Michoacán, the other Little Baja. Clearly, this end of Main Street has been deeded to the Mexicans. Then, on the right, a couple of bars appeared. The first was La Frontera. It had western-style slatted, swinging doors and was open for business. A Mexican man lay slumped nearby on the sidewalk. Gina made a U-turn, pulling up across from the bar. She rolled down her window and caught the sound of Spanish being spoken inside above the strums of a lone guitar. Then she spotted another Mexican man push open the doors and stumble out, nearly falling as he walked down the street. Not long afterward, a man ran out of the bar and started yelling at the first, grasping a beer bottle by the neck and shaking it in a threatening manner. But the first man was out of reach, so the Mexican threw the beer bottle into the street, shattering it to pieces before he went back inside. Gina had seen enough. A small town does not provide the same screening from different worlds as a big city most often does. She needed to talk about what she had witnessed and drove to Margery's as fast as she could. When she reached Margery's door, the clock chimed ten o'clock. Right on time. She peeked in the window before knocking and saw Margery stirring a pot on the stove. Gina walked right in. "Long time, no see."

"I've missed you." Margery continued to stir as she talked. "What have you been up to besides babies?"

"That's what I wanted to talk to you about. But, first things first. Do you have any coffee ready?"

"Let me put some on."

Margery stepped away from the stove and got the coffee started. While it was brewing, she opened the cookie jar and plated some homemade oatmeal raisin cookies. "Here, this will tide you over until the coffee is ready."

Gina sunk her teeth into a soft, chewy cookie rich with raisins, oatmeal, and walnuts. "Mm. This is a great cookie. And the perfect mid-morning snack for someone who skipped break-fast today."

Margery gave Gina a look of disapproval. "You shouldn't be missing meals when you're breastfeeding."

"Today, I had to make an exception. And I want to talk about what I did this morning."

"Let me put the coffee out first so we don't get interrupted."

Gina smoked a cigarette while she awaited her coffee and then began. "You know Marta has been working for me. But did you know that Marta's husband died of a knife wound?"

"Yes, that is not uncommon here amongst the Mexicans. They have fights in those bars down on the south end of Main."

"The Frontera Bar, to be specific. In fact, that's where I was this morning."

Margery shot straight up in her chair, stunned. "You were at the Frontera Bar?"

"Not in the bar. I stopped on the other side of the street and watched it for a while."

Margery let out the breath she had been holding and relaxed. "And what was going on there?"

"Not a lot. I suppose it's a different story at night." Then she recalled what she'd witnessed.

"You got a real slice of life."

"I guess you could say that. At first, I couldn't accept what happened to Marta's husband. It seemed too barbaric."

Margery raised an eyebrow. "And now...?"

"Now, I've learned about their way of life—at least the underbelly of it."

"They all carry knives and know how to use them. Where they come from, they need them for self-defense."

"Back home, we have shootings. But knives seem to be a gruesome way to fight. Imagine plunging a blade into someone's side and having their blood spurt out all over your arm. It's so gory." Gina shivered as she poured out her feelings.

"It's not all that way," Margery said. "Have you ever been to the Sunday evening Mass when the braceros attend?"

"The Mexican farmworkers? No, I haven't."

"They come straight from the fields in their work clothes and sit as far back in the church as they can, perhaps because of embarrassment of how they're dressed. They fill three or four pews. The young men all have handsome faces—chiseled features and piercing dark brown eyes. When they raise their voices to sing, they become a chorus of heavenly tenors filling the church with their joyous song. I always feel transported to another realm. You, of all people, should hear them sing sometime."

"I'll make a point of it."

"Anyway, how's Marta doing?"

"She seems fine. She said she has a big family who will help her through, and that seems to be the case so far. A sister substituted at my house for a few days, and now someone new picks her up after work."

"They do have big extended families, and they seem to help one another. On the other hand, they seem to have more troubles than the rest of us put together."

When Gina returned home, all was quiet. She glanced into the living room and observed Marta praying the rosary. It reminded her of Karl Marx's words—'religion is the opium of the people.' At times like this, they had a ring of truth to them. Gina stole herself into the kitchen—she did not want to disturb Marta's prayers.

Richard pulled into the driveway, eager to relax after a hectic workday. But Ben intercepted him. "I'm sorry to corner you like this, but I needed to alert you."

"Would you like to come in and talk?"

Ben shook his head. "No, this won't take but a minute."

Richard leaned up against the car while Ben continued. "You remember me telling you that your neighbor... the one on the corner..."

"You mean Chuck?"

"Yes, that's the name I was searching for. He's all upset that he's not being allowed into the fly-in with the Korean War jet."

"What's the problem?"

"He's bad-mouthing you around town. I thought you should know about it. It might hurt your chances for a seat on the P&Z."

Richard's face displayed concern. "Go ahead."

"He's saying you don't know what you're doing, and you're not letting good pilots with noteworthy planes into the fly-in.

He's trying to discredit you in any way he can. Not only that, he's trying to pull strings."

"Pull strings?"

"He's trying to get some bigwigs on his side, so he can take you on and win."

"Why doesn't he just come over and talk to me?"

"I think he's intimidated. You know...you being a Stanford engineer and all. I'm not sure he even graduated high school."

"Then it all makes sense. This is like high school stuff he's pulling."

"I hadn't thought about it that way, but you're right."

"It's best nipped in the bud. I'll stop by to talk with him. But he's often on the road, trucking goods around the country for days at a time."

"Now you know, so you can try to do something about it. The last thing we want is people divided on the fly-in. We need all the public support we can get to pull it off."

"Don't worry. It'll come together. Anything worthwhile has a few hurdles to get over." Richard reached in the back seat, pulled out his briefcase, and walked through the gate.

Richard waited for the weekend to visit the Cunninghams. Since Chuck wasn't home, he left a message with Val. Weeks passed, but Chuck did not try to get ahold of him. However, he continued to spread his vitriol around town wherever he could find a sympathetic ear.

Plans for the fly-in were now in their last stage. Ben called another meeting of the Key Three, as he called them, to cover all their bases. Up to now, all their meetings had been in the evenings after both he and Steve had experienced a long day at work and Ben had spent time chasing balls around the golf course. A Saturday afternoon meeting would ensure everyone was fresh and on top of their game.

Richard was the first to arrive at Ben's, followed by Steve. Sylvia had a pot of coffee waiting and some blueberry muffins she had picked up at the bakery. Ben called the meeting to order. "We are less than two months away from the fly-in over Memorial Day weekend. So far, there are about twenty entries, but I'd like to see a few more. The historical stages of flight should be represented."

"I agree," Richard said. "One idea I'm working on is getting a bi-plane that can offer rides to the public—for a fee, of course. Steve, would that require extra insurance?"

"I'll check. But the pilot may carry some. Let's ask about it." Steve jotted down some notes.

Richard said, "What about a model display of the planes throughout the various eras, starting with a model of the Wright brothers' plane?"

Ben let out a burp. "I like that idea, but we're already stretched for time. We need to delegate tasks to other members of our committee. That's one thing I learned in the military— the patrol method—break things down into smaller achievable tasks. Then, when everyone does their part, the whole is complete."

Richard nodded in agreement. "And, I might add, much more thorough."

"While I like the idea of displaying planes from all the various eras," said Steve, "it's more important to focus on the World War II planes, which are part of Watsonville's history. We can start small and then build from there."

Richard looked up from the notes he was taking. "Steve's right. We can't do everything year one. But if we focus on what's important to the town, we'll build enthusiasm and support for the event, which will carry us forward."

Ben had been listening. He took a gulp of coffee and cleared his throat before speaking. "Someone suggested a display of cars as well. What do you think of that idea?"

"This is supposed to be a fly-in," Richard said. "We don't

want it overshadowed by automobiles, especially this year when we'll start small."

"I agree," said Steve. "It's better to stay focused and do that well. By keeping to our primary mission, we'll be able to do that."

"What planes are coming so far?" asked Richard.

"I made sure we'll have the four that were here during World War II—the Hellcat, Avenger, Corsair, and Dauntless. Those Hellcats were something—dominating the skies of the Pacific. They were the preferred night fighters, too. And they were real ace makers. That's because they were built like a battleship and easy to handle. But the top aces of both world wars were Germans—the Red Baron shot down eighty, and Bubi an amazing three hundred fifty-two."

"I guess we're lucky they didn't have more of them," said Steve.

"That's right. They had a couple of aces with a tremendous number of kills. Our aces had few kills—Eddie Rickenbacker only had about twenty-six, but we had a lot of them filling the skies. If one got shot down, there were at least a dozen who could take his place. Put another way, we had great depth to our bench while they only had a few stars."

"Those planes will bring back memories for the veterans, too," said Richard. "After all, we're holding this on Memorial Weekend."

"Speaking of veterans," Steve said, "We could ask some of the guys who were on those types of planes to talk about their experiences. It would be like a living history."

"I like that," said Ben. "I'll get some of my air force buddies up here to take that on."

"Don't forget the locals," Steve said.

"Let's outline tasks and divvy them up," Ben said.

"Here's the list I've drawn up while we talked," Richard said.

"Great. You're always a step ahead of us. Now, before I forget, did you ever get a word in with Cunningham?"

Richard shook his head. "I stopped by his house a couple of weeks ago and spoke with his wife. He was away, so I left both my home and work phones and asked him to call, but I haven't heard a thing from him. Why?"

"He's still bad-mouthing you. He's trying to destroy your credibility."

"If that's all it is, I'm not worried."

"Well, let's hope Cunningham doesn't carry any weight."

"Even better, let's hope he has his rig on the road that weekend."

The first Watsonville fly-in was a success except that Cunningham buzzed the event twice, nearly taking out a biplane tour with the mayor aboard. Now, the town was abuzz with the news about Chuck's crash landing at an airshow near Sacramento. Many were calling Richard a local hero for denying Chuck entry into their show, which averted a town tragedy and all the lawsuits that were sure to follow. Ben scheduled a meeting with Richard later that week to discuss the turn of events. When Richard arrived, Steve was already there.

Ben opened the door to let Richard in. "Take a seat in the kitchen. I'll be right there." Then he walked up the hallway and returned with some papers.

"First things first. Does anyone need anything to drink... coffee or whatever? Of course, I'll have something special for us afterward."

"I'd like coffee," Richard said.

Ben brought out the pot and filled three mugs. "I hope neither of you drinks it sissy style." Steve gave a start. He wasn't used to this type of talk.

Ben shot him a smirk. "I'm sorry. I mean sugar or cream."

"No," said Steve.

"Same," said Richard. Neither of them would've risked taking their coffee any way but black.

"Good. Now we can begin. The events of this past weekend, as sorry as they were, created an opportunity here."

Richard and Steve exchanged glances. Ben caught them. "Not to be mercenary, but this is just the lay of the land. Richard has now emerged as a kind of hero. Heroes are viewed as leaders. Now is the time to get Richard positioned for a place in town government."

"Now may not be the time for me. Gina and I just had twins, and my job is only getting more demanding."

Ben continued as if he hadn't heard Richard's remark. "I had mentioned a possible opening on the Planning and Zoning Commission. And now, I can say for sure that it'll be coming up in the next few weeks. You have the perfect qualifications for it, and there's no doubt in my mind that you'll be appointed if you want it."

"Richard, I've known you a long time," said Steve. "This is the perfect way for you to get involved in running the town and learning more about land for investing. You'll be amongst the first to know. You believe in land ownership as a way to prosperity. This fits with your life's plan."

As Richard stepped out of Ben's house, he gazed up at the sky, not a cloud to obscure the stars that glittered high above. Maybe that was a sign. He crossed the street and thought about what Steve had said. He was ambitious, and a civil engineer's salary alone would not get him to where he wanted to be unless he ended up running the company, and that seemed doubtful. Town government could be the next step to accomplishing his life's plan.

Richard mulled over the P&Z all week. He knew Ben would want an answer soon. He planned to talk to Jack Overton about it but decided against it. Instead, he had a long heart-to-heart with Steve. Richard respected his advice, and, with their long-term friendship, he'd only want the best for him. Steve's advice was full steam ahead.

When Richard was in Sacramento, he dropped in on another college buddy he'd stayed in touch with. Greg Allen was also a civil engineer who worked for a large construction company. But living in Sacramento, a sizeable town and the state's capital, he had little involvement in civic affairs—the town had its long-time power brokers, and there was no room for more. Richard talked the P&Z matter over with him anyway, and he sided with Steve and Ben. That made it unanimous. But there's one more person I need to talk to first—the big boss, Jeremy Edwards.

Richard made an appointment to see Mr. Edwards. He was busy until Friday afternoon. When the time arrived, Richard entered his office, not knowing what would come out of the meeting.

Jeremy sat behind his enormous desk wearing a smile. "It's always good to talk with our engineers, especially one who adds such value to our company. What can I do for you?"

Richard took a seat, taking a moment to compose himself. "I've been approached to fill a vacancy on the town Planning and Zoning Commission. It's a great opportunity, but I wouldn't want to do anything that would compromise the company."

Jeremy leaned back in his chair. "Thanks for asking my opinion. It's a chance to improve your knowledge of the land around here, and you might even get some advance word on a project that could help the company."

"P&Z has to abide by rules and regulations. There wouldn't be any room for creative thinking."

"I know that, but you'll be in a position to hear things. Of course, I never would want you to compromise yourself."

So...he wouldn't want me to compromise myself. But if I obtained insider information and passed it on with no one knowing, then nothing would be compromised. "I understand."

"I'm glad we understand each other. Good luck, Richard. You

have my blessing." Jeremy dismissed him with a wave of his hand.

Richard left the office, grateful it was Friday. He would have the weekend off and only wished he had navy duty to get away from it all. He called Ben and set up a meeting on Sunday afternoon. That would give him time to think things over.

Richard was right on time for his meeting with Ben. This time, Sylvia answered the door and offered him a cup of coffee while he waited for Ben to emerge from his office. When Ben entered the kitchen, Sylvia excused herself. "I see Sylvia already has you pumped up with coffee, so we can get down to it."

"You take the lead."

"Well, Richard, I don't know how much more I can say about the P&Z. You know what it entails. I need a decision from you. Are you interested in the position?"

"I've given it a lot of thought and concluded it'd be an excellent opportunity for me. There's never a perfect time. I'm going to jump in and make the best of it."

"Glad to hear you made the right decision. Now, I need to introduce you to the chairman of the Republican Town Committee. He has to approve you for the nomination to fill the vacancy, and next, the entire committee must agree. Can you give me a resume for him to look over before the two of you meet?"

"I'll need to update it to reflect some of my recent experience."

"When will it be ready?"

"I'll work on it this afternoon if time permits and bring it by tonight."

"That'd be great. We could go over it to determine if there's anything that needs to be added or amended. The committee meets only once a month, and their next meeting is a week from this Tuesday. I'll set up an interview with the chairman beforehand."

Richard headed home and locked himself in his study to update his resume in peace. When he finished, he hustled back over to Ben's to drop it off. "That was quick," Ben said.

"There wasn't much to do. Besides, I don't want anything to hold up the appointment if I have any control."

"You think like a naval officer. And being that this was a navy town a few years back, that should hold you in good stead. I'd like to look over your resume. Can you stay for a few minutes?"

Richard shook his head. "Gina needs my help with the boys. Between my weekly game of tennis, our meeting, and updating my resume, I haven't been available to her today."

"Your priorities are in order. We must keep the wives happy. As the saying goes, 'happy wife, happy life.' I'll call you if there's anything that might be helpful to add. We want to get your appointment through with no problems."

"I don't know what problems there could be."

"Probably none. But now we're dealing with politics, so we need to cover our backsides."

Politics. I only want to have a hand in running the town and getting in on land deals. He left Ben's house wondering if he was getting into something he might regret.

The chairman of the Republican Town Committee (RTC) met with Richard to discuss his interest in serving on the P&Z. He was impressed with how he handled himself. The next step would be to secure the city council's approval, but there was no reason they shouldn't approve him. And that was the way it played out.

The P&Z met on the first Tuesday of the month—a couple of weeks away. In the meantime, Richard needed to do his homework and meet other members of the committee. This is already taking more time than I expected. I hope it's worth it. Then he got a call from the chairman that he needed to do a site inspection before the next meeting on a parcel of land where a developer wanted to build a shopping center, which would require a variance of the wetland's regulations. He looked forward to his first official duty.

The site inspection proved worthwhile. Not only did Richard learn more about land in the town and obstacles to developing it, but he was privy to a lot of side conversations about land deals, politics, and other issues. He realized he was about to become an insider. Mr. Edwards probably realized this, too. But Richard planned to keep what he learned to himself, at least for now. He'd always had a reputation for being tight-lipped, and it had served him well. In this new world of small-town politics, it wouldn't take long for people to figure out who was speaking out of turn. He recalled the motto, *loose lips sink ships*. It's not only important in wartime. That motto can apply to all sorts of situations, especially politics. Richard knew what he needed to do to become a trusted team member and get ahead.

CHAPTER SEVEN

The P&Z Chair put a plan for low-income housing on the upcoming agenda. Steve stopped by Richard's house Monday evening to discuss the issue. "Let's go back into my study where we can talk. Those four boys always make too much of a racket." In the intervening years, Dave and Drew had been added to their brood.

They settled into a couple of leather club chairs in Richard's small study, which was papered in a hunter green plaid to give it some character. On the wall behind the desk, Richard's Stanford diploma hung—a reminder of his achievement. "Now, what's this all about?"

"First, let's go back to the beginning. There have been rumblings for a while amongst the Mexican community that they need more affordable housing in town. Their numbers are growing. Once they get better organized, and they're organizing now, they'll be a force to be reckoned with. Some developers got wind of this notion and are proposing to build low-cost housing now."

"We need a lot of answers first. For instance, where do they plan to put this subdivision? And what will the impact be on the rest of the community? We should do some research."

"You're right. So far, they're only proposing the location on a tract of undeveloped land on Rodriguez Street."

"That's somewhat remote from the main subdivisions of the town. There might not be many objections. But there are going to be financial implications."

"Political implications, too. Already, over the hill in Santa Clara, an effort is underway to register Mexicans to vote, and a Catholic priest is directing it."

"Priest? Why am I not surprised? So many of the coups in Latin America have involved a priest in one way or another—and they all seem to be Jesuits. They're both scholars and activists motivated by social justice."

"Do you think any of the priests in town are involved in organizing Mexicans?"

"I don't know, but we could ask Gina. Honey, can you come into the study for a moment?"

"I'm refereeing the boys. Are you sure you want me to leave my post? They might end up killing each other while I'm away. I worry about Dave and Drew since they're smaller and still can't defend themselves."

"We'll keep our ears tuned. Sometimes, they're better than eyes."

When the boys weren't looking, Gina made a clean getaway, scurrying down the hall. "Okay, now that I'm here, what do you need?"

"Are there any Catholic priests in town who are organizing the Mexican community?"

"Certainly not Father O'Leary. He values participation in his golf tournament too much, as well as donations for the church bazaar. But St. Patrick's has a priest who says the Spanish Masses named Father Garcia."

"That's interesting, isn't it, Steve?"

"Yes, it is. Let's ask around about him."

"I'll ask Margery...oh, I hear the boys mixing it up. I better get back out there."

"If you need reinforcements, give a holler. Anyway, Steve, what do you think?"

"One thing we don't want is for things to get out of control as they did in the 30s with the Filipinos."

"I wasn't around then. What happened?"

"Watsonville had riots that lasted five days. It started with a mob of vigilantes five hundred strong. The Filipino men had been dating white women. That's what set the vigilantes off. The Mexicans joined the whites against the Filipinos."

"We're lucky the Mexicans have families here."

"Not everyone would agree. The young men first came under the Bracero program to work the fields and then went home. Once they found out how good life is here and that a baby born on our soil has all the rights of a citizen, wives came, and they just continued to multiply. When they get a few more numbers and get organized, they'll be the ones with the political clout."

"From what you're telling me, there are a lot of angles to be considered."

"That's right. We don't want unrest in this town. Or even worse, boycotts of our crops during harvest time. That'd cost growers and shippers a fortune, and the town would come up short, too."

"I had no idea when I took the position on P&Z how involved it would be in town politics or how much of my time it would take."

"This is a diverse town with a lot of big business—primarily agribusiness. It gets complicated, trying to balance all the interests. If only we had the wisdom of Solomon."

"I'll talk to Jeremy Edwards about the low-income housing matter. He may have some insights. He'll be interested in who these developers are."

"Whatever you do, go about it discreetly. At the moment, only a few of us are aware of what's coming up. We don't want to stir the pot."

"Do you think we should get Ben's input? He's pretty savvy."

"Let me think about it. I'd like to just keep this between us until the meeting takes place. Then the issue will be out in the open. I better let you go now. It sounds like things are reaching a crescendo in the other room."

Once the boys were put away for the night and Richard had Gina's full attention, he asked her again about Father Garcia. "It would be helpful if you could do some sleuthing for us."

"Sleuthing...you mean spying. Should I wear a trench coat with the collar turned up and dark sunglasses to conceal my identity?"

"You can forget the spy stuff. Just keep your eyes and ears open. Ask some questions. Listen and try to connect any dots."

"Margery mentioned that I should go to the Sunday evening Spanish Mass to hear the Braceros sing. After Mass, I can linger and watch who Father Garcia is talking with. That may tell us something."

"Now, you're following me. And don't forget Marta, too. Has she said anything about organizing or getting registered to vote?"

"No. But why shouldn't they register to vote if they're eligible?"

"That's just it—if they're eligible. Elections are often tainted with fraud. But even if they're eligible, we don't want them to be pawns in someone else's game. They need to think for themselves."

"All I remember is Marta talking about the living conditions. On Bridge Street, the people are crammed into homes resembling flophouses. It's no wonder their kids have so much illness. She told me the men come home dirty from the fields but don't wash because there aren't enough facilities. It's a terrible way to live—and disgraceful in the USA."

"I don't doubt there's a need for more and better housing. We just don't want outsiders coming in and stirring things up, causing trouble. This is a nice community. We all try to get along. Besides, Blackrock has a stake in it since it's headquartered here. We don't want anything to jeopardize that."

"You're always thinking way ahead."

"I try to prevent problems before they start. It's part of being an engineer, the way we're developed to think."

"I'll talk with Marta this week. She has a lot of family here, which puts her on the grapevine."

"And don't forget about the priest. They're educated and hold a church position, which gives them influence over people."

"They also don't have the usual self-interest. Catholics trust priests. That's how I was raised—it's ingrained."

Gina cornered Margery on her way to the car. "What do you know about Father Garcia?"

"Why are you asking?"

"When it's something for Richard's business or town politics, I'm not at liberty to say until the time is right."

"This is my two cents. Father Garcia came here from Guatemala. One time, he talked about his work with the poor and indigenous people. He has a true heart for the underdog in life."

"Is he a Jesuit?"

"He mentioned education and teaching. That's what Jesuits are into, along with social justice."

Gina nodded. "That's true. Many of my best teachers at the College of Boston were Jesuits. They like to get involved with the community. Does Father Garcia have friends here?"

"He often dines with families at the Bistro Mona Lisa. We should go there sometime—their Mexican food gets top reviews."

"We could drag the husbands along and make an evening out of it."

When Richard got home that night, Gina told him what she'd learned.

"My suspicions were right—the priest is a Jesuit. He'll be looking for ways to get involved with the poor to help them better themselves. Checking out that restaurant might be a good idea…Mona Lisa…the woman behind the smile."

"Oh, Richard, now you sound like a secret agent."

Richard squared his shoulders, slipped a hand in his pocket, tilted his head, and gave his most debonair smile. "The name's Bond. James Bond. I couldn't come up with a better name for a restaurant that's got something to hide if I racked my brain all day."

Gina shot him a smirk. "I suggested to Margery that the four of us go there for dinner. I'll make arrangements, and you can do the sleuthing yourself."

"Where's it located?"

"On Rodriguez Street."

"Rodriguez…that's another coincidence. A Rodriguez was given the Mexican land grant that Watsonville sits on."

By the time Gina and Richard arrived at the bistro, Margery and Tom were already seated. "I'm glad they chose a corner table, so we can talk privately," Richard said.

The restaurant had typical Mexican décor—white walls, terra-cotta floors, and wooden tables surrounded by natural rush chairs. Hand-painted flowerpots filled with colorful gerbera daisies added a touch of color. The server left the menus, and everyone began scanning them.

"By the way, did you notice the mural on the outside of the building?" said Gina.

"It's supposed to represent Mexican-Indian history," said Margery.

"I noticed the Virgin of Guadalupe and Christ on the cross. But we went by so fast, I didn't get a chance to take in the entire scene."

"The Virgin of Guadalupe represents hope in times of suffering," said Margery.

"Or," said Richard, "empowerment in times of resistance."

"It reminds me of the mural in San Francisco. A Diego Rivera could be living in our midst," said Gina.

"Don't get me started on that communist," said Tom. "After he completed the *Riches of California* mural, he was commissioned to do one at Rockefeller Center in New York. He had the nerve to paint Lenin's face into the scene. That didn't fly with the Rockefellers, but Rivera wouldn't remove it."

"I, for one, am glad he didn't," said Gina. "Artists can't let themselves be pushed around. Where would the world be if artists couldn't speak their truth?"

"The Rockefellers had the last word," Richard said. "They had the mural chiseled off the wall."

"Not to change the subject, but I hear the enchiladas here are great," said Tom. "I have my eye on the chicken suizas."

"Suizas?" Gina said.

"Swiss-style with green sauce, cheese, and sour cream. Many places don't offer them. Whenever they're on a menu, I go right for them."

"I'll try those, too."

"I'd like a tamale," said Margery. "What about you, Richard?"

"Fish tacos. I hope the fish is fresh today."

"And let's get a big pitcher of margaritas," Gina said. "With glasses all around."

The waiter came and set down a basket of chips with salsa. Then he took their orders. "Oh, and add some guacamole with our drinks," Tom said.

Richard took a moment to scan the small room. Only a couple of other tables had guests, and they were all Mexicans. When the drinks arrived, Gina filled all the glasses. As Richard was about to take his first sip, the door opened. He looked up and spotted a couple of men, gringos, who didn't look like they were from here. He glanced down, fixing his eyes on the table while keeping a corner of an eye on the pair. When the server came over, they seemed friendly. And then the owner appeared to welcome them. There's more here than meets the eye. Then, he turned his thoughts back to the conversation.

"Richard, how's life on the P&Z these days?"

"If you want to get in on the latest, come to the meeting next week. You'll be interested in one item on the agenda, but I'm not at liberty to talk about it just yet."

"You've intrigued me. I'll try to make it."

"Did everyone enjoy their meal?" Richard asked. "What about dessert?"

"We're going to pass," Margery said. "We need to get home to relieve my mother. She doesn't want to be out too late."

On the way out, Richard whispered to Gina, "Look at those two guys over there and remember their faces. If you see them again, let me know."

Gina tried to be discreet as she glanced in their direction. She hadn't seen them before, but one would be easy to recognize. "Did you notice that scar on his cheek?"

"Well, aren't you the observant one? I completely missed it."

Richard grabbed a slot on Jeremy Edwards' calendar for the afternoon. He wished he didn't have to wait since he could think of nothing else all day, making it difficult to concentrate on work. When the appointed hour arrived, he was admitted into Edwards' office without delay.

"Richard, it's good to see you." Jeremy motioned for him to take a seat while leaning back in his leather desk chair. "What brings you here today?"

"Thanks for seeing me on such short notice. But I wanted to talk to you about an important matter coming before the P&Z next week."

Jeremy bolted upright, becoming serious. "Go on."

"Low-income housing. Apparently, some out-of-town developers want to build it. There are a few concerns here."

"Let me guess. First, the Mexican population. Second, these outsiders."

"That about sums it up."

"Let's tackle one matter at a time. I'm sure you'll want to assess what the current housing is like for the immigrant population. Watsonville has always been known for good available housing that is sound and clean. Mexicans are growing in numbers and will be quite a force at some point, and we don't want to get them upset. It wouldn't be good for the town or for business."

"I understand. Right now, this community is one where everyone gets along."

"And I'd like to keep it that way. No one will work here if the surrounding area is a battleground."

"Now, what about the second point—the outsiders?"

"Find out who they are and what they want. If anyone builds around here, it should be us. Heck, we built the Carnegie library decades ago and several other community treasures that I can't name right now. But it could be about more than low-income housing. We don't want people coming into our town and messing with things...stirring people up...creating chaos. I hear there's already an effort going on over the hill to get the Mexicans organized."

"That's my concern, too. I've done some checking around, and last night we had dinner at the Bistro Mona Lisa, where Mexicans gather. I don't know if it's for social purposes or something else."

"The Bistro Mona Lisa, huh? I'd check out the churches, too. You know those priests always seem to be at the center of anything that involves social justice."

"We're looking into it. The Spanish priest at the church just returned from Latin America."

"Just be careful. Sometimes, these things can get ugly. And even more than that...deadly."

. . .

Gina attended the Spanish evening Mass. The braceros sat in the rear pews, just as Margery had described. Gina glimpsed their humble and reverent faces as she took her seat. It's no wonder the Virgin of Guadalupe appeared to one of these men.

Father Garcia processed down the aisle preceded by two altar servers, one carrying the crucifix high for all to see. She heard the braceros' voices forming a chorus as they sang the entrance hymn. Gina's heart went out to these poor men who had traveled hundreds of miles to toil long hours so their families in Mexico could survive, although not all of these men were husbands and fathers. Some were single and educated but still had to do this menial work to get by in their country, where few opportunities existed.

When the Mass ended, Gina lingered on the steps and watched the crowd. The braceros loaded themselves into a few pickup trucks, sitting shoulder to shoulder in the open cargo bays with scant breathing room. Father Garcia shook most of their hands and seemed friendly with them, even calling some by name. Then he descended the steps and turned to walk along the northern side of the church. That's when Gina spotted the gringos following him. She hurried toward the parking lot, which was in the same direction. When she got close, she saw the scar on one man's face. Father Garcia entered the church through the side door—the two men followed.

Richard was right. Father Garcia is involved in town politics. Oh, these Jesuits...then she remembered that some of her favorite Jesuits at the College of Boston were the ones who called the students to act for social justice. Those priests were not just talk—they had been on the front lines of some of the biggest social justice struggles in Latin America. Their Christianity was liberation theology...defending the rights of the poor...working for social and political change. After seeing the braceros and listening to Marta's stories...Gina was beginning to understand. When she got home, she told Richard what she learned.

"I'm not surprised. But I don't want you to get any more involved. I will take it from here."

"Don't you want me to report when I see or hear something?"

"Only if you come upon it. I don't want you doing any more sleuthing—it could be dangerous. You're a mother of four sons—you need to take care of yourself. And, now that you're home, you need to take care of the boys. But I'll help you get them to bed."

After the boys were settled, Richard went into his study to make a call to Steve. "I've got some news for you."

"I was hoping to hear from you before the meeting."

"We're pretty certain that a couple of out-of-town guys—most likely developers—want to build low-cost housing. But the larger issue is we suspect the Mexicans are being organized. The Spanish priest—I think his name is Father Garcia—was seen walking into the back of the church with them. And we saw the same two men at the Bistro Mona Lisa, whose owner greeted them personally. The cafe seems to be a gathering place for activists."

"That's helpful information you've uncovered. It confirms what we've been picking up from other sources. If you don't mind giving up their names, who are your sources?"

Richard laughed. "Just Gina. She went to the Spanish Mass on Sunday and stayed afterward to snoop around. Margery mentioned the Bistro Mona Lisa, so we all went to dinner one night to check it out. I've been making it a point to drive by, and it seems to stay busy even during off-hours. It makes you wonder."

"At least we have a handle on things before P&Z meets. You never want to be blindsided."

The P&Z meeting was held the next week, low-cost housing falling at the bottom of the agenda. The meeting seemed to drag on longer than usual, with a flurry of reports and members asking far too many questions. When the housing issue arose, two men came forward to present their application, which appeared to be very thorough. Richard was impressed and wondered to himself how they had gotten so many details to include. Some members had questions until the chairman cut them off and scheduled a public hearing. "There are legal procedures that must be followed." The meeting adjourned after that, but the two men left so quickly that no one had a chance to meet them. That's unusual, Richard thought. Most of the time, developers want to press the flesh—it helps to smooth the path.

Steve came up to Richard after the meeting. "What did you think of the proposal?"

"They had all their bases covered. I've never seen a more complete report. I just wonder who they're fronting for."

"You're right. For outsiders, they possess an in-depth knowledge of the town."

"And they also understand which buttons to push. Did you notice how some of the commission members nodded their heads in agreement with everything they said?"

"I picked that up, too. Wonder what it means?"

"I plan to do some research on their construction firm."

"Like what?"

"Who the principals are...what type of jobs they've done... their financial profile. That's the type of information that's public knowledge. Then, I'm going to look into what's not so public."

"Now, you're talking. I would imagine, with your connections in the state, you could drill down pretty deep."

"That's what I'm counting on. And if I can't do it...Jeremy Edwards will be able to. He's an ally in this, by the way. Of course, he has a self-interest. He feels Blackrock Construction should build the project since we're headquartered in town and have done previous work for the community. He also doesn't want any race relations problems."

CHAPTER EIGHT

The next morning, Richard ran into Ben on the way to his plane. He had felt a little guilty about not bringing him in on the low-income housing issue. "Ben, sometime this week, I'd like to talk with you about a town matter."

"The developers."

Richard gave a start. "How did you know?"

"I keep my ear to the ground and ask questions of the right people."

"It sounds like you might have some information for me."

"That's right. And the sooner, the better."

"When I'm in Sacramento, I plan to do some due diligence as well."

"I bet your contacts will provide some valuable insights. But don't discount what goes around the grapevine here. I often find it very reliable."

"Okay. I'll call you tonight to set up a time to meet if I don't get back too late."

"Why don't we just say tomorrow night? Do you want to come to me, or should I come to you?"

"I'll come over after dinner around seven-thirty."

"I thought you'd want to get out of the house. That was the beauty of a military career—I got away and had time to myself. You should have stayed in the navy."

"As they say, hindsight is twenty-twenty."

Richard walked across the street to meet with Ben. He was waiting for him, dressed in plaid pants and a polo shirt, looking like he'd just come off the Old Course at St. Andrews. "How was Sacramento?"

"It appears we won the bid for a new state road. But, more importantly, I poked around and asked a few questions about those developer guys and Renfro Construction."

"Don't keep me in suspense—let's hear it."

Richard followed Ben into the kitchen, taking a seat at the table. "Their company is rather small and new. It seems to go after low-income housing in the state—especially in our area. The company is headquartered in Santa Clara."

"That seems to confirm what I've heard except that the money behind the company comes from people trying to organize the Mexicans."

Richard shook his head. "I don't follow."

Ben puffed up his chest and bore down on him. "Don't tell me you're such a novice in the political world that you don't see what this is leading up to."

"Maybe you better spell it out."

"Housing for votes. Now, do you get the picture?"

"There's a lot at stake here besides a building contract."

"That's right. And we don't want this in our town."

"I'm glad we've had this talk. Public hearings must happen before any contracts are issued. That should take a while. In the meantime, we need to deep-six their application."

"This all has to be done on the QT. We aren't sure who else is involved."

"I've got some suspicions."

"Who? Enlighten me."

"The Catholic priest, for one—Father Garcia. They hold community meetings at Bistro Mona Lisa."

"Priests. You're not Catholic, so I can say this. They always figure in those Latin American revolutions. They possess an affinity for the downtrodden and poor that propels them to activism. You'd think with all the prayers that need to be said, they'd be too busy."

"In Santa Clara, a priest by the name of Donald McDonnell has been active in organizing farmworkers for a few years now. Catholic priests are spread all over the state—they're a ready-made network."

"Wait until the grower-shippers get wind of this. They'll go berserk. They're used to running this valley, and they won't stand for anyone one else trying to edge their way in. Besides, many of them are Catholics and big supporters of the church. They will put on the pinch."

"It all comes down to money, doesn't it?"

"Believe me. They still haven't gotten over the lettuce strike in the 30s. They'll do anything to keep that from happening again."

"Ben, we must not give a housing contract to a company that has ulterior motives. But there is little doubt in my mind that better housing for farmworkers is needed. Gina learned about the overcrowded and unsanitary conditions from our house-keeper. That has to change. We just need to provide better housing in the right way with the right construction company."

"What about your company, Blackrock Construction? You've had a long relationship with the town and have earned its trust."

"I'm going to approach the boss about it. He has a commit-ment to the town and only wants to do what's best."

. . .

Jeremy Edwards was waiting for Richard when he walked into his office. Richard took a seat and let Mr. Edwards begin.

"The word's gotten around about the public hearing. We need to have representation. But before that, we should do an end-run."

"End run...what do you mean?"

"I've already done some checking, and that Renfro group does not yet own the land. They may not have the money to take a chance that they won't get awarded the contract."

"Don't they have a tentative bid on it?"

"Most likely. But money talks. I'll make the owners an offer they can't refuse."

"Won't they just find another piece of property?"

"Not in the vicinity. It's all locked up. Anyway, if we get ahold of the property, we can put in our own application and build the housing."

"This is why you're the boss. You think way ahead on everything."

Jeremy gave a smug smile. "Now, we only need to put the plan into action."

The room at the town hall was packed for the public hearing with standing room only as the chair of the P&Z read the application and started taking testimony. The Mexican community had several spokesmen lined up to testify who told of worsening conditions in the community and the need for better housing. Renfro representatives stepped forward to outline their plan. Out of the crowd, Jack Overton, Blackrock's representative, emerged, asking that they have an opportunity to bid on the project.

Richard noticed the Renfro reps exchange surprised glances. Jack went onto say that Blackrock already owned the property described in the Renfro application, and they proposed to build on it. Then he pulled an application out of his briefcase, setting it on the table in front of the chairman. Whispering filled the room that escalated into noisy chatter. The chairman banged his gavel to restore order. "Would anyone else like to speak?" Seeing none, he closed the hearing.

The crowd dispersed, but the Renfro reps waited outside in the hallway. They knew Richard was with Blackrock and held him up on his way out. "What's going on here?"

"What do you mean?"

"Don't play dumb. You blindsided us."

"I did nothing of the sort. It's only business. Now, let me pass."

Richard met with Jeremy to update him on the public hearing. "Those Renfro guys were waiting for me after the meeting. They didn't like what you did at all."

"It's only business, Richard. When you make an offer that someone can't refuse, they accept it. It's as simple as that. Now, what are the next steps?"

"First, the P&Z Commission has to go over the testimony and do a site walk. Next, we need to consider Blackrock's application for the housing project."

"How long until we get approval?"

"At least a month, maybe longer. But I have a hunch it will be approved. All the community representatives were for it. The location couldn't be better behind the lower end of Main Street. I only hope we don't get any trouble from Renfro thugs once the project is underway."

"They're going to be pretty sore after they discover there isn't any other property available where they could build the housing."

"They could always incentivize people to sell."

"I doubt they would have enough clout for that. Grower-shippers own all the properties in the area. They will not cave in once they understand what's at stake."

"And are you going to clue them in?"

"As a matter of fact, I'm going to a dinner party with a couple of them tonight. Once I fill their ears, they will take it from there. Believe me, these guys are tough. They haven't become some of the richest farmers in the country by letting people push them around."

CHAPTER NINE

The Japanese community planned a teriyaki dinner fundraiser for the temple, and Sam stopped by the Povich's to sell tickets. Margery asked Gina and Richard to join them. "We can bring the kids, too. It'll be a great cultural experience."

Japanese lanterns decorated the Buddhist Temple Hall, and all the women wore traditional kimonos, their hair shimada mage style—a bun with a comb, hair sticks, ribbons, and flowers. In one corner, a Japanese garden gave the room a sense of serenity. Tables, set to accommodate large families, had floral centerpieces in attractive arrangements to add a welcoming artistic touch. By the time the Poviches and Bankstons arrived, the crowd was getting thick. Margery said, "Why don't Gina and I find a table and get the kids settled while you get your plates? We'll get ours later." No sooner were they seated than Margery spotted Lynn Matsui from her office, introducing her to Gina. They exchanged a few words before Lynn moved on as they watched her take tiny steps across the floor in zori sandals, the silk kimono fluttering in her wake.

After she left, Margery turned to Gina. "Lynn has an interesting story about World War II. Like so many Japanese, she was sent to an internment camp. But at some point, Lynn was told she could leave if she headed east. She went to Chicago, where she worked for the USO. When the war ended, Lynn volunteered to go to Japan to help during the occupation and reconstruction of the country and was assigned to General MacArthur's headquarters, where she met her husband. They married in Japan and returned here to live."

Gina's face beamed her astonishment. "Now, if that isn't a fairytale ending."

"But fairytales are always in short supply. Take a look around. Most of these people were sent to an internment camp—Poston in the Arizona desert—hot and dusty and crawling with scorpions. Their lives were nothing but misery. Lynn was one of the lucky ones."

Tom and Richard arrived with their plates overflowing. "Besides chicken teriyaki, they have sushi and tempura," Tom said. "They're putting on a show. I guess this means Japantown is back."

"What do you mean by Japantown is back?" said Gina.

"Before the war, there was a Japantown here. Watsonville was one of the few towns that had one. But with everything that happened during the war, some people didn't return, and Japantown dwindled. But now, it appears to be back."

Sam and Ann stopped by the table to greet their guests. "We hope you are enjoying yourselves," Sam said. "We want to make this event an annual tradition."

"If there is anything you need," said Ann, "please ask. It's our pleasure to serve you."

"We couldn't be enjoying ourselves more," said Margery. "Thank you for the opportunity to come and learn more about your culture."

When Sam and Ann moved on to another table, Gina and Margery began to chat. That gave Tom a chance to talk to Richard. "I read that Blackrock is going to be building some low-income housing in town."

"Yes. Our application was approved."

"I heard through the grapevine that some outsiders wanted the project."

"That's correct," Richard said as he dipped a tempura shrimp into soy sake sauce. "But we beat 'em to it."

"Talk is that they want to organize the Mexican community."

"That's how it appears."

"Do you think with Blackrock getting the project, they will give up on organizing?"

"No. I feel certain they will find another way to do it."

"Any ideas how?"

"A few hunches. But nothing for certain."

"I've lived here all my life, and, for the most part, the various races have gotten along. The Japanese were mistreated during the war, but they're rebuilding their lives and holding no grudges. They are models for the rest of us."

"I agree. We have a new engineer at Blackrock, a Stanford grad, running circles around the rest of us. Ken Takata is not only smart, but he has a work ethic that makes the rest of us seem like sloths. He is one impressive young man."

"After going through the war and seeing what people I grew up with had to deal with, it's good to see things moving ahead. But let me tell you, Pearl Harbor changed everything. We all had friends who were Japanese, so it was a difficult time here. They were both ashamed and afraid. And we were angry at Japan, yet filled with empathy for our friends. It was all very complicated."

"I can only imagine how hard it was for everyone here. But no one had it easy. My mother is German, a first-generation American. She always felt under suspicion, even though she was married to an Englishman."

"Both of Margery's parents immigrated here from Germany around the turn of the century. People often say Germans have a superiority complex, but it could be a mask for inferiority or fear of social acceptance. This event here tonight is a shining example of how far all of us have come."

"We've covered some tough topics. Let's hope no one overheard us."

"Nah. Everyone's concentrating on the food and having fun. Besides, I glanced around when we were talking to make sure no one had his big ears up. In a small town like this, you learn that early."

"The boys are getting tired," Gina said. "I think we should pack it in."

They loaded the kids into the strollers and made their way to the cars. The Poviches pulled out of the parking lot first and turned right. Richard turned left.

"Where are you going?" Gina said.

"I thought I'd drive past the Bistro Mona Lisa to see what's going on." And sure enough, the restaurant was packed.

"Look, that's Father Garcia leaving now. It's hard to tell he's a priest, but I caught a glimpse of his collar."

"Once we break ground on the project, we'll be here every day. We'll find out if something is going on or not."

The low-income housing project began with a groundbreaking ceremony featuring speeches by the mayor and other dignitaries and a ribbon-cutting for photo ops. Members of the Mexican community came forward to offer their gratitude on behalf of the entire community. On hand representing Blackrock Construction, Richard was pleased that everything had proceeded smoothly up to this point.

When the ceremony was over, the crowd cleared out to allow construction to begin. First, the big cats prepared the site. The soil was the same sandy loam type found in the fields that is responsible for bountiful harvests. The men understood their work. Within a matter of days, the site was ready to start the framing for the buildings. Even though Ken Takata was the project manager, Richard stopped by every day to check on the project and talk with members of the community who were watching. He learned that one person spent every day on the site. And when he wasn't there, he was taking a break at the Bistro Mona Lisa.

Richard made a point of meeting Hector Lopez. Hector appeared to be in his mid-thirties and had the look of someone who had labored under the sun—skin bronzed and leathery with deep wrinkles around the eyes that had tried to squint out the intense afternoon light. But his hands told the rest of the story. They were the hands of a man who worked the soil—large and muscular, fingers stained black with traces of dirt underneath the nails. In most respects, he looked like the other Mexican farm-workers—short and squatty with jet black hair and piercing brown eyes. But there was something about him that set him apart from the rest, although Richard just couldn't put his finger on it. Was it his bearing that seemed so confident? Was it the way he concentrated on the workmen which appeared so thoughtful? Or was it his awareness of the most minor things, whether it was a phrase of conversation, a passerby, or something else?

After a week had passed, Richard walked up to the man and extended his hand. "I'm Richard Bankston, Vice President of Blackrock Construction."

"Good day. I'm Hector Lopez."

"I've noticed you're here every day."

"Yes, I make it a point to be here."

Richard raised an eyebrow as he looked him in the eyes. "Why is that?"

"I'm not working right now, so I come here to pass the time. I'm an observer for our community."

"I see. What type of work do you do?" Richard asked as if he didn't already know.

"I work on a farm as a field manager. But I had an injury and cannot go to work right now."

"I hope you're seeing good progress on the project."

"Yes, it's being built well."

"Do you plan to live in one of these units?"

"It depends on how they're assigned."

Richard looked away and saw Ken striding toward him. "Excuse me," he said as he made a quick getaway in Ken's direction.

"I spotted you," Ken said, "and wanted to offer a tour of our progress so far."

"Great. Since I spend most of my time in the office, I don't get out on job sites often."

"Well then, follow me. But grab a hard hat first—we must follow the rules."

"I almost forgot—that's how long it's been since I had to wear a hard hat."

Richard and Ken walked through the construction site, making their way around the big cats and other obstacles. The framing was underway, which showed the form the buildings were going to take.

"It looks like everything's in order. You're doing a good job managing the project," Richard said.

"When the men perform their job, it's easy. But the opposite is also true."

"Have you been aware of that guy over there? His name is Hector Lopez."

"Yes, I've seen him here every day for long periods. He has taken quite an interest in what we're doing."

"Is he getting in the way?"

"No. He doesn't even ask questions...just observes."

"Any guess about his purpose?"

"We have not yet spoken."

"Do that soon. I'm eager to learn what he tells you. But the Mexican community should be satisfied with what's happening here."

Ken smiled. "My family has a strawberry farm in the area. We rely on Mexicans to harvest the fruit. They do a good job. When the farm was smaller, the family did all the harvesting...squatting for long hours in the sun. Now, we have to rely on others to help."

"There is no doubt Mexicans are an important part of our economy. We wouldn't get the crops planted and raised and harvested without them. I'll let you go so you can get back to your project."

When Richard returned to the company, he ran into Jeremy Edwards. "I've just been given a tour of our housing project by Ken Tanaka. He's got everything under control."

Jeremy smiled. "He'll be on the rise in this company. Tell me, is there any word from the Mexican community about the project?"

"Not officially, although there is a man by the name of Hector Lopez who's on-site every day. He described himself as an unofficial observer."

"How are the units going to be allocated?"

"By lottery. Families will apply for approval. Expect two requests for every spot."

CHAPTER TEN

That night, Richard had a P&Z meeting. He arrived early to speak with the other commissioners about the housing project and other items of business. He didn't expect to run into Steve, who revealed the sensitivities in town due to the activities at the Bistro Mona Lisa. "That Spanish priest has been seen coming and going several times in the company of outsiders. The grower-shippers are a little nervous."

"One thing you should know is that there's a man named Hector Lopez who's on the worksite every day."

"What's his deal?"

"He watches on behalf of the Mexican community. Our project manager has had no problem with him, nor does he ask questions...just watches."

"I bet he's there for a reason, and we need to find out what it is. It probably has something to do with the organizing that's going on. Over the hill, things are heating up."

"We can talk more about this later. The meeting is about to begin."

· · ·

Richard got home late. As he was getting ready for bed, sirens blared in the distance, but he thought little about them. Gina was asleep, so he slid in next to her. As he was about to doze off, the phone rang. Who'd be calling at this hour? Richard picked up the bedside phone, and before he could say hello, Steve's excited voice shouted, "The housing project's on fire."

"What are you talking about?" Richard said while he rolled out of bed onto his feet, preparing himself for action.

"The fire trucks are on the scene now. I thought you might want to get down there to observe."

"Thanks. I need to make a couple of quick calls first to Mr. Edwards and Ken. Then I'll leave. Will I see you there?"

"Of course. As town attorney, I'm going to be involved, and I need to gather evidence as soon as possible."

"Okay. We'll do it together."

By the time Richard arrived, the firefighters had already gotten a lot of water on the fire, but flames were still shooting up while they tried to wet down areas that had not yet burned. Smoke was filling the air, which caused Richard's eyes to smart and nose to recoil from the putrid odors which always occur when materials burn.

Steve was already on-site, and upon spotting Richard, walked in his direction. Once he was within earshot, he said, "When I got here, it looked like a funeral pyre. I didn't think there would be anything left to save."

"At least half the structures haven't been damaged. It's too bad...Ken and his team were making significant progress."

"I hope they can save half—they're trying to put as much water on it as possible to keep it from burning."

"Do they have any idea what caused the fire?"

"Not yet—it's too early to tell. But they'll find out. Forensics can almost always determine a cause these days. My guess is it was arson."

"Arson? Don't be too quick to come to that conclusion.

There are always combustible materials around a worksite that may not be stored properly."

"Forensics will do its job and reach the right conclusion."

"Is Ken Tanaka around? I'd like to talk to him."

"Follow me, and I'll help you find him."

They came upon Ken, standing amongst the firefighters who were being relieved. He looked serious and worried.

"Ken," Richard called, and the junior engineer turned to look his way, moving toward him. Ken's face said it all. It was not the same proud face Richard had seen earlier that afternoon when they toured the building site. Now, Ken seemed saddened and burdened with responsibility, as if the fire had been his fault.

Richard put his arm around Ken's shoulders. "I'm sorry. You've worked so hard on this project. But don't let this setback get you down. You and your team can rebuild it." Richard didn't feel his words had a lot of effect. The Japanese he had known following the war had such high standards for themselves that it was a devastating blow when they met with even the slightest failure. On the other hand, Americans who hadn't had such standards of excellence had learned resiliency from failure.

Ken took a deep breath and turned toward Richard. "Thank you for your supportive words. You're right. This is something that can be overcome. At least it was only the framing that went up in flames."

"Any thoughts on the cause of the fire? Were there any combustibles left unsecured?"

"I always check the site thoroughly myself before I leave. It is doubtful that the fire started spontaneously."

"Then is it your opinion that it was arson?"

"I'm sure it was not the result of spontaneous combustion."

Richard looked around, and Hector came into view. "What's he doing here?"

"I have no idea. This is the first I've seen of him tonight."

"I'm going to grab Steve and have a talk with him. Maybe

Hector knows something or saw something. From what I've noticed about him, he doesn't miss much."

Richard and Steve approached Hector in as unassuming a way as possible. Richard spoke first. "Hector, why am I not surprised you're here tonight?"

"Sirens sounded, and then someone yelled that the housing project was on fire. I wanted to see things for myself rather than rely on others to tell me."

"Firsthand witness is always best," Steve said. "I heard you were here earlier today. Did you notice anything suspicious?"

"Quien sabe?"

Who knows? Richard was not going to let him get away with that. He spoke some Spanish and understood even more. "Who knows, you say? We are asking if you know anything."

"Tu comprendes Español?"

"Enough to get by. Now, please, answer my question. It's important."

"The only thing I know is that there is a guy in town called the Torch."

"Are you referring to Jewish lightning?" Steve said.

"Not Jewish. Maybe Croatian."

"Can you give us a name?" Richard asked.

"Ivan or something like that."

"Why would he be involved?" Steve said.

"Quien sabe."

"There you go again. Either you know, or you don't."

"My last word is talk to him." Then Hector walked away.

"What do you make of this, Steve?"

"Quien sabe."

"Oh, please, not you, too."

"It's getting late...and I'm getting punchy. But there's a guy who people call the Torch. A couple of businesses in town have gone up in flames under mysterious circumstances—the old diner, for instance."

"I remember that fire. We liked that little hole-in-the-wall diner. But wasn't that old wooden structure just a tinder box awaiting a match?"

"That's the story the insurance company bought when they paid out the claim."

"If the Torch is setting fires, there must be something in it for him—money, for instance. We need to find this character and ask some questions."

"Hold on. First, we don't want to jeopardize the investigation by doing the wrong thing. And second, we don't want to risk bodily harm by taking on thugs. Tomorrow, I'll drop by the police station and talk with the investigator on the case. Chances are, he knows exactly where to find the Torch."

Richard had just sat down at his desk when the secretary stepped in to tell him Mr. Edwards wanted to see him in his office right away. He eyed the stack of mail on his desk, let out a groan, and headed down the hallway. Richard was not prepared for the look he saw on Jeremy's face—a mixture of anger, determination, and suspicion. He slunk into a chair, not sure which emotion would emerge first.

"Richard, I've got to tell you, this fire is upsetting on so many levels, and I don't know where to direct my anger. But more than that, what we are trying to do here for the community is being sabotaged. Ken told me he doubts it was spontaneous combustion because he is careful to store materials safely. I'd like your opinion."

"I agree with Ken. He is meticulous in his management of the project. The fault doesn't lie with him or any of his team. At first, my instincts suspected Renfro. Their reps were not the most upright men I've ever been around. They insisted we pulled the rug out from under them, which, of course, we did."

"Renfro has to be on the list of suspects. But what do they get out of it besides a bit of revenge? What's the payoff? I don't see the risk as worth the reward for them. It won't prevent our building the housing project."

Richard nodded in agreement. "You're right. We got a tip last night from that guy Hector Lopez who's been hanging around every day. He mentioned someone called the Torch."

That got Jeremy's attention. "The Torch...I almost forgot about him. I haven't heard him mentioned in a few years. But if you were looking for a professional to do an arson job for you, he'd be the go-to man."

"Steve is going to talk to the detective assigned to the case today. He said the police would know where to find the Torch."

"My sources tell me he frequents the High Noon Café and bowling alley."

"What else do you know about him? Hector said he's Croatian."

A smirk crossed Jeremy's face. "He's a big, fat Croatian guy who probably eats and drinks too much. I believe he works in one of the apple packinghouses."

"He has connections to the grower-shippers?"

"Most Croatians in the town are related somehow to the grower-shippers even if they're only poor relatives."

"Where do we go from here?" He knew Jeremy would have a plan.

"First, clean up the site. Second, hire security to guard the site at night."

"It might be a good idea to have security during the day, too, as a deterrent in case someone is thinking about making another pass at us."

"That's an even better idea. Can you arrange for security to be there starting immediately?"

"I'll get on it right away. What else?"

"Keep your ear to the ground. If you pick up anything, relay it to me pronto. I suggest you give the town attorney a call today to find out if he has any new information."

When he returned to his office, Richard put in a call to Steve. "Did you have a chance to speak with the detective yet?"

"Detective Moretti is working the case. He's familiar with the Torch, whose real name is Ivan Grizich, and will check him out. But he said this type of fire is not his M.O. because he wouldn't want to touch anything that smacked of politics. It's not a clean fire for insurance purposes."

"He's got that right. Does Moretti have any other ideas about the case?"

"Not yet. He's methodical and will follow every lead."

After he concluded the phone call with Steve, Richard headed out to the project. When he arrived, the men were finishing work for the day. Richard grabbed a hard hat and weaved his way through the debris, finally locating Ken.

"It looks like you got a lot done today."

"Yes, the clean-up is going quite well. We should have it completed in two or three more days and be able to begin again."

"Sometimes, rebuilding goes faster than the initial building, which means you'll be back to where you were in no time."

"Meanwhile, this break gave me a chance to review the architect's rendering."

That grabbed Richard's interest as he moved in closer to listen. "Did your review reveal anything important?"

"Only that there is nothing very aesthetic to the design. We could make a few adjustments that would create a much more welcoming environment for the families."

"What do you suggest?"

"First, we should create more privacy between the patios and balconies, add better insulation between walls. Privacy was one complaint my parents had when they were interned. And they missed a garden—something of beauty. I'd like the exterior to resemble Spanish architecture. We could keep the stucco finish but use red tiles on the roof, wrought-iron railings, and a place to sit in the shade—a patio with a couple of benches, a garden, or pots with flowers."

"All these are wonderful suggestions. Talk with the architect, then figure the costs."

"Often, we don't spend the time to create something of beauty. Even though this is public housing, we can make it a place people will enjoy and be proud to call home."

"Ken, you never cease to amaze me."

Suddenly, Hector appeared out of thin air. He had overheard the conversation and wanted to weigh in. "I wasn't eavesdropping, but I heard what you said about making this a nice place for the community. You have my respect for that, and I want to help in any way I can."

"What are you suggesting?" Richard asked.

"For starters, I'm going to ask some questions about the fire. Someone knows what happened. They won't tell you, but they will tell me. Tonight, there'll be a big meeting at the Bistro Mona Lisa. A lot of community leaders are expected to attend, and I will find answers."

"Will the priest be at that meeting?" Richard asked.

"What does it matter?"

"Forget it. I shouldn't have asked."

Hector answered anyway. "Father Garcia is a friend and helps us in many ways. His heart is always sincere. He only wants to do good. Mexicans consider priests part of their family and want to be involved with them. Not like gringos. We are very different."

Hector walked away, and Richard turned back to Ken. "You made a friend for life. Hector will sing your praises from now on."

"I hope he is my friend. But that was not my intention. I only want to do something good for the families. There's no reason for them to have to suffer if we can avoid it."

"I agree." Richard turned to leave. But he couldn't help

thinking about Ken's desire to make things better for these families. He had learned about life in the internment camps. The inmates lived under dismal conditions—lack of privacy, too much heat or cold, and an absence of beauty so critical to the Japanese soul. This project is an opportunity to do better for people, and Ken has the heart to make it happen.

Even without checking his watch, Richard knew it was late. He entered through the side door and was relieved that Gina was not waiting for him at the kitchen table. Whew. I caught a break this time. His nose told him that dinner was still simmering on the stove. After taking off his boots, Richard padded in his stocking feet toward the living room. Gina was there, surrounded by her brood, all engrossed in the latest capers of *My Three Stooges*.

"Oh, hi, honey," Gina said as she stood to kiss Richard. "You surprised us."

"I can see I interrupted a family bonding session."

"This is the first time I've had a chance to sit all day. Let's go into the kitchen and have dinner. The boys have already eaten."

Richard took his place at the table while Gina dished out polenta topped with chicken cacciatore. She pulled the salads out of the refrigerator and brought the open bottle of Chianti to the table, filling their glasses.

"How was your day?"

"Eventful." Richard took a bite of the chicken, so tender that it almost fell off the bone. "Jeremy Edwards summoned me to his office first thing to discuss the fire investigation."

"Does he have any clues about how it started?"

"He had a couple of theories, but nothing we hadn't already thought of. His first action item was security, which I arranged right after our meeting. Then in the afternoon, I talked to Steve about the investigation."

"Did he have anything to report?"

Richard told her about the detective's plan to track down the Torch and Ken's ideas to improve the project for the families. He then told her about Hector's offer to help and the meeting at the Bistro Mona Lisa.

Upon hearing about the meeting, Gina swallowed hard before speaking. "It must be an important one. Marta said that she and many of her relatives are going to the meeting, too. The bistro will not be able to accommodate too many people."

"That's where standing room only comes in. Did Marta give you any clues about the purpose of the meeting?"

"She only said it's an important community meeting. All the leaders will be there. I suspect it has to do with politics and getting organized to take part in the election."

"Did she say anything about the fire? Who started it and why?"

Gina lifted her glass, but before she took a swallow, she said, "We had little time to talk about anything today. But she said it was politically motivated."

"When Marta comes tomorrow, do some more probing. I don't care if the house gets cleaned as long as we get some answers."

Gina sat Marta down at the kitchen table, gave her a cup of coffee, and pulled up a chair. They talked for nearly an hour about the weather, the children, Marta's family, almost every-thing except what happened at the meeting. Finally, Gina asked her the question she most wanted answered, "Did you find out anything about the fire?"

But Marta just nodded her head and said, "No." Then she added, "I will ask around."

That afternoon, Richard got a call from Steve, who told him there were some preliminary findings on the investigation. "I'm listening."

"It appears to be an amateur job. That leaves out a professional like the Torch. It was started with rags soaked in kerosene. A rope was used as the fuse to ignite the inferno."

Richard paused to mull over the information. "Did they get any other forensic evidence that could give us a clue who did it?"

"Not yet. But they're still working on it. It will take a few weeks before everything is in."

"There was a big community meeting at the Bistro Mona Lisa last night. Gina was supposed to ask Marta about it today."

"Yes, I caught wind of it. The bistro was overcrowded, so extra police were required to monitor the situation."

"What was the meeting about?"

"They only spoke Spanish, which put most of us at a handicap. But the major thrust was voter registration."

"That's pretty benign. Although, they have to be citizens first."

"That's where the Registrar of Voters will have to be very vigilant. We say, one man, one vote, but that should be amended to one citizen, one vote."

"Make some flyers up with that slogan and put them around town."

"You're asking too much. That would require people who can read English."

"Anyway, I'm going to stop by the housing project again this afternoon and nose around a bit. I'll call you if I learn anything."

Richard spotted Hector as he pulled up to the construction site. He hurried out of his car, grabbed a hard hat, and walked in Hector's direction. Hector turned toward Richard when he saw him approach. "Hello, Richard. It seems you come here most days now."

"Once things settle down, I won't be here as often. By the way, what was the meeting about last night?"

"Oh, just some political stuff. Like getting registered to vote and going to the polls on Election Day."

Richard tried not to allow his annoyance to show. "Did you learn anything about who started the fire?"

"Nada. But I have a tip. Check out the St. Francis School."

"A school for seminarians? What are you getting at?"

"Follow the tip, and maybe you will."

Richard pondered the St. Francis School all the way home. Why would seminarians be mixed up in arson? Or perhaps it was someone who worked at the school—a teacher, an office worker, a maintenance man. And what motive would they have? Richard's mind was absorbed in solving the mystery when he reached his driveway. He noticed Tom working in his yard and walked over to ask him a few questions about the school.

"How's it going? Any more information on the fire?"

"That's what I wanted to talk to you about. An informant gave me a tip to check out the St. Francis School."

Tom put down his rake to focus on Richard. "St. Francis School? Those boys are seminarians. Do you understand what that means?"

"They're studying to be priests."

"That's right. I can't imagine they would be involved in arson or anything else like it. In fact, I don't think they're allowed to leave the school except for vacation. They couldn't have done it."

"My informant didn't say it was seminarians, only that I should check out the school. You've lived here all your life. What do you know about it?"

Tom rubbed his chin, trying to remember. "It started as an orphanage for boys in the late 1800s. Then at the turn of the century, they started sending juvenile delinquents there instead of incarcerating them with adults. From those fabled beginnings, it morphed into a school for seminarians. It's named St. Francis after two saints—St. Francis of Assisi and St. Francis de Sales."

"That's interesting...the activist and the mystic...a dangerous combination. Who should I talk to at the school?"

"Father McElroy is the pastor at the Valley Church across the street. He could direct you. But be careful—he's one of the dark Irish priests—all fire and brimstone."

Instead of calling Father McElroy, Richard called Father O'Leary at St. Pats and set up an appointment to meet him in person.

"It is always a pleasure to see members of the church."

"My wife and children are the members. I'm not Catholic." He knew this would make it easier for him to have an open conversation with the priest. He did not hold them on the same high pedestal Catholics did, especially those born to the faith. Converts sometimes had a problem with it, too.

"As a husband and father, I consider you like family. Now, what can I do for you?"

Richard got right to the point. "I need some answers to a few questions about the St. Francis School."

"Have you talked to Father McElroy? He's the pastor for the school and could best help you."

"I started with you since we already have a relationship."

"Your timing is good. Father Garcia and I just spent the day at the school talking about our vocations."

"Oh, really?" Richard leaned forward, prompting Father O'Leary to tell more.

"I talked about my boyhood in Ireland and the many role models I had there. Of course, every Irish family is expected to send at least one boy to the priesthood, and I was the pick of our litter, so to speak. But it was the right choice for me."

"And what is Father Garcia's story?"

"I could not compete with him for inspiration to young people contemplating the priesthood. He spoke of his time in Guatemala, working for agrarian reforms in opposition to the United Fruit Company. The seminarians hung on his every word. He made being a priest sound very exciting...even glamorous. And, of course, it can be, especially when you're placed somewhere like Latin America, living liberation theology, or to put it another way, a concern for the freedom of the oppressed."

"The United Fruit Company. It's the reason there are so many banana republics in Latin America."

"Yes, but the new president of Guatemala wasn't one of them, so the CIA got rid of him. However, as the Chilean poet, Pablo Neruda once said, 'You can cut all the flowers, but you cannot keep spring from coming.' Reforms continued to spread, and another priest who was sharing alongside us, Father Hernandez, worked for them in Honduras."

"Father Hernandez…his name is familiar."

"He is the rector at the school and was also involved in liberation theology. Between him and Father Garcia, more than a few hearts were sown with the seeds of activism."

"Is that so?"

"Some seminarians wanted to get involved in a cause right away."

"Do you think any did?"

"No. They are preparing for their vows, which leaves them no free time."

"Father, I need to ask you this question. Could any seminarians have been involved in the fire at the housing project on Rodriguez Street?"

Father O'Leary bolted upright, shooting an indignant glare at Richard. "Certainly not. We do not believe in being involved in violent activities. Peace is the only way. And there are many peaceful tactics that can affect a situation."

Richard considered his conversation with Father O'Leary on the way back to his office. He wondered if Hector had tried to throw him a curveball or if he needed to do more probing.

The first thing Richard did when he sat down at his desk was to call Steve. His line was busy, which gave Richard more time to reflect. If the arsonist was involved with the St. Francis School and if seminarians are ruled out, who's left? Teachers, office workers, custodians. Anyone else? Richard tried Steve's line again, and this time Steve picked up.

"I got a tip yesterday on the fire. My informant said to check out the St. Francis School."

"Ever since it took in juvenile delinquents, this town has looked askance at that school. It will never live down its past reputation."

"I just met with Father O'Leary and had a talk with him about it."

"Richard, leave the investigation to the police."

"I couldn't help myself and wanted to find out if there was any substance there."

"What did you learn?"

"There was a panel discussion on vocations a few days before the fire."

"So...I don't see any problem there."

"You will. Trust me."

"Just make it quick. I have a lot of work to do today."

"I'll make it as quick as I can. Besides Father O'Leary, Father Garcia and Father Hernandez took part. According to Father O'Leary, both Spanish priests talked about their escapades in Latin America, living liberation theology, and set more than a few hearts on fire with a desire to follow in their footsteps."

"Were they hanging out with Che Guevara, too?"

"Not to my knowledge. But now that you mention Che, I remember that the events he witnessed in Guatemala in the early 50s turned him into a revolutionary."

"How does this involve the housing project fire?"

"Don't you see? The housing project could be a symbol for the United Fruit Company."

"As in Gabriel Garcia Marquez' book *100 Years of Solitude*...a force of suppression?"

"I'm always impressed by your reading list. But that's what I'm getting at. At least it's something to go on..."

"Let me take it from here. I'll talk with Detective Moretti and ask him to nose around out there. Who knows? He may be one step ahead of us."

Steve put in a call to Detective Moretti. "I need to talk to you about the arson case. Can you spare a few minutes?"

"I was headed out, but I can wait if it's important."

"It may be. You'll determine that." Then he relayed what he had learned from Richard.

"All right," said Moretti. "I'll start asking questions of everyone associated with the school. I don't expect to get any answers. But from the evidence we've gathered so far, we assume the arsonist was an amateur, so that fits. Are you suggesting the arsonist is an idealist with a grudge against the establishment?"

"Your guess is better than mine, Detective. But right now, we've come up emptyhanded, so this gives you a fresh trail."

The first person Detective Moretti encountered at the St. Francis School was Father McElroy. He was not well acquainted with the priest but knew to avoid him at all costs. Unfortunately, Father McElroy recognized him.

"What are you doing here, Detective?"

"Just routine, Father. I'm investigating a case."

"Again, why would that bring you here?"

"If you'd like to talk, can we go somewhere private?"

"Can't you just answer my simple question?"

"I'm investigating the fire at the housing project. Someone gave us a tip that we've followed here."

"Then you'll want to speak with the Rector, Father Hernandez. His office is down the hall, second door on the right."

"Thank you, Father."

"I will pray for your investigation, Detective, and hope that it leads to the culprit. This is a house of holiness, not of arson and activism."

Detective Moretti nodded as if in agreement, then turned to walk the short distance down the hall until he reached the correct office. The secretary asked him to wait while she asked if Father Hernandez could meet with him.

The secretary reappeared a few minutes later and ushered Detective Moretti into the room. Father Hernandez was waiting with his hands composed on his desk. He was a delicate-looking Hispanic man who appeared more Spanish than Mexican. His brown doe-like eyes were his most prominent feature. He had high chiseled cheekbones, an aquiline nose, and thin well-defined lips that turned up in a subtle smile. Like the Mona Lisa, Moretti mused as he approached to extend his hand. A mystery behind the smile.

"Tell me, Detective Moretti, what brings you to my office on a beautiful day like this? You should be out walking the beat, listening to birdsong."

"I'm here to ask you a few questions about the housing project fire."

"That was unfortunate. I hope the project is moving ahead again."

"Yes, the clean-up has been completed, and new construction is underway. I'll get right to the point, Father. We received a tip to check out the St. Francis School for a connection to the fire. Is there any reason to suspect someone here is involved?"

Father Hernandez grew stiff as his smile turned into a sneer. "I should hope not. Our seminarians are not allowed to leave the premises, so that removes them from suspicion."

Moretti paused for a moment. "What about the rest of the staff and employees?"

"Most of us can come and go. But you will find no arsonists among us."

"Why do you say that?"

"We are happy that the Mexican community will receive better housing. There would be no reason for us to destroy it."

"Any idea who might have a reason?"

Father Hernandez's body softened as he relaxed. "I'd need time to reflect on it. If something occurs to me, I'll get in touch."

"Just one more question. I heard you were in Latin America practicing Liberation Theology and that you spoke about it during the panel discussion a few weeks ago."

The rector turned serious, narrowing his eyes. "And so..."

"Did you inspire anyone to become an activist?"

"I hope so. We need more priests in difficult places around the world. But if you are asking if anyone got so wild-eyed that they wanted to burn something down right now, I doubt if my words had that much effect."

"I, too, would not want to find the culprit among you." And then he considered the school's previous life as a facility for juvenile delinquents and wondered if these walls still harbored criminals. His mind snapped back to the present when Father Hernandez rose to bid him goodbye. As Detective Moretti walked out, he got an odd vibe, which often happens to him when a criminal element is nearby. Was this just residue from the past or something new? He couldn't tell but would be back to find out.

Months later, the housing project was finished, and plans were underway for a celebration. But the night before the event, Detective Moretti got a call from the project's security force. They had caught a man entering the property with a backpack containing enough kerosene to burn down the entire housing project in minutes. Moretti jumped into his car, put his siren on, and made a mad dash for Rodriguez Street. By the time he got there, the security officers had the man subdued and under control. The detective flashed his badge and began asking questions.

"What is your name?" Moretti asked.

"Jose Salazar."

"What did you plan to do with the kerosene and other items you have in your backpack?"

"I want to talk with a lawyer."

"Okay. We'll do it your way. But you will be questioned one way or the other."

Detective Moretti pulled out handcuffs, put them on the suspect, and read him his rights. Then he called for police officers to come to pick him up. It took only a few minutes for them to arrive, load the suspect in the car, and take him to the station for processing. Detective Moretti followed and settled into his office to make some calls. The mayor was first on his list.

"What do you mean a suspect is in custody? I hope this won't overshadow the ceremony in the morning."

Moretti frowned at the mayor's comment. "I don't think so. We don't know if this is the same person who set the fire a few months ago. This could be a new attempt altogether."

"He has bad timing as far as I'm concerned. Let's keep this hushed up until after the ceremony. This is supposed to offer an opportunity to bond with the Mexican community. The election is not far off, and from what I hear, they're registering in droves. Mexicans will be running this town before long if we don't court them and keep them happy."

"I understand, Mayor. We'll keep everything under control."

Moretti's next call was to Steve to bring him up to date.

"I'm just glad we stopped him in time. Who nabbed him?"

"The security patrol that Blackrock had on duty."

"Is he the same guy who set the fire a few months ago?"

"We need to interrogate him. He's probably had a run-in with the law before because he asked to speak to an attorney. He wouldn't talk or answer questions."

"Did you get anything out of him?"

"Only his name, Jose Salazar. He's Mexican. About fifty years old."

"That name doesn't ring a bell. I'm going to inform Black-rock we have a perpetrator, even though security already alerted them. Give me a heads up when you plan to question Salazar so I can be present."

The public housing ceremony went well. Members of the community were on hand to take a tour. No one mentioned a word about an arrest of a suspect the night before, although Hector was present, looking like the cat that just ate the canary. Richard took one look at his face with that Cheshire cat grin and wondered what more he knew.

The suspect's interrogation was arranged for the afternoon. Steve was there to represent the town while the public defender represented Salazar. Detective Moretti did most of the questioning, but it took a long while before Salazar broke down. He appeared to be a hardened criminal who cared little for society and its rules. Finally, he admitted to setting the earlier fire.

"Yes, I did it, and I'm proud of it. I did it for my people. We have been on this land longer than anyone other than Indians. This town sits on a Mexican land grant. Yet, look at where my people are in the pecking order of this town—at the very bottom. People want us to pick their crops, clean their houses, even take care of their children and elderly, but they despise us. We aren't good enough to live in your neighborhoods. Where is the fairness? Where is the justice?"

"Wow," Steve said when he left the room. "His words were a real eye-opener. I had no idea the Mexicans feel that way. Most are so easygoing and polite."

"You never really know what people are thinking," Moretti said. "But I doubt everyone shares his views. His life has been a mess since the beginning. He started out as an orphan at the St. Francis School."

"The St. Francis connection. Is he still involved with the school?"

"Yes. But he only does odd jobs. He's not very dependable... drinks too much...in and out of jail and mental hospitals."

"I assume his next stop will be Soledad."

"If he's convicted. My guess is his attorney will plea bargain it down. I'm sure Jose has some information he can trade for leniency."

"Like what?"

"Names of drug dealers in town. Mexicans are bringing lots of drugs across the border. We need to nip it in the bud."

CHAPTER ELEVEN

One fall day in 1962, Gina strolled over to Margery's for coffee and a break from her routine. She looked in the window and saw Margery sitting at the table, engrossed in the newspaper. She didn't even look up when Gina entered the kitchen.

"That must be an interesting article you're reading."

Margery pushed the paper aside to acknowledge Gina's presence. "It's a book review about *Silent Spring*."

"*Silent Spring*." Gina thought that was an unusual title. "What's it about?"

"It's about how poisons are affecting our environment and people, too, by causing tumors and cancer."

Gina sat down, contemplating what Margery had said while fumbling for her cigarette pack. "That's terrible."

"Guess why it's called *Silent Spring*? Because there will be no more birdsong. It's like she's talking directly to Pajaro Valley—translation Bird Valley—and issuing us a warning."

"No birdsong. Birdsong is nature's music. I can't imagine not hearing it when new shoots are pushing themselves up through the soil."

"You won't have to worry about that since there won't be any new buds either. Rachel Carson tells a story about apple trees coming into bloom, but because there are no bees to pollinate the flowers, there's no fruit to follow. This book is going to send a shiver through the growers in this valley. Apples are even more precious to them than birds."

"That's just awful to think about."

"Remember, I told you that someone would prove a link between these insecticides and human illness."

"I remember." Gina lit a cigarette as she listened.

"And it's the weakest that are first to be affected...the birds, the bees, the babies..."

Gina caught Margery's voice cracking and saw tears welling up in her eyes as she turned to wipe them away.

"At the turn of the century, there was a company in town manufacturing insecticide. The California Spray Chemical Company was at the corner of Riverside and Walker Streets. They were trying to make an insecticide to kill a moth that was detrimental to apple trees."

"Is it still there?"

"No, they sold it to Standard Oil for its Ortho division. Now, DDT is the poison of choice. Rachel Carson has nothing good to say about it."

"But don't we need these insecticides to protect the crops? Otherwise, there'll be nothing but blight."

"Even Rachel Carson isn't against insecticide altogether. But she's convinced better farming practices can reduce the amount of poison we use."

"I've driven by the fields when crop dusters are spraying insecticide. The bright green lettuce almost turns white," said Gina.

"And imagine those poor farmworkers who have to go in and tend the fields after the spraying. If most of them didn't go back to Mexico and die there, our health care system would be over-loaded. But all this is happening very quietly because the victims retreat into the shadows."

. . .

Gina bombarded Richard with what she had learned as soon as he walked in the door.

"I know all about *Silent Spring*. And Carson's findings will be taken seriously since she's a scientist. I shudder to think what the environmentalists are going to do with this information. Lord knows, in California, we have more of them per capita than birds."

"We spend so much of our lives out of doors—how can we help but be environmentalists?"

"It was a hunter who started the National Park System. Even as Teddy Roosevelt was killing wildlife, he realized how important it was to protect its environment for the future."

"Is there going to be trouble around here because of the environmental concerns over insecticides?"

"From what I've picked up, there's more brewing than just the environmentalists. A guy over the hill named Cesar Chavez just started The National Farm Workers Association. He's organizing the farmworkers to get better pay and working conditions. Insecticides are sure to be one of his focuses."

"I'm worried. I don't want riots to put our lives in danger."

"For right now, everything will continue per the status quo. What worries me are the priests. They could stir up the people. We already know that Father Garcia is involved in meetings at the Bistro Mona Lisa. Next thing, he will be preaching right from the pulpit."

"And I thought we were living in Camelot once Kennedy got elected," Gina said.

"We're still living the good life, but there's always a threat lurking nearby."

Later that fall, everyone learned that John Steinbeck had won the Nobel Prize for literature. His masterpiece, *The Grapes of Wrath,* was cited in the presentation speech along with the keen social perception contained in his writings.

Gina was thrilled when she received the news. "I hope the Women's Club has a book signing at his sister's home. It would be the event of the season."

"Don't count on it," Richard said. "Steinbeck's going to be in demand everywhere now. However, the timing of the award is interesting."

"He deserved it for all of the great books he's written."

"I'm not saying he didn't deserve it. But why now? *Grapes of Wrath* was published over twenty years ago."

Gina shook her head, trying to understand. "What are you getting at?"

"I'm suggesting that it was a political choice timed to coincide with the publishing of *Silent Spring* and the formation of the National Farm Workers Association."

"I'm not as cynical as you are. With Steinbeck, Chavez, and *Silent Spring* all coming together, it's more like the spirit has been guiding the process for the greater good."

"I'll tell you what. Let's not argue about it. Let's wait and see."

In a few years, Chavez would call for the Wrath of Grapes boycott. Because of all the poisons used on grapes that are harmful to farmworkers and consumers alike, he said that boycotting grapes was our only protection and that his weapon was the truth. Union contracts negotiated the ban of DDT and other poisons long before the Environmental Protection Agency banned DDT in 1972.

The Crawfords were hosting a casual holiday dinner party. After the babysitter arrived, Gina and Richard walked the short distance across the street. The Crawford's Christmas tree filled most of their pane glass window, tiny colored lights creating a stained-glass effect. Sylvia greeted them, taking Gina's wrap. Steve and Sue were in the living room having a drink with Ben. They all exchanged greetings as Ben handed each a champagne flute and raised his. "To friendship and continued collaboration." They all clinked their glasses in agreement and settled back into amiable conversation. Sylvia passed a tray of canapés to tease the appetites. Then she called everyone to the table for the first course—shrimp cocktail. Chateaubriand with a béarnaise sauce was next, followed by an apple soufflé, with coffee finishing the meal.

Ben was holding court and threw out the next subject. "Richard, I didn't see any evidence you were around for a month or more this fall."

"You probably have a good idea why."

"Were you called up for that thing going on in Cuba?"

"That's right. The Navy Reserve was on standby."

"The missile crisis wouldn't have happened if Kennedy hadn't blown it in the Bay of Pigs. That whole blundered affair just made him look weak."

"I agree. If we're going to go into a situation, we need to win."

"I give the navy credit—they know how to do a blockade. Those ships weren't letting anything through."

"And we didn't pull out until November 20. We're smarter than to trust diplomacy to do its job."

Ben straightened up in his chair, puffing out his chest. "If you hadn't stayed, those Soviets might have done an end-run, and then where would we be...blown to smithereens."

Steve broke in and switched gears. "On another subject, Hector Lopez stopped by my office the other day."

Richard frowned at Steve as he asked, "What did he want now? I assumed we'd seen the last of him once the housing project was finished."

"Not quite. He's now a community organizer working for that new National Farm Workers Association. He wanted to get a permit to hold a rally."

"I hope you didn't give him one," said Ben.

"After years supporting our country, Ben, you should know

better than any of us how democracy works. People have a right to assemble and to free speech."

"Besides," said Richard, "Hector seems level-headed. I doubt he'll incite any riots."

"Steve, when is this rally going to take place?" asked Gina.

"Not until the weather warms up. He asked for a date in May."

"Could it be Cinco de Mayo?" Ben asked. "The day Mexicans celebrate resistance against imperialism?"

"I don't remember, but it could be," Steve said. "Why, is that a problem?"

"It will be very symbolic to the Mexicans," Ben said. "And that day will draw a large crowd since it's already an annual celebration. Where are they planning to hold this rally?"

"At the plaza."

"Naturally. That's where all the Mexicans will be gravitating to."

"We can't stop what is already in motion. But we can try to manage it."

"That's right," said Richard, "and Hector is someone we already know and can reason with."

"Reason...that's how all you intellectuals think. That's why Kennedy is considered weak, and we will be, too. Some people only understand strength and force."

"Ben, please don't go military on us," said Sylvia. "We're just having a discussion amongst friends."

"That's right," said Richard. "I guess I can play the mediator since I'm half military and half civilian. Often, it is best to let people get rid of a little hot air rather than hold them back until they explode."

"Thank you," Richard. "The mayor shares your opinion," Steve said.

"Maybe we ought to run you next for mayor," Ben said. "It seems you're on a politician's wavelength now. It didn't take long. Just give 'em a little power."

"On that note, we should call it a night," said Richard. "The boys will be up and at 'em early."

As the couples walked back to the street, Steve said to Richard, "Sometimes I find Ben hard to take."

"I know. He spent too much time in the military."

"What do you mean by that?"

"A military man thinks only about the mission. He puts on blinders and blocks everything else, including his own thoughts. Discipline and obedience are the virtues he lives by. In effect, he has turned himself into a machine."

"I guess it's hard to revert back after so many years of that way of life."

"Most can't. They have traded their brain for the heart of a warrior."

"And in the process lost their soul as well."

"Let's be grateful so many men choose the military. And remember, he went in during World War II when our country needed men like Ben to defend liberty. Once war is over, they become obsolete."

"Perhaps that's why the generals are always on the lookout for new wars. Kennedy figured that one out the hard way."

"We're lucky to have a man like Ben around this town. And I'm glad he's a friend."

"Me, too. But Sylvia and I share more in common."

"And she would appreciate your reading list. Just make sure Ben's not around when you show it to her. He'd rip it to shreds."

Richard and Steve met for lunch at the diner. While they waited for their order to arrive, they talked about their families, friends, and future plans. Once their plates were delivered, Steve got serious. "Hector was in the town hall the other day delivering voter registration forms."

"That's interesting," Richard said as he poured himself a glass of water.

"The number of people he's registered is staggering. The registrars are not sure they can process all the forms before the election."

"They have to. They'll need to get more help—that's all." Richard took a bite of his turkey sandwich as he waited for Steve's reply.

"Do you know what these new numbers are going to mean to the town if they vote as a block?"

Richard took a moment to swallow before answering. "They will have a newfound superpower."

"That's right. And it means the character of this valley will change."

"In what way?"

"For starters, it won't be run by the grower-shippers anymore—our primary industry will be threatened. Not only that, our values will be at risk."

"I think that's a ways off, which gives us time to manage the situation. This go-round, we have candidates on the ballot who we can live with no matter how the voting goes. Although there could be write-ins, but that usually isn't successful. It's the next election we have to be more concerned about."

"Can you imagine what will happen to our schools if Mexicans get control of the school board? We've always had excellent education for our children."

"They don't have to get on the school board for schools to change. All they need is numbers in the classroom. I can envision the day when we run the school year based on the migrants' schedule. Right now, Mexican kids are falling behind because of it. Our neighbor, a grade school teacher, thinks they're non-learners—at least that's what she told Gina when she helped with the classroom reading program. On the contrary, Gina found the little boy she worked with excited about books. The problem is language. So, things have to give one way or the other."

Steve nodded in agreement. "You're right. We have people

here a significant part of the year, but they won't grow into good citizens if they don't get an education and learn to speak English. It's a problem that has been brewing for years, but it's reached our doorstep, and the time for action is now."

"We should talk to Hector about it. Since he's a community organizer, he'll have some insight and influence. And, again, he's someone we can work with."

"We've just started into the 60s, but I sense this is going to be a decade of change. No more so than here in Watsonville. I just hope it's a change for the better. But my instincts tell me otherwise."

The November local elections proved uneventful. The mayor and most incumbents, including Richard, were reelected. Even though the registrars worked overtime to process new voter forms, many of the new electors didn't show up at the polls. Hector was disappointed but learned an important lesson.

CHAPTER TWELVE

November 22 was a dreary day in Northern California, alternating between drizzle and light rain. The early fog had given way to a gray, cloud-filled sky that set the scene for the depressing news that President Kennedy had been shot in Dallas and died a short time later.

Richard called home to break the news to Gina as gently as possible. Overcome by the shock and sadness of it all, Gina sought solace the best way she could—with a drink. As soon as she heard the boys return from school, she began to pull herself together. "Get me a cup of coffee," she ordered, and Matt made haste to put a mug in her hand. The caffeine created equilibrium in her that brought some function back. "Come here," she said to the boys as they gathered around her, "I just want to hug you. Today, a great man, our president, died. Let's pray for his soul." And she led them in the Our Father prayer. Then she released them, and they headed outside to play. *If only we could be like little children,* she thought.

When Richard got home, he found Gina still lying on the sofa. Moving in to kiss her, he smelled the alcohol. Of course, she would be drinking upon hearing terrible news like this. Then he asked, "Have the boys been fed?" Gina shook her head no. "I'll order a pizza for dinner," and he placed the call.

The Christmas season brought back the cheer that had been stolen during the solemn November days. Parties and the delight of children brightened even the darkest of moods. Gina threw herself into the spirit of the season with more flair than ever. She bought herself new party dresses, sang with the choir, and spent countless days purchasing presents in her favorite Carmel shops. When the New Year arrived, it was another time to celebrate in style. As 1964 dawned, it was as essential to usher out the old year as ring in the new. Everyone hoped times would get better, but instead, the nation would see the Vietnam War escalate. Camelot would be traded for chaos as the sixties lived up to its slogan—sex, drugs, and rock 'n' roll. Everywhere, cultural decline was evident, including nearby Santa Cruz, where a hippie life-style took hold.

Richard and Gina were thankful their children were still young and under their control. The twins were five years away from high school, at which time they planned to send them to an Eastern boarding school that would keep them under lock and key until the time for college arrived. In the meantime, their lives continued, little affected by the cultural changes, yet change occurred.

Richard came home from work that night looking forward to dinner and a charming evening with his wife. But the minute he set foot in the door, he knew something was wrong. Gina was not in the kitchen, nor did he smell dinner simmering on the stove. Instead, he found the kitchen sink piled with dishes, counters littered with cereal boxes, and streaks of peanut butter and jelly smeared all around. The place was completely trashed. Richard was almost afraid to advance any further, but he forced himself to move on. As he approached the living room, he heard little murmurs and laughs and the scurrying of feet across the carpet. What he found when he entered the living room took him aback. The complete suite of furniture was pushed together in the center of the room, covered with blankets and sheets, forming a fort. More laughter gave away the hiding place as Richard pulled up a corner of a blanket to reveal four pairs of eyes staring back from the dark interior.

"What in the world?" The boys remained frozen in place, trying not to arouse his anger. "Where's your mother?"

"She's in her bedroom sleeping," Mike said.

"Sleeping...at this hour...is she sick?"

"I think so," said Mike, as he cast his eyes downward. The others averted their gaze not to risk their father's temper.

"Come out from under there now and take those blankets off the furniture. We need to put this room back in order. Since you pushed this furniture out of place, I trust you can push it back where it belongs. Now, do as I say—double-time."

At that, Richard turned toward the hallway in the direction of the master bedroom. He opened the door, not sure what he would find. There, sprawled across the bed, lay Gina. She didn't even stir when he entered the room. As Richard drew nearer, he caught the traces of stale beer as his anger mounted. She wasn't sick—she was drunk. She wasn't sleeping—she was passed out. Richard shook her body, but she could not be roused, letting out a moan instead. The situation was hopeless—she'd have to sleep it off.

Richard left the bedroom in utter disgust. He'd been around drunks plenty of times but never a woman. Seeing Gina in that condition was repulsive, a shattering of her feminine mystique. That image would be difficult to erase from his mind. He didn't know if he would ever be able to feel the same way about her.

By the time Richard returned to the living room, the boys had restored the room to its former arrangement. "Put on your shoes. We're going to the diner for dinner tonight." The boys gave him a questioning look. "Your mother isn't well and won't be cooking."

The boys piled into the car for the short ride to the diner. Then they stuffed themselves into a booth at the back of the restaurant. Richard hoped they wouldn't see anyone they knew—he wasn't in the mood for small talk. The waitress recognized a hungry bunch, wasting no time bringing menus and filling water glasses. "Just give us a minute," Richard said.

"What do you boys want for dinner? Chicken fingers, pasta, hamburgers?" He took their requests and gave them to the waitress. "And milk all around," Richard said, amidst the protests by his sons who preferred soda.

While the boys fought amongst themselves at the table, Richard was lost in thought. *This wasn't in my plans. Why didn't I see this coming? The clues were all there. It's my fault. I should have recognized a party girl when I saw one.*

The waitress arrived, balancing a large tray filled with platters of food. Richard had to set aside his thoughts while he sorted out the meals, reminding the boys of their table manners. He dug into his meatloaf, which was always a comforting meal—especially when paired with mashed potatoes and gravy. Whenever he felt low, this was what he ordered, and it never failed to lift his spirits. It transported him home, where his mother would be waiting with open arms to welcome him. No matter how old he got, he never got too old for meatloaf.

Now that he was past wallowing in his pain, he had to come up with a plan. There were four boys sitting at this table who needed care, and they couldn't wait until Gina pulled herself together.

When they returned home, Richard checked on Gina, noting she was still out cold. After putting the boys to bed, and he was certain they were under the Sandman's spell, he snuck out of the house and headed for Margery's.

Margery was at the kitchen sink washing dishes. When he

walked in, she wiped her hands as she asked, "What brings you over tonight?"

"We've got a problem, and I need your advice."

"Is it about Gina?"

"How did you know?"

Margery hesitated. "I've been seeing signs that something was amiss, but I was hoping I was wrong."

"Did they have to do with alcohol?"

Before answering, Margery looked into Richard's eyes to judge if he could take the truth. "If you really want to know, yes. A few times, she came over in the morning with a beer in her hand, and then I witnessed her weaving back and forth as she walked along the driveway. It's a wonder she didn't fall and hurt herself."

"Right now, she's passed out in our bedroom. She's been that way since I got home. This should've been nipped in the bud."

Margery reached out to pat Richard's hand. "Don't blame yourself. People with a drinking problem always try to hide it. How could you have known it'd come to this?"

Richard dropped his head as if defeated. "There were sign-posts along the way. I just ignored them. I guess I was too busy trying to get ahead."

"What now?"

"I don't quite know. That's why I'm here. First, I have to get someone in to take care of the boys so I can work. And then Gina's going to need help."

"Marta is already at your house part-time. I'll ask if she can handle it full-time. I also recommend Gina talk to Father O'Leary. He will have some good suggestions but be gentle about it."

"My head is about to explode."

"I'll be back in a few minutes with some aspirin." But first, Margery needed to help Richard get the boys ready for school.

She ran into Richard in the hallway. "How's Gina?"

"Coming around."

"At least it means she's still alive."

"She's going to feel like she died and went to Hell for several hours. As soon as the boys are off, I'll give her some aspirin and help her bathe. After that, she may be ready to eat a light breakfast."

Margery brought a glass of water to Gina and rummaged through her medicine cabinet for aspirin. "Here, take this." Gina followed instructions, struggling to swallow the pills. Margery started the bath. While the water filled the tub, she returned to the bedroom to deal with Gina. "Can you get up?"

"I'm not sure." Gina's voice was so weak it was barely audible.

"Let's try. I'll support you."

Margery walked Gina the few steps into the bathroom and helped her get undressed. She turned off the water and tested it to make sure it wasn't too hot. "The water's perfect. The bath will relax you and make you feel better. Let me help you in."

Gina was a floppy rag doll. But Margery had little trouble getting her into the tub. She let Gina bask in the warmth but didn't dare leave her alone for fear she might slip under the water and drown. Margery knew that was always a risk with people in Gina's condition. Before the water cooled off too much, Margery washed Gina and shampooed her hair. Now, to get her out of the tub. This always seemed harder to Margery, but she managed. She wrapped Gina in an oversized Turkish towel and laid her back on the bed to rest. "Stay put while I start the coffee. Then, I'll dress you."

Margery helped Gina into a floral bathrobe and pink satin slippers and guided her to the kitchen. She put a cup of steaming coffee in front of her, along with cream and sugar.

"Would you like toast? It will help settle your stomach."

"Whatever you say."

Margery gave Gina buttered toast and poured a cup of coffee for herself before joining Gina at the table.

"Tell me what's going on with you."

"I guess I had too much to drink. But don't worry. I'll be okay."

"Richard is worried about you. And so am I."

"There's no need to worry. I told you that I'd be okay. This was a one-time thing."

"No, Gina, it wasn't, and you know it. You need some help. I'd like you to talk with Father O'Leary."

Gina slammed down her cup, and coffee went flying. "I don't want to talk to Father O'Leary or anyone else. I had too much to drink—that's all."

Margery didn't react to Gina's angry outburst as she wiped up the mess. In a calm voice, she said, "If you wish, I'll accompany you."

"Let me think about it."

"The time for thinking is past. Action is required now. You can't just consider yourself—you have to do this for your family. Your children are young. They need their mother. And they need her to be fully functioning."

Gina began to cry. "You must consider me a terrible mother. And compared to you, I am. I can't handle all this. The boys are driving me crazy, and I'm bored out of my mind staying home all day long. This is not the life I signed up for."

Under her breath, Margery murmured, "It never is."

Margery drove Gina to St. Patrick's Church. Father O'Leary was waiting for them at the rectory. "Gina, my favorite Irish lass. Please, come in. And Margery, it's good to see you as always. Take a seat while we all chat for a moment."

In his gentle, nonjudgmental way, Father O'Leary probed to discern the situation. Once he understood, he asked Margery to step outside. Father O'Leary empowered Gina to solve her problem using the Reflection Method, which involves asking someone a series of guided questions that lead them to their own conclusions. Gina agreed to go to the retreat center in San Juan Bautista, where she would meet with counselors before moving on to a treatment center or Alcoholics Anonymous.

When the door to the office opened, both Gina and Father O'Leary were all smiles. "Margery, Gina realizes she needs help and will start by attending a retreat. I will call the center to enable her to start right away. Can you be ready tomorrow, Gina?"

"Do I have a choice?"

"Let's go home, and I'll help you pack," Margery said. "Tomorrow morning, I'll drive you over."

It took less than half an hour to reach the small town of San Juan Bautista. The mission came into view—white adobe with a red-tiled roof and a three-bell tower acting as a beacon.

"This is the largest mission in California. Its patron is St. John the Baptist. On his feast day in June, they hold San Juan Days to celebrate. Those big barbeques on the lawn grill huge numbers of split chickens for the guests. Before the feast, there's a big parade and lots of other festivities."

"Let's come sometime."

Margery nodded. "See those arches? That's where the monastery is located. The church is built on the San Andreas fault."

"That wasn't good planning."

"They found that out when they had to rebuild after a quake. But they still didn't move it." As they drove along, Margery continued to play tour guide. "That plaza is the only original Spanish plaza left in California today."

"That means our plaza in Watsonville is just a replica."

"But don't tell Marta."

"This is Third Street. It's the primary shopping street in town and also where you'll find the best restaurants. That's it for the nickel tour."

"Nickel tour?"

"This is a tiny town on a postage-stamp-sized piece of prop-erty. You've just seen it all. The retreat center is a couple of minutes ahead near the outskirts. From there, you could walk to town."

Margery pulled her car into the center. She led Gina up the path to the front door, where they were greeted by a nun who was expecting them. Margery got Gina settled before retrieving her suitcase from the car. When she returned, she found Gina in her room crying and asked her what was wrong.

"I just don't want to be here. I want to be home. Father O'Leary tricked me into coming. I won't be able to forgive him for that."

"Please, don't blame Father O'Leary. He's only trying to help you and your family. This is where you'll begin to heal."

Gina spent a week at the retreat center and returned home with instructions to meet with a therapist and attend Alcoholics Anonymous. Margery stopped to check on her progress, asking about her week.

"It was very peaceful. We had Mass every day at the mission. The sanctuary is a very spiritual place—like nothing I've ever experienced before. And did you know the church has a Lady of Guadalupe Chapel? Somehow, she drew me to her. Remember the time we had dinner at the Bistro Mona Lisa, and she was painted in a mural on the cafe's exterior?"

"Yes, I remember. She's a symbol of hope in times of suffering and empowerment in times of resistance. Maybe you sense that about her, too."

"Every day during my retreat, I visited that chapel and lit a candle. I also had some good sessions with the priests, who were very kind and full of wisdom. They helped center me."

"The next step is a therapist and AA, correct?"

"Richard is arranging a therapist for me, and I have the schedule of AA meetings."

"If you wish, I can go with you to your first one. I've done that before for a friend."

"Oh, would you, Margery? It would be so much easier than having to walk in alone."

Margery and Gina arrived at the Presbyterian Church about ten minutes before the meeting was to begin. Margery saw what appeared to be a look of apprehension on Gina's face and tackled it head-on. "Are you scared?"

"Sort of. I'm afraid someone I know will be in that room. It would be easier if it were a roomful of strangers."

"Even if you recognize someone, you have to remember they, like you, are anonymous. You must trust that they won't mention they saw you there or what you said. And you must promise to do the same for them."

"It's just so hard. I don't want to do it."

Margery reached into her purse and pulled out a small, wrapped package. "Here, I have a gift for you that might help."

"Oh, Margery, you are so sweet," Gina said as she opened the box. "It's a rosary bracelet. Thank you."

"It's not just a rosary bracelet, although I bought it because the beads are shaped like roses. But notice that the medal hanging from it is Our Lady of Guadalupe."

"You are so thoughtful. This bracelet has so much meaning for me." Then, she attempted to put it on her left wrist, but Margery reached out and stopped her before she could manage it.

"Gina, I bought this for you to wear on your right wrist since you are right-handed. If you're ever tempted to take another drink, I want you to see the medal of Our Lady who will help you resist."

Gina reached over to hug Margery, kissing her on the cheek. "You will be my strength."

"I'll always do what I can to support you. Now, put out your right arm and give me the bracelet." Margery slipped the bracelet over Gina's right hand, placing it on her wrist. "There. I hope this will help empower you. Now, we need to go to the meeting."

A kind, middle-aged man greeted Margery and Gina as they entered the church hall. They slid into a pair of chairs at the back. Once the meeting started, person after person stood, gave their first name, and said, "I am an alcoholic." When they got to Margery, she stayed silent and prompted Gina to stand. Gina hesitated. Her stomach lurched, and her legs wobbled. Margery grabbed her elbow and helped push her up to a standing position. Gina's face turned pale, and her lips trembled. "My name is Regina, and I'm an alcoholic." When it was over, it seemed she had been standing an eternity with all eyes on her, knowing eyes that looked right through to who she had become. There was no hiding behind a carefully crafted façade. Those eyes could recognize one of their own. A wave of relief washed over her after admitting her weakness. It was a step...a first step...toward recovery. She took her seat, touching the roses on her bracelet until she got to the medal of Our Lady and rubbed it between her fingers.

Richard was pleased to find Gina in the kitchen preparing dinner. He had been worried about what he would come home to but was now relieved. He kissed her on the cheek. "How was your day?"

"You know what I had planned to do."

Richard took a step back. "How did it go? Did Margery take you?"

"It turned out better than I predicted it would. Margery drove me and stayed for the meeting. Right before, she gave me this." Gina held out her arm for Richard to see her bracelet.

"A bracelet...that was nice."

"It's not just any bracelet. It's a rosary bracelet with little rose beads all around and a medal of Our Lady of Guadalupe hanging from it."

"Hmm. When's your next AA meeting?"

"Next week. I got off easy this week, but next time, I have to tell my story."

"You have time to think about it."

"That's just it. I don't want to think about it. It's too painful."

"Pain is part of the process."

Gina started crying. "I've let everyone down—you, the kids, my family, and friends. I'm embarrassed by what I've turned into."

Richard put his arms around Gina and hugged her. "We all want you to become well again."

"I want that, too. But I don't know if I can. It's going to be so hard."

"You have to do like they say—take it one day at a time."

Gina had been anxious about the meeting, resulting in a restless night of panic attacks, and now it was here. She thought *I don't want to go. I can't get up in front of everyone and do this.* By the time Margery arrived to drive her, Gina was in a state of anxiety. Margery felt her forehead and took her pulse, which was racing so fast she couldn't count the beats.

"We have to get you under control before we go anywhere."

Hearing those words seemed to calm Gina because what she needed most was to be in control.

"Have you eaten breakfast?"

Gina shook her head no.

"That's the place to start. I'll make you some hot oatmeal, which always has a soothing effect. Come and sit at the table while it's cooking. Now, let's start with some deep breathing exercises, which will also relax you."

Gina took in a deep breath and let it out slowly. She did this several times until Margery told her to halt. "Now, close your eyes and think about a vacation you had on Martha's Vineyard. Sense the warm sun on your face and the soft sand squeezing between your toes. Now, plunge into the cool ocean—let it embrace you. Take another three deep breaths, now open your eyes. And, voila, your oatmeal is ready."

Gina poured on milk and sprinkled a little sugar over the top. She scooped up a large spoonful, swallowing fast. The warm cereal relaxed her as it slid down her throat. In a few minutes, she had finished the entire bowl.

"That's good," said Margery. "Now, are you better?"

"Much."

Margery looked at her watch. "Let's go, or we'll be late." She took the fastest way there, coming only to a rolling stop at intersections before moving on to arrive right on time.

"Do you want me to come in with you again?"

"Not today. I don't want you to hear me condemn myself. It won't be a pretty story."

"All right. I'll give you a hug and be back to pick you up when the meeting's over."

"Thank you, Margery. I don't know what I'd do without you."

Gina took a seat at the rear again, hoping that everyone would keep their backs to her when her turn came to speak. She didn't think she could bear all those eyes looking into her soul as she spoke. The meeting started with the usual introductions. "I'm Gina, and I'm an alcoholic." Hearing herself say those words sent shivers through her.

The time arrived to tell her story. Gina trembled as she stood. She glanced down at her wrist and focused on the rosary bracelet. Fingering it, she began to speak.

"I had my first drink at twelve years old. We were at a friend's house while her parents were out for the evening. We got a bottle of vodka from the liquor cabinet, which wasn't difficult because it wasn't locked. Vodka was our spirit of choice because, even at age twelve, we knew it wouldn't leave a telltale trace. We poured some in our soda glasses and couldn't tell the difference until we felt the buzz. We all liked the buzz and were hooked.

"From that time on, it was only a matter of opportunity, which was easy in a town like mine. Parents were always off socializing on a Saturday night at their own cocktail parties. We only had to determine which house would be available and spread the word. No one locked their liquor cabinets, and we could always drink to our hearts' content. However, we took care to refill the bottle with water afterward so no one would get suspicious. Four years of high school went along like that—every Saturday night, another drinking party at an unsupervised house. The only problem came when we wanted to go to a school dance or the prom. Of course, there would be chaperones, and liquor was not allowed. We'd have to get some in advance and pre-game, as we called it. That meant we drank until we reached that twilight place where we felt the buzz but could still function and fool all the adults.

"Once I moved on to college, it was even easier to drink since it was legal at eighteen. The frats had big parties every weekend that always featured a punch bowl filled with a specially concocted drink aimed at the fairer sex that looked pretty and tasted even better but packed a punch so powerful that a girl had no clue it was coming. It only took one time to learn your lesson, but the damage had already been done. By the time I graduated, I had earned a bachelor's in music and a doctorate in drinking. Call me a drunk, but I drink only the good stuff.

"After that, I worked for a while and later married. The only fun I had involved drinking. It was what I looked forward to. I began drinking during the day to pass the time. When my sons came home from school and mixed it up, I found my afternoon was more tolerable when I took the edge off with a drink. Oh, and let's not forget my husband, who always kept the pressure on. The only way I could cope was with a drink and, of course, a few cigarettes. What started with one drink moved to two and three and four until this...an alcoholic.

"Maybe I've been an alcoholic for years and just didn't know it. Certainly, I never passed up a drink. And I remember often sneaking an extra drink whenever possible. But I was always careful to cover my tracks and cleverly disposed of the cans and bottles, hiding them in the backyard somewhere where no one would ever look until I disposed of them in the dumpster behind the grocery store. My husband never discovered my tricks. But one day, I overdid things, and he found me passed out in the bedroom. He was confronted with my drunkenness in such a shocking and disgusting way that he was no longer able to ignore it.

"That was a turning point...when I hit bottom, and Richard blew his top. He arranged for our neighbor to take me to meet with our priest, who recommended a retreat. I spent a week at a facility in San Juan Bautista, meeting with therapists, attending masses and prayer sessions, and spending time alone in the garden talking to God about what a mess I had made of my life after all He had done for me. And you know what, He forgave me. He was not that God of vengeance I had always feared, but instead, he was a God of mercy.

"The 2 Corinthians verse came into my mind when He said, 'my power is made perfect in weakness.' He knew my weakness, and He still loved me. After that, I returned home, and here I am confessing to you, too, about what a mess I've made of my life. I pray that God's grace will pull me through. There is no way I can do it alone. I don't have the strength...the willpower. Every time I think of my four sons, I regret that I've let them down. I'm not the mother they deserve. I'm not the wife my husband deserves. I want to be worthy of them. Please, help me be worthy of them again."

After her speech, Gina collapsed into the chair in a burst of tears. The room filled with silence—no one dared breathe. The only sound came from the wall clock as it ticked off the minutes, second by second. Everyone present had been overcome by Gina's emotional journey.

On her way out, the meeting director stopped Gina. "We work in pairs here. It helps us to be more successful. I'm assigning you a partner who will make sure you come to meetings and stay on track. His name is Joe. He'll be in touch."

"His name…Joe. That's a good sign. It's my father's name, too."

When Richard came home that evening, he found Gina in the living room surrounded by her sons. She was reading a story to them, *King Arthur and the Knights of the Round Table*, with Dave and Drew hanging on every word while the older two were restless but willing to sit near their mother, who they were glad to have back. Richard listened from the kitchen until the story was finished. He walked in on the family scene, which almost brought a tear to his eye.

"*Knights of the Roundtable*. One of my favorites when I was a boy."

"It must have been because your mother sent us this book," said Gina, as she opened to the title page. "And here's the proof. Your name in your eight-year-old handwriting, Sir Richard."

"Let me see that." He snatched the book, which he turned over in his hands as if the touch of it would bring back memories. "I hope you boys like the stories as much as I did."

The boys nodded. "But what I liked most," said Dave, "was the way Mom used different voices for each knight and lady. It seemed so real."

"You should have story time with Mom every afternoon. Books can teach you a lot."

"I'd like that," said Dave. And Drew agreed with him.

"What about you, Matt and Mike?"

"Not every afternoon," said Mike. "Yeah," said Matt, "only once in a while."

"You boys won't amount to anything unless you make friends with books. That's what got me into Stanford University."

"When we go to Exeter, we'll start reading books," said Mike. "It's cold there, so we won't want to be playing outside, and there won't be much else to do."

"All right. Gina, we have our work cut out for us making these boys into scholars."

"All we can do is try," she said. "I'll go by the library this week and pick up some books aimed at boys, something like *The Hardy Boys*."

"That's another series I read as a youth—full of action and adventure. Even Matt and Mike will start enjoying books after reading about those boys. Now, is there anything ready for dinner?"

"Oh, I'm sorry. I lost track of time. It won't take me but a few minutes to make pasta."

Richard held up his hand, signaling stop. "Let's go to the diner. I know you had a hard day."

Gina was growing anxious about what was to come. She received a call from Joe the night before the AA meeting, which helped relieve some of her fear. "It's always difficult the week after giving your journey speech," he said, "but once you walk into the room, you will experience the love of all your new friends. We are all there to support you and each other."

Gina told Margery she was ready to solo. When she walked out of the foggy, gray day into the room, she was surrounded by light, and she understood that Joe had been right. Gina took a seat near the back again and waited for the meeting to begin. A Mexican man sat next to her. "Hi, I'm Joe."

Gina did a double-take before offering him a smile. She wondered if she would meet Joe today. It surprised her he was so young and did not expect him to be Mexican. But none of that mattered to her. All she needed was a friend—someone strong who she could lean on. After sizing Joe up, taking in the warmth of his eyes, the strength of his hands, and his humble bearing, she knew he fit the bill. "I'm Gina. It's good to meet you."

The meeting followed the format Gina had experienced in the last two sessions. Everyone stood up, one by one, to announce they were an alcoholic. Then came the journey stories. Two were told today. While each seemed to have their own beginnings, the way alcoholism played out in their lives followed a similar thread, bringing them to the day they hit bottom...just like her. Gina wondered why they had people tell their stories at every meeting. But in the asking, she found the answer—to remember and resist. Again, that word resist. Gina looked down at the medal on her bracelet and gently rubbed it between her fingers.

After the meeting, Joe asked Gina to coffee at a nearby cafe. He said they should get to know each other better to build a bond of trust if ever there came a time when that was needed. Gina accepted his invitation, following him in her car. When they got out, Joe said, "We only meet our partners in public places—that way, we protect ourselves in more ways than one."

"Oh, you mean since I'm a married woman, it protects my reputation."

"That...in addition, there will be no temptation to become drinking partners."

"They have it all figured out, don't they?"

"There are no tricks we can pull that haven't been tried before."

After a quick cup of coffee and a bit of chat, Gina and Joe parted, and she headed for home. She went through the side gate to check if Margery was at home. She caught the glimpse she hoped for and proceeded to the back door, knocking twice before entering. Margery looked up, pleased Gina was getting back into her routine.

"Come in and sit down. Coffee is left in the pot. I'd like to hear how the meeting went today."

"You can hold the coffee. I just had some, and my tank is about to overflow. Cigarettes will do for now." She pulled one out of her pack, struck a match, and lit up. "I was assigned a partner. Apparently, we alcoholics do better with a buddy to keep us straight."

"That makes sense. Who is she?"

"His name is Joe. I just had coffee with him at the High Noon Café, and he seems very nice."

"Is that all you can tell me about him?"

Gina took a puff of her cigarette as she thought a moment. "We're supposed to remain anonymous. But he's in his mid-thirties, and he's Mexican."

Margery's eyebrows shot up at the mention of Mexican. "I hope he's the right partner for you."

"He called last night to remind me of the meeting. And then today, he offered to be there for me if I needed him. But we can only meet in public."

"I can understand that. What's the next step?"

"AA once a week for life. That's the formula that has worked, and that's what I must do."

Margery nodded. "It's not so bad, is it?"

Gina shrugged her shoulders. "Instead, I could be rolling around in a gutter somewhere looking for my next drink."

"Richard would not have let that happen."

"I don't know about Richard. He was pretty shocked when he found me passed out smelling of stale beer. Perhaps disgusted is a better word. Anyway, he wants me shipshape on the double."

"It sounds like he needs some counseling to understand your disease better?"

"He'll never go for it. And he doesn't consider it a disease, even if he calls it that. He believes it's a weakness—a character flaw."

"Then he needs to learn to understand. I read there might be a genetic connection—something inherited that you can't control."

"Richard wouldn't care about that. He believes I have control. I can choose to drink or not. He said if I hadn't started in the first place, I wouldn't be in this situation now."

"Using that logic, he's right. But he has to face facts. He has a wife who is in recovery, and she needs his support."

Gina's problem put a strain on the marriage. She sensed Richard didn't trust her anymore. And she was right. He started calling her during the day to check up on her. When he thought she wasn't looking, he searched garbage cans, cupboards, and other hiding places for evidence of her drinking. And she had to account for her whereabouts when he couldn't reach her. Richard acted like a warden instead of a husband. But Gina realized she had to stay sober for everyone's sake.

As the months passed without a relapse, Richard was less vigilant. Gina's new sense of freedom was like a breath of spring —fresh and full of promise. Life was wonderful. The boys seemed happy. And Richard had a wife again.

CHAPTER THIRTEEN

Richard visited Tom to talk about farmland. This took Tom by surprise, although his real estate agency was known for farm and ranch listings. "Are you thinking about becoming a farmer or simply interested in acquiring property?"

"I suppose it's a bit of both. One reason I moved to this area was because of the fertile land available. As a civil engineer, I really appreciate the land. Perhaps, I'll only speculate, but I may want to do more than that down the line. There's still money to be made in farming."

"That's true. Give me an idea of what you're looking for. Then, I can go through our listings for matches that meet your specifications."

After taking down Richard's information, Tom said, "It'll take a few days to go through the inventory. In the meantime, if you would like to see a real ranch in action, join me for the annual spring lamb roast. There's nothing better than fresh, spring lamb done on a spit. Croatians, like me, are crazy about it."

"What day and time should I mark on my calendar?"

"Next Saturday. Be here at noon, and I'll drive to the Kovic's

place. It'll give us a chance to talk over some properties I've
come across."

Richard arrived on Tom's doorstep on time.

"I have to grab a couple of things and put them in the car.
Admission is minimal, but we have to help defray costs by
contributing to the meal. Can you help with this case of beer
while I grab Margery's apple pie? I bring it by popular demand."
After putting the items in the car, they set out for the ranch. It
was located off Casserly Road, about twenty minutes away.

"I've come across a couple of farm properties that seem to
align with your specs."

"Tell me about them."

"The first one is about forty acres. The land is flat, and there
are already a couple of sharecroppers working it. There's a small
habitable house and a couple of outbuildings which could store
equipment."

"How much?"

"Let's talk price later. The other one has twice as much
acreage and a larger, habitable home, but the land is hilly and not
as suitable for farming, although there are a couple of sharecroppers on it, too. It also has three to four outbuildings and a
paddock for horses. What do you think?"

Richard took a moment to consider the information. "I would
like to look at both. On the one hand, I like the idea of more
land, but the smaller farm sounds as if there's more useable land."

"That's right. When can you go? Tomorrow works for me."

"Let me talk to Gina. After being away today, she may need
me at home. If that's the case, I'll give you a couple of my open
dates."

"I'll be available whenever you are." Tom smiled to himself,
thinking he might bag a big sale from the guy living next door.
Besides, he'd rather spend a few hours out in the fresh air

showing a farm property to a prospective buyer than be cooped up in a bungalow trying to sell its features to a housewife. That often turned out to be a taxing experience. Men who wanted land were far easier to deal with, at least in his experience.

The parking area was almost full when they arrived. "This seems to be a popular event," Richard said.

"It's a sell-out every year. They try to keep it to a hundred or less to give everyone a chance to mingle. And they won't run out of food, which is even more important and the point of the whole thing."

They carried the beer and pie as they headed toward the check-in area. Tom pulled the tickets out of his pocket and gave them to the girl in charge of admissions. She directed them to the location for foodstuff and drinks. Once they unloaded their arms, Tom said, "Let's go grab a drink, and I'll introduce you around." They each pulled a cold beer out of the ice-filled trough and took a swig while Tom perused the setting.

"I see our host. Come with me, and I'll introduce you to Luke Kovic. He's an apple farmer—grows mostly red delicious on a hundred acres of some of the richest soil in the county."

Richard followed Tom while he took in the farm's layout— the Arts and Crafts main house with a towering white oak shading the porch, a big red barn opening onto the corral, a tractor parked in its center, and in the distance, acres of apple trees already in blossom. He was quite taken with the scene. His father's farm in Connecticut couldn't hold a candle to it. Corn stalks turn brown, and ugly stubs cover the fields after harvest. California put romance in farming and rewarded farmers richly.

Tom said, "Richard, I'd like you to meet Luke Kovic, our host for today. Luke, this is my next-door neighbor, Richard Bankston. He's an engineer with Blackrock Construction."

As the two men shook hands, Luke said, "Aren't you on the Planning and Zoning Commission?"

"That's right," said Richard.

"I thought so. You had some trouble with that housing project, didn't you?"

"Yes. But it didn't prevent us from finishing."

"Your company did a good job on it. I just hope that keeps the workers happy. We can't do without them."

Richard did not want to get into a discussion about local politics and, especially, not about growers versus farmworkers and changed the subject. "You have quite a spread here. How many acres do you farm?"

"About a hundred. But I have more acreage that I can use to expand if the market warrants it."

"Where do you sell your apples?"

"We ship them out East. Red delicious are attractive to Easterners, especially New Yorkers, because of their bright red, even color. They're willing to pay for their look."

"That must mean you put them in cold storage to ship."

"You're learning fast. It's the only way to keep them fresh looking."

"What about the taste? Don't they lose some of it?"

"They're certainly not like those fresh off the tree. But Eastern city folk can't tell the difference. They're not attuned to fresh produce."

"That's so true. I grew up in Connecticut on a farm, but we had fresh produce available, although nothing like what you have in California."

"There's no better farmland in the world. It starts with that. Isn't that so, Tom?"

"And you have some of the best. Anyway, thanks for hosting today. I'll take Richard around and introduce him to some of the other guys. But first, we need to check out the lamb. I can smell it roasting."

"It's over there on the other side of that group. We're doing a dozen today. I just hope that's enough for this bunch—you know what big eaters they are."

Tom and Richard made their way over to the roasting spits, where a crowd was gathered around, taking in the aromas. "I've never seen a whole animal roasted before," Richard said.

"It's quite something, isn't it? You should be around when they roast a side of beef in the summer. An animal that size turning on a spit brings out a real primal instinct."

"I would like to witness that sometime."

"One day, you will, I guarantee. Now, I'd like to introduce you to some of the other fellas. Most of them are growers or shippers, but some of them are regulars like me." Tom shepherded Richard around to his friends until he met most of them. "Now that the preliminaries are out of the way," said Tom, "let's get in line because they're already carving up the lamb."

Richard fixed his eyes on the carving station—whole animals, heads and hooves, laid out on the table with part of their sides cut away, exposing ribs and backbone. It was a gruesome sight. But the slice of lamb he was served looked succulent—he was eager to try it. As he continued down the serving line, he filled his plate with an assortment of salads and sides.

Tom was already seated, gorging himself on the lamb. Richard joined him while taking in the plates piled high. These beefy guys have tremendous appetites, he thought. Then he glanced down at his own plate, displaying rather modest portions in comparison. Tom introduced Richard to everyone at the table, but there was little conversation since the guys were much more interested in their food. They did, however, utter words of praise for the lamb—delicious, so tender, unbelievably tasty—in between mouthfuls. Richard was still on his first helping when others were going back for thirds. He had never witnessed such gluttony. They were going to be in for a night of heartburn, stomach aches, and Tums.

Tom and Richard met the following Saturday to tour the farms. They were both near San Andreas Road. While Tom tried to focus Richard on the houses and outbuildings, Richard remained focused on the land. He had all sorts of questions Tom wasn't able to answer—questions a civil engineer would ask but a realtor couldn't anticipate. It occurred to Tom that Richard was a very sophisticated client—maybe too sophisticated for him. He'd have to do some research if he was going to make a sale. So, Tom tried another tack...he'd go question to question. If Richard asked what type of soil the farm had, Tom would ask what type of soil he was interested in. If Richard asked about the aquifer, Tom would ask what he needed water for. And it went on like that. Tom felt Richard was not ready to buy any land, only interested in doing some research— for what purpose, he wasn't sure. He didn't know where he would find either the money or time to farm. But Tom didn't ask Richard any of those questions.

Tom took Richard out a couple more times. He didn't mind since he had a few hours to kill on weekends when Margery shopped with the girls. He would watch Richard take in the land's overview with the eye of a surveyor. Then he would poke at the soil to determine its composition and stoop down to gather up a handful to test for texture. None of the farmers that Tom had dealt with had ever scrutinized the land so closely. But they had experience, knew what they wanted, and recognized it when they saw it. It was going to take Richard quite a while before he could do that. Actually, Richard was playing his cards close to his vest. He wasn't letting anyone in on his private thoughts on a land purchase, including Gina, who he wasn't about to trust to keep his confidence.

CHAPTER FOURTEEN

Margery looked out her window and spotted Gina weaving her way up the driveway. Before she knocked, Margery opened the door, helping her up the step. "What in the world are you doing to yourself? I thought you weren't drinking anymore."

Gina giggled, hiding her embarrassment. "Oh, I just had a teensy-weensy bit—that's all."

"You had a lot more than that. You're drunk. Sit down here. I'll make some coffee."

Gina lowered herself into the chair, careful to maintain her balance. Then she reached into her purse for her pack of cigarettes, attempting to pull one out to light. But her fingers kept missing the pack, which was wavering in her hand until Margery grabbed her wrist to hold it steady. Once Gina had a cigarette in hand, Margery lit it for her. After a couple of puffs, the nicotine seemed to steady Gina. Then she took a sip of the coffee Margery had placed in front of her.

"How do you feel?" Margery asked.

"Better. The room isn't spinning as much."

"Are you still going to AA?"

Gina shrugged her shoulders. "Whenever..."

"Does Richard know you haven't been going?"

Gina held her index finger to her lips, letting out a shh sound. "He doesn't ask, so I don't tell."

Margery shook her head in disgust. "What about your AA partner? Isn't he reaching out to you?"

Gina shrugged her shoulders. "I must have missed his calls."

Margery wasn't going to let Gina get away with her avoidance tactics. "This week, I'll take you to the AA meeting, and I don't want any of your excuses."

Margery tried to get Gina back on track, but she knew she was fighting a losing battle. All the telltale signs were there. Gina couldn't fool her, even if she could fool Richard.

Another crisis struck. Marta discovered Gina passed out in her bed and called the first person she could think of—her cousin Joe. When Joe arrived, he knew he was crossing a line that AA had warned against, but he had to help Marta as well as Gina.

Joe and Marta aroused Gina and helped her to the bathroom to wash up. Marta got her dressed while Joe made some coffee, which he brought Gina to drink. She was coming around, and by the time the boys returned home from school, she was presentable.

"Marta, how did you know to call Joe?" Gina asked.

"My cousins and I have very few secrets from each other. I knew Joe would be home and the best person to help. I hope you're not angry with me."

"No, I'm not angry. It's probably for the best that Joe knows what I'm really like—what I'm capable of doing to myself."

"Miss Gina, Joe does not judge. He only tries to understand. Please, don't feel ashamed. There is no reason for it."

"That's the problem with being sober. I become so embarrassed about the way I've acted when I've been drinking. It's hard to face people who've seen me in that condition."

"Don't worry. Joe and I have seen worse...much, much worse."

Then a terrible thought crossed Gina's mind. "Do you think Richard will suspect I had a problem today?"

"He might," said Marta.

Fortunately, Gina thought, he won't be home until late since he had to fly up to Sacramento today. He'll be too tired when he gets back to notice anything.

Gina kept a close watch on herself until the AA meeting. As promised, Margery drove her. Joe called Gina every day to make sure she stayed sober, giving her tips to get through her day. "It's one day at a time. That's the only way we're able to do it." But twenty-four hours was going to be too long a time to get through without a drink. She just didn't have the willpower to resist. Then she remembered the Our Lady of Guadalupe medal, looking at her wrist. The bracelet was missing. I must have removed it before I went on that binge. She found the bracelet in the bathroom and slipped it on. Help me resist. Give me hope.

Hope without right action would prove futile. Gina had another relapse, and again, Marta called Joe. Marta and Joe were in the bedroom trying to wake Gina when Richard appeared. Joe looked up, locking eyes with him. "What the hell are you doing here in my house?"

"Joe is my cousin," Marta said. "I called him to help me."

"Are you the same Joe that's Gina's AA partner?"

"Yes. Marta knew about us since, as cousins, we talk, and that is why she called me."

"I thought your name was Hector."

"It is, but my friends call me Joe."

"This is a complicated situation if ever I saw one. You and Marta should leave so I can take care of my wife."

Before she exited, Marta asked, "Do you want me to come tomorrow, Mr. Bankston?"

"Yes, please. We're going to need you more than ever. And

Joe or Hector, whatever your name is, Gina is going to need a friend. Since you've been down this road yourself, you may know best how to help."

"All alcoholics travel the same road. If you are in recovery, you may be able to help someone else, and maybe not. It depends."

"Depends on what?" Richard asked.

"It depends on whether the person wants to be helped."

Richard knew he could not leave that decision up to Gina. She had to get help. She had to get better. Everything about their lives was hinging on her sobriety. Richard had already done his research and was now ready to call Lighthouse in Pacific Grove for her residential treatment. *At least this will get her out of the way for a while and give me time to put our lives back in order.* He had to pull strings and was given an appointment for the next day. He told Gina and asked Marta to help her pack a bag. Then he called his boss to let him know he needed a personal day. Jeremy did not ask any questions. *I wonder if he already knows what's happening, but I can't worry about that now.*

They left for Lighthouse after the boys got off to school. Richard tried to keep goodbyes to a minimum while maintaining a stiff upper lip himself. The first half of the ride over to Pacific Grove, they sat in silence, keeping their thoughts to themselves. It was a beautiful summer's day with only a few puffy clouds in the sky. The fields were now full of produce with brown bodies tending the crops, picking nature's bounty. While passing Castroville, known as the Artichoke Capital of the World, they saw the globe artichokes rising out of the earth on tall stalks. Once they caught the first glimpse of Monterey near Fort Ord, the beauty of the seascape released the tension between them.

"Do we have to do this, Richard?" Gina asked.

"Yes. They're experts at treating the disease, so it's our best chance to get you better."

The silence resumed as they followed the road along Pacific Grove's rugged coastline with glimpses of azure waves smashing against the rocks, caps white and frothy. A few minutes later, the Victorian mansion's gabled roof came into view, guiding them to their destination.

"It looks like a B&B," said Gina. "I didn't know it would be like this. It makes me feel like I'm going on a vacation."

"Don't let the façade fool you. This is a serious drug and alcohol treatment center—one of the first in the western U.S. But I think you're going to like some of the activities they provide. Let's get out of the car and go in. I'll come back for your bag later."

They followed the winding path to the porch bordered by pillars, climbing the steps to the entrance. Richard rang the doorbell, which was answered by a middle-aged woman in a ponytail, dressed in a long broom skirt and peasant blouse. "Welcome, I'm Ruth. You must be the Bankstons. We've been expecting you."

"Yes," Richard said as he held out his hand to shake. "I'm Richard, and this is my wife, Gina."

"Pleased to meet you," Ruth said.

"The pleasure is all ours," Gina said, turning on the charm.

"Follow me, please," said Ruth.

Ruth entered the parlor and asked Richard and Gina to sit down. It was decorated in a casual style with lots of wicker furniture, colorful pillows, rag rugs, and plants, some suspended by macramé. Then she rang a bell, and tea appeared. "Please, put the tray down on the ottoman," Ruth said to the young girl who turned to leave as quickly as she had come.

"You must be weary after your drive," said Ruth. "Tea always restores the spirit and smooths the way to acquaintance. Let me pour. Here, Gina, take this cup. Cream and sugar are on the tray. Please help yourself to scones and finger sandwiches. And Richard," Ruth said as she handed him a cup, "here's your tea. Again, please be my guest," gesturing to the assorted sandwiches. Then Ruth poured tea for herself and sat back on the wicker loveseat, adjusting a needlepoint pillow to support her back.

"Let me say that we are so pleased you have come to Lighthouse. Gina, you are going to love your stay here. We have everything to make you comfortable. There's a health and wellness center to learn about healthy cooking and to take exercise classes, even yoga. We offer our guests a variety of experiences such as golf, water sports, horseback riding, and birding. Do any of those activities appeal to you, Gina?"

"I used to love horseback riding but haven't done it in ages."

"That's an excellent choice. Horses can help with your healing process because they can sense when someone is integrated or not."

"I don't follow," Gina said, furrowing her brow.

"I mean, they can tell if you have inner turmoil when it may appear that you look just fine."

"That's true about horses. I remember one favorite mount who just wouldn't perform when it was my time of the month. No matter how hard I tried, he wouldn't go over the jumps. It was like he didn't trust me."

"That settles it. We'll sign you up for horseback riding, and if you have time, you can try something else. Now, where is your luggage?"

"Her bag is in the car. I'll get it," said Richard.

"I'm glad we have a moment to ourselves," Ruth said as she leaned in closer to Gina. "Are there any special concerns or questions you have for me?"

Gina was silent as she considered her answer. The only sound came from a grandfather clock keeping time in the hallway. "It's so quiet. Are there many other guests here?"

"Oh, yes. But they're all out doing activities. We have about twelve guests who stay over and then many more who come in and out different days of the week."

"Will I be able to have visitors?"

"Not right away, but soon enough. We have to give the healing process a chance first."

Richard came back with Gina's bag and took his seat again, placing the bag on the floor.

"Ruth," he said, "can you explain to us what Gina's therapy will involve?"

"We don't use the word therapy here. It's all about healing, which emphasizes the person rather than the professional. Healing is a much more holistic process. It allows the body to do what nature intends it to do."

"Thank you for correcting that. I like your approach. Don't you, Gina?"

"Yes, it all sounds wonderful. I only hope my body responds as you expect."

"It is not how we expect," Ruth said. "It is how you expect. You are the one who holds the power to heal yourself. Now, I'd like to show you to your room. You have a single that looks out on the garden, or would you prefer a sea view?"

"Which one do you think is right for me?"

"The garden view. Where flowers bloom, so does hope."

"That's a beautiful sentiment. I'll have to remember it."

"I wish I could take credit for the words, but they belong to our First Lady, Ladybird Johnson. She has a strong attachment to flowers. Now, where were we? Oh, yes, your accommodation. The room has a terrace that will allow you to sit and watch them grow. But you will take a turn in the garden every day. There is something very healing about working with the earth. Anything that uses the hands is very healing as long as it has positive energy. The hands connect to the heart. They are a conduit to love. And love is what one needs most for healing."

After the first two weeks, Gina was healing. Ruth had been right about love—Lighthouse was filled with it. She realized that was what she was missing in her life. The boys were getting older and more independent. Her husband had grown cold. She felt more at home here than in her own house, which had become a sterile tomb, alcohol her only joy, her only escape.

Richard and the boys came to visit her on the weekend. She was glad to see them, and the boys were especially happy to see a change in their mother. They had either forgotten or never known the joy-filled woman she had been. The burden of responsibilities had buried that side of her. "When are you coming home?" Mike asked.

"When I'm ready," Gina said. "I love you all very much, but I need to get well." He was disappointed, as were the other three.

"Let's go out into the garden," she said. "I want to show you something."

They only had to walk off the terrace to be in the garden. Gina led them around to a bed on the far side. "Look at this beautiful garden I'm creating. I've put in some fairy rose bushes that will bloom all season. The lilies are now in bloom. I'll be adding some annuals for color and some iris bulbs, which will bloom in spring and fall."

"I like all the different plants together," said Mike.

"Yeah," said Matt. "They're a variety of shapes and colors."

"That's the style of a cottage garden, which this is," said Gina.

"We can clear a space so you can create one when you get home," said Richard.

All the boys gave their approval to that suggestion, arguing about who was going to weed the soil, plant the seeds, and water.

Gina let out a laugh. "You can all do all those things. We'll make a work chart to take turns. Now, I'm looking forward to coming home to start on a fun, family project with all of you."

"Dad, what do you want to do in the garden?" asked Matt.

"I can spray to keep the bugs away."

"No, not that," Gina said. "We only grow flowers the natural way. Don't you remember what Rachel Carson said about poisons? They're trying to get rid of poisons here which harm the body, so they don't want poisons that harm the plants and our environment either."

"Maybe I'll just watch the garden grow. That's pretty harmless. In the meantime, I'll order some gardeners' supply catalogs. We can prepare for the garden now, and the boys will help me."

"That would be wonderful," Gina said. "The best homecoming I could possibly ask for."

Dave told Gina to close her eyes as he and Drew led her up the brick path into the courtyard, easing her into a chaise lounge. "What is going on?"

Matt and Mike said in unison, "We're ready. You can open your eyes."

Gina blinked her eyes a few times to focus. "Oh, my goodness. You prepared a garden for me." The little plot had been made ready with topsoil, and the boys had drawn colorful pictures of flowers, attaching them to yardsticks, which they stuck in the ground. The result was a cheerful, simulated garden with animated flowers, some smiling, some laughing, one sticking out its tongue.

"Are you trying to send a message with that one?"

"It's only meant to be funny," Richard said. "We hope you like the garden. It was all the boys' idea."

"I love it. Tomorrow morning, we will begin. Who wants to make a trip to the nursery with me to pick out flowers? I count four hands. What about you, Richard? Do you want to join us?"

"Sure. I can help carry the plants and pack the car. Remember, we need to get an early start to leave time to work in the garden before it gets too hot."

When they returned with the plants, Richard loaded the boys' arms to carry them in. On their way back for more, they spotted Mr. Yamamoto trimming his bushes and waved a greeting. Mike yelled, "We're making a flower garden." Mr. Yamamoto nodded and smiled.

He waited a little while, then wandered over to the Bankston's house and knocked on the gate. Gina looked up. "Sam, I'm glad you're here. We could use your expert advice."

"I would like to be helpful if you think it would be useful."

"Absolutely. Mike and Matt, explain to Sam what we are trying to create and the plants we purchased to do it."

They told Sam about their plan. Then they showed him the plants they had purchased for it.

"The first thing is to determine the amount of sun in your little garden, such as full sun, part sun, or even shade. Then read the information on the plant that is provided. It will tell you how high the flowers will grow, when they will bloom, and how far apart you should plant them. It is best to plant the taller flowers in back and the shorter ones in front. You also want to consider color, shape, and texture for a more artistically pleasing arrangement."

"Sam, what type of sun do we get?" Gina asked.

"The garden will receive part sun. But it will be the hot afternoon kind."

"Of course. I'm out here sunbathing in the afternoon."

"That's all my advice for now. But once you get started, you may come up with more questions. Please ask me. I consider it a privilege to share my knowledge with you. Good luck with your gardening. It will bring you much pleasure and beauty—one of the best things in life."

The next morning, Gina visited Margery. "I'm back," she said, twirling around to show herself off.

"You look great."

"Let's talk about that on my patio. The coffee is already set because I want to show you something."

Margery untied her apron, grabbed her sunglasses, and followed Gina out the door.

"First, I want you to sit down at the patio table and keep your eyes closed. I'll get the tray of coffee and be right back." Margery was curious, but she resisted taking a peek.

"Okay, I'm back, and you can open your eyes. What do you think of our cottage garden?"

Margery put on her sunglasses. "It's beautiful—very similar to the one you were creating at Lighthouse."

"The boys did most of the work. I just love it. This is where you'll find me most of the time—just gazing at the flowers."

"Tell me, how was your stay in Pacific Grove?"

Gina took a sip of coffee before answering. "It was very nice, and everyone was so kind. Riding a horse again brought back fond memories. They gave me a brown gelding named Clarence with the gentlest personality but lots of get up and go. When we loped across the meadow, I felt safe with him—he was very sure-footed. I wanted to bring Clarence home with me."

"The energy of a magnificent animal is so soothing, and it penetrates right to the soul. I still have those sensory memories from horseback riding years ago."

"Horses, Ruth told me, are therapy animals for so many types of needs. Some people consider horses stupid animals, but I've always thought they possessed a special mystical quality."

"I think you're right. Did you get down to the beach? Tom and I used to take the girls to Lovers' Point. We would picnic, suntan on the beach, and swim. The girls would climb all over the rocks and explore tidal pools for starfish, sea urchins, crabs, and other creatures. Afterward, we often stopped by the wharf to feed the seals and watch the fishing boats come in with their catch of the day. Oh, the memories..."

"We had a couple of excursions to the beach. But I think your outings were much more fun."

Margery paused before she changed the subject. "You will resume your AA meetings, won't you?"

"That's something I must do forever. Joe called me last night to give me a reminder."

"You want to stay healthy like you are now. Everybody's rooting for you."

"I'm going to do it this time. I've made up my mind that I can't ever take a drink again. The stuff is poison to me."

"That's a good way to look at it. Anyway, I'm glad you're back. I've missed our visits. But I might be the one stopping by now that the garden is in bloom."

CHAPTER FIFTEEN

Richard spotted the signs again. A hidden liquor bottle, trips to the car to retrieve something, a quick visit to Margery's to borrow a cup of sugar at various times of the day. Gina was backsliding, and the boys were suffering. The twins were merely average students—not the high achievers prep schools like Exeter are looking to admit, and they were entering their teenage years in the 60s—a time of upheaval. And their younger brothers were not far behind. Richard had no choice but to consult an attorney.

When Gina received divorce papers, she was stunned. Richard had not said a word about it. She broke a cardinal rule and called him at the office. "What is the meaning of this?"

"I want a divorce. I can't go on like this any longer, and neither can the boys. You're not the wife and mother any of us need. I'm seeking custody of my sons. You can have the house."

Gina had been blindsided. "This isn't fair. It's not what I want. After fifteen years of marriage, how can you walk out like that?"

"Gina, I have work to do. We can discuss this further tonight."

But when Richard returned home, Gina was gone. He called

Margery to ask about her whereabouts. She hadn't heard from her in a couple of days. Later that night, Gina phoned and told Richard not to worry—she needed time away to think.

Gina returned for the meeting with the attorney. She had not retained her own legal counsel, so Richard's attorney suggested a few names. When the time came for the court date, she was a mess but sobered up for her appearance. The judge awarded custody of the boys to Richard, although he gave her visiting privileges, and she got the house, as promised. The day after the divorce decree was final, Richard purchased a ranch on the outskirts of town. Margery learned about it from Mike, who was bragging about where he was about to move. She asked Tom if he was aware Richard bought a ranch.

"No. I guess I should have known a large sale wouldn't be as easy as our next-door neighbor."

"Do you have any idea how he financed it?"

Tom shook his head. "We didn't talk price and financing when I took him out."

"This is a mystery. I can't wait to see the ranch for myself."

When Richard pulled his car into the driveway, Margery cornered him. "Word is you're going to become a rancher."

"Not exactly. But I suppose someone told you I bought a ranch."

"That's right." She waited for Richard to offer more. "We have to move out of the house—it's all Gina's now. The boys and I need a place to live."

"A ranch is more than a place to live."

"That's true. But I've wanted to be a landowner for some time, and the right opportunity came up." Richard was getting annoyed with the third degree but didn't want to be rude.

"When can we take a tour? We'd love to see it."

"Maybe this weekend. I'll let you know." As he made his getaway, he thought, Margery can be a busybody.

.   .   .

It was two weeks before Margery and Tom got an invitation to visit the ranch, located off San Andreas Road, about twenty minutes away. The first thing that struck them was its rugged, natural beauty. There were oaks and pine trees scattered amongst patches of wildflowers—lupin, Indian paintbrush, and golden California poppies. To the right, a sharecropper was working a strawberry field. But they were taking the road that led uphill, past the horse paddock, past a big red barn, past an apple orchard. At the top, Richard's new home appeared—a hacienda-style ranch built around a brick courtyard. Richard and Mike came out to greet them, followed by two black labs, barking and wagging their tails. The terra cotta tiled great room with rustic beams and a stone fireplace featured a wall of windows with a view across the valley onto the sea. Margery gasped when she walked in. "You've arrived, Richard."

"The tour is only starting. Save your applause for the end." He motioned for them to follow. The kitchen had oak cabinets with wrought iron pulls. A farmhouse sink was set in front of another window that offered a view of the courtyard. The center island, fashioned out of distressed wood, was sizeable, topped with a single piece of granite in a mixture of earthy tones. But the six-burner Aga stove was the star, equipped with a grill top and eight ovens. "I hope you know how to cook, Richard—because this kitchen demands it."

Richard laughed. "Don't worry. If not me, someone will be cooking in here."

Margery didn't respond but couldn't help wondering who that person would be. Now that Richard was single again, he would be in demand.

"Let's go out the kitchen door so you can see the patio. All the rooms have access to it." The patio was quite large, with terra-cotta pots filled with petunias scattered about and a wrought iron dining set near the kitchen.

"I might put in a pool. There's room for it without losing the entire patio. Now, I want to show you the master bedroom." They entered from another door off the patio into a large room with a beamed ceiling and kiva-style fireplace. A large wrought iron bed, festooned with a white gauze canopy, filled most of the space. It had an ensuite bathroom with double sinks, a jacuzzi tub, and an oversized shower that could accommodate two quite comfortably.

"That's the nickel tour. Next, we'll take you on ATVs for a ride around the ranch. Let's head outside."

"That would be swell," said Tom.

"I hate to sound dumb, but what's an ATV?" Margery asked.

"These are. All-Terrain Vehicles. Hop aboard."

Mike had brought up both ATVs while the house tour was being conducted. Tom got on behind Mike, with Margery taking the seat behind Richard. It was a bumpy ride but a great way to get the lay of the land. They set off across the plateau where Richard and Mike stopped. "Follow me," said Richard. And he led them to a rather expansive grass-covered meadow that offered a view of the entire ranch. "Not only is this a great place to survey the ranch, but this is where we plan to plant a garden and grow some of our own vegetables."

"It looks like the soil has never been cultivated," Tom said.

"My thoughts as well. It'll take some hard work, but it can be done. And there's nothing blocking the sun either."

"What about a water source?" asked Tom.

"I might dig another well. But first, I'll try to bring the water up here. There are techniques that should work. Okay, back on the ATVs." They mounted the vehicles and drove side by side as much as possible over the rough terrain, with Richard pointing out distinct features of the property.

Tom asked, "How many sharecroppers are working the land? It looked like a Japanese family down near the road growing strawberries."

"Right now, there are only two. Both are raising strawberries. The Akitas and the Ortegas, who are Mexican."

"Who takes care of the apple orchard?"

"A couple of nearby apple farmers are tending it—but it's mine. I'll give them a share of the crop and sell the rest to grocery stores."

"There are a couple of small houses on the ranch," Margery said. "What are your plans for them?"

"Both are rentals. The Japanese family leases one, and I still need to find a renter for the other. If you know of anyone, send them my way."

"Sometimes, a maiden nurse needs housing."

"I couldn't wish for a better renter," Richard said, beaming a sly smile.

"On second thought, I often come across old bachelors. They might be more suitable out here in the wilderness."

"Now, I know why they call you Marge the Sarge—you have no sympathy. Anyway, let's head back to the house and have some cold drinks while we visit. You look thirsty after being out here in all the heat and dust."

After they stepped off the ATVs, Richard said, "Take a seat on the patio. I'll be right back." He brought out a couple of beers for Tom and himself and a couple of sodas for Margery and Mike, along with a bowl of pretzels. After everyone quenched their thirst, Richard asked, "What do you think of the ranch?"

"You found the best one around," said Tom. "You must have had a good source."

"It was a private deal. Sorry, I wasn't able to do business with you, but you know how it goes."

"That's the game I'm in."

"What I'd like to know," said Margery, "is if you won the lottery. This spread must have cost a pretty penny."

"Not the lottery—I only wish I had—things would have been simpler. Let's just say it took some creative financing."

"I'll say it did," said Tom. "You divorced Gina and gave her the house. Few recently divorced men could then turn around and buy a ranch."

"This has been a long time in the making. It's the fulfillment of a dream. And it will also keep the boys out of trouble in town. There's nothing worse than idleness. And now, with the 60s culture taking over, idleness will result in a terrible end. I've seen it happen too many times. The ranch begs to be worked. The boys will do chores that will build strong bodies and character and, just as important, a work ethic. They don't have that now. That's one reason the twins are such mediocre students. When I was their age, I came home every day and did homework for a few hours. Math, especially, is a subject that is built on previous knowledge. If you miss one of the building blocks, you can't build further."

"I'm happy for the boys," said Margery. "I worried about them. Some of their friends looked like they were going to drag them down. Not all families in town hold high aspirations for their kids like you do. You'll be able to control their friends out here."

"Exactly."

The next morning, Margery went over to Gina's to check on her but, more importantly, to do some busybody work. She wanted to find out if Gina knew anything about how Richard financed the ranch. It was all very curious, and she just couldn't contain herself. She found Gina on the chaise lounge taking a sunbath.

"Gina, I'm glad you're enjoying yourself."

"Oh, I didn't hear you come in. I must have dozed off."

Margery's eyes searched the area and noticed an open beer can hidden under the lounge. "How are you feeling?" That was always her go-to question—her nurses' training had ingrained it into her.

"I'm still at loose ends. Richard up and leaving me like that and taking the boys with him has sent me into a tailspin. I've lost my bearings if I ever had them."

"You need something to do. Volunteer work or a career."

"Right now, I'm not up to anything. Besides, what would I be able to do after staying home for so long?"

"You've got your voice. You could be a church cantor, a backup singer in a band, even a nightclub singer."

"Now, the last one is something I'd enjoy, and the late hours would suit me. I'm not one to get an early start."

"Well, think about it. But I wanted to tell you that Tom and I got a tour of the ranch yesterday."

That got Gina's attention as she righted herself. "You're one up on me."

"It's a gorgeous piece of property with a dream house sitting on a plateau overlooking the valley. What a view Richard has from there, extending all the way to the sea."

"It's just my luck that my ex has it made in the shade while I wallow in the dust."

"Richard never talked finances when Tom took him out to look at farmland. You never mentioned he was rich."

"He's not. His folks own a small farm back in Connecticut. To make ends meet, his father did cabinetry work, and his mother taught school."

"Where did he get the money to buy that ranch?"

"Your guess is as good as mine. I suspect he has investors. He knows plenty of people with money to spare."

"That makes sense. Any idea who they are?"

"His boss, Jeremy Edwards, is one possibility. But there are others who will come to mind once I think about it. The friends Richard surrounds himself with were collected for a purpose. He doesn't waste time unless there's something in it for him. You may not realize that about him."

"No, I never saw that side of him."

"Maybe now you'll understand why I'm in this shape, and we're divorced. I wasn't any use to him anymore."

"That's not true, and you know it. Richard loved you. You and he had one of the best lifestyles of anyone around. You skied at Yosemite in the winter, spent summers on Lake Tahoe, and home was a social whirl. I was pea-green with envy."

"That was because you weren't able to see below the surface. Oh, yes, our lives seemed so wonderful. We had to keep the party going because, if it stopped, the truth would have been revealed. Now, everyone knows, and no one has to be envious any more."

Richard and the boys settled into ranch life. School, however, was a different situation. The twins enrolled in Watsonville High, the public high school since they had not proven themselves to be good students. While not on par with an Eastern prep school, it offered a college-prep curriculum, which many Japanese students filled.

Mexican students, whose migrant parents worked the fields, comprised a significant number of the student population. Moving around, they didn't have a chance to gain competency in any subject, nor learn to speak and write the English language at the level necessary for higher learning.

When Matt and Mike arrived to start their freshman year, it was their first encounter with the Mexican culture that was rapidly taking over the town. They didn't know what to make of it, but they kept their guard up. School became a forbidding place—somewhere they didn't fit in. The less they had to do with school, the better. They were eager to leave as soon as possible, not remaining around for sports or extracurricular activities. Richard hoped farm chores would help develop them along with mandatory study hall.

Dave was in junior high, and of the four seemed to be the most promising student. Drew was still in grade school, and like the twins, preferred playing outdoors to studying. The buses stopped on the road in front of the ranch and transported them to and from school. In the morning, before school, and after they got home, they were expected to do chores. Besides the two inherited horses, Richard purchased a few farm animals to give all the boys enough work. Chickens needed to be fed, eggs gathered, horses cared for, stalls mucked, and goats milked. That was just the start. Then the land needed to be worked as well—trees and bushes cut back, wild berries harvested, land cleared, and vegetables planted.

Mike named himself foreman. He gave Drew the job of feeding the chickens and gathering the eggs. The first time Drew went into the chicken coop, several hens surrounded him, pecking at his feet and legs. It alarmed him, and he kicked to shoo them away. To gather eggs, he had to reach under the hens to pull them out, a delicate maneuver. The hens turned when he disturbed them, pecking at his hands. The process was more like an ordeal that took far longer than it should have. But Drew was determined to have fresh eggs for breakfast. No more store-bought refrigerated eggs for him. Once he tasted the difference, he was hooked and would endure the hardship whatever it took. But from then on, he wore long pants and gloves.

Milking the goats was Dave's job. Mike thought he'd enjoy chasing them around and capturing them in their pen, not to mention milking had its own satisfaction. But Dave found the bucks charged at him, horns pointed, and the nannies often refused. Sometimes, Dave would lead a few goats out to a patch of land that needed clearing of plants or invasive species. Then they were worth their weight in gold. They did that unwanted chore as if they were ranch hands working for wages. Another problem with the goats was that they often escaped their pen. They would search around for a weak spot and then work at it until they had their freedom. Dave found it challenging to outsmart the goats.

That left the horses to Matt. Mike got a bit of revenge on his twin by assigning him the dirty job of mucking stalls. It was a smelly task that Matt found nauseating, but he got used to it.

Fortunately, that disgusting chore was balanced by grooming the horses. He enjoyed washing them down and currying their coats. The horses often responded with nuzzles and neighs. If Matt had time after he finished his chores, he would ride them around the ring bareback. Like his mother, he loved the direct contact of the animal, which had such a soothing effect on him. Afterward, the anger he felt about the divorce would retreat, leaving him with a sense of calm.

Mike gave himself the job of clearing the parcel on the plateau for a vegetable garden. He enjoyed working the land, using tools, and feeling the soil in his hands. Once the land was well-aerated, he wheeled barrels full of goat manure to spread around, enriching the soil. He never felt more alive, spending days in the fresh air and sun.

The physical work showed in the boys' bodies that were becoming lean, muscled, and bronzed. Their hands were well-developed and bore the calluses of hard work. By dinner, they were spent.

Marta had followed Richard to the ranch, where she spent her days. She didn't leave until she served dinner and cleared it away. But she always provided a substantial meal—roast chicken, mashed potatoes, corn, string beans. And she always finished with a special dessert—flan, tres leches cake, or the boys' favorite, churros dipped in hot chocolate. If Richard worked late, she would leave a plate for him warming in the oven. Then she sent the boys to their rooms to study. She never knew if they did their homework or not. But when her ride arrived, the boys were quiet and nowhere to be seen. It was up to Richard to supervise the boys' studies. He was well educated, so he knew what was important.

But Richard's mind was on more than the boys' education. He was concerned about the country. The Summer of Love recently took place in nearby San Francisco. Who knows how that influenced teenagers? The assassinations of two beloved political figures followed–Martin Luther King and Robert F.

Kennedy. Everything was in upheaval. Yet, despite it all, man had landed on the moon, giving hope to the future. However, the Viet Nam War was still raging, and what it might mean to the boys' futures was worrisome. President Johnson escalated the war, putting boots on the ground in 1965.

The twins were still young, but he did not want them to risk the draft. He was hoping they could get a nomination to a military academy—it was always better to be an officer during wartime who would not be on the front lines. Richard's mind was never far from thoughts of war. Although he retired from the navy after earning the rank of commander and was no longer directly involved in the military, he still got reports of the action. In town, he would run into young veterans with shell-shocked faces and, more often than not, missing limbs. Richard didn't want his boys to end up like them. Those veterans had been exposed to Agent Orange and witnessed the gruesome effects of napalm and other horrifying sights. Many would never recover. Richard wanted to protect his boys from the tragedies of war he knew too well but had been lucky to avoid. Eventually, luck runs out.

In 1969, just after the twins started high school, Richard called them into his study for a talk. The oak-paneled study was furnished with a large hand-hewn redwood desk, a chesterfield sofa, and a pair of leather club chairs. Richard's Stanford diploma hung on the wall behind his desk, where his sons would see it whenever they had a discussion. He wanted to motivate them to earn a college degree. "Take a seat," he said. "Now, Matt and Mike, you're getting older, and before long, you will turn eighteen, the age you're eligible for the draft. I'm sure you're aware that the Viet Nam War has not ended. Young boys not much older than you are being sent over there to fight. Some have lost their lives, others a limb, still others have lost their way. I'm sure you've seen them idling around town in their combat fatigues, smelling of marijuana. The war robbed them of whatever ambition they might have once possessed. I don't want you to end up like that. Plan now for your future. I have always set goals for myself which have led to my success—first, as a student, then as an engineer, and now as a landowner in one of the richest parts of the world."

"I don't understand what you want us to do," said Matt.

"For starters, I'd like you to study harder and get better grades to qualify for a military academy appointment."

"I don't want to go into the military," said Mike.

"Then the draft might get you, and you'll end up crawling through the jungles of Southeast Asia, hoping to stay alive."

"I'd go to Canada first. That's what a lot of guys do."

"That's not only unpatriotic but impractical. You'd be undocumented and wouldn't be able to work legally or even go to college. There's no future in it. You might be able to join the National Guard and stay stateside. But even they get sent off to war occasionally...so it's no guarantee."

"Maybe the war will end before we turn eighteen," said Matt.

"You can't plan on that," Richard said. "It's only wishful thinking. I want you boys hitting the books so you can become officers or, at the very least, show an aptitude for something that isn't on the front lines. You may think war is glamorous, but I've seen the brutality of it up close and don't want that for my sons."

CHAPTER SIXTEEN

As the summer of 1970 got into full swing, the United Farm Workers (UFW) called a work stoppage dubbed the Salad Bowl Strike, which featured a series of strikes, picketing, and boycotts. The name, Cesar Chavez, was mentioned in connection with the strike whenever it was discussed. He had growers and shippers rattled. Lettuce rotted in the fields while harvested produce cost three times as much. It wasn't a situation that benefitted either growers or consumers.

Some growers arranged a meeting one night to discuss the situation and look for solutions. Richard and Steve were among those invited because of their involvement in town affairs.

Bud Stanich stood up, calling the meeting to order. "We must do something about this situation, or we'll all be ruined. We can't let this guy Chavez have his way. He has to be stopped."

As he took a breath, applause shot through the room when someone yelled, "Let's run him out of town." Upraised fists pumped the air. The crowd was getting unruly and working itself into an angry mob, hell-bent on vengeance.

Steve stood up and made his way to the front. "Let's settle down," he yelled above the roar. To help, Richard put his fingers in his mouth and blew. The loud, shrill whistle got everyone's attention and settled the crowd. Then, Richard walked up front to support Steve.

"I'm the town attorney," Steve said. "I know you're all angry and worried about what's coming, even though most of you aren't lettuce farmers."

"That's right," a voice in the crowd said. "First, it was grapes. Now, it's lettuce. Next, it'll be apples or strawberries." Loud clapping erupted as Steve tried to regain control.

"We need to be smart about this. There are laws that must be observed. I don't think any of you want to end up serving jail time. As you probably know, it's not just the United Farm Workers involved in the strike over in Salinas. It's the Teamsters, too. We need to bide our time."

Richard and Steve met a few nights later for drinks. "Thanks for having my back at that meeting," Steve said. "Those men were looking for a fight. I've never seen any of those guys like that before—the pack mentality was taking over. It made me realize how close we still are to an animal state."

"I've seen it in wartime. Men can be even worse than animals."

"We certainly witnessed that aspect of their nature. Hopefully, we won't have more trouble with them since the strike seems to be centered on Salinas."

"And, so far, the protesting seems to be confined to the fields, not the towns. The average citizen doesn't feel it and isn't afraid."

"For that, let's be thankful. Now, how are things going with you?" Steve asked.

"The boys are doing well. Ranch life suits them, and they're being instilled with its values. Hard work builds character. It helped me."

"And, if you don't mind my asking, how's Gina? Sue has been worried about her since your divorce."

Richard looked down at the drink in his hands, trying to avoid eye contact. "I don't see her much. But since we're on the topic of the United Farm Workers, I should let you know that she's hanging around with Hector Lopez."

Steve's eyes popped wide open. "You mean the guy at the housing projects?"

"Yes, but he's now a community organizer, and I believe he's involved with the UFW."

"How did she get tangled up with him?"

"AA." Richard's answers were cryptic. He wasn't ready to open up, even to his best friend.

"I don't understand."

"He was the partner they assigned her. And it also turns out that he's one of Marta's cousins. Small world."

"It is a small world around here. Your tenure in town may be too short to realize that lots of people have a long list of relatives. Older generations of Croatians and Italians had ten or more kids. It didn't take long to multiply. And now the Mexicans are doing the same. They never seem to run out of cousins."

"I only hope Gina doesn't let herself get mixed up with them. That's all I need."

In early December, federal marshals arrested Chavez and held him in the Salinas jail. To add to the drama, the widow of Robert F. Kennedy, accompanied by Olympic athlete Rafer Johnson, stopped by the jailhouse to visit him, incurring attacks by an anti-union mob. By the end of the month, Chavez was released only to call for more strikes. In March, an agreement between the UFW and the Teamsters, giving the UFW the right to organize farmworkers, ended the strike.

The following summer, Mike was shopping downtown. Upon exiting Ford's department store, someone handed him a flyer, but before he could read more than the headline, noise coming from the southern end of Main Street caught his attention, and he stuffed the flyer into his pocket. A crowd marched through the street. At first, he assumed it was some sort of parade. But as it got closer, he realized it was a group of United Farm Workers staging a protest led by Cesar Chavez. Until now, he had only heard about Chavez, so he became curious when he saw him in the flesh and followed the crowd. They made their way up Main Street, then wound through the town until they got to the high school field. The marchers streamed in, filling every square inch. Mike stood on the outside and looked around. Then he spotted Joe nearby and asked him what it was all about. "We're marching for our cause—better pay and working conditions for farmworkers. We are here in solidarity with Cesar Chavez, our leader. He will be speaking soon."

The crowd stirred when Chavez held up a megaphone and began to speak, addressing the crowd in Spanish. Mike stood there with a blank look on his face as he didn't understand a word Chavez was saying. Joe said to Mike, "No sabe." Mike didn't react. Then he said, "You don't understand Spanish." And Mike nodded his head. "I will translate for you. Cesar says our cause is important. But it may take a while for success to come. Be patient. We need to practice passive resistance. Nonviolence and noncooperation like Gandhi. Cesar says he is going on another fast for the cause until our demands are met."

Cheers went up from the crowd when Chavez finished speaking. He moved through the crowd, shaking hands and hugging supporters as he went by. Chavez got into a nearby car and left to fast at home.

"What do you think of our leader?" Joe asked Mike.

"I don't know. But people seem to listen to him when he speaks."

"That's because he speaks the truth. Not only that, his heart is in our struggle. He is a leader we can believe in."

"He mentioned a man named Gandhi. Who is he?"

"You don't know who Gandhi is? What are they teaching you in this high school? He was the leader of the independence movement in India."

"We don't learn about India in school."

"Maybe you should. Martin Luther King also followed his method of nonviolent civil disobedience."

"I know about King, but now he's dead. Someone killed him."

"The same thing happened to Gandhi—killed by an assassin's bullet. Both nonviolent men who lost their lives by violence."

"Will Chavez be killed, too?"

"Some people would like him dead. But we are praying for him."

That night, after supper was over, Mike followed his father into his study. "Is something the matter?" Richard asked. "You don't seek me out like this in the evening."

"I just wanted to talk to you about something that happened today."

"Come in and have a seat. Tell me what it's all about."

"Today, I was shopping on Main Street when I saw a crowd marching down the street. It turned out to be the United Farm Workers." Mike told him about meeting Joe and hearing Cesar Chavez speak.

Now, Mike had gotten Richard's attention. "What did Chavez say?"

"He said he was following Gandhi and nonviolence. I asked Joe about Gandhi, but he didn't tell me much. What do you know about him?"

"We'll discuss Gandhi after you finish telling me about what Chavez said."

"He said he was going to fast for the cause until the demands are met."

"Is that so? He's going on a hunger strike. That's nothing but a political ploy to force the growers' hands."

"I don't understand."

"This is where Gandhi comes in. Gandhi fought the British for the independence of India. He used all these same political devices—passive resistance, noncooperation, nonviolence, and fasts."

"Did it work?"

"Yes...in the end, it did."

"I want to learn more about Gandhi."

"Why is that?"

"To learn about his idea of nonviolence. I might want to be a conscientious objector to the Vietnam War. Killing other people isn't the way to handle problems."

"I don't like the idea of killing people either, but sometimes it's necessary to fight evil in this world. But if you want to learn about Gandhi, I suggest you start with the library. Either the high school or town library should have a book on him. Gandhi was an important political figure in this century."

"Joe told me that Martin Luther King followed Gandhi."

"That's true. Gandhi had a lot of influence on many people. Now, what was Joe doing at the parade? Did he say what he's up to?"

"He didn't say, and I didn't ask. But one other thing is bothering me. Will there be any strikes or marches at the ranch?"

"I doubt it. We don't hire many farmworkers. Our sharecroppers do most of the work in the fields themselves. The UFW is targeting the big growers, and they've moved from Salinas to Watsonville. You stay away from those UFW crowds. Even though they talk nonviolence, something could still happen, and I don't want you to get hurt."

After Mike left, Richard sat with his head in his hands. Conscientious objector. I can't let it happen. Mike's too young to understand what impact that would have on his future.

. . .

Mike entered the school library for a book about Gandhi. Since he hadn't set foot in the library all year, he was unfamiliar with the system. The librarian checked the card catalog but couldn't find anything. She called the town library, which had one book on Gandhi, and put it on hold for him.

After school, instead of taking the bus home, he walked to the town library to pick up the book, Gandhi's autobiography, *The Story of My Experiments with Truth*. He stood there a minute, concentrating on the title. Then he realized he had missed his bus and had no way home. While he considered what to do, he sat down in the reading room to page through the book. He passed through the part of Gandhi's early years, his career as an English Barrister, and by the time he got to Gandhi's experience with South Africa, the book was at an end. The story was only about his early years and what formed him. Gandhi felt the rest of his life spoke for itself, relieving him of the burden of writing about it.

One thing caught Mike's eye, however, and that was Gandhi's devotion to meditation. He did Kriya Yoga meditation that was taught to him by Paramhansa Yogananda, a yogi and guru. Kriya Yoga unites the practitioner with God and brings God's love into his life. After reading this, Mike sat still and let it sink in. Then he remembered the flyer that was handed to him on Main Street and pulled it out of his pocket. It was an advertisement for a meditation center near downtown. He folded it, returning it to his pocket. Now, a more practical thought entered his mind. How am I going to get back to the ranch? He had two options— he could call his father and wait until he got off work, or he could call his mother on the chance she'd pick him up right away. What the heck, I'll call her.

Gina agreed to pick him up. The drive to the library should have taken less than fifteen minutes, but Mike waited more than half an hour before Gina showed. He took a quick glance at her and decided she was sober, then got in.

"You'll have to direct me. I haven't been out to the ranch yet."

"You have my promise for the grand tour. But today, it will be too late since it'll be getting dark soon."

"I will count on it. Now, tell me what brought you to the library. You didn't strike me as the bookish type."

Mike explained he was interested in learning more about Gandhi after what Joe told him about Cesar Chavez. He found out his secret was meditation.

"Meditation can be a wonderful thing. I'm meditating now, and it's helping me stay sober."

"You? How did that happen?"

"Joe introduced me to it. He's been going to a meditation center at Mount Madonna. But they also have a center downtown."

"That must be the center on the flyer they handed me yesterday."

"Are you interested in learning how to meditate?"

"Maybe."

"If so, you can come with me sometime. Now, pay attention, so I don't miss your road."

Mike directed Gina to the turnoff. As she drove, she tried to take in as much of the ranch as possible. She saw the apple trees that were in full foliage and wildflowers scattered about. But the road was unpaved and rough, filled with rocks and potholes, jostling her so much that she was about to pee in her pants. To avoid any embarrassing accidents, she slowed down.

When they arrived at the top of the hill, Gina pulled the car directly in front of the house. "I need to use the restroom."

"Follow me," said Mike, as he led her through the front door into the great room.

Despite her urgency, Gina paused. "Margery told me about the view, but I didn't expect this."

Afterward, Gina wandered through the kitchen to check out

the setup Margery had raved about. Marta was preparing dinner. "How are you, Miss Gina?"

"I'm doing well. Joe has probably told you I've been sober quite a while thanks to him."

"Yes, he said something to me but not that much."

Gina walked back into the great room where Mike was waiting. "Come over here. This is the best place for the view." She could hardly believe her eyes. Richard had done all right for himself. *If I hadn't blown it, I'd be living here, too—Queen of the Mountain.*

Mike walked Gina out to her car. As she was about to leave, she rolled down her window and said, "Remember my offer to take you to a meditation class. We can go after school gets out, and I'll drive you home."

"I'll let you know. Thanks for the transport home today."

"It was good to see you and the ranch. What lucky boys you are to have a father who is so successful."

Mike nodded. *But he'd trade all this for a good mother...the mother she had been before her problems set in.*

Mike's curiosity about meditation had been sparked. First, he learned how it helped form Gandhi. Then, he heard how it's helping transform his mother's life. He took the flyer out of his pocket and read every word. *There's no harm in trying it. But I won't call my mother to accompany me, even though transportation home afterward will be a problem.* He didn't care—he'd hitchhike if he had to.

When Mike arrived at the meditation center, he was greeted by a young woman in a white, flowing gown while a flute faintly played in the background. He already felt much calmer, as if he had no cares in the world, as if nothing bad had ever happened in his life or would happen in the future. A sense of peace enveloped him.

The woman led Mike into the main room, where two people sat on pillows, their eyes closed. Mike took his place on a pillow, not knowing what to expect next. He closed his eyes while uncontrolled thoughts raced through his mind. It seemed an eternity until the instructor arrived.

The instructor introduced himself and explained that Transcendental Meditation ™ (TM), a form of mantra meditation, was developed by Maharishi Mahesh Yogi. It involves meditating on a mantra for twenty minutes twice a day, with the benefit being self-development. "The Maharishi has many followers, including the Beatles," he said. After the introduction, there was a slight pause. The instructor came up to Mike and whispered a mantra in his ear. Then he began the guided meditation. Once Mike started using the mantra, he felt his thoughts retreat, calming his mind. The meditation lasted only twenty minutes, but Mike felt refreshed. After a period of relaxation, the instructor initiated a second twenty-minute meditation. More relaxation followed.

The entire session lasted only an hour. When it was time to leave, Mike noticed a difference in the way he perceived others and the world around him. It was an experience he had never had before. He thanked the instructor and left, knowing that he would return.

A few weeks later, Richard called Mike into his study after dinner. "I've noticed you've slacked off on chores, and Marta tells me some days you come home late from school. What is your explanation?"

Mike just stared straight ahead. Richard waited without speaking. Finally, Mike answered. "I've been taking a course in Transcendental Meditation."

"Transcendental Meditation. That's why you're walking around like you're on tranquilizers."

"It makes me more peaceful."

"What you should be thinking about is the war and how you're going to handle your responsibility. As I've told you before, you don't want to risk the draft. That's a guaranteed ticket to a Southeast Asia jungle, which you will most likely not survive intact."

"I don't want to think about war now. I'd rather wait and take my chances."

"Spoken like a teenager who does not understand the consequences of an adult."

"You told me to get a book on Gandhi, so I did. Meditation changed his life and allowed him to have a great impact on the world."

"Gandhi didn't have to worry about being drafted into the Vietnam War. You do."

"Did you know that Mom is meditating? She told me that it has changed her life."

Richard hesitated, processing what he'd just heard. "No...I didn't know that. When did you speak to her?"

"I called her to drive me home the day I went to the town library to pick up Gandhi's autobiography. We discussed meditation, and that's when she told me. Joe introduced her to it."

Richard frowned. "Joe again. I wish he'd stay out of our lives."

"He's helping her, Dad. She seems to be so much better."

"If it's helping her, then I'm glad she's found something that works. But you need to concentrate on your studies and do your chores. If meditation is getting in the way, then it has to go."

They continued to banter back and forth until Mike struck a deal with his father, agreeing to meditate only after chores were done. But not until the course was over in two weeks. Richard brought up the war again, reminding him to think about his future. "Now, what about Matt? All he seems to be interested in is the guitar. When I was your age, I was making plans for my future and taking steps to get there."

"That was another time and place. We see our lives differently than you did."

After Mike left the room, Richard sat still, contemplating how the world had changed. How can any plans be made when nothing remains static? Confucius was right when he said, "If I understand change, I shall make no great mistake in life."

CHAPTER SEVENTEEN

As the twins entered their senior year in the fall of 1972, their futures were still unsettled. Neither Matt nor Mike ever turned into the students their father hoped for, and neither expressed an interest in college. They would turn eighteen at the end of January and be required to register for the draft.

Both boys threw caution to the wind, relying on luck instead. And having a touch of the Irish, the fairies smiled on them. Two important events happened that would send their fates in a different direction. First, the military draft ended on January 27, 1973. And second, they came into an inheritance from their maternal grandparents, who died a few weeks earlier in a car crash on an icy Boston road. The money they were each about to receive was quite sizeable for teenagers, and Richard was not happy about it. For starters, Gina's parents never mentioned the inheritance to her, so neither of them knew about it. Richard could not understand why they would not have consulted the boys' parents before making such a decision. That sum of money in teenagers' hands could ruin them. It should have been put in a trust until they were old enough to handle it.

Of course, Matt and Mike had an entirely different view of their windfall. They both needed to find themselves. Living with an alcoholic mother through their childhood years and the divorce took a toll. As soon as graduation was over, Matt packed a duffle and headed for the nearest commune where he could while away his days playing the guitar and getting high. He didn't have to go far as the Santa Cruz mountains were full of communes—he could have his pick.

Mike took a different tack, setting out for India in search of a guru. He booked a direct flight to New Delhi and took a train to Rikikesh, where he planned to begin his spiritual journey.

Once the train pulled into the station, Mike was awestruck by the beauty of Rikikesh, set at the foothills of the Himalayas along the Ganges River. Many saints and sages had made their way here throughout the ages. The sacredness of the place was palpable—Mike sensed he was about to be transformed.

He grabbed the first rickshaw he spotted, and the old man pulling it got Mike to Ashram Row in record time. Upon his arrival, Mike was disappointed Maharishi was away on a world tour. Nevertheless, he committed to life at the ashram—beginning and ending the day in prayer and working in between. They assigned Mike a job in the garden, tending flowers, especially the roses, which were sold to tourists to help support the ashram. He learned that each plant has a life source and that if he connects with it, the plant will grow strong and healthy. After a few weeks of following that prescription, Mike noticed the flowers responded with lush blooms full of color.

Finally, Maharishi returned. Everyone gathered to hear him speak, often using flower analogies. "Happiness radiates like the fragrance from a flower and draws all good things towards you." Maharishi went onto say, "Success in anything is through happiness." For some reason, Mr. Yamamoto came to mind. He had suffered a lot in life, but growing flowers brought him happiness.

The time came for Mike to leave the ashram. He settled into his train seat and tried to sleep, but so many thoughts whirled around in his mind. He needed to make sense of his experience and all he had learned from Maharishi. It was a lot to process.

He knew this past year had been transformative and that his life's work would involve farming. He connected with the soil, which is so alive with organisms, but more so with plants that have a distinct life force, especially flowers. Maharishi mentioned flowers so often that he felt a strong pull toward them. He tried to remember exactly what the Maharishi said about flowers—something about their fragrance drawing good things to you. What did he mean, Mike wondered. It took some time, but Mike finally arrived at the message—if you look for the good, you'll be happy and draw even more of the good to you. Maybe it's looking at the glass as half full, having an optimistic view toward life, not letting your mind dwell on the negatives, instead surrounding yourself with joy.

Mike arrived in Delhi well past sunset. After a good night's sleep, he was ready for the Gandhi tour. The first stop took him to Birla House, where Gandhi had spent the last months of his life and had been assassinated. The next stop was Raj Ghat, Gandhi's resting place along the Yamuna River, marked by a platform of black marble, topped with an eternal flame. Mike bowed his head and said a prayer to this great man he was just learning about but already admired. He could still sense his spirit, which had never left India, nor the world. A noble life is so much more when it inspires those coming afterward, leaving a path to follow. Martin Luther King and Cesar Chavez stood out. People come to India to find themselves—to find God. But what they find are saints—those living, breathing people who can teach them how to live like Mother Teresa.

One of Gandhi's quotes floated across his mind: "Where there is love, there is life." Gandhi also said that his life was his message. Then another thought popped into Mike's head—his life was about love. Love was his message.

Mike caught a direct flight to San Francisco. A poster of disgraced President Richard Nixon who had resigned over

Watergate welcomed him home. It was odd that no one had removed it. He wondered what other type of welcome awaited him.

After clearing customs, Mike grabbed his backpack and headed for transport. The bus stopped at every nook and cranny on the way, taking forever. In Watsonville, he grabbed a cab out to the ranch. He was eager to see the look on his father's face when he walked in the door—would he welcome him home like the Prodigal Son? He felt he deserved no less.

Mike realized something was wrong the minute he stepped through the door. His father, dressed to go out, appeared in the foyer where they locked eyes. Mike had never seen his father so distressed...so afraid.

"Mike, we didn't expect you. You should have called."

"Is anything wrong? You don't seem like yourself."

"You've come home at a bad time. Your brother had an accident and is in the hospital. I'm going there now."

"My brother," Mike said, wondering which one.

"Your twin, Matt. Someone he was staying with drove him to the hospital in Santa Cruz."

"How serious was the car accident?"

"It wasn't a car accident—he got injured surfing. It happened at Steamer Lane in Santa Cruz."

"Steamer Lane has one of the most hazardous surfs around. Few surfers can handle those waves."

"It wasn't the waves. He saw a fin coming toward him, steered away, and slammed into the cliffs."

"His imagination must have been playing tricks on him?"

"Shark attacks occur around here regularly—by great whites. You were too young to remember, but years ago, a couple of swimmers got attacked at Rio Del Mar. One lost his leg. The other died of his injuries right there on the beach. That son of a bitch had severed all his limbs—they were only hanging by a thread."

"How serious are Matt's injuries?"

"They're serious."

"I'm coming with you. What about Mom?"

"She's already there. Let's get going."

Once they were in the car, Richard didn't bother to ask about Mike's trip before he unloaded. "I knew that inheritance would come to no good. Matt has already run through most of the money. It slipped through his fingers like it would with most eighteen-year-olds. He bought pot and alcohol and loaned money, playing the big shot with whoever was around. And now he's in the ICU—a tomb may be next."

Mike drew a deep breath, trying to calm his fear. For a while, he listened to his father rant. Then he started repeating his mantra, which calmed his mind, focused him, and allowed him to meditate. When they arrived at the hospital, he was renewed and ready to face whatever was to come.

Gina was at Matt's bedside in the Intensive Care Unit when Richard and Mike entered. She had been holding Matt's hand while she leaned over him, stroking his hair, kissing his face, whispering loving words into his ear. When the door opened, she turned and let go of Matt's hand. Gina moved toward Mike with open arms, hugging and kissing him with so much emotion. "Mike, I'm glad you're home."

"Tell me what you need, Mom. I'll be here for you and Matt."

"Richard, it doesn't look good for our son. If he makes it, he might have brain damage."

"No. Not the brain. What did the doctor say?"

"Only that he's lucky to be alive and that he was without oxygen for several minutes when he was underwater."

While his parents conversed, Mike moved close to Matt and put himself into a meditative state to reach Matt's subconscious. He sent out positive energy, prayers, and love. Next, he whispered healing words into Matt's ear as if he were speaking to the ashram's roses. Gina and Richard noticed what Mike was doing and stood by.

"I saw him flutter his eyelids," Gina said as she rushed to Matt's bedside.

"I saw it, too. Keep on doing whatever you're doing because it seems to be working."

"I can work with the energy better if only Matt and I are in the room."

"If you're asking us to leave, we'll step outside. Come on, Gina."

"I don't want to go. I need to be here with Matt."

"Mom, it will be for a few minutes at most. Please, trust me."

Richard put his arm around Gina, escorting her out the door. She broke down as soon as they were by themselves, shedding a waterfall of tears as she tried to express herself in garbled words.

"Don't talk. Let the tears flow. You've got to get them out now so you can maintain your composure when you return to the ICU."

Mike continued to meditate with Matt's subconscious while doing the energy work he had learned at the ashram. He had seen people have amazing results. But none of them were in the shape that Matt was now.

Mike called his parents back into the room. Gina hurried to Matt's bedside to resume holding his hand. She thought he pressed a finger into her palm. "Something's happening."

Richard and Mike watched as Matt's eyelids started flickering. "Go get the nurse," Richard said to Mike.

The nurse rushed in and checked Matt's vitals, noticing an improvement. Matt let out a moan. "Sometimes they do that. Don't get your hopes up."

Don't get your hopes up, thought Mike. What kind of nurse is she, anyway? All we have is hope. And hope is powerful. Mike glanced over at Gina's hand, the one holding Matt's, and spotted the rosary bracelet with the medal of Our Lady of Guadalupe attached. Hope. And roses. Mike had an idea.

"I'll be right back." Mike left for the hospital gift shop, where he planned to purchase a rose. The clerk didn't want to sell him a single rose, so he bought the entire bunch—red, the symbol of love. Now to sneak them into the ICU since they don't like flowers in there. He spotted the men's room and ducked in to prepare for his move. He took one long-stemmed rose from the vase, held it to his nose, and inhaled. It had a lot of fragrance. He tucked the single rose in his shirt and set the bouquet at the nurses' station as a thank you, and he returned to the ICU. The nurse was still there, so he had to bide his time. "You need to leave in a few minutes. Our patient needs his rest."

"Please, let us have a few more moments with him," Gina pleaded.

The nurse nodded and left.

Mike wasted no time pulling the rose out from its hiding place and holding it under Matt's nose.

"What are you doing?" Richard asked, thinking Mike had lost his mind in India.

"I remembered what Maharishi said about fragrance and wanted to try something."

"What did he say?" asked Gina.

He said, "'Happiness radiates like the fragrance from a flower and draws all good things towards you.' If Matt can smell the fragrance of a rose, maybe it would draw the good towards him —all the angels and forces for good that could help him."

Gina looked over at Matt and watched him breathe in the rose's fragrance. In one miraculous instant, he opened his eyes, looked around, and said, "Where the hell am I?"

Once Matt was released from the hospital, Richard took him back to the ranch, over Gina's objection, where he could be cared for by Marta and kept away from friends. He didn't want anyone having access to Matt whose motives were not pure. Under Marta's care, Matt was recovering, at least in body— however, his mind did not seem the same.

"He's not hitting on all cylinders," Richard said to Mike. "I fear he has brain damage."

"I agree. He doesn't seem normal. Let's give it time. I'm also going to show Matt how to meditate if he's willing. It may help his brain recover faster."

"Anyway, that's enough about Matt, let's talk about you. How was your trip to India?"

"It was quite amazing." And Mike recounted all he had done that year until he got to what he really wanted to say. "I found my calling."

"Tell me about it."

"I discovered I have a way with plants. Somehow, I can communicate with them and help them grow. I want to be a farmer."

"Farmer. You'll fit in around here. What type of crops do you want to raise?"

"I want to grow flowers."

"This is a good area for it. There are many flower farms, and even a group called the Monterey Bay Flower Growers Association where you could find some help."

"Mr. Yamamoto could help me."

"He'd be a good person to start with. You'll need to learn about flower growing—everything from the soil conditions to individual species before you do any planting."

"Can I use that plot of land on the plateau that I was working before I left for India?"

"That's as good a spot as any on the ranch. It gets lots of sun and has a water source from that well we put in. We should test the soil to learn what we're working with. I'll take a sample and send it off to the lab."

Mike noticed how his father kept saying "we." *I guess we're going into business together.*

CHAPTER EIGHTEEN

On September 23, Richard received an urgent phone call from Ben Crawford, who wanted to meet with him and Steve that evening. When Richard arrived, he found Ben all worked up. After Steve got there, Ben revealed himself.

"I'm sure you know about this already, Steve. But Richard needs to be alerted. The UFW is striking the Novak apple farm on Green Valley Road. This could be the start of something we don't want around here."

"I thought the growers signed a labor contract with the Teamsters this summer," said Richard.

"They did," said Steve. "Only the farmworkers weren't in on it. And they're the ones who do the work."

"I see," said Richard, shaking his head over the stupidity.

"Not only that, I'm told there are several labor camps around Watsonville with a population of five hundred or more—mostly wetbacks, I'll bet. That means they have the manpower to carry out strikes all over this valley," said Ben.

"What I'm most concerned about," said Steve, "is the Watsonville Organizing Committee that's helping to support the United Farm Workers Union by giving them insider information it would otherwise take months if not years to learn."

"And who's on this committee?" asked Richard.

"They're very secretive," said Steve.

"I bet our man Hector is on it," said Richard.

"Then you should approach him," said Ben. "We've got to head off these strikes. And that brings me to the real reason I asked you here. An election is coming up, and our mayor can no longer stand. He'll step down as soon as we identify someone to appoint. That will give our candidate a leg up at the election since he'll be running as an incumbent. In some ways, we're lucky he won't stand because we need a strong mayor, one who won't take any guff."

"Who might that be?" asked Richard.

"You, of course," Ben said, while Steve stole a quick peek at Richard, catching his frown.

"I'm not your man. Right now, I've got too much on my plate with my job and the boys, especially Matt, who is still having problems. The P&Z Board is plenty of town involvement for me."

Steve turned to look Ben straight in the eyes. "How about you, Ben? You're a homegrown boy, high school football hero, military officer, not to mention a scratch golfer."

"I could do it, I suppose, if there were no other suitable candidate. But you'd need to talk me into it—make me an offer I couldn't refuse."

"We could do that," said Richard. "Right, Steve?"

"You'd be perfect for the job," said Steve. "You wouldn't take any guff. Your physical presence alone would be enough to intimidate anyone."

"I agree. If you showed up at a strike with your old Air Force uniform on, those illegals would run for the hills."

"You flatter me. But I'd like to mull it over and discuss it with Sylvia, not that I require her consent."

By the time October 9 rolled around, the farmworkers had declared victory in their strike, and Ben Crawford had been seated as mayor, running in November as the incumbent. He had the dubious distinction of being elected along with Governor Jerry Brown, a UFW supporter. With this turn of events, Ben knew there was more to come. In May, when Cesar Chavez addressed supporters at E.A. Hall Jr. High School, he told farmworkers to slow down their work in the lettuce fields because victory would come sooner with pressure inside the fields.

The UFW's next move would be to take on Gallo wine. First, they went to stores carrying the wine and asked them to remove it from their shelves—some did, some just covered it up and still sold it upon request. Those that didn't cooperate were picketed.

"The UFW is getting under my skin," said Ben at a meeting with Richard and Steve. "They're making this job of mayor damn difficult."

"We never said it would be easy. I'm just glad they've settled apples for a while so I can get mine picked," said Richard.

"Is that all you care about?" said Ben with a frown.

"I'm a farmer now. I care about the crops."

"Did you track down Hector to ask him about the organizing committee?" Steve asked Richard.

"No, but I will."

Richard asked Marta to arrange a meeting between him and Hector. Richard met him for drinks at the Bistro Mona Lisa. After they exchanged greetings, Hector said, "I heard some of our farmworkers are harvesting apples on your ranch."

"How do you know about that?" Richard asked, thinking that Hector missed little.

"I have my sources."

"As a matter of fact, that's what I wanted to talk to you about. Are you involved with the Watsonville Organizing Committee?"

"What's it to you?"

"We heard it comprises several farmworkers who plan to establish a union strike office here. I thought you might be one of them."

"You already know I'm involved with the UFW. What difference would it make if I'm also part of the organizing committee?"

"Mayor Crawford would like a direct contact with that committee. And if you're in it, maybe you could be that contact."

"Tell him to call me whenever he needs something."

"Hector, we don't want any trouble in town."

"Don't worry. Cesar does not want any violence either. His method is passive resistance."

Richard's tone softened. "Do you still see Gina?"

"Yes, we're friends. She comes to the meditation center. It's helping her."

"I don't want her involved in any of this union business."

"You should tell Gina. I'm not her boss."

During the winter months, while the ground lay fallow, the union laid low in town. But on February twenty-two, the UFW began a march in San Francisco with a few hundred farm workers, and by the time they reached their Modesto destination on March first, they were fifteen thousand strong. That display sent the message intended. Then in the spring, Cesar called for farmworkers to be at the state capitol every Monday to show support for the Agriculture Labor Relations Act. Governor Brown promised to sign the bill once it was passed.

"The bastard sons of Watsonville are doing their part," said Ben. "Every Monday morning, farmworkers meet at the union hall at four in the morning to take trucks up to Sacramento. With all that pressure, I don't see how that bill can't pass."

On June 4, the Agriculture Labor Relations Act was signed into law.

CHAPTER NINETEEN

Richard went looking for Mike and found him tilling the soil on the patch of land that was to become the flower farm. He had the results of the soil survey in his hands.

"Mike, we've got perfect soil for flowers—not too sandy, not too sticky. We may only need to add more organic material to enrich it and help it drain well, so the roots don't rot."

"I've already started a compost pile. It's over there. Marta is saving me her vegetable scraps, and I'm going to talk to the sharecroppers on the ranch about saving me their discards."

"But you still need to do more research before you plant."

"I'll give Mr. Yamamoto a call to ask for help."

"In the meantime, I picked up some books for us to read."

"You can read the books and tell me what I need to know. But I'd rather learn from the farmers who are doing the actual work of growing flowers."

"Certainly, there is nothing to compare with direct experience. With you learning from farmers and me learning from books, we should have our bases covered. When do you plan to plant?"

"If everything is ready, I may grow some flowers that mature in early fall, such as chrysanthemums, which people buy to go along with pumpkins."

"I remember Mr. Yamamoto saying he grows mums. You'll have to pick his brain." Richard left, humming to himself, feeling buoyed by the new flower farm project. He always liked a new challenge that involved obstacles that could be overcome with sound research, planning, and execution. This was the project he had been looking for. Not only would it make money for the ranch, but it was a project that all the boys could be involved in. Richard had always had big dreams for himself, and never were his dreams bigger than becoming a grower who was a major player in one of the richest agricultural counties in the state, if not the world.

Mr. Yamamoto was waiting for Mike's arrival. "First," Sam said, "I want to show you the greenhouse where we grow many varieties of flowers. It will give you an idea of what a large flower farm involves."

"I'd like that," said Mike. "I learn better when I observe."

"We all do. Confucius said, 'I hear, and I forget. I see, and I remember. I do, and I understand.'"

"That saying is new to me, but I agree with it. My dad always wants me to read books, but I find I learn better with my hands."

"Then you will be an excellent farmer. But remember, books are important as well. They contain the hard-earned knowledge that we can learn and benefit from. Now let's step into the greenhouse. Follow me."

Mike's eyes grew wide as he looked at the rows and rows of flowers arranged by variety and color.

"What do you think so far?"

"Your flowers are beautiful. I'd like to learn your secrets."

"Some of my secrets are long, closely guarded family ones.

When my family first came to this country, we were poor, so once we began to sell our flowers, we had to be very clever since there was much competition."

"When did you come to America?"

"We came around the late 1800s and settled in San Francisco, where we attended Domoto College. It wasn't a real college but a hands-on education by the Domoto Brothers in flower growing. After the earthquake in 1906, we moved here."

"Then you've been raising flowers here for over eighty years."

"More or less. Except for the time we spent in the internment camp."

"I don't understand what you mean."

"You must have missed a part of American history. During World War II, Japanese were sent to internment camps to wait out the war under the watchful eye of the federal government."

"I'm sorry, I didn't realize. Were you still Japanese citizens?"

"No, most of us were Nisei and Sansei. Excuse me. Those are words we use for the second and third generation. We were born here. We were Americans."

Not knowing how to respond to this revelation, Mike asked, "What happened to your flower farm while you were away?"

"We were among the lucky ones. We found white friends to take care of our farm, so we did not have to start over when we came back. But many others had no such luck."

"It's terrible what our country did to you. I don't understand it."

"It was fear that brought the internment about. The Japanese had just bombed Pearl Harbor. No one felt they could trust the Japanese."

"What about Germans? Did they have to go, too?"

"It was much harder to identify Germans, but some were also sent to camps. In fact, the U.S. had a program to round up both Germans and Japanese who lived in South America. They were sent, along with a few Italians, to an internment camp in Texas called Crystal City. Later, most of them were deported to their native countries."

"This is something I never learned about."

"That's why books are so important. Not everything is taught in school. Now, you came here to learn about flowers? What types do you want to grow?"

"I might try chrysanthemums first."

"You have chosen to grow a very special flower. The Japanese Emperor sits on the Chrysanthemum Throne. The flower is a symbol of longevity and rejuvenation. It has sixteen petals which stand for the reunification of Japan in the 16th Century."

"Thanks for telling me. I like understanding each flower variety. It helps me to better communicate with it."

"What? Don't tell me you talk to flowers."

"When I was in India, I learned how to meditate, to connect to all things. I worked in the rose garden and spoke to the flowers using kind words, and they seemed to respond."

Sam laughed. "Do you know flowers can also speak to you? The Buddha gave a famous talk called his flower sermon. Basically, everything you need to know is contained in a flower. Now, let's continue our greenhouse tour."

"Is it important to have a greenhouse, too?"

"Some flowers grow much better under controlled conditions where they can be protected from foul weather and pests. You mentioned you are interested in growing chrysanthemums. They are susceptible to several diseases—rust, mildew, mold, fungus, and even viruses. If one of these diseases infects a crop, it is a disaster. Unfortunately, I have had it happen. But no more. A greenhouse is the only way to go."

Mike continued to look around, so he wouldn't miss anything. "I see you are growing mums in here."

"That's right. They will be ready in time for the fall market. We are counting on it."

"If I start now, could the mums be ready for the fall?"

"You are too late, even with a greenhouse. I'll tell you what, if you want to learn how to grow flowers, the best way is to work with someone who has already mastered the art. You can come here and help me. In return, I will give you some seeds and cuttings for your flower business."

"Thank you, Sam. I would be honored to learn from you."

That evening, Marta made her world-famous chicken enchiladas with a side of refried beans. Richard, Mike, Matt, Dave, and Drew gathered around the dinner table for the special feast. Even though this was one of Mike's favorite dishes, he couldn't contain himself and told Richard about his meeting with Sam before taking his first bite.

"Working alongside someone is the best way to become good yourself. It's called an apprenticeship. In the building trades, workmen always apprentice. It would take far longer and many more mistakes to learn to do a trade well without an apprenticeship."

"When I watch and then try something myself, I learn best," Mike said.

"What intrigues me is the greenhouse," said Richard. "I'm going to do some research. The winds coming off that plateau can be pretty harsh. We'll need something to protect the plants."

At the sound of we, the boys exchanged glances amongst themselves. They knew their father was taking over Mike's business, which they also hoped to have a part of.

"We shouldn't get too ahead of ourselves," said Mike. "Sam has a lot to teach me first."

Matt, Dave, and Drew ate their dinner in silence while Richard and Mike conducted their private conversation. But before they left the table, Richard said to Mike, "Why don't you get Matt to help you prepare the field?"

Mike looked at Matt, who was not paying attention. "Matt, would you like to help me?"

"I doubt I'll be any good at it."

"You need to get outside and do some physical work," said Richard. "Now that you're healthier, you should be able to handle it."

"Please excuse me," said Dave. "I've got homework to do."

"This is your senior year when your grades are especially important," said Richard. "I'm glad you're taking an interest in your studies."

"I want to go to college…a good college."

"That's the spirit. I put a lot of value on an education."

Mike and Matt glanced at each other and kept their heads down. They had a lot to prove to their father, and it would be more difficult without a college diploma.

When Mike stepped outside, he felt the cool wind on his face blowing across the plateau as the oak leaves quivered, and he held onto his hat. Dad's right again. We need a greenhouse to protect the plants and a windbreak to protect the soil which was being blown around. I guess man is destined to fight the elements in an attempt to master them.

Mike spent the morning at work in the field. First, he watered the soil to moisten it. Then he dug down about a foot to turn it over, removing rocks and weeds and adding compost. When he finished a section, he laid several inches of mulch on top to protect it from weeds. It was almost noon and time for lunch, so he headed back to the house. Marta made him a couple of turkey sandwiches, which she served with homemade potato salad and rice pudding. Dave and Drew were at school, but Matt heard the commotion and came out of his room with a hungry look on his face. He had slept in, missing out on breakfast. Marta scrambled some eggs with ham and popped some whole-grain bread in the toaster. She presented Matt with breakfast in record time. After he took a few bites, Mike said, "You should've come out to the field with me this morning. I could've used the help."

"I was tired. Besides, Mom is coming to the ranch after lunch to ride, and she wants me to go with her. She says it will be good for me."

"Maybe you can help me tomorrow."

"I'll think about it."

Mike did not reply. He was disgusted with Matt's attitude. He felt he would never get better with the slothful lifestyle he had adopted. But there wasn't anything he could do about it.

After lunch, Mike hopped in the old Chevy truck Richard had bought for farm chores and headed down the dirt road, hitting most of the potholes along the way. When he got to the paddocks, he spotted his mother's car, stopped, rolled down the window, and called to her. She came out of the barn, dressed in jodhpurs and boots, a helmet on her head.

"Mike, I'm so glad I ran into you. Sam has been telling me about his sessions with you. He's impressed by your ability to work with flowers."

"That's where I'm headed now. We have a deal. I help him with the fall crop, and he'll teach me about raising flowers. He even promised to give me some cuttings and seeds to start my nursery."

"I don't want to keep you. Stop by the house sometime for a visit."

Mike continued down to the road and turned toward Sam's flower farm. He found Sam in the greenhouse with a younger Japanese man.

"Mike, I want you to meet my son, Sammy. One day, he's going to take over this operation."

Mike offered his hand. "Glad to meet you, Sammy." He paused a moment. "Sam, are your other sons involved in the business, too?"

"No, sorry to say. They both got different ideas at the university. When they graduated Berkeley, one became a dentist in Monterey and the other an attorney in San Francisco."

"You must be proud of them…so much education."

"Yes, I am proud, but my dream was my three sons working together and building this business for the next generation. We Japanese think in generations, not just the present moment, even though we try to live in the present moment."

"My father would love to trade places with you. He's not happy that Matt and I have not gone onto college."

"One day, he will be very proud of you. Manual labor will be your route to success."

Mike nodded as he reflected on Sam's words.

"Let's get to work. We've wasted enough time talking."

Mike followed Sam into the greenhouse, where the fall flowers were already budding. He paid close attention to everything Sam told him and did whatever he asked. When Mike was watering a plant, he would talk to it using gentle words. He always spoke to one at a time, rarely addressing them as a group. He felt they responded better that way, just like people do. Mike noticed Sam planted nothing in the fields for the fall and asked him about it. "I can control the elements better in the greenhouse. If a drought hits, I would lose most of the crops in the fields."

"Drought," said Mike. "We've had plenty of rain."

"This area goes through periods of drought. You must be prepared. I don't like to take chances. My family's livelihood depends on the profits I can make on my flowers."

Mike continued to show up at Sam's farm every day to help nurture the plants to maturity and then to harvest them. Sam said, "I've never seen a better crop. You brought me luck."

"It's not only luck."

"What do you mean? Was it your talking that did it? You didn't realize I noticed, but I did."

"Words can be powerful. Since you are a Buddhist, you might

not know the Bible, but in Genesis, it says that God spoke and the world was created. He just used His words."

"You are right. I am not familiar with the Bible. But Buddhism holds that everything, even rocks, contains a spirit. It seems you know how to use your spirit to connect to plants. This ability will make you a great flower grower. Now, once we're done with the harvest, I will do what I promised."

"What's that?"

"Don't tell me you forgot. Your reward for your hard work is seeds and plant cuttings. This is the best help I can give you for your flower farm. Look here. I have collected some seeds for you in this box."

Mike peered in, glimpsing hundreds of seeds. He was eager to get them into pots to start the seedlings.

"They are not yours yet. But soon, we will be finished with the harvest, and then you can take them."

That night at dinner, Richard mentioned the research he had been doing on greenhouses. "I've found the one we need. It's from New Zealand."

"New Zealand? Why so far away?"

"It's the best on the market. No one around here uses one, so it will give us an edge. They tend to go for the cheap Chinese models."

"Sam's greenhouse seems fine to me."

"This one will be better. But we need to test it first. Don't mention it to anyone either. If it works well, it'll put our flowers out in front."

"I guess we'll have some family secrets like Sam has."

"That's right. It's nothing new to keep a few business secrets to yourself."

"When will the greenhouse be here? I'd like to get some seedlings started in a few months."

"It will be here by then. I'm drawing up our business plan to determine if we can get a tax exemption on the greenhouse. Every little bit helps.”

“I’ll just stick to farming. My stomach’s growling. What’s taking Marta so long with dinner?”

The greenhouse arrived in the spring. Richard called for all hands on deck to help set it up. He had read through the assembly instructions and felt he knew how to do it. Richard arranged the various components by like kinds and in the order of execution. When the boys arrived, construction began with Richard acting as project engineer. He was impressed with the boys’ ability to follow instructions and even more impressed with their quick grasp of the design concept to assemble the structure effectively. “It’s looking good. Like a real greenhouse.” He hoped this encouragement would motivate the boys to work even harder. Finally, the last piece was in place, and they all stood back to gaze at their finished product.

Mike said, “This greenhouse is so much better than Sam’s. And it’s bigger, too.”

“Let’s go inside,” said Matt, and Dave and Drew followed.

“We could use this as a fort,” said Dave.

“Or a house for outdoor living,” said Matt.

Richard joined the boys inside. “Let’s check all the seams to make sure everything fits airtight.” For the next few minutes, they all busied themselves testing their work to ensure every-thing had been done correctly and there were no design flaws.

“Looks fine to me,” said Mike.

“Great job, boys,” Richard said. “I’ll ask Marta to fix a special dessert for you tonight—you’ve earned it.”

Over the next few weeks, Mike planted the seeds Sam had given him in pots and placed them in the greenhouse. The tempera-ture was always perfect whenever he went inside to water or fertilize the plants. Once he saw the seedlings sprout, he was excited and encouraged them with his words. The seedlings responded with growth spurt after growth spurt until they were mature.

Richard came by to check on the seedlings—he was impressed. "You're ready to begin the next phase."

Mike looked at him, perplexed. "What next phase?"

"I've been thinking and doing more research. You still have a lot of land here that could be planted."

"But I thought we bought the greenhouse to protect the plants."

"That's why I did the research. I discovered statice likes full sun and tolerates drought conditions. Not that we're in a drought now, but the Farmers' Almanac is filled with years of drought for our area. We get good years and bad. Not only is statice perfect for our site, but the florists love it for bouquets—ensuring a good market for us."

"You've thought of everything. All that's left is to buy some seeds and plant them."

"I already bought purple statice seeds."

"Purple...the color for people seeking spiritual fulfillment. Did you know that, or was it just a coincidence?"

"Let's say it was divine guidance along with the fact that florists always need blue or purple in their bouquets, something about the color wheel and how it sets off the other colors."

"Before I start, I should read the planting instructions. I assume you have them somewhere."

"I have them right here." Richard reached into his pocket and handed the instructions to Mike.

"I'll look these over tonight. Then I can start fresh tomorrow. I still have some chores to do in the greenhouse this afternoon."

. . .

Mike got busy the very next day planting the statice seeds in little pots to start the seedlings. When they were ready to transplant eight weeks later, he moved them by wheelbarrow to the field. The field was narrow but wide, which would allow the statice to cut a panoramic swath of color across the land. Mike dug a row the correct depth, sowed the seeds about eighteen inches apart, and covered them with the dry soil. It took all day to plant half the field, and he was exhausted from all the digging, stooping, and pulling of weeds. He was beginning to wonder if this was worth it since the greenhouse was so much more efficient. But he persevered until the entire field was planted. Afterward, he said a blessing for the seeds to have everything they needed to bring forth the flowers they promised. Mike hoped that each plant would yield fifteen stems. If he could get ten cents per stem, which was the going rate, the crop of statice would bring in thirty thousand dollars. It seemed a fortune to him which he would soon claim.

By spring, the greenhouse carnations were already in bloom, bearing large full crowns. They might even be better than the ones Sam had in his greenhouse, Mike mused. He took a small bouquet to Sam to show him how his lessons had paid off. When he arrived at Yamamoto Farms, Sam was standing outside his greenhouse. He wore boots, overalls, and a Cooley hat favored by the Japanese to protect them from the sun. He gave Mike a wave and a smile. When Mike reached him, Sam said, "What brings you here on such a nice farming day?"

"I wanted to show you my carnations. I brought you a bouquet of my first cuttings."

Sam stared at the bouquet, his eyes widening in the silence that stood between them. "You learned your lessons so well that you surpassed your teacher. These are the most beautiful carnations I have ever seen. No one in Monterey Bay grows carnations like these."

"Thank you. Your approval means a lot."

Sam raised his eyebrows. "Is that so? Does my approval mean enough to share your secrets with me?"

"Maybe my secrets are family ones, too."

Sam laughed. "I know you talk to plants, but is that your only secret?"

"We use a special greenhouse, too. That's pretty much it."

"Well then, how much do you charge for storytime?"

"I doubt it's just words—it's my aura that affects them, too, enabling them to grow big and healthy."

"When the word gets around, all the flower growers are going to be coming to you to learn your secrets."

"They might need to spend some time in India first. That's the source of my secrets. Anyway, I just dropped by to give you some of my first carnations in gratitude for your help. In the fall, the chrysanthemums will be ready for you to inspect."

"I look forward to seeing your mums. Only Japanese can grow them well."

When late summer came around, the statice were in full bloom. Richard brought out his camera to photograph the spectacle for publicity. "This looks even more incredible than what I expected. Yard after yard of statice massed together is nothing short of spectacular. I just had to get it on film."

"They took to the soil. The conditions must be right for them," Mike said.

"It was backbreaking work, but it's going to pay off. You'll need help to harvest these for market. A few farmworkers might be available."

"That'd be great. But don't forget the lazy hands right here—otherwise known as my brothers."

"I'll see what I can do to light a fire under them. But you need experienced help to get these flowers to market in good shape."

In a few days, help arrived. Richard came out to watch the harvest, expecting about forty thousand pounds for the acre planted. The two men were experts at handling flowers, having received their training at some of the best flower farms in the valley. They made their way amongst the plants, choosing the ones ready for harvest by noting their bloom and color. They knew to cut the stems as low to the plant as possible and dipped them into a bactericide solution to prevent decay and increase water intake. Then they organized them in packs of ten stems for shipping or selling at the market.

Mike was grateful for the help. But when he went to pay the workers, he learned they were members of the UFW requiring more pay than he had budgeted. Since he had such a small operation, he didn't expect union rules would apply. But the men were very clear about their rights, and he didn't argue.

That night, Richard called a family meeting. "We all need to pitch in to get these flowers to florists throughout California. Matt, Dave, and Drew, I want you to pack them and take them to the shipper. We won't get paid until a customer is satisfied."

"We'll be glad to help," said Dave.

Even though he was younger, thought Richard, he was on the ball, cut from another cloth. Dave had it in him to go to college and use his brain to make a living. "Thanks for cooperating. Matt and Drew, are you all in, too?"

"I'll go along with Dave," Matt said. "This is something I can do."

"Me, too," Drew added.

Mike said, "The hard work is already done, but it will be worth nothing if we don't get these flowers to market."

"That's right," said Richard. "A lot hinges on the three of you. I'd rather pay you than someone outside the family. If we work together, we can build this into a thriving family business— something that will always support you and your families."

"Just look at the Yamamotos," said Mike, "they've been growing flowers for eighty years. About four generations have made a livelihood from it."

"Let's get our action plan together," said Richard, "and execute."

The boys worked together to load the truck with the statice stems for packaging. Mike counted the stems and exclaimed, "Twenty-five stems per stalk, can you believe it? Twenty-five stems per stalk."

Matt, Dave, and Drew turned perplexed faces toward him. They had no idea what he meant. Finally, Dave said, "Can you explain. We don't get it."

"Twenty stems per plant is an excellent harvest. We got twenty-five. It's amazing, just unheard of. At ten cents per stem, we'll make fifty thousand dollars. Add to that the carnations and chrysanthemums in the greenhouse."

They all grabbed each other by the shoulders and started jumping around shouting, "Hip Hip Hooray. Hip Hip Hooray."

During the cheering, Richard appeared on his way to work. "What's all the noise about?"

"The plants produced twenty-five stems," Dave said. "More than usual. We could make fifty thousand dollars on the crop."

"Not bad for beginners. If sales go well, we'll expand the acreage. Mike, the plants must like it here on the ranch."

"So, it seems. Wait until I tell Sam."

"Don't start gloating. The last thing we need is for the long-time growers to get jealous."

After dinner, Richard called a family meeting to discuss the business. "Did you get the statice shipped?"

Dave spoke up first. "Yes, we got it packed well and sent it off to the distributors, just as you wanted."

"We must wait for the invoices to be paid. Then we can reinvest the money."

"Reinvest?" Mike said. "What about our wages?"

"You're getting room and board. What else do you need? If we want to develop the business, we must reinvest the profits."

"What are you thinking?" Dave asked.

"First, we need to clear more land for statice. There's a huge market for it that we've only just begun to tap. Statice can also be dried and sold as everlasting flowers, which makes them very versatile. Then we need to diversify our greenhouse plants to protect ourselves against a disaster—either in the market or a natural occurrence."

"I'll need more help if we're to expand," Mike said. "Matt, can I count on you?"

"What about Dave and Drew?"

"Dave will be in college for the next four years. Drew's still in high school. You're here with nothing else to do."

"I guess I can help somehow," Matt said.

"If you want to continue being fed, you will," said Richard. "We must do a lot of planning over the winter. I'm taking a trip to Holland to visit some tulip farms. Tulips are another spring favorite amongst florists, and they would add to our spring collection. We need something in bloom all three seasons to make a significant profit."

"We might have to buy another greenhouse," said Mike.

"I plan to do a space inventory to ensure we're using our space efficiently. By going vertical, we could make use of all the space."

"Don't forget I have to water and fertilize the plants," Mike said.

"Yeah," Matt added, "he's no trapeze artist."

That comment brought a laugh from the other boys. Matt had a way of putting humor into situations. Although, Richard didn't even break a smile.

"Let's get serious," Richard said. "We're building a flower

business that will compete with any of the current players in Monterey Bay. I want you to know I sent those pictures I took of our statice field to the California Flower Growers Association. A friend told me they were impressed with our first crop and might even use one of my pictures for their brochure."

"I want us to be successful, but growing flowers takes time. As Sam says, it's as much an art as a science. And I'm still an apprentice."

"If we don't plan ahead, we'll get nowhere. How do you boys suppose I've gotten where I am?"

The four of them looked at each other, making resigned faces.

"Your silence tells me you have no clue what it has taken me to get this far. Every step of the way, I set goals and worked my tail off to achieve them. This business is no different. Farmers in this valley aren't just country bumpkins who've gotten lucky. They work hard, pay attention, and are always on the lookout for something that will give them the edge—better equipment, better cultivars, better growing techniques. They don't leave a stone unturned to improve production and, of course, profits."

Before the holidays, Richard called the boys together. "I've gotten all the totals on this year's crops. We made a tidy sum—around a hundred thousand dollars." The boys broke into smiles. "Bravo Zulu."

"What?" they said in unison.

"That's navy-speak for well done. Your work is reflected in the profits. Now, onto next season. Mike, how's the new field coming along?"

Planning ahead, as usual, Mike thought before he said, "I've made a lot of progress clearing it, but the compost needs to be worked in. It should be ready on time."

"Should is not good enough."

"Okay. It will be ready." He's never satisfied no matter what we do.

"That's the spirit. I'm leaving for Amsterdam in early spring to meet with tulip farmers. Tulips will distinguish us from the rest of the growers—none of them are yet raising Holland's finest."

CHAPTER TWENTY

Dave opened the mailbox and spotted the letter he had been waiting for, tearing it open. The College of Santa Clara, the only college he had applied to, accepted him. He stuck the letter in his shirt pocket, gathered up the rest of the mail in his arms, and headed up the road toward the house. Marta was in the kitchen, but he was careful not to give away his news yet—it was going to be a surprise.

After they had all assembled around the table, Marta brought out one of her specialties—tamales. She placed two corn-husk-wrapped tamales on each plate along with a serving of rice. No wonder she noticed nothing, thought Dave. Tamales take hours to make, involving lots of concentration.

"Since we seem to be celebrating with tamales," Dave said, "I'd like to share some good news."

"Is that right?" said Richard. "I could use some good news today. What is it?"

"I got accepted into the College of Santa Clara. That will mean I can come home and help when you need me."

Mike and Matt exchanged glances. While they were happy for Dave, they felt a bit diminished since they had not gone to college themselves. Meantime, Drew hoped Dave hadn't raised the bar on him.

"That is good news," said Richard. "The trust fund your grandparents provided can pay for it. My only concern is you'll be near where the UFW started, and with Santa Clara being a Jesuit college, they'll be involved in any cause that comes along."

"Don't worry," said Dave. "I'll steer clear of any conflicts." But even he knew he wouldn't.

"Since we're sharing news, I leave for Holland this weekend and will be away two weeks. I want to be there for the height of the tulip blooming season in mid-April. Mike, you will be in charge of the ranch while I'm away. But Matt, Dave, and Drew will be here to assist you. Right, boys?"

The trio nodded their heads. They looked forward to Richard leaving, so they could do whatever they wanted for a change. It would be a break for them. But for Mike, it would only mean a heavier load to carry.

The morning after Richard returned from Amsterdam, he went to find Mike at the greenhouse. "I brought you something." He held out some tulip bulbs.

Mike took the offerings in his hand to inspect them. "They look healthy to me. What type of tulips are these?"

Richard shook his head. "I'm not sure. Grow them and find out."

Then Richard pulled an envelope from his pocket and shook a few seeds into his hand. "I also brought these back."

"What type of seeds are they?"

"Tulips. Special ones that are only grown in Holland at the moment. I don't know what they'll look like or even if these seeds are any good. A junkie sold them to me for his next fix. He promised they'd set off Tulip Mania."

"Tulip Mania?"

"Europeans went crazy when they first saw the blooms that

reminded them of Turkish turbans, causing the market to skyrocket. Diplomats serving at the Ottoman court had introduced them."

Mike shook his head. "There's no harm in trying them, I guess."

"That's right. But tulips grown from seeds don't flower for a couple of years. They'll take patience. Now, have you ever thought about growing lilies?" Richard had met a Dutch woman named Sanne, translation lily, and thought the coincidence might be auspicious.

Mike let out a gasp. "Dad, you're getting way ahead of me. I need to concentrate on one thing at a time."

"All right. I'll do a little research on them. But I've noticed hotels fancy the stargazer variety. If we could grow those, we'd move into a whole new realm."

"I'm more concerned about the water situation. Sam thinks we may be in for a drought."

"Let's talk about that tonight. I have to get to the office this morning and am already late."

Richard held court at dinner, entertaining the boys with his travel stories, omitting the one in the famed red-light district that would have piqued their interest. "Now, what is this I hear about a drought?"

"We are low on rain this season, and that's when a drought is likely," said Mike. "Rainfall is only sixty-five percent of the norm."

"I know all about water shortages. My company helped build the California Aqueduct that brings water down from the mountains to the farms and towns below and has helped relieve us during drought periods."

"From what I've heard, the aqueduct won't help us much." Mike wondered if his father had listened to a word he'd said.

"What are the other farmers doing?"

"Collecting rainwater. Recycling. Drilling more wells. Cutting back acreage."

"Let's do the simplest things first, such as collecting rainwater and recycling. We might need to build a system for this."

"I can check with Sam to find out what he's doing. He always has the best ideas."

"Drilling a well will cost money and be more time-consuming. That's a last resort. Thank goodness we planted statice, which is drought resistant." Although, he doubted it would be drought-proof.

"I don't want to lose any of the plants, especially when they're doing so well."

"And I don't want to let our land lay fallow. We won't make any money that way. I want to grow this business, not cut it back."

Matt, Dave, and Drew had listened up to this point. "Is there anything we can do to conserve water?" Dave asked.

"When I lived at the commune in the Santa Cruz mountains, we were always conserving something," said Matt. "I especially remember the rule on toilet water, 'When it's brown, flush it down. When it's yellow, let it mellow.'"

"Toilets use about seven gallons per flush. That's a lot of water," said Richard. "You boys should be able to save on flushes. This is another time I'm glad you're boys, not girls."

"Yeah, we don't even need a toilet," said Matt. And they all laughed.

Dave left for college in the fall, but the drought remained. Fortunately, Richard and Mike prepared themselves for the long haul by setting up drip irrigation systems and hydroponics using recycled water. The drought continued through the following year, making it the most significant drought since the early thirties. When it gave way at the end of 1977, a period of normalcy followed.

"Since the drought is behind us," Richard said, "we can start to expand our business. I want to bring in new cultivars, especially lilies, which are so popular with florists and hotels."

"Sam said we should proceed cautiously. Otherwise, we could be caught blind-sided by another surprise dry spell."

"I've been studying the Farmers' Almanac. These droughts run in cycles. Besides, what we had was nothing compared to those that California has endured in its past. Some lasted as long as ten, even twenty years."

"How do they know that?

"They can tell by studying tree rings, sediment, and other aspects of the natural world. Everything leaves a trail for others to follow and learn from."

Flowers were in full bloom again. Even the tulip seeds had matured—plants bearing flowers with curved petals topped with fringe. They appeared to be the parrot variety, some in bright orange, others near black, all enchanting. Richard was especially pleased with the tulip crop. His trip to Amsterdam had been more than worth it. "We'll cut these and get them to market. Florists will go wild when they see the parrots." And he was right. Florists started asking for more and putting in orders for next year.

Mike hired farmhands to help him right through the fall. First, they helped cut and pack carnations and tulips during the spring. Then they cut and packed chrysanthemums and statice. The statice crop was double last year's, promising to bring in a hefty profit. "Matt and Drew, you need to take responsibility for getting these to market again," said Richard. "And Dave is coming home to help for a few days. We need everyone to pitch in to make it work."

Mike turned his attention to helping the farmhands cut and package the flowers. He noticed the Mexicans had a gift for working with plants. They could work quickly but were also gentle, even tender with the flowers, treating them like fragile, adored babies. They must have developed their hands in the home, handling so many babies who needed to be cuddled and soothed where only the gentlest touch would do. He had a lot of respect for the work they did.

A week later, Richard announced the profits to the boys at dinner. "With doubling our production of statice and by adding tulips, we more than doubled our profits this year. We need to continue expanding into new varieties as well as adding new acreage, maybe another greenhouse. In a few years, we could be one of the dominant players in Monterey Bay."

A source of pride welled up in Mike. Deep down, he knew his work had paid off—that he was the one responsible for the business's success. What is farming without farmers—nothing.

CHAPTER TWENTY-ONE

Cesar Chavez called again for lettuce strikes. This worried both Richard and Mike because they knew their farmhands would be busy manning strike lines to discourage scabs. "What are we going to do when it's time for harvest?" Mike asked.

"That's still months away, but I will figure something out. If need be, I'll go beg from Hector." But that would only be a last resort.

When the spring harvest arrived, the lettuce strikes were still on. Richard confided his concerns to Marta, who was always a good listener. But this time, she had a solution. "I think I have some relatives who could help."

The next day, more than a dozen workers showed up at the field—women who were happy to get away from household chores and make some money while they spent time outside. Mike noticed how eager they were to please and how gifted they were, too, with handling plants. *It's got to be the baby training.*

The harvest was going well, and it was time to get the flowers to market. Dave was supposed to be home to help Matt and Drew, but he didn't show up. "Where the hell is he?" said Richard. "He knows how important this is."

He had his answer a few hours later. Dave was in the Salinas jail. He had been standing in solidarity with the farmworkers and was arrested when a scuffle broke out with the growers' men. "Damn it," said Richard. "Those Jesuits have gotten to him."

Richard hopped in his car and drove over to Salinas as fast as he could, ignoring speed limits and stop signs. Bail had been set at one thousand dollars, and he found a bondsman to arrange it. On the way home, he said, "Dave, what were you thinking?"

"I'm on the farmworkers' side."

Richard frowned. "And why is that?"

"A group of us drove up to Mass at Our Lady of Guadalupe Church and heard Father McDonnell speak about Cesar Chavez and the cause of the farmworkers. It's important for Catholics to support social justice. That's why I came."

"You ended up in jail with an arrest record. Was it worth it?"

"I think so. It wasn't only Father McDonnell's words that moved me. I was moved first by my contact with the farm-workers at the ranch—their dedication, their hard work, all for so little pay that their families barely get by."

"If only the Bracero program still existed. That's when this all worked."

Dave was confused by his father's response. "What do you mean?"

"California used to bring Mexican men up to harvest the crops. Then they would take the pay back to their families in Mexico, where it was worth more. But now that their families are here, they can't survive on what they make."

"That's why they need to make more." To Dave, the solution seemed so simple.

"Profits. It's a question of profits. The more the workers make, the less the growers make."

"The growers are greedy." And Richard let him have the last word.

. . .

The next couple of years gave the Bankstons a clear shot at expanding the business—no strikes and no weather to fight. They were fast becoming known for their ornamental flowers, which only a few growers had in their repertoire. "The ranch is finally paying for itself," said Richard. "In a few years, we'll be among the wealthiest growers in the valley if my calculations are correct, and I would stake my reputation on it."

Mike was pleased that his father had it all figured out. But his gut told him it wasn't going to be so easy.

In 1982, a strong El Niño struck California, bringing snowstorms and heavy rain, causing landslides and rockslides—eighteen thousand were recorded in the San Francisco area alone. The flower farm, while on a plateau, extended down a slope. Mike and Richard worried the rains would start a landslide on the section planted with statice. "We have to build a retaining wall," Richard said.

"Can we get one done in time?" Mike asked.

"I don't know, but we have to try. We need to call the farmhands back to work. I'll draw up plans for a wall and round up the materials for it. We can't waste any time because the rains are already bombarding us. Tomorrow, make sure the workers are here."

The rain had let up, which gave the workers a chance to dig the trench and line it with crushed stone. They covered the stone with stone dust to fill in the gaps, creating a firm foundation. While the rain continued to hold off, the workers took the bricks, tongue and grooved, inspected them, and clumsily tried to fit them together. Richard, who had been overseeing the work, noticed their hesitation. "Here, let me show you how to work with these bricks," he said as he placed a brick with a groove down and fit the one with the tongue into it. "They make a snug, solid fit. The tongue and groove system has been used for centuries, going back to the Chinese in ancient times." Once

Mike and the workers understood how the bricks worked, they created a three-foot-high wall in no time. Richard inspected it, letting out, "Bravo Zulu," to confused looks. But Mike knew what he meant and felt like his father had just given him a big pat on the back.

When the torrential rains returned a few hours later, the retaining wall proved its worth, holding the soil in place that contained the seedlings for the next statice crop. The new concern was that the soil would not absorb the water fast enough, and water would pool, causing the plant roots to rot. Mike and Richard covered the hillside with a tarp to prevent that from happening and then watched as they waited for El Niño to pass.

"I don't know what's worse," said Mike, "a drought or all these rains coming down bucketful after bucketful."

"They're both extreme weather conditions that take their toll on the land. The only good to come of all this is that my company will have projects that will carry it for years. That means job security for me."

Mike drove down the road to check on the sharecroppers. Their fields were flat, so they didn't have to worry about a landslide. Instead, they had to worry about water saturating the soil. It appeared they had been through something similar before because they had their fields covered and had dug trenches to allow the water to flow away.

Mike continued on to check on Sam. He found him in the greenhouse in a fit of anxiety. "These Chinese-made greenhouses turn to crap in a storm. Look at that hole in the ceiling. Pretty soon, the whole thing is going to open up."

"What can I do to help?" He didn't want Sam to risk the flower crop he had tended to so carefully.

"Come up with an idea to save the greenhouse. I could lose everything if we don't do something quick."

"Can I use your phone? I'll ask my father to come and figure something out."

By the time Richard arrived, the hole had doubled in size. He took one look at the situation and knew what to do. "That hole is going to be impossible to fix with the storm raging. Besides, we have no easy way to get up there. We have to create a false ceiling using tarps or large sheets of plastic."

"How are you going to keep tarps from leaking?" Sam asked.

"We'll use duct tape to attach them."

"What's that?"

"It's a kind of miracle adhesive, so strong that nothing can break it."

"Yeah," Mike said, "at the ranch, we use it for everything from patching a hole in a sack to taping a rear-view mirror onto the truck."

"I didn't know about this duct tape before. Sounds like good stuff."

"Once you try it, you'll never be without," said Mike.

"Okay, let's get to work," said Richard. "Do you have any tarps, Sam? Mike, get the duct tape out of my car."

First, they taped tarps to the sides of the greenhouse, then taped them together, using poles to hold them up. When they were done, they checked their work. "We need the center to be higher to allow the water to run off," Richard said as he began placing tall poles along the middle. "Next, let's open up some places along the side for the rain to drain off."

Finally, the false ceiling was completed, and they stood back to watch for leaks. "I don't see any leaks," said Sam. "I hope this cheap greenhouse holds up until I can get a new one."

"I'm guessing our Mickey Mouse solution will work until then," said Richard.

"What?" said Sam. "I don't understand you."

"It's a slang term for a solution that is very simple and uses common materials that are at hand. Third-worlders do it all the time. They're some of the best engineers around, although they lack professional training. As the saying goes, necessity is the mother of invention."

"So true and well-spoken. Today, I am glad a little mouse came to my rescue. But just in case he had only one rescue in him, could you give me the name and phone number of the greenhouse people in New Zealand?"

After El Niño passed, a period of calm followed. The Bankstons' flower business continued to grow with new varieties that were better than any others around. Richard made sure he got pictures to take to the California Flower Growers Association. They had already used one of his pictures of purple statice on a brochure. That credit alone was worth its weight in gold, as so many in the floral industry saw it, putting their name on the map. Orders for their flowers were coming in from all four corners of the country and in between, so much so that they almost couldn't keep up with demand. But Mike was a dedicated farmer, while Matt, Drew, and Dave also pitched in when needed, although they preferred desk jobs running the business rather than raising the flowers.

CHAPTER TWENTY-TWO

Richard was enjoying a cocktail on his patio when the phone rang. He headed to the kitchen to pick it up, expecting one of his sons to be on the line. Instead, it was a representative of a Hollywood producer. "This is Tina Malone. I'm a production assistant on a movie being made this year."

A million thoughts began running through Richard's mind. But he said nothing, just listened.

"The reason I'm calling is that we need a shot of a field of purple flowers, and the California Flower Growers Association recommended you."

Richard took a deep breath to recover his calm. "I'm flattered they recommended us."

"Do you have a field of purple flowers?" she asked.

"We will by the end of August, early September."

"How much acreage do the flowers cover? We need a wide panoramic shot of them."

"There's enough."

"We'd like to scout out the site. You will be compensated for your time, and if we use your flower field, you will be well paid."

Richard wondered what the payment would be, but he hesitated to ask. "When do you want to come to scout out the location?"

"How's next week?"

"Friday would work for me."

"We'd like to come early, say before sunrise, so we can observe the field in all the various lights to determine which one would work best. That means we will be there most of the day."

"Fine by me."

When the call ended, Richard stood still as if in shock. He never expected this in his wildest imagination. Now, his mind was spinning. This could be another lucrative side business—the ranch as an on-site location for movies. He went back to the patio, collapsed in his chair, and slugged the rest of his cocktail as he waited for the boys to come in for dinner.

Marta brought out platters of flank steak, garlic roasted potatoes, corn on the cob, and green beans. Richard said, "Dig in, and then I have a question to ask you." The boys passed the platters, taking large helpings before passing them on. Marta was good at gauging how much they would eat, ensuring there was always plenty to go around. After Richard served himself, he said, "Now for the question. Guess who called today?"

The boys shrugged their shoulders, gave vacant looks, and showed through body language that they had no idea.

"All right. Since you don't want to guess, I'll tell you. A Hollywood producer's assistant."

That got the boys' attention. Dave said, "What did he want?"

After taking a moment to swallow a mouthful of potatoes, Richard said, "She wants to come out and look at our field of statice."

"What for?" asked Mike. He was a little suspicious, thinking some of their competitors might be trying to snoop around.

"They may want to photograph it for their movie. They approached the California Flower Growers Association and asked who had the best field of purple flowers in the state, and they referred them to us."

"That's unbelievable," said Dave. "Your pictures must have had something to do with it."

"More likely, it's the feedback they've gotten from all the florists and even other flower growers."

That comment made Mike feel better. "When are they coming out?"

"They'll be here next Friday. And I want everything ship shape. They plan to spend most of the day, starting at daybreak." A couple of boys groaned when they heard that.

"Why so early?" Drew asked.

"They want to view the field in all the different lights to determine what effect will be best."

"But the light will be different before they can shoot since the flowers won't be in bloom for weeks," Dave said.

"They understand how to adjust—they're experts. Anyway, we're getting in the movie business." He left it at that since he was not yet ready to share more of his plans to go Hollywood.

After dinner, Richard headed straight to his study to make a call. "Steve, it's Richard."

"It's been a while. I've missed you, buddy."

"You know how it is. Work, farming, family life—there's no time left for anything else."

"At least when you were on the P&Z, we saw each other regularly. You should think about getting involved again. With all this terrible weather, we need your expertise with land issues."

"We can talk about that later. But right now, I need some legal advice."

"I hope you and your boys aren't in any trouble with the law."

"No, it's nothing like that. I want you to keep what I tell you under your hat."

"Okay. Shoot."

"Today, I got a call from a Hollywood producer's assistant."

"What in the world? I'm sorry I interrupted. Go on."

Richard explained the situation. "I need contract advice."

"I'll make a couple of calls. Some guys I'm acquainted with practice entertainment law. It should be easy to get answers quickly."

"Thanks. I'd appreciate it." And he paused a moment. "How would you and Sue like to join me for dinner at the Naval Postgraduate School on Friday evening?"

"I'll check with Sue, but I'm sure we'd like to. Will you be bringing a date? Sue will ask me."

"Yeah. I have a couple of gals I see. One of them should be available."

"Then I'll ask Sue tonight and call you back tomorrow."

Richard arrived solo for his dinner with the Hillmans. Upon entering The Trident, he spotted the pair at the bar, engaged in conversation, sharing a laugh, hands touching. Even after all these years, several past their silver anniversary, Steve and Sue seemed in love. Steve didn't look much different than he had in college—same wire-rimmed glasses, same slim build, same brown hair worn in a bowl cut, although he had a few gray hairs around his temple, which only made him appear more dignified. And Sue had maintained her looks and figure, ever the California girl with a tan, toned body, and shoulder-length blonde hair. He wondered how couples like them did it. Was it just luck or a lot of work besides? He did not have the luck Steve had.

"Well, hello, you two," Richard said as he sidled up to the bar. Steve and Sue turned to greet Richard. Noticing he was alone, Steve said, "Where's your date?"

"Babysitter problems." The bartender interrupted to take Richard's order. "Give me whatever he's drinking."

"Our house beer coming right up."

"Do you want to move to a table?" Richard asked.

"Yes, let's," said Sue. As they were about to sit down, they looked around and noticed Ben and Sylvia enter the room. Steve signaled them to come over.

"Long time, no see," Ben said. "I've missed you guys."

"In that case, please join us so we can catch up," said Richard. "Are you expecting anyone else?"

"No. We're alone tonight."

"Then, we'll make a party of it," Richard said.

As soon as Ben and Sylvia got seated, the bartender took their order. He returned with the drinks in no time.

"Here's to us," Ben said. And they all raised their glasses in a toast.

"What's going on with you guys?" Ben asked.

"Richard has some news," said Steve. "Do you want to share it?"

Then Richard told Ben and Sylvia all about the potential movie opportunity while they hung on every word.

The merry group moved into the dining room, and Richard ordered a bottle of champagne. "Let's get this party off to the right start." While they were waiting, Steve asked if there were any specials tonight.

"It's Friday night," Ben said. "That means the navy flies in king crab legs."

"Do you mean they go all the way to Alaska for them?" Sue asked.

"That's right," said Richard. "The navy takes care of its own."

The waiter popped the cork and poured the bubbly into each flute before setting the champagne bottle in an ice bucket, tableside. "Cheers," said Richard, and they all clinked glasses before taking a sip.

"All this drinking has built up my appetite," Ben said. "Let's head to the buffet." They returned with plates full, king crab legs extending over the sides.

"Ben and I come over for the crab at least once a month," said Sylvia. "It's such a treat."

"I don't believe I've ever had it before, but I'm guessing you eat it like lobster," Sue said.

"That's right," said Richard. "You need to crack the shell to get the meat out. A little effort but worth it." He demonstrated the technique.

"How's the flower business?" Ben asked. "You had quite a spell with the weather." While awaiting an answer, Ben dug out some crab, dipped it in butter, and chased it down with a slug of champagne.

"We've had our challenges," Richard said. "But we've stayed ahead of the eight ball and survived. In between, we've been able to grow."

There was a lull in the conversation while everyone concentrated on extracting the crab from their legs, protected by hard, thorny shells. Ben broke the silence. "I'm sure Steve mentioned we could use your expertise on the P&Z again. With all the various weather conditions, we need to review our land-use policies. Now that you're a farmer, you have even more knowledge."

Richard put down his fork, focusing his gaze first on Steve, then Ben. "As I told Steve, I'm up to my eyeballs with obligations. But maybe one day I'll be back. What about you? You've finished serving as mayor."

"I'm at a point where I need to sit back and mentor."

Richard nodded, showing he understood. "Kind of like an elder statesman."

"Something like that. Heck, I'm past seventy. It's time to let the young Turks take a turn." Ben gave a half-hearted smile, thinking he'd prefer to be at the forefront again.

The band began setting up. When they were ready, the singer came out, looking very glamorous, dressed in black lace and pearls. Steve gave Ben a nudge, and he looked up. Loudly clearing his throat, Ben said, "Richard, you better turn around..." At that moment, the singer began singing *Fly Me to the Moon...* and Richard knew who it was without even looking.

"What is she doing here?" But he was thinking that this is my territory—you have no right to intrude.

Of course, Gina had no trouble spotting Richard in the room. When her first set was over, she walked up to his table and asked if she could sit down. "I didn't realize you were singing with a band," Richard said.

"For the last few years, I've been trying to get a career going. This band feels right."

After chatting politely, the band returned, and Gina left to sing another song. When she was finished, she came up to Richard and said, "Come dance with me."

The band began to play a cha-cha, which used to be one of their favorite dances. Why not? A cha-cha doesn't require close contact. It was as if they had never been apart. They moved around the dance floor, anticipating each other's every move. Some things never change. Gina, a woman still in her prime, had all eyes on her. The other couples had left the dance floor to watch as if they were the show. When the music stopped, Gina grabbed Richard's hand to keep him on the dance floor and signaled the band. They struck up a tango, and Richard had no choice but to go along with it. He pulled Gina in close, put his face next to hers, and led her in the dance, dipping and twirling as the music moved them. Richard felt himself becoming aroused with Gina in his arms. There had always been something about her that did it for him. But he thought that was long past. He was surprised she could still bring out his passion. When the dance was over, he sought the refuge of his table where he would be safe.

"You can still cut a rug," said Steve.

"It's something you never forget."

"Well, ladies," Ben said, "who's next?"

"I'd like to take a turn around the dance floor," said Sylvia. "Ben's put up his dancing shoes."

Richard stood up, extending his hand. "Allow me to do the honors. I'm all warmed up." In more ways than one.

After the band finished its last set, Gina returned to Richard's table and sat down. "Can anyone offer me a lift home?"

"How did you get here in the first place?" Richard said.

"I drove with one of the band members. He decided to stay in Monterey tonight to visit a girlfriend."

"You're right across the street from us," said Sylvia. "It wouldn't be out of our way to give you a ride."

Gina ignored Sylvia's response. "Richard, you seem to be by yourself. Would you be willing to drive me home?"

Richard felt put on the spot. He didn't want to be alone in a car or anywhere else with Gina. But how was he going to get out of it without looking like a jerk?

Gina recognized his hesitation. She added, "The reason I asked you is I'd like to talk about the boys. We haven't done that in so long, but I think it's about time."

She knows how to maneuver. "Of course, I'd be happy to give you a ride." Richard looked across the table at Steve, who seemed to be reading his mind. Steve knew his entire story with Gina and was afraid Richard might be falling into a trap.

Once in the car, Gina started talking about Matt. "I'm still worried about him. I don't think he's fully functioning since the accident. He comes horseback riding with me, which I think is helping. But he needs something more. Just what, I haven't a clue."

Before he responded, Richard pulled out of the lot onto the road. "I've noticed the same thing. The question remains, is it permanent brain damage, or does the brain just need more time to heal?"

"I think he needs to see a specialist." Gina reached for her cigarette pack, then had second thoughts.

"There's no way to force him. He's an adult and can do what he wants."

"We need to convince him—that's all. And another thing, both he and Mike are almost thirty, with Dave right behind them. What's going on in their love lives?"

Richard wished he could have driven home in silence. But he continued to answer Gina's questions. "Dave has a girlfriend in Monterey who he sees pretty often. Drew has become a real ladies' man and plays the field. Mike farms from dawn to dusk and doesn't find much time for anything else. And it's going to take a special girl to take on Matt's case."

"I know they're helping you build a business and all, but I worry they won't have a family to call their own when it's all over. All those years we were married, we had such a wonderful family life. I don't want them to miss out on that joy."

"Unfortunately, they were young and probably don't remember those years very well. Have you forgotten we've been divorced for over fifteen years?"

"Has it really been that long? I still remember when you first brought me to California, showing off your old stomping grounds in San Francisco before settling me in Watsonville. We had some great times back then, didn't we?"

"The early years were great. But then things began to fall apart." He hoped that would put an end to this conversation.

"It's all my fault. But I couldn't help myself. I started drinking so early in life that it became a habit—one that got worse and worse. But I'm sober now and have been for years."

"That's good. I'm glad to hear it."

Richard pulled up in front of his old house and kept the engine running, hoping Gina would get out and say goodbye. But instead, she invited him in.

"I need to be getting home. A lot is going on at the ranch, and I have to get an early start tomorrow."

"Oh, yeah, like what?"

"Like the ranch might be used for a movie."

Gina looked at him, begging to hear more.

"It's true. A production crew was there today, scouting the property. We'll know soon if they want to use it."

"It seems I have no choice but to let you go. Make me a promise."

"What's that?"

"Let me know when they plan to film. I'd like to come out and watch. I always wanted to be in the movies. This may be the closest I get."

"Don't worry. You'll be among the first. Good night."

As Gina stepped out of the car, she turned her head and said, "By the way, you can still move a girl around a dance floor. I had forgotten what it's like to be in the arms of a master."

Richard just rolled his eyes. He wanted to say, don't waste your charm on me, but he bit his lip instead.

Gina had been counting the days until the film crew would be at the ranch, and when the time arrived, she got an early start and brought Margery along.

Gina drove up to the ranch house. "I'll run in and tell Richard we're here," she said.

She knocked and turned the handle to let herself in. No one was anywhere in sight. She walked down the hall toward the master bedroom, where Richard suddenly appeared. Before she had a chance to make herself known, Marta followed him out of the bedroom, dressed only in a flimsy nightgown.

Marta gave a start. "Oh, Miss Gina, I didn't know you were here."

I bet you didn't, Gina thought. "What's going on here?"

Richard kept walking toward the kitchen.

Marta said, "Mr. Richard and I have no spouses. Sometimes, we comfort each other."

"Is that so?" said Gina. She made an abrupt turn to exit. As she passed the kitchen, she said, "Margery and I will wait outside."

"I'll be right out," he said with a grin of manly pride.

Once she was out the door, Gina paused to take a deep breath to calm herself. She didn't want Margery to suspect anything was wrong.

In a few minutes, Richard appeared, taking slow strides as if he didn't have a care in the world. He stopped at Gina's car, motioned for her to roll down the window, and told the women to follow him. "The film crew is already here and setting up. It might be over in an hour, or shooting could take most of the week. Let's hurry...we don't want to miss anything."

Gina followed Richard's Jeep, but it was clear her BMW wasn't made for this rough terrain. That old station wagon she drove years ago would have had no problem. But somehow, they made it since the earth was hard-packed. Gina spotted Mike right away, assisting the crew. Matt, Dave, and Drew were right alongside trying to help. Gina parked where Richard directed, and she and Margery got out of the car.

Richard came up to them, motioning with his arms. "Let's stand back until everything is in place. Otherwise, we'll be in the way."

Gina and Margery followed instructions and just observed. Most of the people working on the movie appeared to be production people—cameramen, producers, technical assistants —along with a wide assortment of gofers. There didn't appear to be any actors around. But a black woman standing off to the side sparked Gina's curiosity because she didn't seem to have any role with the crew. "Who's that?" Gina said to Richard.

"I don't know, but Mike should. We can ask him when he comes by."

But before Mike greeted them, he went over to speak with the woman. They seemed to be engrossed in a deep conversation, which surprised both Gina and Richard. They had never seen him so talkative and wondered what they were discussing. Finally, Mike made his way over to them.

"Who is that woman you were talking to?" Gina asked.

Mike gave her name. "She's the author of the book the movie is based on."

"As many novels as I've read, I've never heard of her," Gina said. "What's the title of her book?"

"It's called *The Color Purple*."

"That explains why they want to photograph your field of purple flowers," said Margery.

"What were you two talking about?" asked Gina.

"Her book."

"What did she say?"

"She said her book is about God."

"God?" Gina said. "No wonder I've never heard of her book —it mustn't have been a bestseller."

"But what's purple got to do with it?" Margery asked.

"She said purple is always found in nature. It represents all the good things that God has created for us to enjoy. Besides, it's the color of spiritual fulfillment. It contains the key point she wanted to make in her book."

The boys joined Richard, Gina, and Margery as they watched the moviemaking. The crew began filming at dawn when the field of statice appeared black. As the sun rose and spread its light, the blossoms revealed more and more color until the sun reached its zenith, the flowers exploding into the most brilliant shade of purple any of them had ever seen.

"It was amazing to witness how light changes things and brought out that spectacular shade of purple," Margery said. "No wonder the Bible says to let our light shine."

"I think that was what this whole shot was about," said Mike.

Richard added, "It reminds me of a Mori saying a navy buddy once used—face the light and the shadows fall behind."

"That's beautiful," said Gina. "If only we could do that— focus on the good and cast a blind eye to the bad."

"It's our minds that won't let us do that," said Mike. "That's why it's so important to meditate and calm them. Our thoughts can be our worst enemies."

"Or even our best friends if we think good ones," said Margery. "It's human nature to dwell on the negative, not to appreciate all the good things we have in life."

While they were engaged in conversation, they had not

noticed that the crew stopped filming until someone yelled, "It's a wrap."

"What," Gina said, "are they already done?"

"It appears so," said Richard. "Boys, help them pack up."

"Aren't they even going to stay for lunch?" Gina asked.

"I doubt it. The director said he wanted to get down to Carmel after this. That's the only reason he's here. He plans to spend a night or two at Clint's place," said Richard.

"Wouldn't that be nice?" Margery said. "I suppose they'll have dinner at the Hog's Breath Inn tonight."

"Clint hangs out there often from what I hear," said Gina.

"That's right. But, of course, he owns the place."

"Let's go over and say goodbye so we can press the flesh of a famous Hollywood director."

They all stood together on the plateau and watched as the movie crew pulled out, leaving the ranch behind. The director, dressed in a leather-brimmed hat and khaki jacket, appeared to be channeling Indiana Jones as he drove away in his Jeep.

"That was quite an experience. Let's hope the footage doesn't end up on the cutting room floor," Richard said. "Now, would you care to join me for lunch?"

Before anyone could answer, Gina said, "No, thank you. Margery and I have to get going."

Margery frowned. She was hungry and didn't have to be anywhere soon. But she followed Gina to the car. "I don't understand," she said. "We skipped breakfast, and now you want to pass up lunch."

"We're not passing up lunch," Gina said, "just moving on."

"What? Spell it out."

"How does the Hog's Breath Inn sound to you? My treat."

Mike was inspired to grow cosmos after watching *The Color Purple*. He mentioned his idea to his father, who said he would do some research. Meantime, Mike sought out Sam.

"Cosmos," said Sam, "I don't grow them, but they can do well here. They are both drought and pest-resistant. But you have to guard them from the wind."

"Do florists like them?" asked Mike.

"They are very popular in wedding bouquets because they symbolize love."

"You've sold me on trying to grow them."

When he returned to the ranch, Mike ran into Marta near the house. "I hear you might grow Cosmos," she said.

"Do you know that flower?"

"Oh, yes. It grows all over Mexico. I believe my country was the first to have them fill our meadows. Cosmos means beautiful, and we give them to the ones we love."

"I like everything I've learned about cosmos. Sam said they would do well here. I'm going to grow them in honor of you and your people, Marta, to show my love."

"Mike, you are such a nice boy. The beautiful flowers will be in so much demand they will make you rich."

"I'm going to send away for some seed catalogs to find the ones I want to grow."

"They come in many colors—pink, orange, red, yellow, and even white."

"I would like a dark pink to complement the purple statice."

"Yellow would be a good choice, too. It is purple's opposite on the color wheel, which would make them very striking. In addition, they would look like little sunflowers. I love sunflowers."

"Thanks for the advice. I have time to decide on the color."

"It might be a good idea to talk to a florist. They know what sells best."

In the spring, Mike planted cosmos seeds on the land he had cleared over the winter. Richard had learned that cosmos need to be protected from wind, and he was concerned that this would be a factor because of the field's location. He drew up plans for a windbreak they could construct. The windbreak was in place by the time the seeds sprouted, protecting the delicate new stems emerging from the soil. The plants grew gracefully, and by the end of summer, their blooms full of pink petals filled the field next to the statice. Breezes blew through the crop, creating currents that moved the plants in a slow dance but didn't blow hard enough to pull the roots out of the soil or the petals off the flowers. At harvest time, words of love flashed through Mike's mind. These flowers remind me of love—what's important. Corinthians 13 came to mind—his mother's favorite Bible verse—but the only words he could recall were "love never fails."

The flower farm continued to grow as they added new varieties to their mix, many of which were not being grown anywhere in the area. Sam told Mike, "You are the talk of the Monterey Bay Flower Growers. Everyone wonders how you can grow all these varieties." That made Mike proud. He knew there was both a science and an art to flower growing. It was possible to have quality soil, an abundance of nutrients, and everything else flowers needed, but without the connection to each individual plant, he would not have as much success. The spiritual component was the key. Love made the difference.

CHAPTER 23

In 1987, another drought hit California. But this time, they were prepared for it. Richard had constructed a system for collecting rainwater and recycling water. The ranch, like others nearby, was independent. It didn't need to rely on government help, which often was no help at all.

But despite the water system, rain was important. At dinnertime, Richard and the boys would listen for it. When the leaves from the oak rustled, they'd run out to look, only to find the wind had picked up. The land was becoming parched, and even the mighty oaks with their deep tap roots were showing the strain, leaves turning brown. They were glad a large part of their farm was planted with drought-resistant flowers. And the greenhouse was under their control.

"I never expected farming to be such a challenge," said Mike.

"It always has been," said Richard. "Weather, pests, labor—they always figure into the mix, no matter where you farm. If you listen to the old-timers, you'll hear them talk about the cycles they've been through. Then there's always the Farmer's Almanac, which is good at forecasting, too. What we need to do is 'make hay while the sun shines,' which will enable us to weather the next storm."

"We make a great team," Mike said. "I farm, and you problem-solve."

"That's right," Richard said. "And with Matt, Dave, and Drew in the mix, we're building a family business for generations to come."

On the afternoon of October 17, 1989, Mike was finishing a few chores in the greenhouse. It was the time when all the flower harvests had passed, and he was preparing for the next planting season, which would still be months away. Mike had looked at his watch moments before. Later, he could recall the exact time it started, 5:10 p.m. He felt the earth tremble and at first thought a large vehicle must be driving up the bumpy dirt road. But the trembling continued and escalated. That's when he realized it was an earthquake.

He crawled under one of the large trestle tables to wait out the motion. It seemed an eternity. Instead of leveling off, the shaking gained momentum, almost like a wave in an ocean that would build energy for the finale. When the quake crested, letting go of its fury in a mighty fit of vengeance, it registered 7.1 on the Richter scale, a massive show of the earth's power. Mike had experienced small tremblers but never anything that came close to this. Perhaps, because he was lying on the ground, he felt the quake's intensity even more than most, leaving no doubt this had been the Big One for the notorious San Andreas fault. After the shaking stopped, Mike stayed in place, gathering his wits while waiting for an aftershock. A few minutes later, he decided it was safe to come out from under his shelter, only to discover the greenhouse had collapsed and he needed help to protect it from further damage.

He hurried to the house, hoping to find his father at home. Opening the door, he yelled, "Dad, Dad, where are you?"

There was no immediate response until a faint voice said, "I'm in here."

Mike found his father seated in his favorite easy chair with his eyes fixed on the television's black screen.

"What are you doing?" asked Mike. "Don't you realize we just had a big earthquake?"

"I was watching the baseball game. Then the screen went blank."

"Who cares about the game? I need your help. The greenhouse collapsed."

"Dave and Drew. I need to find out about Dave and Drew."

"I'm sure they're fine," said Mike. "They could be heading up to the house right now."

"They were at the game."

Mike felt a shiver go through him. "What are you talking about?"

"Yesterday...someone gave Dave tickets to the World Series."

Mike's face turned sober at that news while a million scenarios ran through his mind—none of them good. He pulled himself together for his father's sake and said, "They'll be fine."

"Not if the stadium collapsed. Do you know how many times that has happened around the world?"

"But this is America. We build things to last. Of all people, you understand that."

"I hope the reinforced concrete held out," Richard said. "That would make all the difference."

Words failed Mike. He just stood there in silence.

At last, Richard rose from the chair. "I need to make some calls."

The first person Richard called was Gina. "How are you?" he asked.

"I'm fine, but the chimney fell down—Margery's, too. Are the boys all right?"

"Mike's fine. He's here with me. Marta left early to go to a doctor's appointment."

"And what about Matt, Dave, and Drew?"

"That's why I'm calling." He heard her gasp. "Dave and Drew were at Candlestick for the game."

"Candlestick…Oh, Richard, they might be trapped in the stadium. And with all the hazards, they might not find a way home."

"Try not to worry. They aren't babies anymore. Together, they should be able to get back safely." But he wasn't so sure.

"Is there any news about the stadium or the roads?" Gina said, on the verge of hysterics.

"Not yet. But if I hear anything, I'll call. Just sit tight."

After they hung up, Gina said to herself, "Sit tight? I'm heading to the ranch." She didn't want to wait alone.

Before Richard could make another call, his phone rang. It was Steve, who seemed to be in a state of panic. "Richard," he said, "I need you here. Things are bad in town. A lot of homes have been damaged. Many won't be habitable until they're fixed. Downtown's a mess. Ford's department store is in a shambles, along with some of the historic buildings. One woman ran out of the bakery during the quake and was killed by a flying brick."

"Any other casualties?"

"Not that we know of, but we must set up some tent cities for people to live in for a while."

"What about the Red Cross and the Salvation Army?"

"They've been contacted, but it may take some time for them to get here. Until then, we're on our own."

"Okay. I'll be there as soon as I can. We've had some damage that requires my attention first."

Richard returned to the living room, where he found Mike glued to the TV. The news was reporting, and because the Goodyear Blimp had been in place for the game, it was now turning out earthquake footage.

"Dad, they said both the Bay Bridge and Nimitz Freeway were damaged."

"Anything about Candlestick?"

"They showed people leaving. That must mean the stadium survived."

"Let's hope. Thank God the boys don't need to take the Bay Bridge or Nimitz home. Maybe their path will be clear. Let's examine the greenhouse. Then I'll head for town where there's been a lot of destruction."

Richard and Mike jumped into the Jeep and headed toward the fields. Even at a distance, Richard suspected the greenhouse was a total loss. "Let's take a closer look," he said.

After surveying the area, Richard noted, "The structural pieces gave way and punctured holes in the greenhouse walls. We can't let it stay like this because the wind will tear what's left to shreds."

"What should we do?"

"Somehow, we need to secure it. Let me think a minute. While I'm thinking, walk around and inspect for other damage."

Mike reported that the retaining wall had given way, and some of the soil and plants were sliding down the hill.

"That can wait," said Richard. "But I've got an idea for the greenhouse. Get some twine."

Richard and Mike removed the mangled supports and secured the greenhouse fabric to whatever they could—a pole, a table—anything that offered stability.

"That should hold. Now, I have to get to town."

"Can I come with you?" Mike asked.

"You should stay here in case your brothers call and need help. And check on Matt. Who knows what happened to him?"

It was past sundown by the time Richard got underway. An eerie feeling enveloped him as he drove along the carless streets, houses dark and silent. Occasionally, he would catch the flicker of a candle flame, the one bright spot. Richard arranged to meet Steve at the town hall. When he turned onto Main Street, crews were already clearing the street of debris. From what he could make out, some buildings had collapsed, but it was too dark to tell the full extent of the damage.

The parking lot at the town hall was packed, but Richard got a spot as someone pulled out. He made a beeline to Steve's office.

"Well, look who's here," said Ben. "It's a sad day for a reunion, but I'm glad the Three Musketeers have another mission."

Richard extended his hand to shake Ben's. "You and Steve are the ones I'd want at my side during a disaster like this one."

"That's what we need to talk about," said Steve. "We have to put a plan in place for the recovery. The mayor asked Ben to head it up and include the two of us."

"I wonder where he got that idea?" said Ben.

Steve glanced at Richard and then moved on. "This is going to be a major recovery effort. From the preliminary report I received, it will take years to rebuild. But for now, we've got hundreds, if not thousands, of people in need of shelter, food, and clothing. Over a thousand homes were destroyed or damaged."

"What about the army? Have you contacted them?" said Ben. "Those generals at Fort Ord, who I play golf with, are always bragging they can get a platoon placed anywhere in the world in just a few days. Since they are less than thirty miles away, they should be here already."

"The mayor contacted the commandant, who said he's scrambling to send troops to help with the cleanup," Steve said.

"In the meantime, who do you have?" said Richard.

"Believe it or not, Hector rounded up a bunch of farm-workers who are doing a bang-up job. In fact, they're doing work no one else would do. And they're not afraid to go into crumbling buildings to check for survivors, although once the fire department got organized, it wouldn't let them in if there was too much risk."

"Good old Hector," said Richard. "He's a double-edged sword."

"Right now, he's saving our hide," Ben said.

"As they say," said Steve, "sometimes fact is stranger than fiction. But I suppose they aren't doing it for gratis."

"Next thing you know, Cesar Chavez will be marching around for higher pay and better work conditions," said Ben.

"Enough small talk. Let's sit down at the conference table and start putting a plan together. Then we can determine the action steps."

Before he did anything, Ben posted a map of Watsonville on the wall. "There. That will give us a good visual. No war room is ever official without a map."

Richard arrived home in the wee hours of the morning, beyond exhausted. The house was quiet—no sign that Dave and Drew had returned. He wanted to keep a vigil for them, but his body beckoned toward bed. It's the right thing to do. I'll be needed tomorrow and for many tomorrows to come, and I have to function. Who knows what tomorrow will bring?

He woke up to the smell of bacon frying. He wondered if Marta had returned to make sure he was cared for. She was so kind-hearted that she always thought of others first. But when he walked into the kitchen, it was Gina he found at the stove. "Good morning. You must have gotten home late. I waited up as long as I could, then I just had to get some sleep."

"Yes, it was a late night." Richard wondered what her real motives were for being here. "I met Steve and Ben to put together a recovery plan. The mayor asked Ben to head the Task Force, and then, of course, he pulled Steve and me into it."

Gina grabbed the tongs, turning the bacon. "Of course, he would do that. He knows he can depend on you. Did you get a sense of the town's damage?"

Richard paused, shaking his head. His face wore a sad, depressed expression. "Watsonville is in a shambles. Many people are without homes. In fact, some of them have put up tent shelters in Ramsey and Callahan parks. On top of everything else, sanitation is going to be a big concern."

"Margery said she volunteered to help the Red Cross with their relief efforts, which will focus on food, clothing, and shelter."

"Shelter is going to be a problem. The town was already lacking because of land availability. We can't take precious farmland for it. Regardless, it takes time to build houses and apartments."

"I remember how involved that low-income housing project you did years ago was. Do you know if it held up to the quake?"

Richard shrugged his shoulders. "We'll know after inspections today."

Gina set the table, coffee mugs first. "Take a seat and start drinking your coffee. I'll have a farm breakfast ready in a few minutes. The blueberry muffins only need a few minutes."

She plated the bacon, eggs, and home fries. When the timer rang, she pulled the muffins out of an Aga oven and placed them on a serving tray. Then she put everything on the table and sat down to eat with Richard.

"Waking up to this breakfast is a treat. Thank you. I'm going to need a full stomach to get through this day."

"Any more news about Candlestick or the roads back to Watsonville?"

Richard swallowed before answering. "Not a thing. But remember, no news is good news." Although, he wasn't sure in this case. Authorities had so much to do that notifying next of kin would receive low priority.

Gina put down her fork and let out a sigh. "I guess. Until we're informed otherwise, there's hope."

Richard and Gina sat in silence for a few minutes, alone with their thoughts. Mike broke the mood when he stumbled into the kitchen, looking groggy and unkempt. "Something smells good." His presence changed the mood.

"I'll make up a plate for you," said Gina, as she stood and turned toward the stove. "Sit down. It won't take but a minute, and grab a glass of orange juice while you're waiting."

All three were still sitting at the breakfast table when a car rumbled up the road. They lifted their heads, pricking up their ears like hunting dogs trying to make out the sound. When the engine turned off, Mike peered out the kitchen window. "It's them," he said. "Dave and Drew are back from the dead."

Gina and Richard rushed to the front door, followed by Mike. They swung it wide open and dashed to the car. The dogs ran up the road, barking as loud as they could. They were the first to reach the boys, jumping up and licking their faces.

"You made it home," said Gina, as she hugged each boy and kissed him.

Richard looked on, noting how exhausted they looked. "I never doubted you'd make it back," he lied.

Gina ushered the boys into the kitchen, where they collapsed into chairs. "You must be famished."

"We had a hot dog before all the confusion started," said Dave, "but nothing else, not even water."

"You better hydrate yourselves," said Richard. "Let's get them some water and take away the coffee—it's dehydrating."

Mike grabbed Gatorade from the cupboard. He handed each of his brothers a bottle. "Drink this. It will help your electrolytes."

"I can make you a full breakfast," said Gina. "Blueberry muffins are already on the table. Or if you prefer, I could make blueberry pancakes."

Dave and Drew looked at each other and then chimed, "Blueberry pancakes."

"You got it with bacon on the side."

Once they finished their breakfast, Gina, Richard, and Mike asked for details of their ordeal. Their story sounded like something out of the Apocalypse.

"At first," said Dave, "we didn't know we were having an

earthquake. Most people thought someone had started the Wave cheer, causing the motion."

"Yeah, but when we saw an announcer jump from his perch, we knew something was wrong. Next, someone yelled earthquake," said Drew.

"How did you get out of the stadium?" Richard asked.

"We walked," said Dave. "People were staying pretty calm."

"That can make a difference. In so many of these types of situations, people panic. I'm assuming the stadium held up to the stress."

"We didn't notice anything collapsing or breaking off," said Dave.

"What about the drive back?" said Mike.

"Roads were closed, lights were out—I don't know how we made it home," said Dave. "If we hadn't been together, we wouldn't have. What I didn't know, Drew did, and vice versa. Two heads do make better than one."

"I think that's enough talk for now," said Gina. "You two boys need to go to bed and get some sleep."

Richard looked around. "Are we missing someone?

"If you mean Matt, he's probably still in bed."

Richard and Mike drove through the ranch, checking outbuildings for structural damage and land for fissures and slides. They found the horses had kicked through their stalls and gotten into the paddock. They seemed spooked and agitated. "We need to make a list of repairs. Here's a notebook, Mike. Can you put the barn on the list? Most of the other outbuildings seem in good shape." They stopped by the flower farm to check for more damage. They found nothing new—just the greenhouse, the retaining wall, and some minor landslides. Afterward, they made their way to the sharecroppers. The Mexican farmers were out in their fields tending crops when Richard and Mike arrived. Mr. Ortega waved and then walked up to meet them.

"How did you fare during the earthquake?" Richard asked.

"Not too bad," Mr. Ortega said. "One of our living room walls got a crack, and some of our pottery fell off the shelf and broke. But other than that, we are fine."

"We're doing better out here than the town did." And Richard explained.

"That's too bad. I will pray for them."

As they were leaving, Mike glimpsed a young, attractive woman, most likely his daughter. And he vowed to return later to check on them again.

Next, Richard and Mike stopped by the Akitas' place. The Akitas, too, were working their fields when they arrived. Mrs. Akita came out of the house to greet them. "Would you like to come in for some tea?" she offered.

"No, thank you. We only want to check on your welfare. Any damage from the earthquake?"

"A very sad thing happened. The altar for our ancestors toppled over, and some urns cracked."

"That's terrible," said Mike. "What can we do to help?"

"We fixed everything. None of the ashes escaped."

"Was that the extent of the damage?"

"Everything else is minor in comparison," she said.

As Richard and Mike left the property, they noticed an enormous gaping hole in a wall of the house and other damage—a collapsed chicken coop, fences down, a side of the barn missing. "Remember," Mike said, "this is all minor in comparison."

When they arrived at town hall, Richard sent Mike in search of a crew that was heading out. Mike found one right away and ended up on Main Street alongside Hector's crew. Everyone was telling stories about what they had experienced. Mike told about his brothers' ordeal getting back from Candlestick. That was one story they hadn't heard.

Richard met Steve in his office. Ben followed close behind, hobbling on a cane. Richard hadn't noticed the cane before and then realized that time had moved on. Ben had to be near seventy-five, the age many men use canes. My time will come before long, too.

"Now that you're all here, let's get to work," said Steve.

"Who's running this Task Force anyway?" said Ben.

"You are," Steve said.

"That's right. I'll call the shots—first, an update. The Red Cross is in place, and Margery Povich is their point person. They're helping to offset the demand at the hospital, besides providing for basic needs. Lots of people are showing up with a case of nerves. But the big concern is looting."

"Looting," said Richard. "That shouldn't be a surprise since it always happens at times like these. People are desperate. They need food and other necessities."

"And let's not forget the opportunists," Ben said. "Those who intend to profit off other peoples' misery."

"We deputized a few men who can help provide security downtown and in other areas likely to be targeted," said Steve.

"Who are they?" said Ben. "Not just anyone can do that sort of work. That's why we need the damn army here."

"They're ranchers—they own guns and know how to use them. They've gotten their training defending their homes and properties against the strikers."

"Has anyone been out to the tent cities to check on those folks?" Richard asked.

"We've offered them food and shelter at sites we've set up around town. But they've refused to move from where they've planted themselves," said Steve. "I'm not sure how we're going to handle their situation. And before I forget, your two colleagues, Ken and Jack, came by earlier looking for a place to lend their talents. I put them on the crew checking buildings on Main Street."

"That should be a good role for them," said Richard.

"Any word yet from the governor on disaster aid?"

"The mayor is working on that," said Steve. "But I don't think there's any doubt we'll be declared a disaster area."

"Yeah, but the question is, how much are they going to give us to clean up and rebuild?"

"Any updates on the Catholic church?" said Richard.

"The church may have to be condemned," said Steve. "It's a shame, but there are so many other problems to deal with. We've had fires popping up. The Struve Slough Bridge Collapsed on Highway One, and there's a landslide on Highway Seventeen that closed the road. It's all overwhelming."

"While it may be overwhelming, we will overcome," said Ben. "Remember all the rebuilding after World War II. It has been done before, and it will be done again here."

A few days later, President Bush signed a 1.1-billion-dollar earthquake aid package for California. Relief was on its way.

A couple of weeks later, when the Task Force met, there was much to report. "I hate to tell you this," said Ben, "but the Red Cross has mucked things up. Clothing donations are stored sky-high in the Ag building, but they haven't figured out how to distribute them. Margery tells me they're thinking of handing out cash cards instead. But where are they going to shop? Downtown isn't available. The Pacific Coast Mall in Santa Cruz is a disaster zone, even if there is a road to take you there."

"The problem is," Steve said, "no one has seen anything like this before. They're learning on the job, and by then, it's too late."

"We can't do everything for people," said Richard. "They need to take care of themselves as much as possible. Those who do will come out of this intact."

On Sunday, Cesar Chavez led a march through town to bring attention to the peoples' needs. It was one more headache for the Task Force.

"I won't say I told you so," said Richard.

"Let him march," said Ben. "Then maybe he'll know what it's like to be a soldier. That reminds me, where is the blasted army?"

"Your guess is as good as mine," said Steve.

"Again, we have to be self-sufficient if we want to accomplish anything. There's enough talent and labor in this town to get the job done," said Richard.

Chavez marched into the tent camps and held meetings there. Since the campers didn't want to move, food and Red Cross help came to them.

Eventually, the Army showed up too—a month after the disaster struck. "When I see those generals," Ben said, "I'm going to give them hell. How they can brag about putting a platoon anywhere in the world in four days when it took them four weeks to go less than thirty miles...what were they doing, crawling on their bellies?"

Richard laughed. "Don't they say an army travels on its stomach?"

"They must have taken the saying literally," said Steve.

"Well, at least the army's here. Where are they assigned?"

"The tent camps—they're digging latrines."

"After all the time they took to get here, they deserve a dirty job. But that shouldn't take long. What's their next assignment?"

"Main Street still needs cleaning up."

"Put the army on that next. They can provide security as well."

That night, Richard returned home to find Gina in the kitchen with pots on the Aga sending out savory aromas throughout the house. He was secretly pleased he had a good home-cooked meal waiting for him.

"Dinner will be ready in a few minutes," Gina announced.

"I'll wash up."

"Please tell the boys to be ready." Then she added, "As long as you're working two jobs and are without Marta, I plan to be here providing meals." And she thought, comfort, too, on an as-needed basis, although she wasn't sure if that would be his or hers.

Richard was too tired to get into a tete a tete with her about her meal plan. The last thing he wanted was her camping out in his house. But since the earthquake, that's what many people were doing. It was the new normal, so why should he care. Gina's meals had always been outstanding. Besides, arroz con pollo had run its course.

Richard was in a new routine. He'd head to the office early and work most of the day estimating bids for projects which were coming out of the woodwork since the earthquake. In the late afternoon, he would meet with the Task Force for a couple of hours before returning home. Wednesdays, he flew up to Sacramento to put in state project bids. It also gave him a chance to meet with state officials about aid for the town. He spent weekends touring cleanup sites and inspecting buildings. It was lucky that this was a downtime for the ranch, but it would soon be time to turn his attention to the flower farm. Rebuilding the town was going to take years.

At the next Task Force meeting, Ben announced, "I have some good news and bad news. First, the bad news. Ford's Department store is going to be torn down—it's a total loss."

"Some people will be upset about that," said Steve. "They like to eat at the lunch counter where they'll run into people and pick up a bit of gossip."

"And it's doubtful they'll rebuild," said Ben. "The store manager told me business had shifted away from Main Street to suburban malls, so Ford's would have been closing its doors anyway. But it's a real shame, no matter how you look at it. Ford's, after all, was Watsonville's first business. Its loss marks the end of an era."

"When disaster strikes, it is a double-edged sword," said Richard. "But it also gives people a chance to reimagine things. Of course, the old-timers won't like it, but time moves on."

"That's right," said Steve. "At one time, the Irish and Croatians dominated the town. Now, it's the Mexicans, and they have different wants and needs."

"It's also a time to build better, like after the 1906 San Francisco earthquake. Most of the buildings that were built with the new codes withstood this earthquake. I'm glad Candlestick was built on bedrock."

"But if they had known about those winds that Willie Mays claimed robbed him of countless home runs, the park would have been sited on sandy soil a few hundred feet away," said Ben.

"You don't need to tell me about sandy soil," said Richard. "If that had been the case, the stadium would have shifted and cracked, and my two boys might not be alive."

"Let's hear the good news," said Steve. "We need to be uplifted."

"We're going to be able to save St. Patrick's Church," said Ben. "The community will be elated when they hear that."

"I can't wait to tell Gina," said Richard. "Currently, she's attending Mass in Notre Dame School's gym. During the week, the gym is used for a distribution center, and crates of canned goods are stacked around the perimeter. She knows the church is doing its best, but she misses St. Pat's. Not to mention, the acoustics in the gym are so terrible that the choir is almost afraid to sing."

At dinner, Richard told Gina the good news about St. Patrick's Church. "It can't be rebuilt soon enough for me. Last Sunday, I went to the Valley Church with Margery and Tom. That angry Irish priest, Father McElroy, is still there."

"You mean the one who breathes fire and brimstone?"

"He's way beyond that now. It's more like he's turned into a doomsday prophet, spewing negativity and nastiness."

"He's somewhat of a radical."

"That's right. When he arrived in the 60s, he stripped the church of all its statuary and adornments and hung banners in their place. And they're still there over twenty years later."

"Is Father McElroy saying anything I should be aware of?"

"He keeps talking about the plight of the people and is encouraging them to organize and make demands."

"That's all we need...by the way, where are the boys? Why aren't they eating dinner with us tonight?"

"They called and said they were staying in town with friends so they could work late and start early."

Richard's eyes widened as he took in Gina's words. "Well, I'll be. They've developed a work ethic after all."

CHAPTER 24

Gina put on her sexiest negligee and tiptoed down the hall to Richard's room. She opened the door and slipped in, making her way toward the bed where Richard was sleeping. What her next move was going to be, she wasn't sure. But somehow, she needed to get into the bed to arouse him. Gina eased herself onto the mattress while she contemplated her next move. Before she could execute, arms enfolded her and pulled her in. "I thought you would never get here."

When Richard entered the kitchen in the morning, he heard Gina humming to herself. He walked up to her and kissed her on the cheek. Gina turned around. "Is that all I get after last night?" Then she put her arms around his neck and gave him a deep, passionate kiss.

Richard had a million things on his mind as he drove to work, but thoughts of Gina kept sneaking in. Last night reminded him of old times. She was always so sensual, bringing out his primal instincts. Her body made him whole. He had always known that and tried to avoid her once they divorced. But the world changed, and fate brought them together again. The earth moved on October seventeenth, and it moved again last night. He could feel the shift in himself and knew it was pointless to resist.

Before Richard stepped into his office, his secretary stopped him to say that Jeremy Edwards wanted to meet with him right away. Richard set his briefcase down, turned around, and headed for the boss's office. Ken Tanaka and Jack Overton were there, engaged in conversation while everyone awaited Richard's arrival. "I'm sorry if I'm late."

"You're right on time," said Jeremy. "Let's get to the purpose of this meeting. It's been over a month since the earthquake. Requests for projects are coming in from all over. Somehow, we need to prioritize them. And then there's Watsonville, the town where we're headquartered. We need to give back. Since all of you have been on the ground, I'd like to get a report on the status of the cleanup and condition of the public buildings and the housing situation. Then, I'd like to get some recommendations on the best place to put our resources. Who would like to start?"

Jack and Ken looked at Richard. "I guess the ball's in my court. You know I serve on the Task Force." Then he filled Jeremy in on the state of the town. He concluded by saying, "Housing is the number one priority. For a variety of reasons, we can't have people living in tent cities for long. Unrest is certain to develop if we let things fester. And, besides, Cesar Chavez has already been here, making demands on behalf of the Mexicans living in substandard housing, and he will be back. I don't care if he believes in peaceful means—many of his followers don't, and there will be violence to contend with."

"Jack and Ken, what's your opinion?" Jeremy asked. "Do you agree with Richard?"

"Richard has a good handle on the situation," said Jack. "I agree with his recommendation on housing."

"I remember when we did the low-income housing project

years ago," said Ken. "It was very well-received by the community. It would be a sign of goodwill toward the Mexican residents of our town if we put our efforts into another housing project."

"In addition," said Jack, "it would give them hope for the future."

"And it would be a visible sign of our response to their needs," said Richard. "I hate to go all political on you, but that's the reality I've learned after years in town government. It should help satisfy Chavez so he can put his efforts elsewhere."

"I'm glad to see you're all in agreement. Housing was my preference as well, which puts us on the same page. Or another way of saying it, all great minds think alike."

The three men each gave a subtle smile, trying to appear humble. We're all smiling like the Mona Lisa, as if we know something we're not telling, Richard mused.

Mayor Bob Thomas arrived ahead of the Task Force. When Richard stepped into the room, he said, "Bob, what brings you here tonight?"

"I only want to sit in and listen, and maybe I can add something. I sort of feel like we're sitting on a powder keg waiting to go off."

"What do you mean?"

"The people are getting restless—everything's taking too long. They don't have the patience to wait much longer."

"I might have some good news for you. But I'll wait for the others to arrive."

Ben rolled in, looking beat, leaning on his cane. "I'm getting too old for this nonsense. My phone rings day and night. Sylvia and I can't catch a break."

Steve arrived last, stressed.

"Anything wrong?" Richard asked.

"I just learned that a fight broke out at Callahan Park, and they're transporting the injured to the hospital as we speak."

"What was it about?" the mayor asked.

"Some men were playing cards and had too much to drink. One called the other a cheater, and then blades were drawn. People trying to break up the fight also got injured. This is just more proof that tensions are riding high."

"Let's all sit down and discuss this calmly," said Ben.

"The men don't have enough to do," said Richard. "It'll be months before any crops are ready to be picked. They need work to keep themselves occupied."

"What do you propose?" asked the mayor.

"I'm not sure," said Richard. "I'll have to reflect more on it. They need a job that uses up their physical energy to the point of exhaustion. Then they'll be too tired to pull out their blades."

"You need to think fast," said Ben. "We need solutions now."

"Blackrock Construction has come up with one. Mr. Edwards is offering to do some pro bono work for new housing."

"That's something we can build a PR campaign around," said the mayor.

"I assumed you'd see it that way," said Richard. "It will get people to focus on something positive, and they will see progress being made."

"As you know," said Steve, "a housing project doesn't just go up overnight. There'll be a lot of planning involved."

"I don't care," said the mayor. "It gives us something to offer. We have to throw the people some sort of lifesaver. When people are grumbling, it's never a good sign."

"Let's move on," said Ben. "I see three action items we have to get on right away—tent city security, work for the men, and a PR campaign about housing."

"How do you want to divvy this up?" Steve asked.

"You take on the security issue since the town may also have some liability. Richard, you suggested a work program— that's your baby. And Mayor, you know all about campaigns and have the staff to help you. I assign you the housing project PR. This meeting is adjourned. Let's get to it and meet again tomorrow night and every night until the situation is under control."

Gina and the boys were waiting for Richard to arrive home for dinner. Richard found that this was now his favorite time of day. His house was more of a home since Gina took up residence. Not only did she cook fabulous meals, but she added little touches like a vase of fresh-cut flowers, candles, a pretty table cloth—all amenities only a woman would provide—a woman who considered the house her home. Now that the boys were grown men, Richard enjoyed bantering ideas around with them. Gina always added her opinions, mixing in her sense of humor that enlivened heady discussions and small talk. She was fun to have around.

After dinner, the boys paraded down the hall to their rooms while Richard lingered in the kitchen as Gina cleaned up. Dave said, "Have either of you noticed something different around here?"

"What do you mean?" said Matt.

"I mean Mom and Dad. Do they seem like they're getting along better?"

"It's more than just getting along," said Mike. "I spotted Mom leaving Dad's bedroom the other morning. She didn't see me, but I saw her wearing a sexy negligee."

"Then I was right," said Dave. "Something is different. But I like things better this way."

"Yeah, I hope it lasts," said Drew. "It's good Mom is around again, especially since she seems to be her old self."

"We lost a lot of years during her addiction," said Mike. "Do you remember all those happy times we used to have in the house on Buena Vista Drive?"

"The Bible says not to look back," said Dave. "The present moment is the only thing available, and, of course, the future.

But we should appreciate what we have instead of what we've lost."

"That's how I'm living my life since the surfing accident," said Matt. "I can't always remember, so I live in the moment. In a way, the accident has set me free."

Meantime, Richard and Gina continued talking into the night. Gina said, "The holidays are coming up. I'd like to throw a Christmas party here if you agree. With all the stress of the past few weeks, we need some good cheer."

"What type of party are you thinking of?"

"I'd like to invite a lot of people, so a dinner party is out. It could be a cocktail party, but again, that's not such a good idea either. Perhaps something during the day—brunch or lunch after church or a late afternoon dessert party. The view from the living room is so fabulous that it would provide a good backdrop. Everyone loves Christmas cookies, and I make some of the best ever since Margery shared her recipes."

"Think about it and decide. But a day party sounds like it might be best."

By the time they finished talking, it was late. Richard was exhausted and needed his sleep more than ever. He knew tomorrow would be a big day with the mayor's announcement and the aftermath of the camp fight. He kissed Gina goodnight and went to bed alone.

The mayor's announcement was set for noon. Richard took his lunch break and headed to the town hall to listen. Ever since he met Bob Thomas years ago, he thought he would make the ideal politician. He was a polished public speaker, congenial, and politically correct. His years as a banker had trained him well in measured speech and restraint. Even in a game of tennis, he did the politically correct thing and double-faulted so he wouldn't beat an opponent he was doing business with. Bob was in his element on the podium—the moment he had trained for all his life had finally come.

Richard grabbed a seat up front. When he heard the scuffling of dozens of feet, he turned and saw a group of Mexicans pouring into the room, packing it to its fullest capacity. Hector Lopez, along with some of his operatives from the Watsonville Organizing Committee, was there, and he appeared to be in charge of the group. Most of the people were carrying placards. *This is all we need—an angry mob demonstrating for all the world to see.* He knew the mayor had invited the media to attend, and now TV crews were arriving and setting up. *I better have a word with Hector.*

Richard made his way to the back of the room and called Hector aside, noting a ripe odor emanating from the tent crowd. "We don't want any trouble. The mayor is trying to do a good deed for your people. This is not the time to raise complaints."

"You know this housing project will take a long time. People need help now, and they feel they are being ignored."

"The mayor and the rest of us are doing our best. But after a disaster like we've had, it takes a while to address all the needs."

"Your best is not good enough. Winter is coming. If we get spring rains, the people will be at risk. We've seen it before, and we don't want our babies and old people dying because the town took its time."

Richard grimaced. "I'll tell you what, rather than make a scene here this afternoon, come to our Task Force meeting tonight with your list of grievances."

"Unless we demonstrate first, we are not taken seriously. We are just sidelined and forgotten. That's why Cesar came—to raise awareness of our situation. And he'll come again whenever necessary until problems are resolved."

Before they could finish their conversation, the mayor and his entourage streamed in, signaling the press conference was about to begin.

"I'll be at your meeting tonight," said Hector, as Richard was leaving to retake his seat. "Don't worry. We practice passive resistance." Richard shook his head. He had tried. Now the ball is in Hector's court. Richard was only too glad to get away from the stench. These people need baths.

Mayor Thomas strutted up to the podium, an American flag on his right, the California Bear Republic flag on his left, the town motto centered on the wall behind him—*Opportunity in diversity. Unity in cooperation.* The mayor began by welcoming the crowd. "I especially want to thank former Mayor Ben Crawford and Richard Bankston for being here. Along with our town attorney, Steve Hillman, they make up the Task Force I assigned to plan our recovery. And they are doing an excellent job. I also see Hector Lopez, one of our community organizers, here with a group of concerned citizens. Welcome to town hall, and thank you all for coming. Please be aware that I asked your representatives on the city council to be here today—Juan Martinez and Tony Perez. Hector, I would like to invite you and your group to meet with us after this meeting in my office. I know there's a lot on your minds, and we are here to help."

He's good, mused Richard. And it was all off script unless he was tipped off beforehand that Hector was here in full force. Of course, politics runs in Bob's blood. His father and both his grandfathers were involved in state and local politics. He learned from the knee. Politicians are born, not made.

Mayor Thomas acknowledged the hardships the earthquake had brought on everyone, especially those who had lost their homes and were now living in tents. Then he moved on to say what is being done to help relieve some of the anxiety people in the room were feeling. Finally, he announced the housing project Blackrock Construction had offered to do for the town pro bono, adding his pledge to cut through red tape to get it done as soon as possible. He concluded with more words of sympathy for the suffering people are experiencing. Then he called forward Father O'Leary to offer a prayer for a speedy end to suffering and a return to normalcy.

Richard couldn't believe it, but Hector's group had been respectful throughout the mayor's address. His soothing words had defused their anger. As the group left the meeting room, they held up their signs for the cameras, but otherwise, they were quiet and calm.

Richard followed the crowd to the mayor's office but stayed outside to listen as he held a handkerchief over his nose, which only helped to filter the smell so much. The mayor continued to soothe the crowd while he listened to what they had to say. The mayor, along with Councilmen Martinez and Perez, pledged to improve their living conditions in a timely manner. After that, the crowd dispersed while Richard headed back to the office.

Hector followed up on Richard's invitation to attend the Task Force meeting. "We need a better solution to our housing than tents. What are you going to do about it?"

"We're working on it," said Ben.

"What about moving us into the buildings at the fairgrounds?" said Hector.

"If it were a short-term matter, it might make sense to do that," said Steve. "But those buildings belong to Santa Cruz County—we can't just take them over for our personal use. They will be needed for the annual county fair and other events. Besides, the Ag building is bulging with donated clothes. There's no room to put people."

"All I know is my people are losing patience. They can't wait much longer for your solutions." Then Hector turned and left.

Ben, Richard, and Steve exchanged looks while they waited for Hector's footsteps to disappear down the hall.

"Have you come up with any ideas to put the men to work?" asked Ben.

"I think they should start taking over the responsibilities for their day-to-day living," said Richard. "What I mean is, they should be cooking their own meals and cleaning up after themselves. We could purchase camp stoves to cook outside."

"I don't know," said Ben. "That could lead to another fiasco."

"I think both the men and women will feel better about themselves if they can be more independent," said Richard.

"That's right," said Steve. "If we don't help them achieve independence, after this is all over, we might find we've created a class of helpless dependents."

"Moochers, you mean," said Ben. "I could see that happening."

"We need to bring up morale, too," said Richard.

"Wasn't it Eisenhower who said, morale is the greatest single factor in successful wars?" asked Steve.

"Most likely," said Richard. "He should've known what it takes after leading the allies to victory in Nazi Europe."

"We need to distract the tent people from their misery. Raising morale might just be it," said Ben. "If the powder keg we're sitting on explodes, it won't make much difference what else we accomplish. We could have permanent race problems."

"I just had a brainstorm," said Richard. "Maybe we should consult the Japanese community and ask them for some ideas. They spent time in internment camps and may have thoughts on what these people need."

"That's a great idea," said Steve.

"One of you will have to take it on," said Ben. "I still don't trust Japs after what I experienced in the war."

The next day, Richard left work early to talk with Sam before the Task Force met that evening. He found him near his greenhouse. "Sam, got a minute?"

"I can always make time. Would you like to come in for some tea while we talk?"

"I don't want to trouble you. Let's sit down outside on a bench."

"The wind is blowing. Let's go into the greenhouse. It will be more comfortable inside."

After they sat down, Sam said, "What's on your mind? Is the flower farm going well?"

"This is not about the flower farm. I have some questions that might help the town better manage the tent cities. But I don't want to pry. If you feel uncomfortable, please let me know."

"I don't understand what you mean. Why not start with your questions?"

"We are concerned that the people in the tent cities are becoming impatient with their situation, which could lead to all sorts of problems. We want to build up their morale and thought you might have some ideas since you spent time in an internment camp during World War II."

"Now, I understand. You cannot compare the situations. We were fenced in with armed guards in towers watching our every move. We had no freedom to leave like the people in the tent camps. They should experience internment before they complain. The earthquake was an unfortunate act of nature. People should be happy they and their loved ones survived and they can all live together, even if only in a tent. The house does not make the happiness, the family does."

"You are right. What did you do to raise morale?"

"First, we were self-sufficient. All of us had jobs at the camps, from maintenance to gardening to cooking. Whatever needed to be done, we did it. But sports helped keep our morale up—baseball, football, even hide and seek. The arts, too, can help—painting, music, sewing. And, of course, books, but not all of us could read English, which is the same problem with the Mexicans."

"These are all good ideas, Sam. Thank you for sharing them with me. I hope my questions didn't bring up painful memories."

"Not all my memories are painful. I met my wife, Ann, at the camp, and our first son was born there. God works in mysterious ways."

"Maybe he's even working in mysterious ways now. I must pay more attention."

When the Task Force assembled, Ben said, "Richard, did you get anything helpful from Mr. Yamaguchi?"

"Yamamoto," said Richard, "better known to me as Sam. And he offered some good ideas. Real pearls, in fact. Camp chores, self-sufficiency, and sports."

"That's great," said Steve. "At Callahan, there's a baseball field."

"Except tents are posted on it," said Ben.

"Tents are easy to move," said Richard. "Although, we'll have to get their buy-in to do that. We don't want to create even more friction."

"What did he think about arts programs?" said Steve.

"Sam recommended those, too. But for the men to burn off their energy and keep under control, something physical like baseball would be best."

"Soccer would be a winner with them, too," said Ben. "As it is, they kick soccer balls around when they have nothing better to do, which is most of the time. Now, enough with the ideas. Let's draw up a plan to put them into action."

"Let's get Hector in here to be part of this," said Richard. "If there's one thing I've learned from politics, it's to be inclusive, especially when you're at the conceptual stage."

"You possess great instincts," said Ben. "Why waste our time doing a plan if Hector and his crew are going to shoot it down?"

"I agree with that point," said Steve. "We all have better things to do, even if it's only getting a little more shut-eye."

"Any more word from your boss about the housing project?" said Ben.

"No. I think it's up to us to take it forward from here. Do you have any ideas for a site, Steve?"

"Over by Riverside and Bridge Street, there are a lot of

houses down. We'd need to determine the property owners. We might have to take it by the power of eminent domain."

"Let's hope it doesn't come to that," said Ben. "The press would drag us through the wringer. No one likes government taking private property. There's almost something un-American about it."

"I'll ask our Town Clerk to do a title search, which should turn up the owner."

"Is that all for tonight?" said Ben.

"The holidays are coming up. It would be a gracious gesture to provide a Thanksgiving feast for the tent dwellers. Or at the very least provide families with turkeys," said Steve.

"A chicken in every pot like Hoover promised in his '28 campaign," said Richard.

"Something like that. We Stanford men can't help but be influenced by Hoover, our college's first student."

"Let's not forget he also promised a car in every garage," said Ben. "But I suppose we can be excused since the tent dwellers don't have garages."

Hector came to the next Task Force meeting to discuss the ideas for raising morale at the tent camps. "Most Mexicans don't have a clue about Thanksgiving or what to do with a turkey even if our Aztec ancestors ate them. Chicken is our choice for a feast. But no one will turn down a good meal. Plan a dinner everyone can enjoy."

"Thanks for your input," said Ben.

"Perhaps we could use it as an opportunity to teach the meaning of Thanksgiving," said Richard.

"And the deeper meaning as well," said Steve. "About sharing and taking care of each other, which is what we're trying to do here in town. The takeaway will be that they get it."

"The people will be happy with a good meal. You don't need to get all symbolic about it," said Hector.

"Now that's settled, let's move on to our other ideas. Richard, do you want to take it from here?"

Richard paused for a moment before he spoke. He didn't want to go into the whole Japanese internment issue. Hector wouldn't understand, and it would take too long to explain, so he cut to the chase. "We were thinking sports and other games would be a diversion that would raise morale. Baseball would be a good one, and there is even a diamond at Callahan Park."

"You know people are camping there," Hector said.

"We know that, but tents can be moved."

"My advice is to wait. Mexicans always go back to Mexico for the holidays, and now, more than ever, they want to get out of here. Let them pull up their own stakes."

"That's the best news yet," said Ben. "When will your people leave?" It won't be soon enough.

"Various times."

"Will they wait for the school vacation?" said Richard.

"No. They go whenever they feel like it. They just pull the kids out of school. No one seems to care since they think the kids are too stupid to learn anyway."

"That's not true," said Steve.

"But it is," said Hector. "A gringo who volunteers in the school said a teacher called a Mexican boy a 'non-learner' just like his brothers. She probably leads a cheer when her Mexican students stop showing up."

"She's just ignorant," said Steve. "She doesn't understand that migrant children miss a lot of time in the classroom, besides trying to learn a new language."

"Let's just say she's a donkey. Unfortunately, she is not alone."

Hector was right. Even before the Thanksgiving feast took place, Mexicans began to leave town. Their cars, packed to the brim with containers hanging off the roof, left in a series of caravans headed for El Michoacan. The state, in southwest Mexico on the Pacific Ocean, is where Monarch butterflies fly to in winter. As many as a billion butterflies travel up to two thousand

five hundred miles to arrive for Dia de los Muertos, Day of the
Dead, on November first. According to legend, the butterflies
are the souls of loved ones returning to earth. Upon departing
earthquake-ravaged Watsonville, one Mexican was overheard to
say, "After surviving Dia de los Muertos, we are the loved ones
returning to our homeland."

The Thanksgiving feast took place at the high school cafeteria,
which was the biggest public space in town with a kitchen. Gina
and Margery went to lend their culinary skills, but beforehand,
they had baked pies for days along with many other women to
have enough desserts to go around. As they placed their pies on
the table, decorated with pumpkins and gourds, a couple of
Mexican women were perusing it. "Pies," they were overheard to
say, "what's with all the pies? We like flan for dessert. Don't they
know that by now?"

Despite the comment, the pies were all consumed, as was the
rest of the feast. Gina and Margery were cleaning up in the
kitchen when they heard tables being moved while music played
in the background. When they came out to look, the room was
filled with couples dancing the samba. "This is some Thanksgiving celebration—" Before Gina could finish her sentence,
Hector whisked her onto the dance floor. "We always dance at a
celebration," he said, "or any other time a group of us gathers—
even after political meetings." The dancing lasted until the wee
hours of the morning. No one, including the police, had the
nerve to clear them out.

Hector showed up unannounced at one of the Task Force
meetings in early December. "It is just as I told you it
would be."

"Just spell it out," said Ben. He did not like people who spoke
in riddles.

"My people are leaving to spend the Christmas holidays in Mexico, and they have pulled up stakes."

"Both literally and figuratively, I assume," said Steve.

"Yes. The baseball field is empty," said Hector.

"So, let the games begin," said Richard.

"Not yet. First, we have to celebrate the feast of Our Lady of Guadalupe."

"When is that?" Ben asked.

"December twelfth. Even though many of us are not practicing Catholics, we are devoted Guadaloupeans."

"Gina will want to know about this," said Richard. "I think she has become a Guadalupean, too."

"I know," said Hector, "she showed me the bracelet she always wears with Our Lady's medal on it. She told me she often goes to San Juan Bautista mission to pray before the image of Our Lady in the Chapel of Our Lady of Guadalupe."

"Is that so?" said Richard.

"Yes, the image is a copy of the one Our Lady gave to Juan Diego. It has been in the mission church for three hundred and fifty years and is a very powerful icon. Many people attribute miracles to it."

"Well," said Ben, "from what you tell us, this feast is very important. You can take the lead, Hector."

"I do not need to lead it. The feast almost leads itself after all these years. The priests of St. Patrick's know what to do, and so do the parishioners. But there is still much preparation."

"My understanding is, we don't need to do anything for the campers until after New Year's. Is that correct?"

"Mas o menos."

"What?" Ben said. "Someone translate."

"More or less."

At four o'clock on the morning of December twelfth, thousands of Mexicans gathered at the plaza to pray the rosary. Then they marched in a procession behind a picture of Our Lady of Guadalupe—a reproduction of one made by Diego Rivera, with Juan Diego above her head and red Castilian roses at her feet. Since a large section of Main Street was still cordoned off, they could not follow the normal route, nor could they attend Mass in St. Patrick's Church. The procession had to take side streets around town until it came to the Notre Dame School gym, now serving as the church. It was an overflow crowd with everyone carrying a bouquet of red roses in their arms to present as an offering to Our Lady. More Mexicans attend Mass on this day than on Christmas. In anticipation of the large showing, bleachers and speakers had been set up outside, where a carved wooden statue of Our Lady presided. Many of those gathered pinned Milagros on her, little metal replicas of an intention used to ask a favor or even a miracle. In no time, the statue was covered with the metal charms—a heart, an arm, even a dog— whatever needed the prayers. Mexicans have many superstitions dating back to their Indian culture, and the use of Milagros is just one of them.

The Mass included a reenactment of the miracle by school children and singing of the Mañanitas. Father O'Leary told the devotees that by attending this Mass, they were fulfilling their vow to make a pilgrimage to Our Lady of Guadalupe Shrine in Mexico City, which they often promised when praying for a cure or special favor. Afterward, the procession continued to the high school cafeteria, where the crowd feasted on a variety of Mexican dishes, including menudo, tacos, tamales, mole poblano, arroz con pollo, and the all-time favorite dessert—flan. Next, followed shots of pulque, tequila and mescal, while not on the menu, were available, nonetheless. The only thing left to do was to take a siesta. Not a tent flap was up that afternoon.

CHAPTER 25

Sam held a big red potted poinsettia in his arms. "This is to thank you for inviting us to your party." Gina accepted the holiday plant and asked Sam in for coffee.

"I can only stay a few minutes." Sam followed Gina into the kitchen and sat down at the table. Soon, Richard joined them before he headed out to work. Noticing the poinsettia on the table, he asked Sam about it.

"It's a thank you gift for the very enjoyable afternoon we had yesterday with so many friends. It's from my own nursery."

"Your nursery. I didn't know you were growing potted plants in addition to cut flowers."

"We are trying to diversify our business. That's what my son wants to do to protect it in the event the market changes."

"That's smart." But Richard thought the cut flower market is where most of the action is.

"In the spring, we will have some more potted plants that are attractive to the garden centers. My son is deciding which ones we should raise—maybe hydrangeas or lilacs. He will do the research before making a choice."

"I wish you luck with it. Now, I must be off."

Sam followed right behind.

Before dinner, Richard called the boys to his office. "We need to make the most of this next growing season and plan early. I'd like us to expand acreage to increase profits."

"First, we need to replace the greenhouse," said Mike. "The old one cannot be mended."

"That's why we need to increase our production," said Richard. "Order a new greenhouse. We should be able to get the cost covered by insurance. By the way, Sam came by today. They're raising potted plants. Did you know about that?"

"No," said Mike. "Perhaps I should talk to him about what he's doing. It may be good for us, too."

"He's diversifying," said Dave. "He's playing it safe."

"What do you mean?" asked Matt.

"Word is spreading around the Monterey Bay Flower Growers that Congress may enact legislation to give a trade preference to Latin American countries if they grow flowers instead of drugs. A lot of the old-timers are worried it may hurt their livelihood, so they're devising ways to safeguard their business. The Japanese growers, in particular, have learned from previous experience to be wary of the government. Growing potted plants is one way to protect themselves."

"That means less competition for us in the cut flower industry," said Richard.

"Adding potted plants would require more nursery space. Right now, the farm can support only one greenhouse since the rest of the land is on a slope," said Mike.

"We can't spread ourselves too thin," said Richard. "We need to focus on what is working right now."

The new greenhouse arrived before spring, and it was an improved version, stronger and more spacious. Richard and the boys had it set up before the seedlings needed shelter. In early spring, the much-awaited rains came. It was a mixed blessing. To the farmers, it meant crops would get the nourishment they required, and they wouldn't have to leave acreage unplanted to conserve what water they had. But for the tent camps, it meant mud and breeding grounds for mosquitos and other vermin. Not only were things dirty, but the conditions allowed for the spread of disease. Fortunately, the farmhands had work again to keep occupied and provide a living.

"We've got to get these camps cleaned up," Ben said to Richard and Steve. "We don't want workers striking now that we're finally getting on our feet."

"We could get the army back," said Steve.

"We can't wait months for them to show up," said Ben. "We need action now."

"Let me talk to Jeremy Edwards. He may be able to spare a crew or two to do the cleanup," said Richard.

"It just seems like it's one thing after the other," said Ben. "I'm getting too old for all this nonsense."

"You may be old, but you're wise," said Steve. "And right now, it's wisdom we require."

"Go ask Solomon. He's the one known for wisdom."

"Give me a number, and I'll call him. But right now, you're it."

"That's telling him," said Richard. "Let's wind up so I can get home in time to call Jeremy before he hits the hay."

The Blackrock crews got out to the tent camps right away, digging trenches for the rain and spreading hay to cover the muddy soil. Meantime, the men were back to work in the fields, and once the rains stopped, baseball began, which kept everyone engaged until sunset. At the seventh-inning stretch, Mayor Thomas made an announcement. "We will break ground for a new housing project next week, and if all goes well, the apartments will be ready by fall. And, we are looking for another site for a similar project." The mayor expected cheers to erupt when he finished, but people only smiled a little and nodded. On the way out, he spotted Hector. "Your folks did not get excited about my announcement. Should someone restate it in Spanish?"

"No. That's just how they are. They're more interested in the baseball game right now. You should not have chosen the game for your speech. But don't worry, I will spread the word, so everyone knows. They will be happy when they hear the news."

The mayor left, feeling let down. He had expected appreciation after all the work he had done to secure the project.

The following week, Richard and Ken went out to inspect the site and do preliminary planning. "Just like old times," Ken said.

"That right. But let's hope a fire doesn't set us back this time," said Richard.

At that moment, Hector appeared. "Don't worry. I'm posting guards. No one is going to mess around with this project."

Richard turned his concerns to the flower farm. The past season had been a profitable one with the weather a partner instead of a foe. He called the boys into his office to go over the books.

"We've done very well this year, thanks to all of you and Mother Nature smiling down on us. The business has been showing steady growth these past few years, despite all the challenges."

"Is that what you call it?" said Mike. "Challenges—droughts, worker strikes, and one of the worst earthquakes in history."

"I'm surprised we still have a flower farm," said Matt.

"Don't count your blessings too soon," said Dave. "Congress is about to screw us."

"What do you mean?" asked Mike.

"I mean the Andes Free Trade Act," said Dave. "All the flower farmers are talking about it."

"I know they think it will help curb drugs, but they need to realize those Latin American growers have been using flowers to smuggle in the drugs. If they can ship even more flowers, it follows that they will ship even more drugs," said Richard.

"That's not what President Bush thinks. He has declared a War on Drugs, and he plans to convince growers in Columbia, Bolivia, Ecuador, and Peru to use their acreage to grow flowers instead of drugs."

"Well, we're making hay while the sun shines," said Richard. "We have a solid business that is close to becoming a major player in the California flower industry, one of the biggest in the country. At this rate, I may own the land outright in a few years."

"We're on our way to becoming millionaires," said Drew.

"Not if Bush has his way. Just don't count your chickens," said Dave.

"What are we going to do if the law goes into effect?" asked Mike.

"We'll stand together and fight it every step of the way," said Richard.

"Some Monterey Bay Flower Growers Association members plan to go to Washington DC to lobby against it. I want to be with them," said Dave.

"I may tag along, too," said Richard. "I've had a good deal of experience trying to sway politicians."

The following year proved to be another successful growing season. Mike introduced a few new varieties while focusing on his best sellers. In the fall, Richard and Dave, along with Sam's three sons, made the trip to Washington DC with members of the Monterey Bay Flower Growers Association to lobby Congress against the passage of the Andes Free Trade Act. Richard said to Sammy, "It makes sense why you came to lobby, but I don't understand why your brothers are taking part."

"My father believes in a family business, even though my brothers chose other occupations. Bruce, an attorney, is very skilled in the powers of persuasion, which may be helpful. My other brother, Phillip, can offer an incentive, so to speak."

"I don't follow," said Richard.

Phillip overheard the conversation, stepped closer, and opened a tote bag. In one quick motion, he pulled out what appeared to be a dentist's drill and yelled, "Banzai! And if that doesn't work, I'll threaten a root canal—without anesthesia," he said with a sadistic grin.

The group met with their lawyers in Washington to go over their strategy before hitting Capitol Hill. The consultants had targeted the members of Congress who had not yet taken a position. Each flower grower was handed a packet containing background information, personal stories, and talking points. The California delegation hosted a reception to give them tips and a pep talk to show their support for the flower growing industry, which they hoped would make generous contributions to their upcoming reelection campaigns.

When they arrived on Capitol Hill, they spread themselves out between the House and Senate Office Buildings and started making calls. Rarely did they get a chance to speak with a Member—it was usually staff—some young kid just out of college handling legislative affairs.

Despite their lobbying efforts, the Andes Free Trade Act passed both houses of Congress. In December 1991, President H.W. Bush signed it into law.

"I know all of us did our best to convince Congress otherwise," Richard said to Dave, "but this is going to hurt us."

"Maybe we should move into potted plants like the Yamamotos."

"We need to keep raising the best cut flowers like always," said Mike. "The florists are particular and know the difference."

"We'll have to wait and see," said Richard.

Their sales declined during the next couple of growing seasons while the Andes countries' market share increased, forcing most U.S. flower farmers out of business. The Act dealt a near-fatal blow to American growers.

CHAPTER 26

One day in the fall of 1993, Richard walked the familiar path from the ranch house to the flower farm, lost in thought, trying to plot his next move. The purple statice was in bloom, and with the bright sun overhead, it was the most brilliant shade of purple he had ever seen—even more so than the day it was filmed for the movie. He tried to recall what the author of *The Color Purple* had said about purple. That was so long ago, a time they were riding high, everything lining up in their favor.

Gina came up behind him, catching him unawares. "I've been looking everywhere for you. Margery called with the most incredible news."

Jolted back to reality, Richard uttered, "Huh, what?"

"A Mexican woman claims to have seen an image of Our Lady of Guadalupe on an oak tree at Pinto Lake. People are going there in droves—setting up shrines, leaving devotions, praying novenas. Margery and I are heading out there to take a look for ourselves."

"That's good. Then you'll know if it's a hoax or not."

"I should bring some flowers. Do you have any red roses?"

"No, but you can have all the purple statice you want. In fact,

I'll fill the back of the pickup with it, and you can dump the load at the base of the tree. They might as well rot there as here."

"Purple statice? That's perfect. Didn't that author say the color purple stood for love...for God?"

"Something like that," his memory recalling her words.

"They've named her Our Lady of Watsonville. The Mexicans believe she came to give them hope since they're still struggling after the earthquake."

"We could all use some hope."

"That's right. Wasn't it Emily Dickinson who said, 'hope inspires the good to reveal itself'? After all the tragedy, we need something good to happen."

Richard entered the greenhouse and grabbed an armful of cut purple statice. "Here, take this." Then he went back and got another armful. "If this isn't enough for Our Lady, there's plenty more to offer her." Carrying a bunch of flowers under one arm, Richard put his other arm around Gina as they walked back toward the house. He helped her load the flowers into the trunk of her car and gave her a tender kiss on the lips. "Remember, purple stands for all the good things God created for us to enjoy. I'm looking forward to some enjoyment with you later."

"That's what it's all about," Gina said. She pulled out one stem and handed Richard the flower. "Meditate on this until I get back."

After visiting the shrine at Pinto Lake, Gina dropped off Margery and headed back to the ranch. Her thoughts drifted from the image she had seen of Our Lady to Richard and the afternoon ahead. She hoped he wouldn't be too depressed over the flower business to use his energy making love to her.

Gina had been paying such scant attention to her driving that she almost missed the turnoff for the windy road through the canyon that she loved to drive—giving her the feel of a race car driver as she powered around one turn after the other.

Miles ahead, three boys had left their home for a bicycle ride. "Stay in a single line," cautioned their mother, "as far to the right as possible so cars can get by." The brothers nodded to show they understood but, being boys, their mother never could be certain they would obey. She stood on the porch and watched as they turned onto the road, one after the other, in a single file line.

Gina knew all the landmarks, and after a few more curves, she would be at the turnoff. Suddenly, as she came around the next curve, there they were, the boys, riding three abreast, taking up her entire lane. She was going too fast to avoid hitting them. She needed to go around them, but as she swung left, a pickup truck loaded with gear appeared, heading straight for her. In a split second, she had to decide. Should she get back into her lane and risk killing the boys or make the ultimate sacrifice? A divine force seemed in control as Gina pulled the wheel hard left, crossing the oncoming lane, briefly contacting the truck as she did so. When she passed over the edge of the cliff, Gina felt herself falling, everything in slow motion, all her senses heightened. She noticed every rock and root on the way down, the sun peeking through the leaves, a bird calling in the distance. Images of her mother and father appeared...her sons...Richard. Mike was whispering something in her ear. She strained to listen, but she couldn't make it out. Even so, his words soothed her. The last sound she heard was a loud thud when she hit a boulder and came to an abrupt stop. Now she was floating over her body, over the car, lighter than air. Higher and higher she went until she had a bird's-eye view of the world. She focused on the crumpled BMW, her bloody body slumped over the steering wheel, the massive rock, black yet gleaming in the sun. Then, as if carried on the wind, she heard Mike's voice murmur a single word...love. I must be dead. When she saw the bright light coming toward her, she no longer had any doubt.

A policeman knocked on the door of the ranch house. When Richard answered, a shiver ran through him. His intuition told him it was about one of his sons. After the officer gave him the news, he let out a terrifying primal cry—his heart had been broken.

Gina's funeral was held a few days later. Father O'Leary said she has joined the saints and angels in heaven. Not only that, "She is a saint, for she gave up her life for others." Richard would never forget those words. They helped sustain him even as he mourned her passing and the time that had gone by not marked in the way either of them had hoped. Why had the world not welcomed the lovers as the song promised?

But Richard was mourning more than the death of Gina. He was agonizing over the loss of the flower farm and the impending foreclosure of the ranch. I've worked so hard following my dream, but it's ended in a nightmare.

Mike walked into the great room, looking for his father. He found him collapsed in an easy chair, staring out into space. "Dad, I want to remind you that the reading of mom's will is this afternoon. Are you coming along?"

"No, go ahead. Officially, we were divorced. There should be no reason I'm named a beneficiary."

Mike left to gather his brothers, and together, they set off to meet with Gina's attorney. None of them expected much except what would be left from the sale of the house after paying her bills. Knowing their mother's spending habits, there would be little remaining. But they had been taken by surprise.

A few hours later, the boys returned to the ranch in triumph. Richard stood up to meet them, taken aback by their upbeat moods. "Don't tell me. Your mother won the lottery and left you all her winnings."

"Better than that," Dave said, "we inherited the ranch."

"What do you mean? I don't understand."

"The lawyer told us that mom's father had arranged a syndicate to back your purchase of the ranch. Before he died,

Granddad bought all the shares you didn't own and put them in a trust. Mom was paid an allowance from the trust. But the ranch stays in the family forever. Apparently, Granddad thought the land would keep us together and insure future generations."

Richard could hardly believe his ears. This was the best news ever. Now, he could begin planning again. Heck, he thought, I'm only seventy. Many world leaders are older than I am. Who knows what I can accomplish before my time is up? He recalled a Confucius saying in a fortune cookie from long ago. "When it is obvious the goals cannot be reached, don't adjust the goals, adjust the action steps." A smile came to his lips as Confucius' words gave him renewed hope. His mind was on fire, figuring solutions. He headed to his study, full of ideas, to lay out a new set of action steps.

During the past months, Richard had been spending almost every waking moment in his study, drawing up a new business plan for the ranch. When Mike came by, he knew where to find him. "Dad, I want you to meet someone."

Richard looked up to focus on Mike and his guest.

"This is Miranda Ortega, the daughter of the sharecropper on our ranch. She's also a schoolteacher and, more importantly, Marta's great-granddaughter." She was a lovely young woman with long dark hair, wide-set amber eyes, nearly white skin, and full lips painted a soft shade of pink. As she stood before him, Richard's eyes scanned her voluptuous figure, and his heart skipped a beat.

Before any more was said, Mike stepped out of the office and returned with a baby in his arms, swaddled in a purple blanket. "And this is Regina Marie, your granddaughter."

Richard's eyes grew wide, and his mouth dropped open, but words did not come. Regina Marie—for the grandmother and the Lady. He stood up, trembling, and moved toward them, holding out his arms.

Mike looked down at the baby, "Regina, I'd like to present your grandfather."

Richard took the baby and clutched her to his breast. As he gazed upon Regina's face, he thought, hope—what would life be without it? And, as if carried on the wind, the words came to him—'hope inspires the good to reveal itself.'

I hope you enjoyed reading Where Flowers Grow *and would appreciate your honest star rating on my Amazon or Goodreads book page.*
Thank you.

ALSO BY BARBARA ANNE KING

The California Immigrant

The Apple King

AUTHOR'S NOTE

Where Flowers Grow is the first novel I ever wrote, a labor of love inspired by the memory of people long gone. With a bulky first draft that clocked in at over 150,000 words, it took time to shape the novel into a well-told story. At last, *Where Flowers Grow* is ready for publication—coincidentally, during the 80th anniversary of the California Flower Growers and Shippers Association.

As I imagined the story, I realized I was not only telling the tale of a family but of a town—one whose history has been shaped both by the people who lived there and the land. Many know Watsonville as an agricultural area. And it certainly is that. Apples first put Watsonville on the map and then it was strawberries. But Watsonville and the entire Monterey Bay are also flower growing areas. Japanese, Chinese, and Italians were the early flower farmers. And despite Alien Land Laws, Japanese persevered until World War Two internment disrupted their businesses. Today, California is known as the flower garden of the United States, producing eighty percent of cut flowers.

This novel is a tribute to flowers not only through farming but also through faith. Our Lady of Guadalupe, a symbol of hope, is woven throughout the story. Her miraculous act that caused red roses to bloom in winter proved Juan Diego's vision.

The title, "Where Flowers Grow," is the first part of a quote by Ladybird Johnson. The second part is "so does hope." It is my hope that you will enjoy reading *Where Flowers Grow* as much as I enjoyed writing it.

With best wishes,
Barbara

Barbara Anne King is the author of *The California Immigrant* and *The Apple King*, historical fiction novels that take place in her home town.

Barbara was born and raised in Watsonville, California, set on the magnificent Monterey Bay. After graduating college, armed with a political science degree, she headed east for a job on Capitol Hill. But while she may have left California, it never left her and she remains a *California Girl*.

Now she lives in a New York City suburb with her husband in the place they've called home for over 25 years. After raising three children, she's reinvented herself as an author so she can share her stories with readers wherever she finds them.

www.barbaraanneking.com
author@barbaraanneking.com